M000219345

CATACLYSM

FOUR HORSEMEN
BOOK FOUR

SARAH BAILEY

Cataclysm Copyright © 2021 by Sarah Bailey

All rights reserved. No part of this book may be reproduced in any form or by any electronic or mechanical means including information storage and retrieval systems, without permission in writing from the publisher. The only exception is by a reviewer, who may quote short excerpts in a review.

This book is a work of fiction. Names, characters, places, and incidents either are products of the author's imagination or are used fictitiously. Any resemblance to actual persons, living or dead, events, or locales is entirely coincidental.

Please note the spelling throughout is British English.

Cover Art by Sarah Bailey

Published by Twisted Tree Publications
www.twistedtreepublications.com
info@twistedtreepublications.com

Paperback ISBN: 978-1-913217-26-6

To those who live under the night's sky, who experience darkness in every corner, who have been through hell and back and who are ready to walk into the abyss with me
You are who this tale of the men fated to bring the apocalypse and their goddess of the night is dedicated to
Blessed be your dark little hearts

ONE

Scarlett

ELEVEN MONTHS AGO

"One more day in the darkened cell. One more day in hell. One more day in the pitch-black cell. One more day…" I sang almost brokenly, my voice hushed and hoarse.

The room was cold. There were no windows. No way of letting the light in. Only me and the darkness.

I curled in on myself in my corner, trying to preserve what little heat I had. Who the hell knew how long I'd been in here? The minutes passed slowly, time ticking away without me. The world outside was nothing to me. I hadn't left the estate in nine years. This prison where my parents held me under lock and key. It was a lonely existence. One marred by violence and pain when I stepped out of line. Like now. That was the reason I was here in the darkness. I'd done something they didn't approve of.

Arguing with my father was always futile. The older I got, the less patience I had for his rule. This time it had been about me refusing to stay out of sight when they had guests over. Dad caught me sneaking down to the kitchen. I'd been thrown in here for my sins.

Now I was cold and utterly alone, wishing I was anyone else, anywhere else. All I'd ever wanted was to leave the estate. To see the outside world. I'd only ever seen it on a fucking TV or computer screen.

I sighed and buried my face in my knees, curling my arms tighter around them. Everything hurt with the chill in the air seeping into my bones. Closing my eyes, I tried not to let the agony consume me. Tried not to allow myself to fall apart. The futility of my life was most pronounced when I was in this room. It haunted me. Made me feel like I was nothing. Nothing and no one.

I faintly heard a noise coming from a few feet away. The sound of the door opening and closing. The shuffle of footsteps was followed by someone placing things down on the floor. Then a body settled next to me.

"Scar."

I opened my eyes slowly. Mason sat beside me. He'd brought in a lamp with him. I didn't turn to look at him, but I could see him out of the corner of my eye.

"Let me see."

I didn't want to show him. All I wanted was for everything to go away. I wanted to… die. Then perhaps I would be free of this hell.

Letting out a sigh, I raised my head and met his brown eyes. There was so much sympathy in them, it threatened to decimate me further. He leant closer, capturing my chin between his fingers. There was a small damp cloth in his hands. With absolute gentle care, he wiped away the blood from my chin. I'd accidentally bitten my tongue after Stuart smacked me in the face. I'd spat the blood at his feet. It only earned me another fist and the reward of being thrown in here.

My face hurt, but I was used to the pain now. Used to being beaten and left to nurse my own wounds. Well, Mason usually snuck in here when everyone else had gone to bed and cleaned me up. He was the only person who gave a shit about me, even if he never protected me from Stuart's temper. His violence. His fists.

After wiping my face up, he applied some cream to the bruise forming on my jaw. Then he sat back, having put both the cloth and the tube of cream down next to me.

"Do you know what day it is?" he asked, his voice hushed.

I shook my head.

Mason shifted, turning to grab something from behind him. When he presented it to me, I stared at the plate with the little cake sitting on it with a lit candle.

"Happy birthday, Scar."

I took the plate from his hands, stretching my legs out and staring at the cake he'd clearly had the chef, Gio, make for me. I could see it had little chunks of apple running through it. Leaning closer, I inhaled the scent. Apples and cinnamon. It made me bite my lip. My favourite scent in the whole wide world.

"Go on, blow it out and make a wish," he encouraged me when I didn't say a word.

There were so many things I wished for in this world, but two things stuck out more than anything else.

I wish for freedom and to remember who I was.

I blew the candle out and set the plate in my lap.

"I hope it was a good one."

"It was," I whispered.

My eyes remained on the cake, staring at it with abject misery. My chest ached with a longing that threatened to have me turning into a sobbing mess. I couldn't cry in front of Mason on a day like this. He had no idea of the void inside me.

I was missing something. Missing something huge. It left a giant gaping hole in my heart. In my whole soul. There was no escaping it. No hiding or running away. It annihilated me every single time. Today marked the tenth year I'd had to experience it. And for the first time, I could admit to myself it wasn't only one thing. It was four separate voids. My missing pieces. I didn't know what or who they were, only they weren't here with me.

Shoving all of my emotions down, I plucked the candle from the cake and picked it up, taking a bite. The burst of flavour soothed me a fraction. It couldn't heal the holes in my heart, but it could make me feel less... empty. Even if it was just for a moment.

"Good?" Mason asked.

I nodded around my mouthful.

"Gio made it especially for you."

I swallowed and picked at the cake.

"Thank him for me... please."

Mason would have asked Gio to do it in secret, considering I was in the doghouse with my parents. No doubt they'd

4

forgotten it was my birthday. I didn't care about whether they did or not. I spent most of them with Mason. He was the only friend I had.

Mason nodded as I bit into the cake again. It was the only food I'd had in god knows how long. A small slice of heaven. A small treat in my otherwise lonely and tragic existence.

We sat in silence as I finished the rest of the cake. I handed him the plate when I was done. He set it beside him and took my hand, running his thumb along it.

"I'm sorry I can't do more to help you celebrate today."

I shrugged.

"S'okay. It's not your fault... it's mine."

"Scar..."

"I should have done what Dad said and stayed in my room."

His sympathetic look made my chest ache. I didn't want his pity. I just wanted to leave this place and be free. For this void inside me to be filled. To find the missing pieces of my soul.

"You shouldn't blame yourself."

"I know better, Mase. I've always known better. I'm just tired. So tired of everything. Sometimes... sometimes I want to disappear completely."

He reached out and put his hand on my thigh, giving it a squeeze. I looked down at it, feeling slightly uncomfortable from the direct contact.

"I don't want you to disappear."

I didn't ask him to help me escape my parents. It was another futile endeavour. I'd tried before and he'd told me to stick it out. Said he couldn't interfere with what Stuart wanted. Mason gave with one hand by taking care of me when things

5

got out of hand but took with the other by refusing to do anything about the abuse. And so my feelings towards the man I thought of as a brother figure were all fucked up. A mess of conflicting emotions I buried to survive.

"I'm still here, aren't I?"

He withdrew his hand as if sensing it made me uncomfortable. Then he shifted to his feet, picking up the things he brought in here, including the lamp.

"Yeah, you are. But I wish you wouldn't say things like that."

I didn't answer him. He didn't understand my pain. I don't think anyone could. Turning away, I stared at the wall, wishing he would leave me alone again. While I appreciated his gesture, I wanted to cry myself to sleep and pretend it wasn't the one day of the year that made me feel like I was dying. Birthdays should be a happy event. Not for the first time, I wished I didn't feel so empty from it.

"I'm sorry I can't make today better for you."

When I continued refusing to respond to him, Mason left, taking all the light with him. The door shut and tears slid down my cheeks.

Please… if there's someone out there, set me free. Please, set me free.

One day… one day I'd find my freedom. I'd find those missing pieces. And I'd hold on to them tight. Then we'd never be separated again.

TWO

FRANCIS

Setting my book down on the bedside table, I looked over at the clock. My brow furrowed when I realised Scarlett had been gone for well over an hour. I didn't think her conversation with Drake would take that long. It needed to happen, but the Scarlett-sized void in my bed had me feeling off.

I got up, slipping from bed and stretched. My gut told me to find out where she'd got to. My feet carried me over to my bedroom door. I yanked it open and stepped out, almost running headlong into Drake. He stepped back and gave me an odd look.

"What's wrong?"

I rubbed my face before looking up and down the hallway. My eyes went back to Drake. Unease spread across me, gathering speed like a tsunami was about to hit. Like it was about to drown us all in a fresh new hell.

"Isn't Scarlett with you?"

He blinked.

"No, I sent her to bed like twenty minutes ago."

My stomach churned.

"She was meant to come back to me after she spoke to you."

Drake's brow creased, his indigo eyes filling with concern.

"I didn't see her downstairs. You don't think she got intercepted by Pres or West?"

I couldn't imagine why. She'd spent all day with West. And Prescott wouldn't have wanted to interrupt my night with her.

"No, but we should check with them."

Somehow, I knew she wouldn't be with Prescott or West, but where else would she have got to? Scarlett had no reason not to come to bed with me. I'd told her I loved her. I already knew she loved me, but us exchanging those words had been a profound moment for me. Now, I wanted my girl in bed, curled up against me while I fell asleep. I already missed her beautiful face.

Drake nodded and walked towards Prescott's door as it was the closest and knocked rapidly. A minute later, a rather rumpled looking Prescott dressed only in boxers appeared and openly glared at Drake.

"What do you want? I was asleep."

"Is Scarlett with you?"

"No, why would she be? She's spending the night with Francis." His eyes darted over to me. Then his expression changed. "Why isn't she with you?"

Drake's expression grew grim, but he ignored Prescott and strode towards West's door, slamming his hand down on it twice. It took less than thirty seconds for the door to be wrenched open.

"What the fuck do you want?"

West looked ready to go to battle, even if he was also only in his boxers.

"Scarlett."

"What about her? I thought she was spending the night with Frankie."

It was then I finally allowed myself to panic. To truly feel the dread curling in my gut.

"She's not with you."

"No."

"Fuck."

West stepped out and looked at the three of us, his irritation morphing into concern.

"What is going on?" Prescott asked, putting his hands on his hips.

Drake didn't respond. His hands clenched and unclenched at his sides as if he was trying to control his reaction to learning Scarlett might be gone. Hell, I knew it in my fucking bones. She wasn't here.

"We are not going to jump to conclusions. She could still be here."

"Drake, what the fuck is going on?"

I rubbed my arm before deciding I wasn't going to stand here and hash it out with them. We needed to find out what happened. And we needed to do it now.

"She went to see Drake on the roof an hour ago and was meant to come back to me. Drake said he sent her down to bed twenty minutes ago. So excuse me if I want to jump to fucking conclusions," I ground out.

Then I was moving towards the stairs, heedless of the fact I wasn't fully dressed. Nothing was more important than finding her.

"You can't go around the building dressed like that," Drake called after me.

"Get me some fucking clothes then," I shouted back, taking the stairs two by two.

Scarlett would have left the roof by the stairwell. Only very few people had access to it. You had to have the right code to open any of the doors. Of course, in an emergency, they would unlock. There was another stairwell in the building, but this one was for our personal use.

I shouldered open the door, walking into it and looking around. Drake hadn't noticed anything untoward, but maybe he hadn't been paying attention. I walked up the first flight of stairs, trying to see if there was anything different. I don't know why I was so sure she was gone. My body felt her absence. It was as if I was attuned to her on some cellular level, which was fucking crazy. When you grow up with coincidence like the circumstances of our birth, it made things like fate and destiny seem real. Feel fucking real. I didn't care if it was crazy. I fucking knew.

"Francis," came Drake's voice.

"I'm up here."

"We should check the security footage to see where she went."

"Where's Pres and West?"

"Getting dressed."

My eyes searched the stairwell, but I couldn't see anything out of place. Quietly cursing to myself, I searched up the next set of stairs. Drake had closed the roof door. I wasn't going to check outside. There was no way she was still up there.

I made my way back down the stairs and found Drake with a pile of clothes in his hand.

"Put this shit on and we'll go down to my office to pull up the security feeds."

Taking the clothes out of his hands, I hurriedly pulled on the t-shirt and shorts before following Drake down to our office floor. We walked along to his office. The place was silent. No lights were on, just as we'd left it earlier. He sat down at his computer while I stood next to him.

It took him a few minutes to get into the security feeds. West and Prescott joined us as Drake brought the feeds up on the screen. He found the cameras in the stairwell and rewound it back until we could see Scarlett entering from the roof. We watched her walk down the first set of stairs. As she approached the second, a body slammed into her. They wore a hood. We couldn't see their face and their back was to us.

"Do we have another angle?" I asked as the person put a hood over Scarlett's head and looked like they jabbed something into her neck.

"Yes," Drake replied, fiddling with the screen and bringing up the camera covering the next part of the stairwell.

We still couldn't see who it was, but what they'd done to Scarlett was clearer. They'd covered her mouth with their hand and stabbed her with a needle.

"They fucking drugged her," West ground out.

I glanced at him, finding a furious expression on his face and his fists clenched into balls at his sides. Anger was simmering in my veins too, but there was worry there too. Worry for our girl.

My eyes went back to the screen. Scarlett had stopped struggling. The person picked her up in their arms and carried her down the stairs, disappearing from view.

None of us were going to state the obvious. Someone had taken her from us. Again. Fucking stolen her. Again.

"How the fuck did they get into the stairwell? No one should be able to do that," Prescott said, waving his hand at the screen.

"We need to check everything surrounding the stairwell from the last hour and a half. And I mean everything," Drake said, ignoring Prescott's question.

He sounded like he'd shut down all of his emotions and was trying to stay level-headed, but I wasn't fucking level-headed right now at all. Our girl was gone. Fucking gone. And I wanted to kick some fucking heads in.

You sound like West.

I didn't care. Scarlett was the most important person in my life. I'd do whatever it took to get her back and keep her safe.

"We should be going after her," West said.

"How the fuck do you think we're going to find her if we don't know who took her and how?"

West didn't respond, glaring at Drake even though he was right. We couldn't find her without knowing who took her.

"What if it was Stuart?" Prescott said. "He threatened to come after her. To come after all of us."

It was the logical explanation, but Stuart wasn't the type of man who acted quickly. He had always been calculating in his approach to us. However, perhaps now he knew Scarlett had remembered the past, the thing he actually wanted, he may have acted faster. Somehow, it didn't sit right with me. We couldn't rule it out, but we needed to look at every possible avenue.

"It could have been him, but we have to find out how they gained access to the building and the stairwell first."

Drake sighed and started bringing up more cameras.

"Look, I know. Someone has taken our woman and I'm fucking mad about it, but I am not going off half-cocked without a plan or knowing what happened. Our position is already precarious in the first place with Stuart threatening her. We need to be thorough. Now is not the time to be reckless."

West paced away towards the window. The tension lining his shoulders spoke volumes. This was not what any of us wanted. It was the second time she'd been stolen from us. We were meant to protect her from any and all threats, but how the fuck could we have known someone would infiltrate our building. We had security to prevent this shit from happening. Clearly, we needed to re-think it. Maybe increase it in the future.

"What about Mel? Shouldn't we check in with him?" I asked.

Melvin was our weekday night-time security guy.

"You're right. Call him. I'll keep going through this. There's no point checking the tracker on her phone since she didn't have it on her, did she?"

"No, she left it in my room."

It had been on my bedside table before I left my room. We couldn't track her, and it frustrated me no end. I should have insisted she took it with her. Maybe then we wouldn't be on the back foot. Then again, whoever took her would have probably checked her for a phone and got rid of it. We were going to have to work out a better way to track our girl. Something more discreet. I'd talk to the boys about it when we got her back. We were going to find her. I was in no fucking doubt of that. We would move heaven and earth to get to her. This time, we wouldn't fail Scarlett. We would never fail her again.

I picked up Drake's office phone and rang down to the front desk. The longer the phone rang without being answered, the more concerned I grew. Melvin normally answered straight away unless he was taking a toilet break.

"He's not answering."

"Go down and check on him. Take West with you."

We could have checked the feeds, but it was going to take Drake long enough to go through the footage as it was. I moved over to West, pulling him by the arm. He came willingly, even if he looked about ready to unleash hell upon the world. I was fully on board with that fucking idea. Heads were going to roll when we found out who had taken her. This time, we weren't going to allow her to go missing for ten years. Even ten fucking seconds was too long.

I swear to you, Scar, I swear on my fucking life we'll find you and bring you home.

"I know Drake's right," West murmured as we walked along the hallway towards the lifts, "I know he's fucking right, but I am going to murder the motherfucker who took her. I will tear him apart."

"How do you know it's a him?"

West gave me a look.

"I have a very good idea of who took her, Frankie. In fact, I will put fucking money on it."

I eyed him as I pressed down on the button to call the lift. "Who?"

"Think about it. Think long and fucking hard and you will come up with the same idea I have."

"Why didn't you say anything to Drake?"

West shrugged.

"You know what he's like. He will need proof. But I know in my fucking gut." He pointed at his chest. "I fucking know."

The lift arrived and the two of us piled in. I didn't ask him again as we rode down to the ground floor. West wasn't going to share his thoughts with me when he was in this kind of mood.

When the doors opened, both of us stepped out and walked over to the reception desk. My eyes darted around, seeing no one about. West made his way behind it.

"Frankie."

He disappeared from sight, making me race over to find out what was happening. The marble floor was cold under my bare feet, but I didn't give a shit. West was kneeling down next to Mel, checking for a pulse. There were no visible injuries on his body.

"Is he…?" I asked, pausing by his chair.

"He's alive." He slapped Mel's face lightly. "Hey, come on, wake up."

Mel didn't stir.

"He must have knocked him out with the same shit as Scarlett."

West put his arms under Mel and hauled him up, getting him sat down in the chair. Mel's head lolled on his chest. There wasn't much we could do about that. I picked up the desk phone and called up to Drake.

"Yeah?" Prescott answered.

"Mel is unconscious, but he's alive. We think he was drugged like Scar."

"Fuck, okay... Drake's still checking the footage... wait, hold on, go back."

I stood, my body tense as I waited for Prescott to say something else. Pressing down, I put the phone on speaker so West could hear too.

"There... stop there," Prescott said a moment later. "Isn't that...?"

There was a muffled voice from next to him, so I assumed Drake was answering. When neither of them said another word, I prompted them, wanting to know what the fuck they'd found.

"Who is it?"

And when Prescott replied to me, my blood ran cold. My eyes met West's, who had a rather grim expression on his face.

"Is that who you were thinking?" I asked.

"Yeah. It fucking well is. And mark my words, he's a dead man walking."

THREE

SCARLETT

My neck was stiff and achy when I regained consciousness. For a second I lay there, trying to remember what the fuck happened, then my eyes flew open. Above me was a white ceiling with swirly decorative plastering. I blinked twice, then sat up. My eyes went around the room, trying to work out where the fuck I was.

I was on a bed with a ridiculous amount of throw pillows on it. It was a wooden four-poster with white see-through material suspended from the top end to the bottom. The room was decorated in light blue pastel colours. The covers had little blue sailing boats all over them. A dressing table sat to my left with a glass top and under it was one of those resin images of a beach and a swelling tide. On the opposite side sat a wall of wardrobe doors. At the bottom of the bed was a driftwood ottoman. The whole room was light and airy. And it gave me the fucking creeps if I was honest.

Looking down at myself, I found I was still in the same dress I'd put on when I'd gone up to the roof to see Drake. Still with no knickers or bra on. It made me feel even more uneasy, but at least I hadn't been touched… I hoped.

I wasn't tied down to the bed, so I got up and walked over to the door. My hand went to the handle. It turned. Swallowing hard, I pulled the door open and looked out into the corridor. It wasn't very long. There was a door opposite it, then another at each end. I stepped out and went towards the open one where I could hear the faint sound of a TV. My bare feet on the carpet made very little sound as I padded towards it.

Why haven't I been locked up? This doesn't feel right.

I'd been kidnapped from Fortuity by an unknown person. I thought it might be one of Stuart's men, but in reality, I had absolutely no idea. And the fact I was in a well-kept home made me nervous. I was going to be brave, though. I had to. Not just for me, but for the boys. I had to make sure I could get out of here alive, so I could go back to the men I loved. There was no other option. I didn't want to be separated from them again.

The moment I thought about them, my chest caved in. They would be going crazy knowing I'd been taken again. After what it had done to them last time, I dreaded to think of how it would affect them this time. I knew in my heart they would do everything in their power to find me. And I would do my best to escape, regardless.

I reached the door and peered into the room beyond. It was an open-plan kitchen/living space. I could see the flickering screen of the TV and a figure sitting on the sofa watching it.

My breath caught in my throat. My lungs constricted painfully, and my hands shook.

Sat on that sofa was someone I recognised. I would know the back of their head anywhere. And it made me sick to my stomach.

"Hello, Scar."

Mason turned his head and looked over at me standing in the doorway. His expression was open, and he smiled at me. It made me want to retch. My trembling hand went to my stomach, trying to fight back the urge. Trying to process what I was seeing. Trying to understand what the hell was going on.

He stood up from the sofa and walked around it, coming closer to me. His hands dug into his pockets as he continued to smile with a horrifying glint in his eyes.

"How are you feeling? Are you hungry?"

You fucking kidnapped me and you're acting like there's nothing wrong. Like this is just a normal fucking day. What the fuck?

"You look a little pale. Come, sit down and I'll make you some breakfast."

He went to take me by the arm, but I stepped back out of his reach. How on earth could he be so casual about this? The man had kidnapped me. Actually taken me away from the men I loved. And now he was being nice, like we were… a couple. That would never happen. In fact, I would rather die.

His expression darkened even though he kept smiling.

"Come now, Scarlett, you need to eat."

I couldn't find my voice. It was all too fucked up and surreal.

This time when he reached for me, I was too slow. He gripped my wrist and forcibly dragged me into the room. I

19

barely had a chance to resist. He tugged me to the dining room table just off the kitchen and physically sat me down in a chair.

When he let go, his expression cleared, and his eyes softened.

"What would you like for breakfast?"

I stared up at him, feeling completely out of my depth. This man had cared for me for ten years and yet the things I now knew about him made my skin crawl. They made me want to run as far away as possible.

"I know, I'll make your favourite, shall I? You deserve a treat."

I flinched but didn't respond to him. The fact he knew those things about me was a blessing and a fucking curse. He gave me a warning look before he moved into the kitchen. My eyes went to the table, staring down at it as I tried to process everything. I could hear him banging around in the kitchen, but I didn't look back. I didn't move.

There were things I had to establish. First of all, I needed to know where he'd taken me. Where the hell I was. Then I could make a plan to escape. And I needed to find out why he'd taken me. Was he keeping me here for Stuart? What was his plan?

You need to stay calm. Don't make him angry.

The last time I'd angered Mason, he'd hurt me. The risk of it happening again was far too great. I had to keep a level head. Had to keep him onside until I made my move.

"Where are we?" I asked, trying to keep the panic out of my voice.

"Home."

"Home?"

"Mmm, yes, home, Scar. Do you like it? I decorated it especially for you."

My eyes roamed around the space, finding everything was exactly my style. And it made me feel worse. So much fucking worse because I didn't like it all. I hated it. Everything about this situation was horrifying.

"It's nice... but where is home exactly?"

"Look out the window."

I didn't know if I was allowed to get up from the table, but when I looked back at him, the man was smiling at me. He waved towards the patio doors to our right. Slowly, I rose from the chair and walked over to it. My eyes darted around the landscape, finding we were set off a little way back from the edge of a cliff. And beyond that? It was the sea. A very rough sea. The waves were high with whitecaps, and the water looked grey. Rain battered against the glass as a storm raged outside, but I couldn't see anything else near us.

We were on the coast somewhere. And we were isolated.

Fuck. Oh... oh fuck!

"Mason, where are we?"

This time, I couldn't keep the rising alarm out of my voice.

"The northwest coast of Scotland."

My stomach was on the floor in a matter of seconds. Mason had basically taken me as far away from my boys as we could get without leaving the country.

"And this place is yours?"

"Ours, and yes, I bought it five years ago. I finished redecorating it earlier this year, so it was ready for you."

I turned around and met his eyes.

"Ready for me?"

Then I remembered what Stuart had told me. How he intended to hand me off to Mason like I was a prize for his loyalty. A fucking trophy.

"Yes, this is our home, Scar."

He said it like it was something I should have known already. And it was the creepiest fucking thing I'd ever heard come out of his mouth. This man had bought this place with the sole intention of bringing me here and keeping me under lock and key. Of that, I was certain.

"Mason, this is…" *It's creepy. It's so fucking creepy.* "Really lovely of you. Thank you."

His smile made me want to throw up.

"I'm so happy you like it. Now, sit back down."

I did as he said on automatic. If I did anything sudden right now, I didn't think it would end well for me. My mind was rioting, rebelling against everything I was seeing and hearing. This wasn't Stuart's doing at all. Mason had taken me for his own reasons.

He's obsessed with you.

I realised it was probably hypocritical of me to be alarmed by Mason's obsessiveness when West was obsessed with me too. However, I'd grown up with West. I knew him inside out. He wasn't a threat to me. He'd killed for me, and he would do it again. In fact, I was relatively sure this would be the final straw when it came to Mason, regardless of the fact his father was the Met Police Commissioner.

Besides, I was in love with West. Even after he told me about his diagnosis, it didn't change my feelings. He might be a little psychotic, but I could see how the past had shaped him. How guilt had eaten him up inside. To me, he wasn't crazy or lacking remorse or empathy. He had those two things in spades… for me. No one outside of me and the boys knew the truth of the night I'd fallen. They didn't understand him. I did.

Fuck, I miss you. My heart burns for you. All of you.

Mason brought over a cup of tea for me, along with French toast with apples and cinnamon. I didn't want him to think I was ungrateful, so I thanked him. It was one of my favourites, and I couldn't fault him for it. He sat down across from me and watched me eat. It tasted like ash in my mouth. Only because this whole situation had me on edge.

"Good?" he asked me after I'd finished, having forced the food down. I needed to keep my strength up.

"Yes, thank you."

He gave me a smile, getting up and collecting my dishes. I watched him walk into the kitchen.

"Um… is it okay if I have a shower?"

Mason was turning the taps on for the sink.

"Of course, it's the room across from our bedroom. And there are clothes for you in the wardrobe."

"Thank you."

I got up, giving him a nod. Then I walked out of the room, trying not to break down on the spot. My feet carried me to the bedroom. I pulled open the wardrobe doors. The sight I was met with made my body tremble. He'd bought me so many clothes, I could barely count them. Not wishing to think too hard about it, I pulled out some jeans, a t-shirt and a jumper, along with underwear. I hurried into the bathroom and locked the door. There were towels on the rack and all the toiletries I could need.

Dumping the clothes on the floor, I stripped out of my dress and got in the shower. I turned it on, not caring that the water was cold at first. When it warmed up, I stood under the spray and allowed myself to feel the fear seeping into my veins. Tears mixed with the water as I washed, wishing I could rid myself of the horrors awaiting me outside the door of the bathroom.

Mason had planned this for years. He'd watched me, bided his time and waited until he could take me away from my life. So he could hold me captive, just like Stuart had done. Only I had the distinct feeling he wanted to play house with me. It meant he would expect me to be his... girlfriend? Wife? Neither of those things sat well with me. The implications had me clenching my fists at my sides.

I will not break. I will not fall apart over this. I will be strong.

West called me his little warrior. I was going to be exactly that. A warrior. All I had to do was bide my time and play nice. Then I could question him about what the fuck he thought he was doing. And I would find a way to get myself out of this situation. I wasn't going to wait for them to find me, but they would come for me. They would fight tooth and nail to get to me.

I was going to rescue myself too. I wasn't a fucking damsel in distress. I was a queen. And it was time to put on my crown.

I finished washing, dried myself and got dressed. Instead of drying it, I braided my wet hair and left the bathroom. I walked back into the living space and found Mason watching TV again. Going over to him, I sat down and curled my legs up underneath me. He gave me a smile as if to show he was pleased with me.

24

CATACLYSM

Time to begin with a charade. You will think I'm compliant. And I will make you let your guard down. When you least expect it, I will burn you to the ground, Mason. Just fucking watch yourself.

FOUR

SCARLETT

I was climbing the walls after only two days of being here with a man I could no longer stand. Everything about this wore on me. When I'd been kept prisoner by Stuart, it had been all I'd known. There was nothing I had to compare it to. Now, I knew what freedom was like. Being denied it again had left me with very little patience.

While I knew the boys would come for me, I didn't know when. It made my situation precarious. I didn't know how long Mason would tolerate not sharing the bed with me. For now, he was content to sleep on the sofa bed in the living room. No doubt it wouldn't last long, and he'd want to share the bed with me. It meant he would try to do things to me. Things I didn't want from him under any circumstances.

The only people I wanted to be sexually intimate with were my boys. The four men who owned my heart. The thought of Mason trying to kiss me, let alone touch me, made my skin crawl.

I'd remained obedient since I'd been here. Perhaps that was why he hadn't tried anything with me. It didn't mean the whole experience hadn't creeped me the fuck out. The way he talked about this place being ours and how we'd live the rest of our days out here was unnerving, to say the least.

I took a seat next to him on the sofa, turning his way as he fiddled with something on his laptop. I wasn't allowed to touch it. He kept it locked up in his office when he wasn't using it. A place he'd refused to show me.

There wasn't exactly much I could do in the house. I couldn't go outside as it had been raining non-stop, battering the house with its intensity. It made this whole experience even more miserable. I had to hand it to him. If you wanted to hold a girl against her will, what better place? It was remote and the nearest neighbours were miles away.

"Mase?"

He glanced at me.

"Mmm?"

"Can I ask you something?"

He put his laptop on the arm of the sofa and turned to me fully.

"Of course."

I fiddled with the hem of my jumper, rubbing it between my fingers. Having to wear the things he'd bought gave me an icky feeling, but I had no other choice. At least it was my style and not skimpy dresses or underwear. I didn't know what I would have done if I'd found that in the wardrobe. Maybe run away screaming.

"Are you taking me back to Stuart?"

"No. He wants to kill you. I can't allow that. You're too precious to me."

I wanted to look up at him, but I didn't. Better he thought I was scared and meek right now. He might be more inclined to be candid if I wasn't confrontational.

"When did he tell you?"

"The day I rescued you."

Rescued me? You didn't fucking rescue me. You kidnapped me like a fucking thief in the night. Drugging someone doesn't make them compliant.

I had to stay calm and not alert him to my real feelings.

"What else did he tell you?"

I glanced at him under my lashes. His brow was furrowed, but he didn't seem put out by what I was asking.

"You remembered."

"The past?"

"Yes… have you?"

I nodded. There would be no point keeping it from him. I didn't want to hide it either. I was me again. Perhaps a different version of the Scarlett from ten years ago, but I was her. And I wasn't going to pretend I was someone else.

"Do you know what happened to his sons?"

"No."

My answer was automatic. There was no way in hell I was telling Mason I knew what my men had done to Ray and Ryan. They were his friends, according to the boys. I couldn't put them in danger by revealing the truth.

"Are you sure about that?"

"Yes."

"Stuart seems to think you do know."

"Well, I allowed him to think that. It doesn't matter, anyway. You're not taking me back to him, so I'm safe, aren't I?"

Mason reached out and patted my thigh. It took everything I had not to react. Not to flinch and move away from him.

"Yes. I won't let anything happen to you, Scar. Not like what he did before."

My eyes met his.

"Why did you let him hurt me for all those years?"

Mason's eyes darkened and his expression turned grim.

"You know why. I couldn't do anything about it. What did you want me to do?"

"You could have told me the truth."

"The truth is complicated."

I dug my nails into my thigh.

"Trust me, I'm aware. The truth is way more fucked up than I could have ever imagined."

There was a wariness to Mason's face I hadn't been expecting. Like he was trying to work out if I knew everything or not and he wasn't sure whether to ask me about it.

"You didn't want me to take you away from them."

He knew the answer to that question. It was obvious. I wanted to stay with the Horsemen. They were my family. The loves of my life.

"Why did you?"

"You're not safe with them. Not with Stuart planning to come after you."

I almost laughed, but then again, Mason had got to me at Fortuity. What's to say no one else could have? I didn't blame the boys for what Mason had done. They couldn't predict that someone would manage to get into their building given all the security they had in place. I hoped they found out how. Asking Mason didn't seem like a good idea right now.

"Are you sure it's not because Stuart promised me to you?"

My tone came off accusatory. I couldn't help it. The knowledge had stung. It drove the knife in further. Mason wasn't on my side. He was on his own.

"You weren't supposed to know about that."

"Well, I'm so sorry Stuart decided to spill your sordid little secret."

He didn't exactly look pissed off at my sarcasm, but I could tell he wasn't happy.

"That's not the only thing I know about you, Mason. Oh no, I've found out many things and you're going to be honest with me about them."

As much as I wanted to launch myself at him, tear his fucking face off and give him hell, I would settle for the truth. I needed to know if everything the boys and Stuart had told me was accurate.

"What else did he tell you?"

"Stuart? Nothing. Though, I suppose he doesn't know about you and Phoebe, does he?"

Mason sat up straighter, retracting his hand from my thigh and giving me a pained look.

"What about me and Phoebe?"

I raised an eyebrow.

"Your affair with her. And don't try to deny it. I've seen evidence. How long has that been going on, huh? Real smart to fuck his wife behind his back. Oh, and let's not forget she

31

was your best friends' mother too. I mean, that's just the icing on the cake."

Perhaps I shouldn't have said it like that, but I didn't care. If he was going to attempt to hide the truth from me, I wasn't going to give him a fucking inch. While this was playing a dangerous game, the ten years I'd known Mason had to count for something. We'd been friends. Or at least, what counted for friends under the circumstances. He knew way too much about me, and I knew nothing about him.

"She came on to me."

At least you're fucking admitting it.

"Right… that makes it so much better and explains everything."

His eyes drifted away from me to the window, where the rain was still hammering down.

"It happened after the twins disappeared. She was lonely. Then there was you to contend with too. The fact you didn't remember. And Stuart's decision to pretend they were your adoptive parents. She didn't want to go along with it at first, but he was so determined to find out the truth. He knew those four had something to do with the twins going missing."

Mason rubbed his arm.

"He became so single-minded about the whole thing. It's like his need for the truth and revenge was fuelled by his grief. He directed all of that at them. And… took it out on you."

I flinched. Stuart had taken it out on me all right. He'd done it with his fists. But it wasn't enough for him, clearly. He needed to destroy my men. He wouldn't be satisfied otherwise.

"He neglected everything else, including his wife. So she turned to me, the only connection she had left to her sons.

32

That's how it started. It's not like it has been a constant thing for the past ten years, Scar. Just when Stuart got too much for her."

I didn't feel sorry for Phoebe, but I could understand her situation.

"What did you get out of it?"

"Guess it was my way of saying 'fuck you' to him over the way he treated you."

"You could have stopped him."

"I didn't have a choice."

For a moment, I wondered why on earth he wouldn't have a choice in the matter. Then it became clear. Mason was complicit in my kidnapping. He was complicit in everything going on. Stuart likely held it over him.

It didn't make it better. The fact was, Mason had been interested in me when I was a teenager. He was six years my senior. It made it creepy and downright disturbing. I wasn't going to forgive him for it. Mason couldn't redeem himself in my eyes.

"You had a choice. I didn't. I've had no agency in my life for ten years. And just when I get some…"

Mason's eyes narrowed. I wasn't going to finish my sentence. It was clear. He'd taken me against my will and was holding me here. It would be stupid and dangerous for me to try running. Where would I even go? He'd come after me unless I could incapacitate him. And given he watched me most of the time, I wasn't sure how I could do that without hurting him. It's not as if he let me near any of the kitchen knives or anything sharp.

33

I shouldn't have qualms about hurting him, but the memory of thinking I was killing him the night the boys had forced me to prove my loyalty left me feeling reluctant to take it that far. Going through the pain afterwards wasn't exactly worth it. It would be more darkness staining my soul. Another thing to feel guilt over. Taking a life wasn't easy for me the way it was for the boys.

Are you going to leave it for them to do?

I didn't have an answer to that question. I hadn't considered how it would feel to kill again, given I didn't think I would be put in that situation. And I had unresolved issues regarding having thought I'd killed Mason. Sitting here in front of him made me see that. My conflict remained. I wasn't sure what it would take to push me in either direction.

"There are no good choices in life, Scar. I thought you would have realised that by now."

His words made me shiver. My life hadn't had any good choices in it, but I knew what side I fell on in this war.

"Does Stuart know you took me?"

"No. He can fight it out with them. They can burn for all I care. I'm done with Stuart and his revenge shit." He reached out and took my hands. "I have all I need right here."

His response made me feel worse. I wanted to pull away. His touching me had my skin crawling. And I had a feeling my time would be up very soon. Mason wasn't going to let me get away with keeping him out of the bed.

"Isn't it lunchtime?" I asked, wanting to divert his attention away from me. The look in his eyes made me ill.

He dropped my hands and smiled.

"It is. Stay here, I'll make us something nice."

As he got up from the sofa, I shrank back into it. There was a lot I had to think about in light of what he'd said to me. Hearing about Stuart's reasoning for everything made me hate him even more. Yes, the boys had taken away his sons' lives, but it didn't justify the things Stuart had done because of it. Especially when he didn't know what the boys had done to the twins. He didn't have any evidence or proof. He had made a bunch of assumptions, and not knowing the truth had only fuelled his need for revenge. There was nothing Stuart wouldn't do to bring down the Horsemen and destroy me in the process. He'd more than proven that now.

Grief did funny things to people. It twisted them into people their former selves might not recognise. I had a feeling when I finally dealt with my own grief regarding my mother, I wasn't sure I would recognise myself either. And I wasn't sure how I felt about that... at all.

FIVE

SCARLETT

The wind whipped my hair around my face as I stood close to the cliff's edge, staring out at the sea. Three days had passed since my conversation with Mason. It meant I'd been away for a week at this point. Mason told me it took him a day to travel here from London when I'd asked him about it.

I hugged my woollen cardigan closer around my body, shielding myself from the breeze. It was freezing out here, but I didn't care. It had finally stopped raining and glimpses of the sun broke through the clouds every so often. Being locked up in that damn house for days on end was wearing me down.

The sea was rough, the waves crashing against the cliffs. Birds were flying around, cawing, but those were the only sounds in the air. The wind, the sea and the wildlife. Having spent half my life in a city and the other half in the countryside, this place felt far bleaker than anywhere else I'd been. The thought of existing here for the rest of my life, cut off from everything I once knew, had tears springing to my eyes. I didn't want that again. To be locked up. Only this time, it was far more remote.

There was another reason I was out here all alone with my thoughts. Last night my luck ran out. While Mason hadn't tried to touch me, he spent the night next to me. I'd been so terrified he would do something to me in my sleep, I'd been awake for most of it. After he got up, I was able to sleep the morning away. Of course, he could have done something to me at any point but having him right there left me feeling vulnerable and unprotected.

I needed to get away from here. I had no other choice but to find a way to escape him. Who knew how long it would be until he decided he wasn't going to wait any longer? Was he planning on trying to woo me or something? There was no way in hell I would ever willingly sleep with him. The thought of it made me ill. His friends had tried to force themselves on me. Did he even know about it? I hadn't asked. It didn't matter in all honesty. What fucking difference would it make? It wouldn't change the situation I was in. It wouldn't make him buying this house away from everyone else to keep me in any less disturbing. I think that was the worst part of all. He'd planned this for years. He knew how I felt about being locked away. He fucking knew. And even knowing that, he'd done this.

I shivered, shoving it all out of my head. The more I thought about it, the more I wanted to cry. The more I wanted to run and never look back. But Mason would come after me. He'd chase me the fuck down and then where would I be? In a worse situation. He would probably stop being nice to me. I couldn't have that.

I turned to look out over the landscape behind the house, trying not to judge how far I'd have to run. There were hills everywhere, but it didn't mean there were many places for me to hide. The track to the house was dirt. Who knew how far the main road was from here?

Movement in the distance caught my eye. I blinked, then squinted. Unless I was seeing things, four figures were walking this way. My heart lurched, imagining it might be my men.

Had Prescott, West, Francis and Drake found me?

"Scarlett."

My head whipped around to the house. Mason stood by the patio door. My eyes went to what he was holding. I swallowed. My heart thumped hard against my ribcage, making me even more nervous.

Why the fuck does he have a shotgun?

I'd never seen a gun in real life before. The sight of him with one made me fear for my life.

"What is it, Mason?"

"Come inside."

I didn't want to. Not when he had a fucking gun on him. Why did he even need that? What was the reason he had it out right now?

My eyes went back to the figures I'd seen, but they weren't there any longer. I must have been seeing things.

"Now, Scarlett."

Letting out a sigh, I made my way towards the house. I couldn't take any chances. Not when he was brandishing a shotgun like it was normal behaviour.

When I reached Mason, he looked down at me with annoyance written all over his face.

"Get in the house."

"Why on earth do you have that?"

He looked down at the gun.

"I was cleaning it."

"No, I mean, why do you have it in the first place? I didn't know you owned a gun. Do you even have a licence for it?"

He looked slightly taken aback by my questions. They were valid as far as I was concerned. The only reason people in this country owned rifles or shotguns was for hunting or sport. Mason wasn't interested in either of those, as far as I knew.

"Of course I have a licence for it."

"Well, how am I supposed to know? You could have a stash of illegal handguns."

He let out an exasperated noise.

"Where do you think I'd get hold of one?"

"Well, you shouldn't have one, considering who your father is. But oh wait, you helped a man kidnap me, so excuse me for being sceptical."

I probably shouldn't have been giving him attitude when he had a shotgun in his hands, but I didn't think it was loaded. He said he was cleaning it. Didn't make me feel any better about him having it. Not to mention I was a little on edge after thinking I saw four people in the distance.

"My father…" he paused and scowled. "They told you."

"Of course they fucking told me, Mason. How do you think I found out about you and Phoebe?"

He stepped closer.

"What else did they tell you?"

"That you used to watch me when I was a teenager and have been obsessed with me since before my accident."

I didn't mean to blurt those words out, but apparently, my common sense had fled. Mason's eyes narrowed on me. I didn't step back. Despite the fact he had a weapon on him, I wasn't going to be a meek, obedient girl any longer. It was time to stand my ground.

"And you believed them?"

"What's not to believe? Unlike you, I've known them my whole life."

"They lied to you for months about not knowing who you are."

"I was there to destroy them. They couldn't trust me. I couldn't trust them. Go figure. You've lied to me too, so don't you stand there and act like you're on some moral high ground."

His expression hardened to stone.

"Get in the house, Scarlett. Now."

"Or what?"

"Or I will use force and I don't think you want that."

I wanted to fight him. I really fucking did, but I didn't think I would win. Besides, this argument wasn't getting us anywhere.

I shoved past him and went inside. Mason glanced around outside before he followed me, shutting the patio doors and locking them.

"You're not going back outside without me. Is that understood?"

"Why? Do you think I'm going to run off?"

"Yes."

I crossed my arms over my chest.

"Well, you shouldn't exactly be surprised considering you're keeping me here against my will."

His hands tightened around the gun. I should be scared, but I wasn't. He wasn't going to kill me.

"I've had about enough of your attitude today. Get in the bedroom and stay in there."

"You've had enough of me, huh? Well, I'm sorry to disappoint you, but this is what you're getting. I did not ask for this. And I don't fucking want you."

Mason walked into the kitchen and placed the shotgun down on the counter. Then he turned and approached me, his hands clenched into fists at his sides. I didn't back away. He needed to understand I wasn't going to be a willing victim.

"Get in the bedroom, Scarlett, before I do something I regret."

I raised an eyebrow.

"What a way to take responsibility. Blame your inability to control yourself on me because you don't like how I'm talking to you. Did you think I would be the same sad little meek girl once I remembered who I am, hmm? Did you think Stuart broke me so I'd be an obedient girl for you?"

I saw it coming from a mile off and yet I did nothing to stop it. His hand came up, and he struck me across the face. My head snapped back, but I took it. I let him do it because it proved my point. He was as bad as Stuart.

I turned my face back towards him. Then I smiled before I spat blood at him. He glowered, then took me by the arm and dragged me along to the bedroom. He threw me into the room and slammed the door shut behind him.

I went over to the mirror on the dresser and looked at my face. Opening my mouth, I found the source of the bleeding. The impact of his fist had knocked my cheek into my teeth. I rubbed my jaw and got a tissue to wipe the blood from around my mouth. Stuart had hit me in the face enough times for this to be a minor assault as far as I was concerned.

Provoking Mason hadn't been my smartest idea, but I was no longer in the mood to be nice. Not after the way he'd behaved. Not after he'd kidnapped me. I was done being a pawn for other people. No, I was a warrior. I'd survive this shit and get back to my men.

I went over to the bed and lay down, staring at the wardrobe, and wondered how long Mason intended to keep me in here. He needed to cool off, so I wasn't going to go out and ask him.

I must have fallen asleep because I jolted awake to a faint tapping sound. Looking around, I couldn't locate the source of it. It had got dark, but the room was lit by the moon streaming in through the windows.

The noise came again. I hopped off the bed. Something was tapping against the glass. I walked towards it and realised there was a hand there. I looked out, but I couldn't see who the hand belonged to. I almost jumped out of my skin when something slammed against the glass. It took me a second to register that it was a piece of paper. I peered at it, wondering what the fuck was going on.

Open the bathroom window. Get the shotgun. Bring it to us.

It was gone a moment later. I stared at the space it had been for a long moment. There was only one logical explanation for who had written that. They were here. They had to be here. The four figures I'd seen in the distance had been them.

Oh shit!

They'd found me. My heart burnt in my chest, but I shook myself. I had to do what they'd asked of me. I couldn't let them down.

Turning away, I walked over to the door and carefully opened it. I could hear the noise of the TV coming from the living area. Hopefully, it would mask the sound of my footsteps. My feet were silent as I crept into the bathroom. I had to lean over the sink to reach the window. Thankfully, this one opened as the ones in the bedroom didn't. It wasn't big. I didn't know if anyone could actually fit through it. I took it off the latch and pushed it open. Then I retreated into the hallway, pulling the door to behind me. As far as I knew, Mason had left the shotgun on the kitchen counter. I wondered if he'd moved it. Then again, they wouldn't have asked me to get it if it wasn't still there, would they? No, they wouldn't have. I didn't think it was loaded, but we couldn't take any chances.

I got to the doorway of the living area and looked in. Mason was sitting watching TV. He didn't look around, so he hadn't heard me. My eyes went to the kitchen, finding the gun resting on the counter. He hadn't moved it.

Lowering myself to the floor, I shuffled into the room, trying to be as quiet as possible. I kept checking the sofa to make sure Mason had stayed where he was. It took me some time to make my way to the counter. I hid behind it for a long moment before carefully peering over it. Reaching out, I gripped the gun with both hands and lifted it off the counter. I slowly brought it towards me before dropping back down behind the counter again.

My heart raced at a million miles an hour as I crouched there with a fucking shotgun in my hands.

You can do this. You can get back into the hallway without him noticing. You have to. This is the only way you'll escape.

I looked out at the sofa. Mason had his gaze fixed on the screen. I moved, inching along towards the door while keeping my eyes on him. It wasn't exactly easy with a gun under my arm, but I had to make do. Mason let out a noise, making me freeze until I realised he was laughing at something on the TV. I tried to keep my breathing even as I moved again, a little faster this time.

By the time I made it into the hallway, I was panicking and wanting this to be over with. I rose to my feet and crept back along to the bathroom. The moment I reached it, a hand reached out and yanked me inside. The gun was removed from my hands before I had time to blink.

Standing in the small space were Francis, Drake, West, and Prescott. Drake held the shotgun. He checked if it was loaded. There were no shells inside. He looked at me for a second, then he was signalling to the others to move.

"Stay here and be quiet," he told me in a hushed whisper before they all piled out of the room, leaving me staring after them with my heart in my mouth.

They were here. They'd come for me. And now… they were about to confront Mason.

Oh fuck.

SIX

WEST

I wanted to fucking storm the place and kill the son of a bitch for taking Scarlett, but Drake had put a stop to that when we saw Mason and his shotgun earlier. Instead, we'd waited until nightfall, hatched a plan to enlist Scarlett's help, and got into the house without Mason's knowledge. Now we were going to fuck that cunt up. Well, I had no intention of allowing him to leave here alive, but I'm not sure Drake would agree with me on that point. I didn't care what he had to say about it. Mason had got away with his shit for far too long.

Kidnapping Scarlett from Fortuity was the last fucking straw.

I was done with excuses.

Mason Jones was going to die.

And that was fucking that.

The four of us walked into the living area. Drake aimed the shotgun at Mason's head while Francis and Prescott stood behind him with me. Francis already had the ropes we intended to restrain Mason with. It was time to show this fucker he wasn't going to get away with shit.

"Hello, Mason," Drake said, his voice completely calm and very much at odds with his expression. He looked like he was ready to rip Mason to pieces.

Considering he was the last person to see Scarlett before Mason took her, he'd taken it personally. Drake had been a boar the whole week, but we'd all been stressed out and on edge, so I didn't exactly blame him for it.

Mason whipped his head around, his eyes going wide when he spied us. Then he was up off the sofa and backing away until he hit the TV.

"Did you think you could hide from us?" Drake continued, taking a step forward. "You should know we would tear apart the world for her by now. Or maybe you thought we wouldn't find out it was you. After all, Stuart threatened her life. Isn't that why you took her?"

Mason flinched, then glared at the four of us.

"Fuck you. That's not even loaded."

I scoffed and stabbed a finger in his direction.

"What a fucking comeback. I'm so scared. What you going to do now, Mason? Four of us and one of you. Those odds aren't really in your favour."

Mason didn't say a word, just continued to glare.

"Tie him to one of those chairs," Drake said.

I stayed back while Prescott and Francis approached Mason. They knew I would probably rip his face off if I went near him. Drake had warned me about us not causing any further trouble for ourselves. The last week had been fucked up enough with us trying to track down where Mason had taken Scarlett after we'd seen him on our security footage.

He didn't struggle as Prescott dragged one of the dining chairs over and Francis pushed him into it. Our rope boy tied Mason up, securing him to the chair so he couldn't go anywhere. Then Prescott put tape across his mouth because we weren't in the mood to hear what the fuck the cunt had to say to us.

Drake put the shotgun down on the kitchen counter.

"You can come out now, Scarlett," he called down the hallway.

A few moments later, our girl walked into the room. My eyes immediately went to her jaw, where a bruise was forming. It took two steps before I was next to her and gently tipped her chin up towards me. Her hazel-green eyes were full of conflicting emotions.

"Did he hit you?" I murmured, trying to suppress the urge to stab Mason in the face.

"Yes," she whispered. "He would tell you I provoked him, but I'm not responsible for his inability to control himself. I took it because it shows he's as bad as Stuart."

I stroked her jaw.

"My brave little warrior."

Tears welled in her eyes. I wrapped my arms around her, holding her against my chest. Her fists bunched in my coat.

"Thank you. Thank you for coming for me."

"I told you, I'd tear apart the world to find you, my little Scar. You're mine."

"Yours. Always yours."

I held her closer, giving her what she needed. She was so fucking brave. I had no idea what he'd put her through while she'd been here, but I was sure she'd done everything in her power to keep herself safe. Scarlett wouldn't take anything lying down. Not now she was free of fucking Stuart and his fists.

I could hear Drake, Francis, and Prescott talking behind us, but I ignored them. Scarlett needed me. I would never let her down again. She didn't blame me for her accident, but I was still responsible for what happened that night.

"I want to go home," she whispered into my chest. "I want to go home so fucking much."

I stroked her hair.

"We'll take you as soon as we're done here, okay? I promise."

She nodded, clutching me tighter for a long moment. Then she pulled away and smiled. I stroked her arm. If she wanted us to take her home to Fortuity, we would, but we had to deal with Mason first.

Both of us turned to look at the others. They were watching us. Mason was glaring behind the tape over his mouth. Scarlett moved towards the boys. Then she was bundled up against Prescott's chest and he was murmuring how much he loved her before kissing her like it was the last time he would. When he let her go, she went to Francis. There were similar sentiments shared between them.

She looked at Drake. His expression was dark, but his eyes softened. She stepped closer, running her hand up his chest before cupping the back of his neck.

"I've missed you."

Drake dipped his head and pressed his lips to her forehead. "Me too," was all he said in response.

"Won't you kiss me properly?"

It took a moment for him to relent, bowing his head and pressing a chaste kiss to her lips. She pouted when he pulled away, but he was already moving towards Mason.

"You have caused us no end of fucking trouble," he ground out. "And you're fucking lucky you're Garrett's son or we wouldn't hesitate to end your sad, sorry existence, because trust me, I'm having a very hard time finding reasons to keep you alive."

Drake towered over Mason, staring down at him with hatred glowing in his indigo eyes. The mask had dropped. He wasn't playing games today. Out of all of us, Drake was the most sleep-deprived, having spent hours upon hours tracking down where Mason had taken Scarlett. His patience was at an all-time low.

"In case we hadn't already made it very clear to you, Scarlett belongs with us. She's ours. And you should have known you couldn't keep us from hunting you the fuck down when you took her."

Mason's eyes were full of rage, and he struggled against his bindings as if he wanted to throw himself at Drake.

"You are pathetic, you know that? You've wanted her for years. I know unrequited love can fucking suck, but helping a man kidnap a sixteen-year-old girl, pretending to be her friend whilst biding your time until you can have her makes you a sorry excuse for a human being."

Drake turned away from Mason and levelled his gaze on Scarlett.

"Did he do anything else to you other than that?"

He pointed at the bruise on her jaw.

"No." She sent Mason a dirty look before turning her attention back to Drake. "What now? Are we going home?"

"We will… after we search the place and decide what to do about this fuck."

"He wouldn't allow me into his office."

"Then we'll start there. Francis, you come with me. Pres, watch West and make sure he doesn't do anything stupid."

I scoffed and crossed my arms over my chest. If he thought I wasn't going to punish that little shit Mason while he was out of the room, he was clearly putting far too much trust in Prescott's ability to keep me under control.

Drake gave me a significant look before he and Francis left the room. If this was Mason's hideaway, no doubt he had shit here he didn't want anyone else seeing.

I turned to the man himself, giving him a smile.

"Why do I get the feeling you have no intention of listening to Drake?" Prescott said as he came to stand next to me.

"Because I'm not."

"You can't kill him."

"I can punish him in other ways. After all, this fucker has been after Scar for years and quite frankly, he deserves a little torture."

Prescott raised an eyebrow. Scarlett looked at both of us with a raised eyebrow.

"Come here," I said to her as I walked around the other side of the dining table.

Scarlett approached me with caution in her eyes. She probably should be suspicious as fuck right now.

I took her by the arm, pulling her closer and stroking a hand down her cheek.

"Do you want to help me punish him, little Scar?"

"How?"

I leant closer and whispered in her ear. When I pulled back, her cheeks were pink.

"Are you serious?"

"Very. After all, you like being watched, don't you?"

Her cheeks darkened to red. Her eyes darted away for a moment.

"I need… I need you to make me," she whispered.

My lips curved up into a smile. She wanted to be my reluctant but willing little victim. Well, I could certainly play that game. Scarlett liked to be humiliated and degraded. What better way than to fuck her in front of the man who had pretended to be her friend for ten years.

"Do you want a safe word?"

She shook her head, looking up at me with wide eyes.

"I trust you."

I slid her cardigan off her shoulders and threw it on one of the chairs. She was wearing a t-shirt and jeans. It pissed me off to see her in clothes he'd clearly bought for her, but at least he'd given her something decent. I would have smacked him around the head if he'd bought her skimpy shit to wear. She liked to be comfortable.

My hand went to her hair, fisting it behind her head and forcing it back so she met my eyes.

"Is my little slut desperate for dick? You've been without for far too long, haven't you?"

Her lips parted, but no sound came out.

"Mmm, I know you are."

I let go of her hair, took her arm again and pressed her face-first onto the dining table. I held her down on it with her arm pinned behind her back.

"You got something to gag her with, Pres?"

Prescott stared at the two of us with heat in his eyes, then dug his hand in his pocket, pulling out the tape. I grinned and indicated her with my head. He moved closer, pulling off a piece of duct tape. He leant over and secured it across Scarlett's mouth. She whimpered into the makeshift gag.

"Hold her down for me. Wouldn't want my dirty little slut trying to escape whilst we're teaching Mason a fucking lesson."

Prescott took over, pinning her arm to her back and grabbed her other one, securing it in his hold too. Then he turned to Mason and gave him a wink. The little shit looked incensed, struggling against the ropes holding him to the chair. He had a grand old view of Scarlett's face.

"Make sure she doesn't look away from him," I said to Prescott. "I want him to see how much she loves my dick. I want him to watch her come all over it."

My hands went to Scarlett's jeans, unbuttoning them and pulling them down her legs, along with her knickers. I ran my hands over her bare behind, stroking her skin. Then I slapped my hand across it, making her jerk.

"This is what you want, isn't it, Mason? You want to fuck this pussy. Too fucking bad. This slut belongs to my dick. I'm the one who gets to abuse her, not you."

The way he struggled harder had me chuckling and smiling at him. Scarlett shifted, spreading her legs wider for me.

54

"Well, look at you, slut, offering your pussy up to me like a fucking sacrifice."

I ran my thumb along her wet slit, almost groaning at the feeling. Fuck, how I'd missed her sweet little body.

"See this?" I brought my thumb up, letting Mason see it glisten. "This is all for me."

I watched him making noise behind his gag and smiled wider. Then I slapped Scarlett's pussy, making her cry out behind the tape.

"You ready for dick, slut? Show me how much you want it and perhaps I'll give it to you."

Scarlett raised her hips off the table, trying to encourage me. I slapped her pussy again. Prescott was no longer looking at Mason. He was staring at my hands on Scarlett, spreading her so we could both see how dripping wet she was.

"Fuck," he muttered.

"Do you think she deserves to get fucked?"

He looked up at me, his blue eyes shining with mischief and desire.

"Show him what he's missing."

SEVEN

WEST

Prescott was clearly as into punishing Mason as I was. The sick fuck had stolen our woman. We weren't going to lie down and let him fuck us over like this without exacting retribution. Drake had banned us from killing him, but he said nothing about making Mason suffer. Right now, the cunt was going to topple over the chair we'd secured him to with all his protesting behind the tape secured to his mouth and wriggling in his restraints.

"You want me to make her come over my dick, huh, Pres?"

Prescott's pupils were blown as he stared down at Scarlett's exposed holes.

"Make her come so hard, she cries."

I winked at my voyeuristic friend. It's not like Mason could see too much of what was going on since I'd made sure to place Scarlett head on to him, but it was enough to torture the fuck out of the little shit. I didn't want him seeing the view I had, anyway. He didn't deserve it. Hell, he barely deserved to see her come, but it would drive him fucking insane. That's exactly what I wanted. For him to fucking feel the pain.

"You hear that, my little Scar? Pres wants me to make you cry."

She moaned against the gag, shifting against the table. Prescott tightened his grip on her with one hand while he held her chin with the other. I'd told him to make sure she didn't look away from Mason.

My hands went to my jeans, unbuckling my belt and undoing the buttons. My dick was so hard, it fucking ached with the need to be inside my woman. My little Scar. The owner of my soul. There was nothing I wouldn't do for this woman. And being without her for almost a week was fucking crushing. It damn near ruined the four of us. We'd just got her back and this fuck deciding to steal her again made us even more determined to end this war between us and Stuart fucking Carver.

I freed my dick and ran it up her slit, almost groaning at how wet she felt.

"Do you want my cock, slut? Did you miss it? Did you miss us?"

She nodded profusely despite Prescott's hold on her face. I stroked her hip with my free hand, reassuring her I missed her too. Fuck. I didn't know what I'd do without this woman. I'd been more stable since she'd been back. Less inclined to lose my shit. She was my balm. The calm in the storm that was the four of us. The guiding fucking light of our lives.

"Mmm, don't worry, you'll get thoroughly fucked by all of us when we get home, I promise."

"After she's rested," Prescott murmured. "All of us need to."

I gave him a nod. Scarlett could sleep in the car, but we all needed to rest. None of us had been sleeping very much over the past week with our desperation to find out where the fuck Mason had taken her.

"You ready to show Mason how much you love my dick?" I asked Scarlett, leaning over her and running my hand up her spine.

She moaned into the tape. I bit my lip before notching the head of my dick at her entrance. Then I was pushing in, unable to help the groan erupting from my lips.

Prescott turned his attention to Mason, giving him an evil smile.

"You should see how she stretches around his dick. Such a fucking sight."

"Pres' favourite game is watching," I added.

The death glare we both got from Mason was worth every moment.

I slid deeper, impaling Scarlett completely. My hands went to her hips to give me leverage to fuck her. She cried out into the tape when I pulled back and slammed inside her. Her hands shifted against Prescott's, but he had a firm hold of them.

"That's it, little lamb, you're doing so good. Take his dick nice and deep."

She rubbed her face against his fingers. Prescott released her chin to cup it instead. He leant closer and nuzzled her hair.

"Good girl," he whispered in her ear. "Such a good girl."

Then he moved back, releasing her chin. Scarlett didn't look away from Mason. She stayed where she was, allowing me to fuck her as deep and rough as I wanted.

"Let go of her hands," I said a moment later.

Prescott did as I said. Scarlett laid them on the table, taking everything I was giving her without complaint. His hands went to his dick instead, adjusting it. I smirked and gave him a wink. Watching always got him going.

"You going to make him come, little lamb? You want him to fill you up with his cum?"

She nodded. It made Mason spit out a bunch of intelligible noises behind the tape. Prescott moved closer to him.

"You see that?" He pointed at us. "He had her first, you know. And I'm not talking about now. When you were busy leering over her, he was taking what's rightfully his. Scarlett has always been ours since day fucking one. We were born as one. We'll die as one." He gave Mason an evil smile. "And you? You're nothing but a fucking waste of space wanting what he can't have. She's never been yours. Never will be. Time to get that into your thick skull."

Prescott turned back to us.

"She's going to come all over his dick because she likes being told she's a dirty little bitch who loves cock. She's our corrupt queen. And she's taken her rightful place by our sides. The Four Horsemen and their goddess, Nyx."

I ran my hand up her back and gripped her hair, tugging her upright until her back was pressed to my chest. I wrapped my hand around her throat while still pumping my hips, letting her feel how much I needed her sweet little pussy wrapped around my dick.

"You hear that, little Scar? Our goddess. That's what you are."

She reached behind us, gripping my coat between her fingers. The low whine coming from behind the tape only made me shove her back down on the table, my body going with her. I leant over her, keeping her pinned to the wood while I hammered into her pussy.

"You like that, don't you, slut? Being ours. Letting us use your little body the way we need."

I ripped the tape from her mouth, making her cry out.

"I want to hear you. Tell him how much you love my dick, slut."

My hand went back to her neck, holding it and squeezing.

"I love your dick. The things you do with it make me scream," she choked out. "I can't live without it… or you."

I looked over her shoulder at Mason. The fucking broken expression on his face was exactly what I wanted to see.

"Tell him how much you like to get fucked by more than one dick at once," I whispered in her ear. "Tell him the truth."

Scarlett's grip on my coat tightened, keeping me against her.

"I can't wait to get home so you can fuck me together. I want all of you inside me. I need it so bad."

"Such a filthy little slut. So needy for cock."

"Yes," she moaned, "I need it."

Prescott was rubbing himself through his clothes, watching us with no shame.

"You want to come, slut?"

"Please."

My fingers tightened around her throat.

"You going to come for Pres, hmm? Show him how much you like getting fucked?"

"Yes, yes!"

"Tell him."

She turned her attention to Prescott who moved away from Mason, coming closer to us again.

"I want you to watch me come over his cock."

Prescott bit his lip and smiled at her, his gaze absolutely wicked.

"Mmm, then you better be a good little lamb. Show him you deserve it."

He leant over the table and stroked her hair. It was as if Mason was no longer there. It was just the three of us. And so it fucking well should be. Prescott and Scarlett were far more important to me than that piece of shit we had tied up.

"I want to see you. Show me how hard you are."

His smirk as his hand went to his jeans was devious. He had as much shame as I did, which was zero.

"Do you want him in your mouth?" I murmured in her ear. "Want him to come down your throat?"

"Please."

"You've been such a good little slut. I think Pres should reward you with his cum."

She moaned, letting go of me and reaching for Prescott.

"Hold on, get up on the table, Scar, then you can suck his dick."

I pulled away from her. She crawled up on the table and I got up on it behind her. Prescott had his dick out and knelt on the table too, shifting closer to Scarlett. I gripped her hip, pressing back inside her pussy. Scarlett reached out and stroked Prescott's cock while he gathered her hair between his fingers.

"So hard for me," she murmured, licking the head of his dick.

"Always, little lamb."

She took him in her mouth, letting go of his dick so he could control the action. I met Prescott's eyes over her body. He gave me a wink before shoving his dick so far down Scarlett's throat, she let out a low whining sound around it and gagged.

"Such a dirty little slut you are, taking his dick so deep," I taunted as I fucked her with brutal strokes.

She was trapped between us now, getting thoroughly railed from both ends. And she did nothing to stop it. No, our girl took every inch of our dicks.

"Look at you, crying so sweetly, lamb. Such a good girl," Prescott said. "You deserve a reward."

"Give it to her."

"Only if you make her come."

I grinned, reaching around and strumming her clit with my fingers.

"With fucking pleasure."

Scarlett bucked between us, trying to impale herself further on my dick. I held onto her hip tighter to stop her from moving while I claimed her pussy with my cock and stroked her needy clit. She was moaning around Prescott's dick, her hands scrabbling against the wood.

"Come for us, little lamb. Soak his dick," Prescott ground out, fucking her throat harder with his hand still fisted in her hair. "Give it to us."

It took another minute. Then she was crying all over his dick, her pussy clamping down around mine and her body trembling with her orgasm. She was wild with it, shifting and bucking in our hold. Prescott didn't let up with his cock in her throat. He kept ramming it down while I continued to fuck her pussy with as much brutality.

"Fuck," he groaned a moment later.

"Don't swallow it all yet, slut," I ordered as he came violently down her throat.

Prescott held her in place for a moment longer, before letting go of her hair, his dick popping out of her mouth. I gripped her hair instead, pulling her upright against my chest. I gripped her chin and turned her face towards Mason.

"Show him."

She opened her mouth, cum dribbling out of it down her chin.

"Good slut. Now lick it up and swallow."

Scarlett did as she was told while my hand went to her throat, holding it as an anchor while I continued to fuck her.

"Make him come, lamb, I want to see him flooding your pussy," Prescott told her as he sat back and watched the show now he was spent.

Scarlett wrapped her hand around mine on her throat and leant into me. I held closer with my arm wrapped around her middle.

"You hear that, slut? Pres wants to watch me come inside you. Do you want that? Want my cum running down your fucking thighs?"

"Yes," she moaned.

"Dirty, dirty little whore. My little bitch is in heat, isn't she?"

She whimpered but nodded against my shoulder.

"Good thing I'm about to feed your pussy then, isn't it?"

My hand squeezed around her throat as I felt it building. I fucked her harder, making her cry out from the intense pace. Then I was groaning in her ear as I erupted in her wet little pussy, coating her insides and making her squirm in my hold.

We stayed that way for a long moment after I was spent. Then I lowered Scarlett back to her hands and knees, leaning over her as I forced her to look at Mason again.

"There's something you need to know, little Scar," I whispered in her ear. "And you're not going to like it… but it's time. The truth needs to come out."

Scarlett tensed in my hold as I continued to whisper to her, watching Mason's grim expression to see what he thought of our little display. He had no idea what I was about to unleash on him. This was my final hurrah. My fucking ace. It would hurt Scarlett. I knew that, but my need to get revenge on this sick fuck was far more important.

She would forgive me… but she wouldn't be forgiving Mason for it.

Not by a long shot.

He was about to find out the reason I called her my little warrior. And why he should have never messed with my woman in the first place.

EIGHT

SCARLETT

I stared at Mason, my entire world falling to fucking pieces as West whispered the dreaded words I never wanted to hear in my ear.

"Mason killed Lylah. He killed your mother on Stuart's orders. She was making too much noise over your disappearance. It was all over the news. She kept harassing the police to do more. She wouldn't take it lying down, Scar. She was determined to get you back because she loved you so much. You were everything to her. And Stuart couldn't let that stand when he realised you couldn't remember what happened that night. When he kept you to punish us."

A tear leaked out of my eye. This time it was one of grief and not pleasure.

"He had Mason kill her and stage it as a break-in gone wrong. He stabbed her to death, Scar. It was brutal and bloody. It's an unsolved killing because that fuck was good at covering his tracks, but we knew. We fucking knew it had to be Stuart's doing. When we found out Mason had done it on Stuart's orders, that he was the one who killed her, we were fucking livid. But we couldn't touch him because of his fucking daddy."

Mason had killed my mother. He'd killed my fucking mother. Rage, hurt, and pain echoed around the void in my chest where she should be.

"I'm sorry, my little Scar. I'm sorry you have to find out this way, but I'm done hiding the truth from you. Done with secrets. You need to know why we hate him so much. Why we wish he was fucking dead."

They'd asked me to kill him once. Or, at least, they made me think I was killing him. And now? Now I wanted to rip his fucking face off. I wanted to tear him to pieces. The red mist descended. I did nothing to stop it. Nothing at all.

"Let me up."

West moved off me and the table without hesitation. He tucked himself away as I crawled off the table. I could feel his cum leaking out of me, but I literally did not give two shits about it. Pulling my clothes back on, I zipped up my jeans and stared at West. His expression almost decimated me. As if his words hadn't already done the trick. But I wasn't angry with him. No, I was fucking livid at Mason.

"Give me your knife."

"Little Scar."

"Thank you for telling me. Now give me the knife and don't get in my way."

West slid it from his pocket. I knew he would have it on him. He never went anywhere without it. I put my hand out. He placed it in my palm but didn't let it go.

"You're not angry with me, are you?"

I shook my head, then I reached out with my other hand and ran my fingers down his chest.

"No. I promise I'm not."

He released the knife. I stared down at it. Then I flipped it open and gripped it in my fist, my eyes turning towards Mason. He was looking between us with confusion. I had enjoyed Prescott and West fucking me in front of him. It gave me a high to see him so tortured over it after all the shit he'd put me through.

And now… now I was going to kill him because he'd killed my mother. I was going to avenge her death. It was the least I could fucking do. My mother would have never given up searching for me. Never. Mason had taken her away. That was unforgivable.

I walked around the table with the knife clutched between my fingers and approached Mason. I don't know what he could see in my expression, but it couldn't be anything good. Then I ripped the fucking tape off his mouth.

"Scar—"

"Oh no, I didn't take that off so you could fucking talk," I ground out, cutting him off.

"I'm—"

I slapped him across his face.

"You killed my mother. You killed her in cold fucking blood."

He tipped his face up towards me as the blood drained from it.

"I…"

"Now you can't talk? Fuck you! Just fuck you!"

69

"I'm sorry."

The fact he'd even tried to apologise to me was rage-inducing.

"You're sorry? You're fucking sorry? You murdered her for him. You took away my only fucking family after he stole me."

The abject misery on his face didn't fill me with sympathy or compassion. In fact, it made me want to kill him more. To make him feel every ounce of pain my mother must have felt. She'd looked for me. She'd wanted me back, and he made sure I could never be reunited with her. All for fucking Stuart Carver.

"Scarlett..."

"I hate you!" I screamed in his face. "I fucking hate you!"

My hand came up with the knife in it. It sailed through the air and hit my target. It hit him right in the fucking chest. For a moment, neither of us did anything. Then he looked down at the knife. I choked on my own breath before I ripped it out of his chest.

"I hope you burn."

Everything went still for the briefest of moments, then I stabbed him again. And again. And again. It reminded me of killing the man in the warehouse, but this time, I was in control. I knew what I was doing.

I was aiming to kill.

"Guess what, fucker? They killed your friends for me. They fucking murdered them. And now you're going to die. Die drowning in your own fucking blood."

I heard footsteps followed by an exclamation behind me, but I ignored it. Mason's expression was horrifying, but I didn't care. My heart was frozen over. He had shown himself to be nothing and no one. A selfish piece of shit who never cared about me. He only cared about himself. And I was his fucking reaper.

He choked a minute later, blood gurgling from his mouth. I watched the life drain from his eyes. They were wide with shock like he never expected me to be the one to take his life. Well, it served him fucking right.

"Scarlett!"

Drake's voice broke through my blood-fuelled haze. I stepped back, ripping the knife from Mason's chest one last time. He was a dead, bloody mess. And it was fucking glorious.

My chest heaved as my arm dropped to my side. I turned my head and saw the four of them staring at me.

Francis had a proud look in his eyes, but he was trying not to show it. Prescott's pupils were blown and his lips curled up into a smile, like the sight of me murdering Mason was hot as fuck. Drake looked like he wanted to blow a fucking fuse. But West? Well, he looked at me the way he had always done. Like I was the only thing in the world that mattered to him. And he loved me.

My feet advanced forward before my brain even registered I was on the move. I dropped the knife on the table then I was on West, my bloody hands in his hair tugging him down until my mouth crashed against his. I pressed myself against him, forcing him into accepting my affection. Into accepting my kiss.

West was frozen for a long moment, clearly unprepared for me to attack his face like this. Then his arms were around me and his tongue was in my mouth. He backed me up against the table, shoving me down on it and covering my body with his.

He kissed me like he was drowning, and I responded in kind, moaning into his mouth. His fingers tangled in my hair, clutching me to him as if his whole life depended on it. I couldn't get enough of this feeling. Of the sensation of his tongue against mine, devouring my mouth with each swipe. It was messy. My hands were in his hair, covering him in Mason's blood, but neither of us cared. All I could think, see, and feel was him. All I could do was grind against his body and kiss him until I could hardly breathe.

West pulled back slightly, his amber eyes full of heat and his mouth smeared with blood.

"There's my little warrior," he murmured.

Then his mouth was back on mine, kissing me with such gentleness, I almost cried. It was the way he'd kissed me when we'd been sixteen. His grip on me was still rough, but his mouth was so soft and sweet.

My West. My West is back. This... I need this... I need you. Fuck, do I need you.

I wanted to tell him, but he was too busy making me feel like I was his only one. The only girl in this entire world that he needed and wanted. He put me back together, piece by piece, with his kisses. Repairing the part of my heart that had broken when faced with the knowledge Mason had murdered my mother. West made me feel whole again.

I love you, West Greer. I don't think my heart ever stopped, even when I couldn't remember you.

When he finally released me, he smiled, and I couldn't help grinning back.

"West..."

"If you two have quite finished, we need to talk about this," came Drake's voice from behind us.

West straightened and looked behind him at Drake.

"Oh, I'm sorry, did you want a turn?"

His eyes went pointedly to Drake's crotch as I pushed myself up on my elbows. Drake glared at him and turned away slightly, trying to hide the fact the sight of all the blood had aroused him. All of us could see and were very aware of his particular... kinks.

"You can kiss me too... if you want," I said, giving him a wink.

I was still caught up in the kiss with West and my stabby-fest. Adrenaline coursed through my veins, making me reckless. And I sure as fuck wanted to push Drake's buttons because of it.

For a second, I thought he might tell me to turn over so he could spank me in punishment for giving him attitude.

"Come here." His voice came out low, gravelly, and commanding all at the same time. "Now."

I scrambled off the table, West stepping back to give me room. The moment I got within two feet of Drake, he had me by the arm and dragged me closer. He leant down, his indigo eyes full of suppressed desire.

"You are such a little brat," he murmured.

"Yes, Daddy."

He stopped right before his mouth met mine. I'd said it quietly so no one else could hear me. It's not like I had a daddy kink but knowing it would piss Drake off was the only reason I said it.

"What the fuck did you just say to me?"

"You heard me."

"You'll be the death of me, little wisp."

He gripped my hair in his fist, then he kissed me in that savage way of his, completely heedless of the fact he was doing it in front of the others. The grip he had on my hair made my scalp burn, but I didn't care. He was punishing me for my remark.

When he released me, he nuzzled my face.

"I'm going to thoroughly redden your pert little arse when we get home," he murmured, "and I'm going to fuck it afterwards, you hear me?"

"Yes, sir."

"Brat."

"You love it."

He stroked my cheek.

"You're lucky I do," he whispered, finally admitting it for the first time.

I pressed my mouth to his before smearing the blood I'd left on him across his cheek. He let out a little growl in response, then pulled away and looked over at Mason.

"That is a mess we didn't need, little wisp."

"He killed my mother."

Drake straightened and looked between West and Prescott.

"Which one of you told her?"

"Me," West replied with a shrug.

He stood next to Prescott while Drake was mauling my mouth. I wanted to press myself against West and never leave his side. He'd finally allowed me to kiss him and it had been everything. And this stubborn man in front of me had given

74

me a real kiss too, like I'd wanted from him earlier. I was on cloud nine, even if I'd just killed a man in cold blood.

Drake turned his attention back to me.

"We'll talk about that later. Right now, we need to clean this shit up. It's lucky he put in wooden floors. Francis, go get the car from where we left it. Prescott, you can take this one to clean herself up whilst West and I deal with Mason since we've already got his fucking blood on us."

"Are you sure you don't want me to help?"

He looked at me for a long moment.

"No, you can help Francis and Prescott with the stuff in Mason's office."

I raised an eyebrow.

"The stuff in his office?"

Drake stroked my cheek with his fingers.

"Yes. We're taking it with us to look through at home. There's too much there for us to deal with right now and from what Francis and I have seen… well, let's just say it's rather useful."

I wasn't sure what Mason could have that would be useful, but I was going to take Drake's word for it.

"Strip out of that first. We'll need to make sure we destroy all the evidence."

Francis moved towards the front door while Prescott went over to the kitchen and started looking in the cupboards. I imagined it was for Mason's cleaning supplies.

I let out a sigh and started removing my clothes, leaving them in a pile on the floor. When I was bare, I wiped my feet down to make sure I wasn't trailing blood everywhere, then moved towards the hallway. Prescott had piled a bunch of things on the kitchen counter for Drake and West. He followed me to the bathroom and flipped on the shower for me.

"Are you okay, little lamb?" he asked, stroking my arm to get my attention.

I had to think about it for a moment. I'd killed another person. Last time, I'd fallen apart over it. Somehow, this time, it was different. There were no feelings of regret or remorse. I merely felt a sense of peace washing over me.

Wherever you are now, Mum, I hope you're happy. I avenged your death. And even if that puts a black mark on my soul, I don't care. It was worth it.

I looked up at Prescott and gave him a smile.

"I'm good... I'm glad he's dead. And I don't feel bad about it."

Then I stepped into the shower and let it wash away the evidence of the slaughter I'd left in my wake.

NINE

DRAKE

W hat a fucking shitshow. The past fucking week had been one, but what we'd just had to clean up was even more so. That wasn't even the end of it. Scarlett had set in motion a tidal wave of fuckery none of us could run from. She'd cast the first stone by killing Mason. And now the consequences would come galloping in like a fucking storm with hellfire in its wake.

Yet... I wasn't angry at her for it. In fact, I was proud of the way she'd handled herself. She hadn't hesitated this time, according to West. She'd asked for his knife to kill Mason with. When Francis and I had heard screaming, we'd run into the living area to find her stabbing the guy to death with calm fury written all over her face. Scarlett knew exactly what she was doing. She wanted him to die. Needed it. How could I ever begrudge her revenge on the man who'd helped steal her from her life? Who'd murdered her mother to cover up her kidnapping. Who had done nothing but lust after her since she was a teenager. There was no redeeming a man like Mason Jones.

We'd spent a couple of hours dealing with Mason's place, making sure we scrubbed it thoroughly of our presence and loading his papers into the Jeep. Now all I wanted to do was get home and sleep in my own fucking bed. However, we had a stupidly long journey home to contend with, not to mention there was a body in the back of the car.

West had called Penn when we were finishing up. He'd given us details for someone he knew who could help us dispose of Mason's body. I didn't question how or why he knew someone in Scotland. The guy was resourceful. He was London's best known and most sought after Fixer for a reason. No wonder he basically lived in Zayn Villetti's pocket, according to West.

It wasn't the first time I'd been thankful for his friendship with West. Penn might be batshit crazy, but he was useful as fuck. He'd helped us out on more than one occasion. We still owed him a favour, and no doubt he would come to collect when he was ready.

Francis was taking the first few hours behind the wheel. Prescott had fallen asleep with his face smashed against the window in the front seat a few minutes after we'd set off. He'd barely got any sleep since we'd left home, so it was unsurprising he was the first one to crash out. West was dozing in the back with me and Scarlett, who was sitting in the middle. She was curled into my side with her head resting on my shoulder. I'd covered the both of us with one of the blankets we'd brought with us so she didn't get cold.

I needed her close to me. Needed her body against mine. I was the last person to see her, and it killed me to know she'd been taken right after the moment we'd shared on the rooftop. After she'd given me exactly what I needed. To punish her, fuck her and hold her afterwards. She was my heaven, wrapped up in a beautiful human being who loved fiercely and gave everything to those she cared about. And having her gone for a week was a fucking wake up call.

"Drake?"

I looked at her. It was dark outside, but I could just about make out her wary expression. Her voice was hushed as if she didn't want to disturb the others.

"Yes?"

She curled an arm around me, stroking my side with her fingertips.

"How did you find me?"

My mind circled back to the past week. The hours we'd spent tracking down Mason's place. It wasn't an easy task, by any means. He'd covered his tracks well. The house wasn't even in his fucking name. It made finding it far more difficult than it should have been.

"We saw you being taken on the security footage and after trawling through it, we got a good look at who took you. He not only drugged you but one of our security guards. It took us some time to work out how he got into the building in the first place. After we went snooping around Tonya's old place, we found she'd leaked our building plans, along with our security details, to him. That's how he got to you."

I decided to lay it all out for her. Scarlett should know the lengths we went to in order to find her.

"You searched Tonya's?"

"Mmm, we broke in. I wasn't going to ask Fletch, even though he has the keys. I'm not fucking talking to him after he landed me in the shit with my mother."

Scarlett's stroking grew more insistent. It was making me uncomfortable, but not because I didn't want her touching me. My problem had to do with the fact she'd looked like a damn queen when she'd butchered Mason. All that blood covering her clothes. The blood that had got on me when I kissed her. Not to mention the provoking words she'd come out with. All of it fuelled my desire to paint her lithe little body with welts and fuck her until she cried from my brutality.

Fuck, I need to rein this in.

"When are you going to tell her about me?"

"After we've handled Stuart."

"Are you going to be honest about all of us being a thing? You know, we can't exactly hide that from her, Rosie and Frankie's parents."

I hadn't exactly thought about it, even if she was right.

"I don't see how we can keep the truth from them."

"I can't even imagine what she's going to say."

I didn't want to. In fact, it was a conversation I would quite happily avoid forever. Our families likely wouldn't approve of our unorthodox relationship with Scarlett. And they would be unhappy about us hiding the truth about her return from them too.

"Are you going to let me get on with telling you about the past week?"

She nodded, her hand leaving my side and running down my stomach. I tensed under her exploration, not wanting her to find out what her proximity was doing to me right at this moment. Before she could get too far, I removed her hand from my stomach and placed it on my thigh instead. Scarlett didn't protest, but I could feel her eyes boring into the side of my head.

"Once we worked out how Mason gained access to the building, we had to put in extra measures to prevent anything like this from happening again. We're going to keep you safe this time, little wisp. We don't care what it takes or the cost. We won't let anyone take you again."

"I know," she whispered into my shoulder. "I trust you."

Her hand curled around my thigh, her fingers stroking along it. I fought against the urge to press her hand against my cock. It was getting really fucking uncomfortable now.

"It wasn't easy to find you. Mason has a property in the city, but the one he took you to isn't in his name. We searched his London flat for clues about where he'd taken you. Then we tracked down his associates when we turned up nothing. West beat some sense into them, but even they had no fucking clue. Francis searched his flat again and had to break into the safe he had hidden under the floorboards. That's where we found the deed. It was in his mother's name. And his mother isn't Garrett's wife. Not his real mother, anyway. We found his birth certificate there too. Quite the fucking scandal Garrett had to cover up there."

Even as I told her this, all I could focus on was where her hand was. I didn't question why I found Scarlett so fucking distracting. She was my very own siren. A woman I couldn't resist under any circumstances.

"He had an affair with a woman he worked with, and she ended up pregnant. Two months after she gave birth to Mason, she was found dead in the canal by a single gunshot wound to the back of the head. It was from a police issue weapon, so pretty fucking suspicious, but they never found her killer and Mason was raised by Garrett alone."

"No wonder he turned into such a creep."

I almost snorted. Mason was more than a creep, but that was neither here nor there.

"The moment we found out where you were, we came for you, little wisp. We drove all night to get to you. None of us has slept much in the past forty-eight hours."

Her hand moved higher as if she wanted to soothe me with her touch.

"You must be exhausted. I'll let you sleep."

I caught her hand in mine, pulling it away so she wouldn't notice how fucking hard I was for her. Scarlett shifted next to me, tugging her hand from mine. I thought she was going to move away from me, but no. The girl damn well decided she was going to touch me right where I was aching for her.

"Or not. Did I do that?"

"You know very well you did," I muttered, trying not to groan when she started stroking her hand along my length.

You are going to kill me one day.

"Was it all the blood?"

I felt like telling her to quit it, but it felt too fucking good.

"You, the blood, watching you kill again. All of it, little wisp. You make me so fucking crazy."

Our voices were low, so they didn't carry to the front. West was still asleep. We weren't exactly disturbing him, either.

"Then let me take care of it for you."

Scarlett shifted and started unbuttoning my clothes without a second fucking thought. The moment she wrapped her small hand around my cock, I gritted my teeth. This wasn't going to do. I didn't want to come all over myself. Gripping the blanket, I tugged it up before planting my hand behind her head and shoving her underneath it.

"Wrap your lips around it," I hissed before settling the blanket over her.

I almost fucking died when she complied. Her hot little mouth was heaven. She stroked what she couldn't fit between her lips. I wasn't going to make her gag on me. It might wake up Prescott and West. My eyes went to the front of the car and met Francis' through the rearview mirror. He gave me a look that spoke volumes. He knew what was happening. I gave him a shrug, placing my hand over Scarlett's head underneath the blanket to keep her working my cock with her mouth.

Francis shook his head and turned his attention back to the road. Probably a good thing he was the one driving. If it had been Prescott, he would no doubt be encouraging us right now. I didn't have time for his voyeuristic antics. Not when it felt so fucking good to have her mouth wrapped around me.

"Little wisp, don't stop," I whispered.

She hummed, the sensation making my dick throb in her mouth. I had no problems letting her set the pace and be in control right now. All I wanted was to come down her fucking throat after being tormented by the sight of her bloody form earlier.

The moment she cupped my balls with her free hand, my head hit the headrest and I couldn't help the low groan escaping my mouth. It was a mistake because West opened his eyes and glared at me. Then he looked down at what Scarlett was doing. A smirk appeared on his face as he glanced into the front to find Prescott still fast asleep.

"And here I thought you would be giving Mr Voyeur a show," he murmured, tugging the blanket he had on up higher around him.

"Fuck off," I hissed. "Go back to sleep."

"How can I when you're getting your dick sucked next to me?"

"Easy, pretend you didn't see it and close your eyes."

Scarlett popped off my dick and sat up, pushing the blanket off her head.

"Would you shut up? I can't make you come if you're busy arguing with West."

West snorted, giving me a wink.

"Yeah, Drake, listen to Scar and keep your mouth shut if you want to get off."

I was about to open my mouth to retort when I was rudely interrupted.

"All of you shut up or you'll wake Pres," Francis hissed from the driver's seat. "Did you forget he literally had no sleep at all on the journey up here?"

West turned away from us, rolling his eyes, and settled back down. Scarlett dived back beneath the blanket and wrapped her mouth around my dick. My hand went to her hair, pushing her down on it. She sucked me harder, making me grit my teeth so I wouldn't make any further noise.

It didn't take long before I came with a low grunt down her throat. While it felt fucking good, it wasn't quite the most satisfying experience given we'd been interrupted by West. I reminded myself when we were home, I had planned to punish her. The knowledge of it would tide me over until then.

Scarlett pulled back, swallowing before she tucked me away. Then she settled herself on me, her arm around me as her head burrowed against my chest. I covered her with the blanket, not wanting to tell her off for the way she was draped over me. My hand went to her hair, stroking her as I leant back against the headrest.

I closed my eyes, feeling content with her there. The motion of the car, Scarlett's soft breathing and her lithe body on mine lulled me to sleep. And I realised before I dropped off, it had been a very long time since my mind was empty enough to allow me to rest without any worries crowding my head.

TEN

FRANCIS

I was too fucking tired for words by the time we got back to Fortuity. The stress of the past week and the lack of sleep had left me needing to hibernate in bed. The relief we all felt having Scarlett back with us was palpable. There was no stone we'd left unturned in our search for her. We weren't going to allow her to be taken from us again. Not after the past ten years without her. Not when we were in love with the girl we'd grown up with. If anything, that made it even more imperative we got her back.

Drake pulled the Jeep up under Fortuity in the carpark. I looked over at the car next to us, finding Penn leaning against it with a smirk on his face. That tattooed bastard was useful, even if he was a headcase. We all got out and West went over to greet him. Prescott took Scarlett's hand and pulled her towards the lifts. Drake had told him to take her up to bed while we dealt with Penn.

"Am I not allowed to say hello to your little lady?" Penn asked West.

"Don't fucking flirt with her."

Penn gave West a wink before he took a few steps towards the lift where Scarlett was clutching Prescott's hand and looking dead on her feet.

"I hear you've had quite the adventure."

"You could say that," she replied.

"Did you meet my friend?"

She raised an eyebrow.

"The one who grunts more than actually talks?"

"Yeah, that's him."

We'd stopped on the way to deal with Mason, so we didn't have to drive all the way back here with a dead body in Prescott's Jeep. Well, for the most part, anyway. Penn's "friend" took Mason's body out of the back of the Jeep and returned half an hour later with one of those freezer bags containing ice packs and a decapitated head. Drake had asked him for that and to dispose of the rest.

"We did, though he didn't say much. I liked his house. I wouldn't want to be tucked away surrounded by the woods. This is my home." She waved around at the place. "But if you wanted peace and quiet, it'd be perfect."

Penn gave her a nod.

"Haven't been there myself. He lived down here for a few years. That's how I met him. He's a useful sort."

"You seem to know a lot of those."

"Part of my job… say, did West talk to you about getting tattooed yet?"

Scarlett's eyebrows shot up. Her eyes went to West, who merely shrugged. Drake was busy getting the freezer bag out of the back, but I could see him listening to what was being said.

"No, he didn't."

The lift arrived, the doors sliding open.

"Well, just so you know, the offer is there if you ever need my services."

Penn gave her a wink as Prescott pulled her into the lift. She didn't respond, just gave him a little wave before the doors closed.

"If you're quite done flirting with our girlfriend," Drake said, giving Penn a hard stare.

Penn merely smiled at Drake and walked back over to us.

"If you think that was flirting, I clearly need to give you some lessons."

West barked with laughter. Drake scowled. I put my hand over my mouth. Drake and flirting did not go hand in hand.

"I'd love to see you try," West said when he settled down. "Drake's not a very good student."

Drake merely shoved the bag at Penn, who took it with a graceful smile.

"You can shut the fuck up, West. And you... look after this for us," Drake ground out, pointing at the bag. "We haven't decided what we're going to do with it yet, but we will be sure to let you know when we do."

Drake didn't wait for an answer. He stalked away to the lift, hitting the button to wait for it to come back down.

"Someone clearly got out on the wrong side of bed this morning," Penn said with a grin before he opened the boot of his car and stuffed the bag containing Mason's head inside it.

"None of us has really slept," I said with a shrug. "Not to mention West interrupted Scar giving Drake head in the car. Think that soured his mood."

Penn snorted. Drake would probably kill me for telling him that, but I didn't care. All I wanted to do was take a shower and fall into bed.

"He did get off though, right? I'm sure she's not the type to leave a man hanging."

"Don't talk about her like that," West ground out, giving Penn a look. "But yes, he did." He walked towards where Drake was standing. "I'll call you."

I gave Penn a nod, watching him walk around and get in his car before joining the other two. The ride up to our penthouse was silent. Drake was clearly brooding. Neither me nor West wanted to piss him off further. I trudged up the stairs when we left the lift. The five of us had stopped for an early dinner on the way at a service station, so I was ready to sleep.

When I slipped into my bedroom and shut the door, my eyes went to the bed. I stilled when I saw a lump in it. My heart thumped in my chest. I hadn't expected her to be here. Our night together last week had been rudely fucking interrupted by Mason. Her coming to me had me wanting to get into bed, curl myself around her and never leave again, but I needed a wash first.

I padded into the bathroom, trying not to be too loud as I stripped out of my clothes and got in the shower. The hot water soothed me. I didn't linger after I'd washed myself, eager to be with my girl even if we were just going to sleep. Drying as fast as I could, I pulled on a pair of boxers, turned out the lights and slid into bed behind Scarlett.

I wrapped myself around her back, curling my arm around her and pinning her to my body. Nuzzling her hair with my face, I breathed her in. She didn't smell of her usual cinnamon, but that was okay. I was just happy to have her here.

"Frankie," she breathed out.

"I'm here."

She turned in my arms and buried her face in my chest, clutching me to her body.

"I missed you so much," she choked out a moment later. "I know you're tired, but please kiss me. I need you."

I took hold of her chin, tipped her face up and found her hazel-green eyes teary.

"Shh, shh, don't cry. I'll give you anything you need, Scar."

Capturing her mouth with mine, I held her close and kissed her, trying to be gentle and sweet, knowing it was what she needed after everything she'd been through.

"I love you," she murmured against my lips, "I love you so much."

She kissed her way down my jaw and buried her face in my neck, breathing me in.

"You're my favourite scent in the whole damn world, you know that."

I chuckled. Knowing she loved it, I'd slapped on some of my cologne before getting into bed.

"I'll let you in on a secret. I've been having it specially made for years. Your love of apples and cinnamon is something I'll never forget. I wanted something that reminded me of you wherever I went. It kept me from falling apart and losing hope that we'd get you back one day."

She tipped her head back, staring up at me with wide eyes.

"That's... fuck, Frankie, why are you so sweet?"

I reached up and stroked her face.

"Because I love you."

She leant back into me, brushing her lips against mine.

"Tell me again."

I flipped her over onto her back, pressing my body against hers and running my tongue along her jaw.

"I love you, little whore."

My fingers tugged off the little lacy knickers she'd worn to bed. Yes, I was fucking exhausted, but her body was too tempting and sinful for me not to be aroused. I couldn't help myself when it came to Scarlett.

"I love you." I pressed my lips to her pulse point. "I love you." My boxers were discarded next to us within a matter of seconds. "I love you." I stroked my fingers between her legs, finding her wet for me. "I love you forever."

She let out a moan when I slid home, clutching my shoulders with her small hands. Her legs wrapped around me, encouraging me to give her what she needed... me. I wasn't going to be rough with her today. I wanted to make love to her. To show her how much I missed her. How I needed her as much as I needed air to keep breathing.

Rocking into her, I stroked her hair back from her face before cupping her cheek. I stared into those eyes I loved so much, trying to communicate my feelings without words. She looked up at me with so much fucking open love and affection, it was almost too much to handle after being away from this beautiful woman for a week.

"Mason ruined our last night together," she whispered, stroking her hand down my back. "He can't ruin anything for us ever again."

"You made sure of that."

"I did… and before you ask, I don't regret it. He got what was coming to him."

I pressed my lips to hers.

"He deserved to die."

"I know I shouldn't, but I liked it. The heat of the moment, watching the life drain from his eyes. It made me feel like a god."

I took her hands and pinned them to the bed. Hearing her talk about killing made my dick throb. And while I wanted to be gentle, her words had me needing to give it to her harder.

"It's a heady feeling, being the one in control of someone's life like that."

She arched up into me, asking for more. I thrust deeper, knowing exactly what she needed.

"Intoxicating… like a high you know you shouldn't feel, but you do because he deserved it. He deserved the pain. I gave it to him. I hurt him. Made him feel my pain. And all that blood everywhere, fuck… Frankie, it made me feel like a queen being covered in it."

"You looked like a goddess, my fucking goddess."

I wasn't going to lie. Seeing her kill was hot. It's not like Scarlett and I hadn't talked about killing before. She knew my feelings on the matter. Knew how it fuelled me when I took someone's life. How it did something to all of us.

"Tell me… tell me how she died."

She was talking about Chelsea. It was on the news a few days ago about how Chelsea McDonald had killed herself. Except she hadn't really. It was me who'd killed her.

I pressed my face into Scarlett's neck, keeping up my pace. She felt so hot and wet as I fucked her. Talking about this was turning both of us on further. Scarlett linked her fingers between mine, holding onto me right back as if she craved the deep connection we'd forged with each other.

"I wore gloves to her house so I wouldn't leave fingerprints. The moment she saw me, she knew why I was there. And, of course, she was a bitch to me about it, but I didn't care. She threatened my family."

Scarlett moaned as I shifted the angle, hitting the right spot for her. I noted what she liked whenever we fucked, so I could make her feel good.

"I made her write a suicide note whilst I tied the noose I'd fashioned to the bannisters on the landing next to the stairs. Then I placed a chair underneath it and made her stand on it. She put the noose over her head and tightened it like I requested… then she was still giving me shit, so I kicked the chair from under her. I guess I got a little impatient to get it over and done with."

Scarlett's nails dug into my back with my words, like hearing me say those things only made her want me more. Her chest heaved against mine, her body moving with me. I kissed her neck, licking her skin to taste her.

"I watched her die, Scar. I watched her, and I didn't care that I'd taken a life. I didn't give a shit. She knew the rules, and she broke them. I will kill anyone who fucks with my family.

And I'll torture anyone who fucks with you before I end them."

"Why is that so hot?"

I grinned, pulling away to look at her.

"You're in the darkness with us now, little whore." My hands pressed hers down harder into the mattress. "Embrace it as I have. Be ours."

She smiled up at me.

"The goddess and her horsemen?"

I leant closer, running my nose up hers.

"That's right... Nyx belongs with Pestilence, War, Famine and Death."

"Always."

I kissed her. It was rough and raw. Her tongue clashed with mine, our bodies moving faster together like we were both pushing each other to the edge. I let go of one of her hands and pressed it between us to reach her clit. Scarlett cried out at the extra sensation.

"Come for me, little whore," I murmured against her mouth. "Show me you belong to me."

She wrapped her now free hand around me, stroking it down my back. Her nails dug into my skin a minute later, making me grunt. I fucked her harder in response and she exploded for me. Her pussy clenched around my cock. I couldn't hold back my own climax with her bucking against me.

"Fuck," I ground out, feeling it race up my spine before I erupted inside her.

I almost collapsed on top of her when I was spent. Then exhaustion really did set in. I don't know where the extra burst of energy came from, but we'd both needed this. To reconnect with each other after Mason had ripped her away.

Shifting off Scarlett, I made myself get up and pull her with me into the bathroom to clean up. We got tucked back up together afterwards, holding each other like our lives depended on it. I buried my face in her hair, never wanting this moment to end as I closed my eyes.

"Love you forever," she whispered against my chest, pressing a kiss to my heart.

"Love you for eternity," I murmured back as sleep claimed me and my beautiful girl, who ruled my soul.

ELEVEN

PRESCOTT

I awoke for the first time to the sound of my sheets rustling. Opening my eyes, I found Scarlett crawling into my bed. Her hair was sleep-rumpled, and she had a tired smile on her face. I lifted my arm up, allowing her to tuck herself up next to me, and pulled the sheets over us. A minute later, I drifted back off, content to have my girl next to me.

Waking for the second time, I discovered Scarlett sprawled across my body, her hair fanning over my chest. Her tiny fist was pressed against her mouth, making her look so fucking adorable. I didn't want to disturb her, even though I was curious why she'd left Francis' bed to come to mine this morning. She'd told me it was important they got to have their night together after Mason had interrupted it when he stole her. I respected her wishes, although I wanted her with me. When you were in a relationship with a woman who was also in one with your three best friends, selfishness wasn't an option.

Reaching up, I stroked Scarlett's hair with gentle fingers, not intending to wake her but needing to touch my girl all the same.

"I've missed you, little lamb," I whispered.

Her being gone had left us in a fucking state. It made it all the more clear she belonged with us. We didn't function right without Scarlett. The way we'd been for the past ten years no longer worked for us. Not now the five of us knew what it felt like to be together. Sure, we still had conflicts, and Scarlett hadn't exactly completely resolved her relationships with Drake and West, but between me and her, things were perfect. Same for Francis now he'd declared his love to her. He'd told me about it during some downtime we'd had in the search for Scarlett. I got why it was a big deal to him after everything he'd been through with Chelsea.

Scarlett shifted on my chest, her hand uncurling from her mouth and flattening on my skin.

"My wolf," she murmured.

I couldn't fight the grin spreading across my face. She opened those hazel-green eyes of hers and gave me a soft smile when she saw I was awake too.

"Dare I ask if Francis knows you're here?"

"He does... he had his fill of me last night."

"I bet he did."

Scarlett rolled her eyes. The next thing I knew, she'd moved to straddle my lap and lean over me, placing her hands on either side of my head.

"Jealous?"

"Not in the slightest." I ran my thumb along her bottom lip. "I already got to fuck this pretty little mouth of yours."

She nipped my thumb before sucking it into her mouth and swirling her tongue around it. I licked my lip. Of course, I'd woken up sporting an erection, what with Scarlett being on top of me. This wasn't helping it go down.

"Don't start something you can't finish."

My words only made her suck my thumb the way she'd suck my dick.

Fuck me.

"You're a bad little lamb."

She slid my thumb out of her mouth and gave me a salacious look.

"Maybe your lamb wants her wolf."

I groaned, wanting so fucking badly to take her up on that offer, but we promised Drake we'd all go through the boxes from Mason's house we'd brought with us today.

"My lamb is going to have to wait until later… and if you'd like, I'll quite happily chase you around the penthouse."

She grinned and leant closer, pressing her mouth to mine. Her tongue chased mine down. I allowed us a moment of passion, running my hand down her back, and making her wriggle on top of me.

"And what about the woods?" she asked as she pulled away and rolled off me.

"Mmm, I can arrange that soon."

"I wasn't asking for tonight." She hopped off the bed and went over to my wardrobes. "We should go when it rains next."

I sat up and watched her open the door. She pulled out a few things for both of us, placing them on my armchair.

"You want me to chase you in the rain?"

The wicked look in her eyes had me adjusting myself.

"I want you to make me extra dirty when you catch me and fuck me in the mud."

I jumped out of bed and went over to her, capturing her up in my arms.

"I'm pretty sure you've been taking lessons from Francis."

"Lessons in what?"

"How to be a secret deviant."

She snorted and shoved my chest.

"He's just smart."

"Too fucking smart for his own good. I swear his imagination knows no bounds."

Going up on her tiptoes, she pressed a kiss to my mouth.

"That's one of the things I love about him."

I raised an eyebrow.

"And what do you love about me?"

She licked her lip.

"You're always putting me first, taking care of me, being sweet and kind and the way you love me is... I don't have words, but it's the best feeling in the world."

My hand drifted from her back to her behind. I gave it a squeeze.

"And you're dirty as fuck, so there's that too," she added.

"That's more like it."

"Aww, Pres, do you not like having nice qualities?"

"No, I like being bad."

She laughed and kissed me again.

"You can be bad to me later." She skipped out of my arms and gathered up my clothes. "For now, let me dress you."

I didn't object as she helped me into a casual pair of dark chinos and a black polo shirt. She stroked my chest when she was done, giving me the once over before dressing herself in a little black jersey dress. I noted she hadn't put on any underwear underneath it. Her nipples stood out against the fabric. I stroked one when she passed by me, only earning me a scowl.

"You can play with them later," she stated before she flounced out of the room, leaving me trailing behind her.

When we got downstairs, Drake was already up and had laid out the boxes all over the dining table. In the kitchen, he'd left a selection of brunch items for us on the counter.

"Well, someone has been busy this morning," I commented as Scarlett, and I made our way over to the kitchen.

"No time for slacking off," Drake muttered, his head buried in some papers.

I didn't know if it was a dig or not, but I decided to ignore him. Scarlett set about making us some tea and a coffee for his majesty. She took it over to him, placing it down by his hand and leaning down to kiss his temple.

"Morning, grumpy."

"I'm adding that to your list of offences, Scarlett."

She grinned at me before pushing his arm off the table so she could straddle his lap. Drake stared at her with cold eyes. She merely stroked her fingers through his hair.

"Are you going to write it all down and present it to me, so I know why I'm being punished?"

"If that's what it takes to get you to behave."

"We both know you don't want me to behave, Drake. Let's not pretend otherwise."

I snorted, picking up two plates for me and Scarlett and bringing them over to the table. I made some room for them before grabbing our teas and sitting down.

"Go eat your breakfast."

She leant closer to him, brushing her lips over his.

"What if I want you to feed me?"

"You're trying my patience."

"Is it so bad I want to spend time with you?" she told him, her voice cracking on the words. "I need you, Drake. Don't you understand that?"

For a moment I thought he might push her off him and tell her to go sit with me, but he reached up and stroked her hair back from her face.

"You need me."

"Yes... a lot more than you realise. The only time you give me your undivided attention is when I push your buttons. Is it any wonder I'm always doing it?"

He leant his forehead against hers and sighed.

"I'm sorry. I didn't think. I'm not used to being... needed."

She wrapped her arms around him and buried her face in his neck.

"I'm not trying to ask you for things you can't give me but spending time with me is non-negotiable. And a little affection wouldn't hurt either."

He curled his arms around her.

"Like this?" he asked, nuzzling her hair.

"Exactly like this. No more statue Drake. I don't like him."

"Statue Drake?"

She pulled away and looked at him.

"Yes, sometimes you're like a stone and I'm not here for it. Warm, fuzzies Drake who kisses me without restraint is who I want."

"I don't do warm fuzzies, Scarlett."

She bopped his nose with her finger. He scowled but didn't make a move to stop her.

"You do with me. Now, about feeding me."

"Don't push your luck."

She cupped his face with both hands and gave him a bright smile.

"It's what I do."

He didn't get a chance to respond. She kissed him, making him accept her affection. And he did, tangling his hand in her hair and angling her head to deepen their kiss.

Watching Scarlett handle Drake was rather amusing. He clearly wasn't sure what to do with her when she was like this. I had a feeling he also liked the way she pushed him. In fact, he needed it. She was the only one who could wrap him around her finger without him realising she was doing it.

I turned when I heard a noise from the stairs finding West and Francis walking downstairs together, talking in low voices. Scarlett slipped out of Drake's lap and came over to me, taking a seat in mine instead.

"Are you expecting me to feed you?" I asked, turning to her as the other two went into the kitchen.

"No, but we can eat whilst we look through this shit."

I wrapped my arm around her waist before sipping at my tea. Then I dragged over a stack of papers and started looking through them. West and Francis joined us a few minutes later.

The five of us were silent as we ate and looked through everything we'd brought back from Mason's.

"Holy fuck," Francis breathed out, making me look up.

"What?"

He flipped around a photo he was holding to show me. It was taken in a hospital room and showed a patient lying in a bed with Garrett Jones standing over her. Next to him was Stuart. There was a window in the background, and it was dark outside. It took me a minute to register that the person in the bed was Scarlett.

"Is this what I think it is?"

"I'm pretty sure that gives us undeniable proof he was involved."

"What I want to know is how far down the rabbit hole did he go with Stuart."

I handed it to Scarlett, who looked incensed.

"What the fuck? Why did he take a picture of this?"

"Maybe Mason wanted some collateral."

Scarlett gave it to Drake. He eyed it with no small amount of suspicion.

"We've never been able to hit Stuart head-on because of his relationship with Garrett," he said after a moment. "This isn't enough, though. We need more. If Mason had this, he could have a lot more shit on his father. Find it."

"And then what?" West asked. "I mean, I wasn't judging when you asked to keep Mason's head. Hell, I'd want a trophy too, but what are we going to do with it?"

Francis snorted.

"I think we should have kept his balls if you wanted a trophy because you lot certainly emasculated him."

West barked with laughter and gave Francis a wink. We'd told Drake and Francis about the whole fucking her before she'd killed him business.

"I merely showed him what he couldn't have. Voyeur boy over there made it into a spit roast. I'm surprised Mason didn't come in his fucking pants at the sight of it. He was too busy cursing us behind his gag rather than enjoying the show."

Scarlett blushed and buried her face in my neck. I stroked her hair. She enjoyed being watched by us, but I was pretty sure the Mason thing was a one-time deal to punish him for everything he'd done to her.

Drake gave us all a look before he stared down at the photograph again. Then he rubbed his chin and sat back, placing the photo on the table.

"What are we going to do with it?" He cracked his knuckles. "Tie a nice little bow around his face, package it up and have it hand-delivered to Stuart."

"That's going to force him into coming after us, and antagonise the fuck out of Garrett," I said.

Drake smiled, his indigo eyes glinting.

"That's the whole point. Stuart threatened Scarlett. We're going to show him we're not to be messed with. Are you in?"

The rest of us looked at each other as Scarlett turned her face from my neck to stare at Drake.

"As long as I get to torture the fuck when we finally nail him, I'm in," West said with a shrug.

"I wouldn't expect anything else."

"I'm ready," Francis said.

"Me too," I put in.

All of us looked at Scarlett. She had to be on board with it too. We did it all together or not at all. Those were the rules. And she was one of us. They applied to her too.

She leant forward, placing her palm down on the table.

"Let's show him who's boss and kill that motherfucker."

West gave Scarlett a smile.

"As my little Scar wishes. I'll text Penn and get the ball rolling."

"Good," Drake said as he sat forward and picked up the pages he'd been looking through again. "It's time we declared outright war on those fuckers once and for all."

And fuck if it wasn't satisfying to know we were all going to take that cunt down or die trying.

TWELVE

SCARLETT

I jumped down the last couple of steps, looking back to find Prescott on my tail. My feet carried me into the kitchen, squealing as he made to grab me, narrowly missing catching hold of my dress. I ran around the counter to avoid him.

"You're making this far too easy, little lamb."

I raised an eyebrow, watching him walk around it while I dashed away towards the dining table.

"We don't have enough room in this place," I countered.

"Excuses, excuses."

I grinned and gave him a wink, moving around the table as he came at me. We were on either side, staring each other down a moment later.

The door to their gym opened and out walked a shirtless Francis, who shoved his dark hair back from his face. My eyes immediately went to his chest, watching sweat drip down to the grooves of his abs.

That should not be so hot, but it is. Holy fuck.

The fact I even got distracted by the sight of Francis shirtless was my downfall. Prescott took advantage of my momentary distraction, ran around the table, and caught me against his chest, nuzzling my ear and pressing his hard dick into my back.

"You made that far too easy, sweetness."

"Blame him." I waved at Francis. "Coming out here looking all hot and shit."

Prescott looked over my shoulder at Francis, who had paused by the stairs to eye both of us with a wary expression on his face.

"Well, if I was into dick, I would be distracted too."

"What are you two staring at?" Francis asked, raising his eyebrow.

"You," I said like it was obvious.

"Me?"

"Mmm, yeah, our girl is staring at your abs," Prescott replied, waving at him.

Francis looked down at himself, then back up at me. Then a smirk appeared on his face.

"You can come touch them if you want."

I looked up at Prescott, who was grinning.

"Go on, show me how much you appreciate Francis' hard work in the gym."

He released me, letting me make my way over to Francis while he followed behind. The moment I got close to him, I ran my fingers along Francis' stomach, getting them covered in his sweat. I didn't care. He was far too attractive for his own good. And besides, we both got rather sweaty together in the bedroom.

"Don't stop there," Prescott murmured in my ear. "Perhaps you want to get on your knees."

I lowered myself to them on his order, sliding my fingers into the waistband of Francis' shorts and tugging at them. Prescott put his hands on my shoulders, pushing me closer to his friend. I looked up at Francis, who was breathing harder now. Those grey eyes were full of desire.

"Make him hard for me, little lamb."

I ran my hand along the slight bulge in his shorts, making Francis let out a harsh breath. His hand went to my hair, fingers digging into the strands and stroking my scalp. I kept stroking, feeling him stiffen under my caress.

"Good girl," Prescott murmured from behind me as I continued to stroke Francis.

I didn't look at him. My body heated. I enjoyed being watched as much as he enjoyed watching me, but I wanted to know what he saw one day. Maybe I'd ask him to take me somewhere we could watch together. Prescott was definitely the type of person who would be aware of such places.

My fingers went to the waistband of Francis' shorts again. I tugged them down, along with his boxers, freeing his cock. My tongue flicked out, running up his hard shaft.

"Fuck, Scar," he ground out, his fingers tightening around my head.

"Push him down on the stairs so you can straddle his lap, little lamb. I want to see him slide into your wet little pussy."

Francis didn't object when I directed him closer to the stairs and made him sit down a few steps up. Nor did he when

I crawled into his lap. My dress slid up my thighs. Prescott came closer and leant down behind me, tugging it up further so it sat around my waist. He stayed there, staring down between me and Francis, waiting for me to carry out the second part of his instructions.

My hand wrapped around Francis' dick, holding it so I could lower myself onto him. He let out a grunt. I moaned with the stretch.

"That's so fucking hot," Prescott whispered. "Ride him for me. Make him feel good."

I did as he asked, moving my hips and up and down. Francis' hands went to them, helping guide me. One of my hands went to Francis' shoulder to hold myself steady, while I moved the other behind me, finding my way to Prescott's dick and stroking it through his clothes. He growled in my ear.

"Naughty lamb."

"Punish me then, wolf."

He chuckled, and I felt him shift behind me.

"Oh, why would I do that when I can just get Drake to?"

My eyes went to the top of the stairs, finding Drake standing there watching us with a raised eyebrow.

"Is this what we're doing now? Openly fucking anywhere in the house when we feel like it?" he asked a moment later, digging his hand into his pocket and leaning against the bannisters.

"You complaining?" Prescott asked as I continued to fuck Francis without missing a beat.

"No, by all means… continue."

"Well, there's one for the books. Drake not complaining about our sexual antics," Francis said with a grin as he looked up at his best friend.

Drake watched for a moment, not saying a word in response to Francis. I continued to stroke Prescott's dick, making him let out a harsh pant in my ear.

"Take her dress off."

Prescott looked up at Drake again. Then his hands were tugging at my dress, pulling it up my body. I put my arms up to allow him to take it off and toss it on the bannister. He cupped my breasts, rolling the nipples with his thumbs before he licked my neck. I watched Drake's expression. His indigo eyes darkened with lust.

Francis' grip on my hips tightened, making me ride him harder. His eyes were fixed on Prescott's hands on my breasts, like the sight of it mesmerised him. Being wanted by these men was a high I never thought I'd experience. Being back with them after my ordeal with Mason had me wanting to savour every moment. I needed to feel them this way. It helped calm the raging storm in my mind. The thoughts and worries I had about our next course of action.

Sex was my way of escaping for a while. And connecting with the people I loved. Because I loved all of them. I might not have said it to Drake or West yet, but I felt it. My heart belonged to them in the same way it did to Prescott and Francis.

Drake walked down the stairs until he was level with us. Then he sat on the step next to Francis and stroked his fingers down my arm. My hands were back on Francis' shoulders to hold myself steady.

"My beautiful little wisp," he murmured, leaning closer and pressing a kiss to my shoulder. He kissed his way up my neck until he met my ear. "I've missed the way you light up a room with your intoxicating spirit."

I shivered at his words, turning my face into his. Drake didn't hesitate to kiss me. Hearing him admit those things to me freely was more than I could take. Perhaps he'd taken my words from this morning to heart. I hoped so. I wanted him to spend more time with me outside of sex. To make me a priority in his life. I deserved to be. And I wasn't going to take no for an answer. He was going to be a better boyfriend to me. I didn't care what Drake said. These men? They were my boyfriends. They were all mine.

My hand left Francis' shoulder and went to Drake's thigh, giving it a squeeze. My hand drifted up his leg, getting closer to his cock. Prescott must have noticed as he nuzzled my ear.

"I want to watch you suck him off, little lamb," he whispered.

I released Drake's mouth and looked back at Prescott.

"Who, Drake?"

"Yes."

"And are you going to join in the fun too?"

Prescott growled, rubbing himself against my back.

"Do you want all your little holes filled, lamb?"

I nodded. I didn't just want it. I needed it. Wanted to feel that connection between the four of us... and maybe even five if West came downstairs. He'd disappeared after dinner earlier, probably to go smoke a joint, but who knew. We hadn't talked after I'd kissed him. While he'd actively participated, I wasn't entirely sure how he felt about it, given he'd told me on

112

numerous occasions he didn't kiss. Had he been waiting for me to do it? Did he need me to push him the way I had been doing to Drake?

You already know the answer to that.

Prescott chuckled and released me before standing up.

"Let's move this party to the sofa, hmm?"

I shifted off Francis as Drake stood up, helping me to my feet. The four of us made our way over to the sofa. Francis sat down and I straddled his lap again, sinking down on his hard cock. Apparently, Prescott had stashed lube down here because he pulled it out of a drawer in the coffee table and knelt behind me.

I got distracted from what he was doing by Drake leaning over the back of the sofa and capturing my chin between his fingers. He stared at me with so much affection, I just about died on the spot. I leant towards him, wanting to be closer.

"I thought you didn't do warm fuzzies," I murmured.

"I don't."

"Could have fooled me with your sweet words and the look in your eye."

The way he broke out into a grin made my heart thump against my ribcage. He moved closer, brushing his nose against mine.

"I'm not sweet, Little Nyx."

He gripped my chin tighter and kissed me. We both knew that was a lie. He could be sweet to me if he was so inclined. I adored the soft side of Drake. It told me my Drake from my youth was still in there. I had to draw him out completely and make sure he stayed that way. He could be cold-hearted to everyone else outside of these four walls, but with his family? Well, that was a different story.

I pulled away, grinning back at him before I looked down at Francis. He was watching us with a wicked glint in his eyes, so I leant down and kissed him too, for good measure. His hand tangled in my hair, pulling me against his chest as his hips thrust up into me. I moaned around his tongue, feeling Prescott lube me up from behind with his body pressed to my back.

"Less kissing, more fucking," he said in my ear.

I released Francis and gave my voyeuristic king a look over my shoulder.

"I'll ban you from my lips if you're not careful."

He gave me a wounded look, so I kissed him. When I turned back, Drake had stood up and was busy undressing. I watched him. The way his muscles flexed with his movements. His long fingers unbuttoned his chinos. My body shuddered at the thought of him wrapping those big hands around me. To say I was a little obsessed with them would be an understatement.

Feeling a little daring, I reached out towards him when he was bare. He came closer and looked down at me. I took his hands, pulling him against the back of the sofa. His brow furrowed slightly as if he was wondering what on earth I wanted. I placed his hands on my shoulders, forcing him to lean down to reach me.

"I want you to hold me down."

"What?"

"I… I like your hands. I mean, in general, I can't stop looking at them but right now I'd like them on me."

For a long moment, he didn't react. Then his fingers curled around my shoulders. I let out a long breath, feeling the tension leave my body.

"And what is it about them you like so much?"

I let out a little moan as Prescott pressed a third finger inside me.

"They're so... big. I feel small compared to you and the fact you can easily overpower me is a turn on, okay? I just find them attractive, and this is officially embarrassing."

My cheeks were burning, but I maintained eye contact with him, not wanting him to think I was scared of telling him the truth of my feelings.

Drake raised one of his hands from my shoulder and cupped my face with it. The simple gesture made me tremble.

"Do you like it when I wrap them around you?"

I nodded, catching my bottom lip between my teeth.

"When I punish you with them?"

My head kept bobbing. Drake smiled in such a deviant way, I almost wanted to faint.

"Then I shall endeavour to make you happy by giving you what you need, little wisp."

He released me and I was about to protest, but he walked around the sofa and sat down next to me. Then he was pulling me closer and running his hands all over my torso, squeezing them around my sides and my breasts. I choked on a moan. All three of them touching me had my body feeling over-sensitised and drove me closer to the edge, especially when Drake slapped me across my breast, making it sting.

"Fuck," I hissed. "Do it again."

He did. The pain made me crazy in the best way possible. My hand went to his cock, stroking it. I needed to feel him as he touched me. He grunted but didn't tell me to stop.

"I see you all started the fun without me," came a voice from behind us.

I knew exactly who it was.

"Then you better make up for lost time," I replied, not even looking over my shoulder.

And the moment I heard West's chuckle, I knew I was in for another mind-blowing experience with these four men.

THIRTEEN

SCARLETT

I felt him before I saw him as West approached our little gang of four. He sat down on the other side of me from Drake, his amber eyes glinting with mischief. He stroked my shoulder and gave me a smile.

"I'm sure these three can satisfy your urges, little Scar," he murmured and didn't move to join in.

My attention was stolen by Drake squeezing my breast and running his thumb over the nipple. And then I cried out because Prescott entered me from behind without warning. It didn't hurt, as he'd prepared me, but I hadn't been ready for it. My hand tightened around Drake's cock, the other squeezing Francis' shoulder.

"That's it, little lamb," Prescott said. "Such a good girl."

I preened at his praise, rubbing myself against his chest as his arm came around me and he thrust deeper. Being filled by both him and Francis was my heaven. Having any of them this way was. It helped me from spiralling out of control. My thoughts were a demon I could only escape when I was with them this way. When they fucked me with brutality and the only thing I could see was them.

The very thought of this being taken away from me had me trying not to choke. Stuart had already stolen me from them once. Mason had tried to again. They couldn't keep us away from each other forever. Fate wanted us together. It demanded the five of us remain by each other's sides. And we couldn't escape it. Nor did I want to.

"I've missed you all so much," I blurted out, my voice sounding all small and helpless. "Please... don't let anyone take me away from you again."

All of them stopped moving. My words hung in the air, making us all tense. I didn't blame them for what happened to me ten years ago. I didn't think placing it on anyone would get us very far. It was what it was. We couldn't go back and change it. The future was important, not the past.

Francis was the first to move, sitting up slightly and pulling me into his arms. Then I had Prescott embrace me from behind. The next thing I knew, Drake and West joined in, all of us holding on to each other like we never wanted to let go.

"Never again, little Scar," West whispered against my hair. "And even if it does happen, we'll find you. We'll bring you home every single time."

A little sob erupted from my lips. I couldn't help it. The weight of being kidnapped by Mason, killing him, and the very real threat Stuart posed to us came crashing down on me. The past week had been awful without them. Now I was with them, I was safe, I couldn't hold back my emotions any longer.

"Shh, little lamb, we've got you," Prescott murmured.

"I don't know what I'd do without you," I told them. "I tried so hard to be brave when he took me, but I was so afraid."

One of them stroked my hair, soothing me with their gentle touch. Prescott shifted, pulling out of me, and moving my hips, so Francis slipped free too. Clearly, he knew I needed to get whatever was going on in my head out and sex was the last thing on my mind now.

"He was going to keep me in that place like his little pet. He planned it all. Bought the house, did it up and furnished it the way he knew I liked. But it wasn't nice. It was super fucking creepy. And... and the night before you came for me, he slept next to me. I thought he was going to force himself on me."

I choked back tears, not wanting to cry over it.

"He didn't, but I spent the whole night awake. I was fucking terrified he would. I knew you'd come for me. I really did, but it didn't stop me from worrying about what he'd do. A part of me knew I might have to save myself before you came for me... before... before he made me do something I didn't want to."

The whole week I'd been on high alert. Now I was home and rested, I felt safe again. I could fall apart and show them my vulnerabilities because they were mine and I was theirs. It didn't make me weak, just human. A woman who'd been through an ordeal and her men who'd tear apart the world for her. Maybe I was fucked up for wanting the four of them after everything they'd done to me. After everything we'd been through. I didn't care. We were a family and we loved each other.

"The idea of anyone going to those lengths, plotting to keep me captive in a remote location, especially knowing what

I'd already been through for the past ten years… it's fucking horrifying. I want to be free. The only time I feel that way is when I'm with all of you. I don't feel like I'm trapped here. I want to be with you. I need you so much, it hurts."

Their arms around me tightened, reminding me of the way Francis' ropes always calmed me. They must know I needed this. Francis always did. He gave me the safety I'd always craved when I'd been locked away.

"Thank you for coming for me. Thank you for all these years you kept fighting for me. I know it all got so fucked up, but it's okay… I forgive you. I don't care about the past. I need you. I just want us to be able to live normal lives without all of this shit hanging over our heads."

It was my only desire going forward. For us to be free. For this shit to end. I'd got rid of one threat. Now we had to get rid of the rest. We had to fight to survive and hope they didn't kill us before we got to them.

"We will," Drake murmured. "I promise, little wisp, we will."

None of us moved for a long time. We needed a moment of stillness together. Reassuring each other our family was together. We weren't going to let anyone pull us apart again. They didn't need to say a word for me to know they understood my feelings. It was in the way they held me close and didn't let go.

While I might have things I needed to resolve with all the boys, I didn't want to be away from them. We were stronger together.

"Do you want to continue, little lamb?" Prescott asked, rubbing my shoulder. "It's okay if you don't."

I hadn't meant to ruin the mood by getting all emotional.

"Maybe," I whispered, "I don't really know."

Prescott pulled away. The next thing I knew, he'd plucked me out of Francis' lap and settled me between Francis and Drake. He knelt between my thighs and rubbed them. Leaning down, he kissed his way up my leg.

"How about I reward you for being such a good girl, hmm? I want you to make my face messy, little lamb."

I shuddered when he spread my thighs further and lowered his mouth to my pussy. Those blue eyes of his glinted as he stared up at me. The other three watched Prescott slide his fingers into my wet hole while his tongue flicked out, running over my clit, and making my hips buck.

"Pres," I breathed.

"Let us make you feel good, little whore," Francis murmured as he leant over me, kissing his way down my collarbone.

I had Drake touching me on the other side, wrapping his lips around my nipple and biting down on it. One of my hands went to Prescott's hair, stroking through the soft strands. My gaze went to West, who was watching me with a pensive expression as if my words from a few minutes ago were still playing on his mind. I reached out to him over Francis' head. He took my hand and pressed a kiss to it before entwining our fingers together. Having that connection with him had me relaxing against the back of the sofa, allowing them to make me feel good like Francis had told me to.

I whimpered when Prescott grazed his teeth across my clit, his fingers pumping harder inside me. Both my nipples were now occupied by two mouths. The sensations drove me closer to the edge. My eyes closed and, in my mind, I hovered over the abyss. The tendrils pulled me down, sucking me into the void. It's why I didn't immediately register movement next to me. It was only when a hot mouth pressed against mine, I opened my eyes and found West leaning over Francis to get to me. His lips were soft. I yielded immediately, sinking into his kiss like our mouths belonged together.

In a lot of ways, they did. West had been mine since the moment we'd laid eyes on each other at five years old. It was an instant thing. We both knew but it had taken years for us to act on those feelings. They were innocent when we were young. They grew into more as time passed. He buried himself in my heart as I buried myself in his. There was no way to extract each other. And I didn't want to. Despite everything that had happened, I wanted him right there, nestled inside me where he should be.

"West," I moaned against his mouth, letting go of his hand so I could cup his face, pulling him closer.

His fingers dug into my hair, holding my head in place as his tongue slid into my mouth. The extra sensation of him kissing me sent me over the edge. I whimpered into his mouth, bucking into Prescott's face with my climax. He kept fucking me with his fingers, drawing it out while the other two continued to suck my nipples until I was pushing Prescott away from my pussy.

All four of them released me, West leaning back to allow Francis to sit up properly. Prescott sat back on his heels, smiling up at me with my arousal glistening on his lips. I licked my own in response.

"Do you want to go to bed, little lamb?" he asked, stroking my leg with his fingers.

I nodded. I was drained now. All I wanted was to curl up under the sheets.

"And who would you like to take you?"

My eyes immediately went to West. I wasn't done kissing him. In fact, I wanted to be wrapped up in his arms with his mouth pressed to mine. Asking for that, however, had me swallowing hard, trying to find the words.

Prescott kissed my thigh and stood up, reaching to grab his clothes. Francis and Drake stood with him, moving away, and leaving me and West staring at each other. I didn't have to ask. They knew the moment I looked at West, I wanted him. As the others moved away to get dressed, West shifted closer and cupped my face with one hand.

"I want to stay with you," I murmured.

He nodded, then he got up and picked me up in his arms. Before he carried me to the stairs, he turned me to the others one at a time, letting them kiss me goodnight. We were silent as he took me to his room. He pulled back the covers with one hand and set me down on the bed, tucking the duvet around me a moment later. Then he walked away towards the window and stared out over the city.

"What were you doing up here before you came down?" I asked when he didn't say anything.

"Thinking."

"About what?"

"Everything that's happened in the past week." He let out a sigh but didn't turn around. "I know what you said when I asked, but I'm still wondering how you really feel about the way I told you of Lylah's death."

I stiffened. Thinking about the fact Mason had killed my mother to stop her from making too much noise hurt me. I didn't blame West for it, however. It was all on Stuart and Mason. They were responsible for her death.

"I'm not upset with you over it. I mean, it wasn't exactly the best time to tell me, but I don't know if I would have... killed him if you hadn't."

West turned around. He hadn't turned the lights on, but I could see his features from the city lights spilling in through the windows.

"I wanted him dead. Drake made us swear we wouldn't hurt him, but he said nothing about you." He took a step towards the bed. "I need you to know I told you because I wanted you to kill him. I was counting on it."

"And you think that might upset me?"

He shrugged, digging his hands into his pockets.

"Last time I made you kill someone, you weren't very happy with me."

I slipped out of bed and walked over to his wardrobes, trying to get my thoughts straight. Opening one of the doors, I pulled out one of his t-shirts and slipped it over my head. I lowered my face and breathed in. It smelt faintly like their detergent and West. Closing the door, I rested my forehead against the wood.

"I'm grateful you told me the truth. I had trouble confronting it. The fact that my mother is dead. And that made it real. Knowing he killed her made it... real."

Tears welled in my eyes. This time, I didn't hold them back as one slid down my cheek.

"I miss her... so much."

My knees threatened to buckle, but I put my hands on the door to stop myself from falling to the floor. I'd tried to keep my grief inside me. Tried so hard not to allow it to burst through. I'd held onto my anger towards Mason so I didn't have to deal with it, but now... now I couldn't hold back any longer.

My mother was gone. Murdered. It happened when I had no idea who she was. That was the very worst part of all.

FOURTEEN

WEST

Watching her struggle with her composure made my chest hurt. I wasn't good at this shit. Being there for people. It had been a long time since I'd needed to. And Scarlett had been the only one I'd ever comforted.

I walked around the bed and reached out to her, placing my hands on her shoulders while she tried to hold in her emotions. All I wanted to do was take away her pain. To end her suffering. She deserved more than life had given her. I would do everything in my power to give this woman a better future.

"Little Scar."

"I've lost so much already. Almost half my life was stolen from me. I lost you… I lost us. Why did I have to lose her too?"

I pulled her away from the door, turning her around and tucking her against my chest. She clutched my t-shirt and let out a hiccup.

"I want you back," she choked out. "I can't have my mother back or my old life, but I want you, West. I just want you."

I didn't know what the fuck to say. Didn't she know I was right here? Didn't she know she had me? Every part of me?

No, because you haven't fucking told her.

It should be simple. Telling her I loved her. But the truth was… I still struggled with myself over it. Scarlett reminded me of the boy I'd been. She dragged him out into the open. The boy I thought had died the night she fell. The man I'd become had all but been labelled a sociopath. And yet, I was capable of feeling human emotions. I felt them for Scarlett. Her pain. I understood it. I felt it inside me, like a festering wound unable to heal. And it was killing me.

I didn't know how to define myself any longer. How to navigate these waters I'd found myself in. Maybe I wasn't supposed to do it alone. The world had given me Scarlett back. Given me the one person who had always filled me with the hope I wasn't completely fucked in the head. She told me she didn't see me differently because of my diagnosis. So why did I still see myself as unworthy of her love?

"Tell me how to give you that, little Scar," I whispered, pressing my face into the top of her head. "Tell me, so I can give you me."

Her body shuddered against mine. I could feel her tears soaking my t-shirt, but I didn't care. If she wanted to cry on me for hours, I'd let her. Fuck, I would do anything at this point. Anything to make her smile again. To see those hazel-green eyes full of joy, love, and affection. I'd forgotten how much I need that from her. How she was the only person in this world capable of keeping me on an even keel. Maybe it had everything to do with me loving her.

"Why wouldn't you kiss me before? Tell me the real reason."

I stroked her back. If we were ever going to get back to where we were before, I had to be honest with her.

"Do you remember the night you came to me after the twins tried to assault you?"

She nodded.

"You kissed me first, little Scar. I guess I needed you to be the one to do it again… then I'd know you'd forgiven me for everything. That you still felt the same way you did all those years ago. You still saw me as… yours."

She let out a choking sound before she looked up at me, forcing me to straighten.

"You needed me to be your little warrior?"

I gave her a smile.

"You were always the one who kept us together. You were good at this stuff. I'm not. I don't know how to be a good… boyfriend to you."

Being vulnerable wasn't easy for me, but I was done hiding away from her and my feelings.

She blinked back her tears, letting go of my t-shirt to wrap her arms around my neck instead.

"I don't think you ever stopped being my boyfriend. We technically never broke up. And you were pretty good at it when we were younger, even if our time got cut horribly short."

"Was I?"

My girl rose up on her tiptoes and nuzzled my jaw with her lips.

"Yeah, you took care of me, West... always."

I allowed her to press a kiss to my lips.

"Look, I'm not asking for you to be anything other than who you are now. I happen to like you this way. I won't lie. Sometimes you scare the shit out of me, but we both know that turns me on. That night you pushed me way past my limits because I asked you? I trusted you implicitly in those moments. You and me... we have something special. I don't want to lose it or you."

"I never wanted to lose you."

She sighed, pressing her face into my neck.

"But you did... the night I fell."

I nodded, clutching her tighter.

"I'm sorry you suffered all these years without me when I had no idea who you were. I'm here now... and I'm never leaving you again, West. Never. I promise. I'm yours."

My heart slammed hard against my ribcage. I didn't think I'd hear those words from her mouth, uttered so freely as if it didn't cost her anything.

Leaning down, I clasped her thighs and picked her up, carrying her over to my bed. I set her down under the covers and tucked them around her. Scarlett reached for me when I straightened.

"I'm not going anywhere, little Scar. Let me just take this off, okay?"

She settled back against the sheets, watching me as I moved towards my wardrobes and undressed. I walked back over to her and got into bed. She immediately moved closer, tucking herself up in my arms. Scarlett turned her head up towards me and I leant down, capturing her mouth as if it was natural. As if I'd never gone without kissing her all these months since she'd been back.

The simple act was all I needed, no matter how much her body against mine aroused me. Scarlett needed to sleep, not be mauled by me. Funny to think weeks ago, I would have done whatever I wanted with her, but not now. Not when I knew she needed this. Needed me to kiss her and hold her against me while she fell asleep.

"This feels like when we were teenagers," she whispered to me when she pulled away.

"Is that a good thing?"

Her hand slid from my back to my chest.

"It's like coming home, being in the place I was always meant to, right here in your arms."

Her eyes clouded over a moment later, making me stiffen.

"Am I still your curse?"

I shook my head.

"You were never a curse, little Scar… you were always my destiny, just as I'm yours."

"You make it sound like we're in a world where fated mates exist."

I snorted, stroking my hand down her back.

"Maybe that's what the five of us are, even if it's ridiculous and farfetched."

"Who knew you, of all people, could be sappy as fuck."

Leaning closer again, I nuzzled her nose with mine.

"For you, Scar, I'd be anything and everything."

She grinned, pressing her mouth to mine in a series of kisses, leaving the both of us breathless. Maybe I was being sappy or whatever, but a part of me had always known Scarlett and I were soulmates. I'd just been lucky enough to find her when we were young. Lucky enough to know who I would spend my whole life loving with every inch of my being.

We lay cuddled together in silence for a long while. It had been years since I had this sort of contentment in my life. There was no driving need for violence filling my insides when she was in my arms. Well, perhaps not the type of violence involving death and destruction… sex was an entirely different matter. Scarlett had given me an outlet I didn't realise I needed until now. The way she craved degradation fed me. Instead of violence with my fists, it was with my words. It didn't mean I wouldn't relish killing that cunt Stuart, but I didn't need to hurt, maim and torture quite so much when she was near me.

The balm to my soul. That's what you are, little Scar.

I pressed a kiss to her forehead, nuzzling her hair and pulling her tighter against me. She reached up and stroked the scars she'd given me. They were healing nicely. Scarlett had taken care of them, just as she'd promised. Although, while she'd been kidnapped, I'd had to do it myself, not that I minded. It was painful as fuck having to pick off my own scabs, but whatever. I could take it. The pain reminded me I was hers.

"I understand why you scarred me," she said after a moment. "Your little warrior needed a battle scar from her warring horseman."

Even though I'd always thought that fucking moniker was ridiculous, it was fitting for the five of us. The horsemen and their warrior woman. We would ride into battle upon four horses, white, red, black, and pale, with the goddess of the night in our wake. And we would destroy our enemies for good. Nothing would be left standing in our way now.

"Will you go to war with me if I asked it of you?"

"Always."

I pressed a kiss to her hair.

"I'll make the world safe for us," I whispered. "I won't let anyone hurt you. None of us will."

She snuggled even closer, pressing her lips to my chest.

"I want to burn his empire down and dance amongst the ashes."

"You will. I'll make sure of it."

Scarlett closed her eyes and wrapped her arm around me.

"Did she ever stop fighting for me?"

She was referring to Lylah. My heart twisted for her. My poor girl never got a chance to see her mother again or say goodbye. After everything she'd had to endure, that was a fucking travesty I couldn't forgive. I was glad Scarlett had avenged Lylah's death by killing Mason.

"No, never. She was advocating for you until the very end. She loved you with everything she had, little Scar. There's nothing in this world she wouldn't have done to get you back. Nothing at all. And we continued that fight for her. We brought you home."

She nodded, shifting in my embrace before settling down again. I stroked her arm as I watched her fall asleep. My perfect little woman in my arms. And I promised myself I would do my best to keep opening up to her. To keep being vulnerable. If there was anything in this world she deserved, it was that.

She deserved to be treated like my partner. My equal in every sense of the word. If she could be open with me, I could do it for her.

I pressed one last kiss to her hair before settling down to sleep myself. And wondered as I drifted off if Stuart would enjoy the little package he would have delivered on his doorstep tomorrow. After all, it wasn't every day you were sent a severed head accompanied by pictures of his affair with your wife. If only I could be a fly on the wall when it happened, but I would settle for knowing it would fuck with him. And we'd continue fucking with Stuart until we could end the man. He deserved nothing less.

FIFTEEN

DRAKE

I stared down at the phone for a long moment after being informed we had a guest. Well, I wouldn't exactly describe Garrett Jones as a guest, but we would be treating him like one. After all, it wasn't every day you had a personal visit from the Met Police Commissioner. The fact he'd come alone spoke volumes. He would have sent officers if he was here to arrest us.

Standing from my desk, I straightened my suit jacket, dusting off a piece of lint on the sleeve. I sent a group text out to the boys and Scarlett. I took a breath then strode out of my office towards the lobby where our guest would be arriving shortly. Scarlett peeked her head out of her office. I paused when she stepped out.

"Do you need me?"

"Get the rest of them into the meeting room before I bring him in, then make yourself scarce. We don't need him to suspect you."

She nodded, moving away to Prescott's office as I continued down the hallway.

I knew exactly why Garrett was here. It might have taken him a few days to turn up at our offices, but we'd known he would come. There was no way he would let what we'd sent Stuart go unanswered. I smiled to myself as I waited by the desk in the lobby. Quite the present we had delivered on his doorstep by Penn's men. It wasn't as if they could trace it back to us, but they would know we'd done it all the same. No two fucking ways about it.

My features were schooled when the lift doors opened and out stepped Garrett Jones, his light brown hair slicked back, blue eyes dark with irritation. He wore a pinstripe suit with a trench coat over the top of it.

"Good afternoon, Commissioner," I said, giving him a nod.

He came to a standstill near me. I didn't offer my hand since I knew he wouldn't take it.

"I'm not here for niceties nor do I offer them in return."

"No, of course not. Please come this way."

I put my hand out towards the hallway before leading him towards the meeting room. If he didn't want niceties, I would endeavour not to give him any. He would probably hate us even more by the end of his time here, but who gave a fuck.

As I entered the meeting room, I found the other three sat at the table. Francis had a pile of documents in front of him. I waved at a chair as I crossed the room to sit next to Prescott, but the Commissioner remained standing. He looked over at the four of us with narrowed eyes.

"I expect you are aware of why I'm here."

"Why don't you enlighten us… Commissioner?"

He'd asked to see the four of us directly. It meant he had no idea of Scarlett's involvement. I was counting on that.

"Let's not play games," he ground out, leaning on the table with one hand flat on the wood. "I should have you all arrested."

"On what grounds?"

"You dare ask me that? I shouldn't be surprised." He straightened and glared. "You were never ones for telling the truth, even when you were boys."

West clenched his fist on the table. Francis nudged him. I needed West to keep his fucking temper in check. We couldn't have Garrett suspecting a damn thing. Nor would violence solve this problem. If he remained calm, we could get through this unscathed.

"If you tell us why you're here, perhaps we can help you."

I knew my nonplussed attitude was pissing him right the fuck off. If we riled the man up, that was fine with me. We had the upper hand.

"I know it was you who sent Stuart my… my… my son."

"Your son?"

"Don't play dumb. This is not a game. You sent his decapitated head to Mr Carver along with pictures of his wife's affair."

I raised my eyebrows.

"Did we?"

He threw his hands up.

"Look, you can sit here and deny your involvement all you want. We know what you've done whether or not there is proof."

137

I sat back and tapped my fingers on the table.

"Is that why you came alone? You don't have evidence we were involved in any of the things you and Stuart have accused us of. We're innocent until proven guilty, Commissioner. You, of all people, should know that. So tell me, are you here to arrest us for a crime you have evidence for or did you just want a little chinwag?"

He slammed his hand down on the table, making Prescott jump.

"You killed my son. I can't prove it, but I know you did."

There we had it. The real reason he'd come in person. He wanted to look us in the eye and see if we'd admit or deny it. The thing was, we didn't kill Mason, we'd just covered it up for our girl. Just like we'd made sure Penn covered up the man we'd made her kill. There was no fucking way we would ever allow our girl to be arrested for any of this shit. We'd always been thorough when it came to killing and knew exactly how to get away with it.

"I'd bet you'd love to pin it on us," Francis said, giving Garrett a cold, hard stare. "Just like you tried to pin Stuart's kids disappearing on four sixteen-year-olds who witnessed their best friend almost die."

Garrett didn't look cowed at all by Francis' statement, but his expression turned grim.

"What happened to that girl was a tragedy. It doesn't change the fact you had it out for the twins and are the only ones with motive."

"That girl, huh?" Prescott interjected. "She has a name. I'm pretty sure you're fully aware of it."

I gave him a look, but Prescott ignored me, continuing to stare at Garrett with disgust written all over his features

"Scarlett."

Prescott gave him a sweet smile and his gaze fell on Francis, who picked up a photo from the pile of documents in front of him and slid it across the table towards Garrett. It took a minute for him to pull it closer and stare down at it. His eyes narrowed. It was the photo of him standing over her bedside with Stuart.

"You remember when that was taken, don't you?" Francis asked with a hint of reproach in his voice.

Garrett said nothing.

"Well, let me enlighten you." Francis slid another photo across the table, showing Garrett and Stuart in low conversation near Scarlett's bed. "You being there shouldn't raise any eyebrows, but him? Well, he should never have been anywhere near her."

Garrett looked up at us then, after eyeing the second photograph.

"This proves nothing."

"Are you going to deny you knew he took her?"

We'd always planned to turn this around on him, but they were meant to let me lead the conversation. Clearly, Francis and Prescott weren't in the mood for placating the Police Commissioner. No, they wanted to go on the offensive.

"Because if you are, we have plenty more proving you not only knew he took Scarlett, but you also aided him in stealing her from the hospital and made sure no one ever found out where she went."

Francis slid more of the pages he held across the table. Garrett made no move to take them. Mason had quite the damning evidence against Stuart and his father. We weren't going to show our full hand, but we had enough here to get him to back off. At least, that was the aim, anyway.

"What do you want?"

I smiled and leant forward.

"We all know Stuart will never stop coming after us. He wants us dead and no doubt if he does succeed, you'll make sure he's never prosecuted for it."

Garrett didn't acknowledge my statement, but it was the truth. He wouldn't allow his best friend to go to prison after all the shit he'd done. He was just as embroiled in the sordid affair as Stuart. They were as bad as each other. Too many fucking skeletons in their cupboards.

"You have as much to lose as he does if any of this becomes public knowledge." I waved at the pages in front of us. "We'll keep this from coming out provided you turn a blind eye to what happens next."

He looked down at the pages. Then he pulled out a chair and took a seat, steepling his fingers together.

"This is blackmail."

I shrugged.

"You didn't come here today as the Commissioner. If you had, it would have raised a lot of eyebrows. This is personal for you, just as it is for us."

He pulled the rest of the documents towards him and rifled through them. The more he read, the more incensed he looked. We had pages upon pages proving he'd helped Stuart kidnap Scarlett. How he'd covered up everything Stuart had done. How he'd made sure the site where Scarlett's accident happened was kept cordoned off until the developers went bankrupt. We knew who owned the land and the surrounding buildings now, after doing a little research. No doubt that was a deal Garrett made in exchange for turning a blind eye to money laundering.

I almost shook my head. I hadn't cared about that fucking site until recently. To be honest, I wanted to forget it ever existed, considering it was an ugly reminder of the worst night of my life. Discovering it was owned by none other than Zayn Villetti put a whole new spin on things.

Everyone liked to think the mafia wasn't a big thing in this country, but they kept a low profile. Knowing the Met Police Commissioner was likely in bed with the kingpin himself, Gennaro Villetti… well… it was obvious how they flew under the radar now.

Garrett leant back a moment later, staring down at the table for a long moment before he met my eyes.

"You're asking me to turn a blind eye to what, exactly?"

"What we do about Stuart."

He tapped his fingers against the arm of the chair.

"I don't owe you any loyalty."

"No, but you do want to keep your job, don't you?"

If he had been any other man, we would have butchered him to get him out of our way. We didn't kill members of the police force. That was just asking for trouble. It took enough coordination to kill a normal citizen and not get caught. It would be infinitely more difficult to kill an officer of the law and get away with it.

"We're fair men, Commissioner. We understand betraying your lifelong friend is no easy matter, but you would be stripped of your position and go to prison for all of this. Do you really want to destroy the reputation of the force?"

He didn't answer for a moment, but I knew I had him there. Besides, if he refused, we would go public with not only this but everything else. We would ruin his reputation for good. We could do that to Stuart too, but we wanted him dead. He deserved it after the way he'd treated Scarlett.

Garrett stood up and straightened his sleeves. His eyes went to me again.

"You have my word I will not interfere in your plans for Stuart." He paused and fidgeted for a moment. "What did you do with the rest of my son?"

"Who said we did anything with him."

"We both know I cannot tie any of you back to it."

I leant forward.

"Your son took her with the intention of keeping her locked away for the rest of her life. Not to mention he murdered her mother on behalf of Stuart, something else you covered up. And yet *we* still did nothing to him."

I wasn't going to admit it was Scarlett who'd murdered his son in an act of revenge, but if Garrett read between the lines, he would see the truth.

His eyes narrowed.

"I see."

Garrett took a moment to look at all of us before he nodded.

"Keep to your word and I keep to mine, not that I trust any of you, but this doesn't come out in the open." He pointed to the papers. "Are we clear?"

"Very."

"Good."

Then he strode from the room, leaving the four of us staring after him. West got up and walked to the door. He stayed there for a long moment as if he was making sure Garrett didn't go looking for Scarlett. Then he turned to us.

"Well, that was easier than expected."

"I don't trust him," Prescott said, leaning back and scowling.

"We shouldn't," I replied. "But that's one hurdle we've overcome for now. Next… we go after Stuart head-on."

"We should sit down with Scarlett later to discuss what we're going to do," Francis said.

I nodded and stood. I'd speak to her now and make sure she was okay. No doubt I didn't trust Garrett Jones as far as I could throw him, but we'd given him and Stuart more reason to fear us. Perhaps our greatest enemy would finally understand we were not to be messed with. Nor were we ever going to back down.

SIXTEEN

SCARLETT

I t had been several days since the Police Commissioner
had visited Fortuity. We'd not heard a peep from either
him or Stuart, something that had put all of us on edge.
The boys were in the midst of coming up with a plan for what
they were going to do going forward about Stuart with my
help. We knew we wanted to go after him directly. We all
wanted him dead. The only problem was the how of it. We
didn't want to get caught. Killing a man with a profile as high
as Stuart Carver required careful planning and precision. Drake
didn't want to go off half-cocked. I was inclined to agree with
him. If we were going to rid the world of Stuart Carver, it had
to be done as cleanly as possible.

Today, as it was the weekend, I'd persuaded the boys to let
me go see my mother's grave. I'd asked them about where she
was buried a few days ago. Drake had insisted on taking me
since he didn't trust I would be safe on my own. After being
kidnapped by Mason, I agreed with him and didn't complain

about it. I was sure Prescott wanted to accompany me, but if anyone was going to go with me, the stoic one was my choice, anyway. Drake would keep silent while I said goodbye to my mother. He wouldn't interfere or offer me platitudes and comfort. I didn't want those. All I wanted was a space to tell her everything I never got to when she was alive.

The cemetery was on the outskirts of London. For a city of millions, it was a quiet, peaceful place with trees planted amongst the graves. Drake parked the car in the car park next to the crematorium in the middle of the cemetery and took my hand.

He'd become more affectionate towards me after I'd told him I needed him, not hesitating to give me casual touches and kisses. Every morning when I brought his coffee into his office, he'd make me come around his desk so he could kiss me before he got on with his day. I didn't know where this side of him had come from, but I wasn't about to start complaining. He'd made the effort to give me what I'd asked for. And every time he smiled at me, it made my heart go all funny in my chest.

"Why do you look happy?" he asked after we'd been walking for a couple of minutes along the road running through the cemetery.

I glanced up at him. His dark hair was a little messy like he hadn't bothered brushing it this morning. I admired his casual attire of black jeans, a dark jumper and a black coat, along with a pair of trainers. It was the first time I'd seen him be so careless with his appearance. It was really fucking hot. While I probably should not be thinking about how much I wanted to jump his bones when I was visiting my mother's grave, I needed a distraction. The thought of saying goodbye was making me anxious.

"I'm with you."

"Being with me makes you... happy?"

"Um, I hate to break it to you, Drake, but you make me happy even when you're being all domineering and shit. I'd be kind of worried if you didn't, considering you're my boyfriend."

I smiled more when I noticed a slight blush appear on his cheeks as he looked away.

"So you're definitely set on calling me that then."

"Do you have a problem with being my boyfriend? Or is it because I have four and you don't feel special enough?"

He gave me a reproachful look.

"No, I don't have a problem with it, nor you being with the others. You know that."

"Do I though?"

He pulled me to a halt and took my chin between the fingers of his free hand, making me meet his eyes.

"Are you mine, little wisp?"

"Yes."

"And am I yours?"

"Yes."

"Then don't ask stupid questions."

He let me go and took off again, his long legs eating up the road and making it difficult for me to keep up with him.

"How is that a stupid question?"

"I have never given you any indication I have an issue with you having a relationship with West, Prescott, and Francis. I don't know why you would ever think that about me."

147

I tried not to laugh even as I had to jog to keep up with him.

"I don't."

He stopped abruptly, making me almost crash into him.

"Then what are you playing at, Scarlett?"

"It's fun to see you get worked up."

He huffed and gave me a disapproving stare.

"Are you capable of going one day without being a brat? Not that I'll complain about fucking the attitude out of you later, but is this really the time? We're about to get to Lylah's grave."

I bit my lip and looked away.

"Maybe I was deflecting."

The next thing I knew, I was gathered up against Drake's chest and he was pressing a kiss to the top of my head.

"I know this must be difficult for you, little wisp, but you asked to come here today. I'm just trying to give you the space you need to say goodbye, okay?"

"Are you really going to fuck the attitude out of me?"

"Scarlett…"

"I'm just asking."

"Yes."

"Okay. I'd like that."

I heard him chuckling while he held me tighter.

"You are a reckless little troublemaker."

"That's what you lo… like about me."

What the fuck? Were you just about to tell him he loved you?

I almost winced. Drake hadn't expressed his feelings towards me, at least not like that. I knew he wanted me, but as for love? Fuck knows. My heart was his. He might be grumpy, overbearing and drive me crazy at times, but the glimpses of the younger version of Drake I had made it impossible for me not to fall in love with him. He was trying his hardest when it came to me. I appreciated it so fucking much.

"I like a lot of things about you. I always have."

"Even though I'm a brat?"

"You're *my* brat, little wisp. Mine. No one else's, just mine."

Jesus, I swear you're trying to kill me. How am I supposed to not melt in a pile of goo at your feet right now?

We stayed locked together for a long moment before Drake pulled away and looked down at me.

"You ready now?"

I nodded. He took my hand and led me down a small path into the trees. I swallowed hard as we approached a little wooden plaque. Drake's hand tightened in mine as we stared down at it.

"She wanted a woodland burial," he said when I didn't say a word. "We all came to the funeral. It was... I don't really know how to describe a funeral, to be honest."

I had to smile at his words.

"It's okay. You don't need to."

I looked up at him. His indigo eyes were full of sorrow as if he was remembering the day it happened.

"Would you mind if I have a few minutes alone?"

He shook his head, letting go of my hand to cup my face in both of us. Leaning down, he pressed a kiss to my forehead.

"Take all the time you need, little wisp. I'll just be over there keeping watch."

I tipped my head up to catch his mouth before he could let go. My hand slid around his neck, keeping him there. I kissed him until my heart was beating so hard in my chest, I thought I might pass out.

"Thank you for bringing me," I whispered when I pulled away and let him go.

"You're welcome."

His cheeks were flushed, but he gave me a soft smile and backed away. I watched him walk a little way off to give me some space. While I wanted to do this alone, I didn't want him to be so far away I couldn't see him. A part of me didn't feel safe without one of them near me after being stolen from them twice in my life already. That was the best part about having four boyfriends. One of them could always be near me, no matter what. It gave me a sense of peace to know the four parts that made up my heart were close by.

I squatted down and placed my hand on the grassy area by the wooden plaque.

"Hi, Mum... it feels kind of weird talking to you because you're not really here, but I'm going to do it, anyway."

I sat down on the grass as I didn't want my legs to give out. Leaning my head on my knees, I stared out over the woodland burial area.

"I miss you, Mum. It's like there's a hole in my heart where you should be. I hate that you died before we ever had a chance to be reunited. It feels so unfair your life got cut short because of all the shit that went down."

I sighed and let out a breath.

"At least I remember you now, hey? Would have sucked if I'd gone the rest of my life without knowing who you are... not that my life hasn't sucked already. I mean, I'm okay now, I guess... no, I am okay. I have the boys." Reaching out, I stroked the grass again. "They found me and brought me home."

I smiled to myself.

"You know, you always told me one day I was going to have to choose between the four of them. Maybe if I'd never been kidnapped, West and I could call ourselves childhood sweethearts. You knew it was him, didn't you? I made it kind of obvious. Don't get me wrong, I loved the others too, but he… he was the one."

My gaze went to my fingers, wondering if West and I would have grown up, got married and had two point five kids like you're supposed to. Then I remembered we'd never ascribed to society's values or rules.

"It seems kind of fucked up to say I'm not entirely sorry I was stolen from them, but I don't think things would have happened this way otherwise. I mean, I don't think I would have ever been okay with being with all of them. Fuck, it feels so weird to admit that out loud. Who'd have thought I'd have four boyfriends."

I let out a little chuckle. Most people would probably think this was crazy. A rather unorthodox relationship. And it was… but it didn't matter. I loved them. They wanted to be with me. What difference did it make to the rest of the world? We were happy. It was all that mattered.

"We've always said we were born to be with each other. I just didn't think it meant like this. But I wouldn't have it any other way, Mum. They're my family. They understand me and my needs. That's what's important. Being with the people who give you everything you've ever needed. And if it's from all four of them, then it's not wrong. A love like ours is never wrong. It just came in a different package."

It struck me then how true that statement was. People would have you believe anything that deviates from so-called traditional values is abnormal and should be stamped out. But life wasn't about absolutes and strict adherence to a moral code. It was so many shades of grey and everything in between. Real happiness only comes from being your true self. Mine happened to be a woman who'd fought through hell and was now able to stand by the sides of the men known as the Four Horsemen. The ones who'd see her through to the end.

"I'd like to think you would be okay with this, Mum. That you were happy I'd found them again. You can rest easy knowing we'll spend the rest of our lives bringing each other joy, contentment and... love. It's all anyone can ask for. A family that sticks together no matter what. That's what the boys and me are."

I raised my hand to my mouth, pressing my lips to my fingertips before placing them back on the ground.

"Thank you for never giving up, even when your life was stolen from you. Goodbye, Mum."

I stayed there for a long moment before I looked back at Drake. He was leaning against a tree, fiddling with his phone, but I could tell he was still alert and checking our surroundings. He shoved off the tree when he noticed I was looking at him and walked over to me, his brow furrowed.

"You okay, little wisp?"

I nodded and put my hand up to him. He helped me to my feet and stroked my hair as if to reassure himself I was good. I tucked myself into his side, wrapping an arm around his waist and pressing my face into his coat. There was no need for tears or angry words about the injustice of her death. I'd already avenged it by killing Mason. Now, I merely felt a sense of relief that I'd been able to talk to her. To tell her how I felt about the boys. And to know, despite everything, I was okay.

The wind blew, ruffling my hair, but I stayed close to Drake, appreciating his warmth despite his icy exterior.

"Scarlett."

"Mmm?"

"We need to talk about something."

I looked up at him. Drake's eyes were full of hesitation. It made the skin at the back of my neck prickle.

"What is it?"

"I should have told you this when you spoke to us about it the day Stuart called."

His expression clouded over further. My skin grew cold.

Has he been keeping more things from me? What the fuck? I thought we were done with secrets.

SEVENTEEN

DRAKE

Now was likely the wrong time to talk to her about this, but it couldn't wait any longer. I didn't want to keep shit from her. Not when it was important we were open about things. After all her teasing regarding my feelings about her being with the others, I was reminded a relationship would only work if we had honesty.

"Told me what, Drake?"

Scarlett was tucked up against my side, but I had a feeling she'd be pretty fucking mad at me the moment I told her.

"When you told us you can't have children… we already knew about it."

Her eyes narrowed and her mouth thinned. Then she extracted herself from my grasp and took a few steps back, putting space between us.

"You knew."

"Yes."

Her tiny hands clenched into fists at her sides, like she was trying to keep her anger in check.

"I don't want to jump to conclusions, so you better tell me exactly how you found out."

I dug my hands in my coat pockets. This had been playing on my mind since the day we'd found out about Stuart's abuse. Since she'd openly admitted to us she was unable to have kids.

"Drake, spit it the fuck out."

It was now or never. I had to rip the bandage off.

"We bribed the doctor Stuart got for you to give us access to your medical files. We saw everything… all of your injuries, how the scarring from the way they pinned your pelvis together all but destroyed your ovaries, how extensive your rehabilitation was, everything, Scarlett. There's nothing we don't know about your medical history. I know that's really fucked up. I know it's an invasion of privacy and I'm sorry."

Scarlett's fists didn't unclench. She stared at me, her expression dark and full of anger.

"Sorry. You're sorry. Jesus Christ, Drake! What the fuck next, huh? When are these secrets going to end? Are you going to tell me this has all been a fucking ruse and when this is over, you're going to leave me in the dust because I can't give you children? Or that you never really wanted me in the first place?"

"What? No!" I took a step towards her, putting my hands out. "Hey, no, don't do that. Don't start accusing me of wanting to leave you. I'm trying to be honest with you here."

She backed away, but I caught her by the arm. How could she think that of us? We cared about Scarlett above all else. Hell, I'd fallen so hard for her, it was un-fucking-real. I didn't think I was capable of such emotions after everything fell apart, but my long-buried feelings for her resurfaced when she'd arrived back in our lives. When she'd ripped open the ice casing around my heart and made herself at home in it.

"Let go of me!"

"No. You listen here, I made you a fucking promise I'd never leave you no matter what happens. I don't give a shit about children, Scarlett. I never have. I don't care about destinies or fate. I literally couldn't care less what anyone else thinks about our relationship. The only thing in this entire world I care about is you. Only you. Forever. You hear me? For-fucking-ever."

For a second, Scarlett didn't react to my words. Then she put a hand to her mouth as if she was trying to hold back her emotions. Her eyes were wide and her chest heaved. I decided to press on. To admit things to her I would have never done so before, but she needed to get stupid shit like we'd leave her out of her head. She was it for the four of us.

"I've spent almost my whole damn life wishing you were mine. It might not have looked that way to you, but it's the truth. Why do you think I turned down all the girls at school? Why do you think I wasn't interested? The only person I've ever looked at and thought 'she's it for me' is you."

Unable to help myself, I cupped her cheek, drawing her closer to me.

"I've been trying so hard to give you what you need. To give you parts of me no one else has had before. You're the only person I trust with them. I am yours. I will be yours for as long as you want me. For as long as you need me in your life, little wisp."

I should tell her I loved her. I should fucking say it, but the words wouldn't come. It didn't matter. I hoped I was getting my point across. She didn't need to worry or be afraid we'd walk away. We'd fought to get her back for ten years. I couldn't allow another ten years to pass without her in our lives. Without her by our sides.

I need you. I really fucking need you. Damn it, Scarlett. I'm in love with you.

"You... you... you *liked* me, liked me?"

"Yes."

"Holy shit."

"I never thought you ever saw me that way... saw any of us like that. West didn't even tell us about you and him until recently. I had no idea."

She blinked.

"I told Frankie. He knew I loved West."

I half-smiled.

"I know that now."

She put her hand to mine on her cheek and pulled it away. Her eyes went to it as she fit her small fingers between my much larger ones. It reminded me of how she'd said she liked the way my hands fit around her. I had to stop myself from smiling at that little detail.

"I'm sorry I kept all this shit from you, but I meant what I said. You are what I need. Nothing more. Nothing less. Just you."

My little wisp of a woman stared up at me with conflicting emotions racing across her face.

"Can I ask one thing about you knowing my medical history?"

"You can ask me anything."

Not like I was planning on keeping anything else from her.

"Is that why all of you decided it was okay to just..." she faltered and looked away.

"What was okay?"

"To not use protection and not even talk to me about it."

I tried not to smile.

"Yes. You never brought it up either."

She met my eyes again and gave me a disapproving look.

"Oh yeah, because that was the first thing on my mind when I woke up tied to a bed naked. I wonder if they're going to use condoms."

I tucked my free hand around the back of her head.

"Do you want us to use them?"

"No!"

I leant closer.

"So... you like it when we—"

She slapped a hand over my mouth.

"Do not say it."

I removed her hand and captured her mouth with mine. She didn't protest. Her body melted into mine as I wrapped an arm around her back. Her fingers clasped the front of my coat. The little moan sounding in the back of her throat made me want to shove her up against a tree and put my hand down her jeans. I wanted to make her come on my fingers while she rubbed herself all over me. However, I didn't think it was a very appropriate thing to do in a cemetery where anyone could come upon us.

"Drake," she moaned against my mouth.

The temptation was almost too much. I had to pull away and catch my damn breath.

"Take me home," she whispered, her little fists still clenched around my coat.

"Have you forgiven me for keeping another secret?"

She nodded, releasing my coat and stroking her hands down my chest.

"Then let's—"

I heard rustling from behind me. My body went on high alert. I whipped around, shoving Scarlett behind me. And for good fucking reason. Three men appeared out of the trees. They did not look like they were here to exchange pleasantries with us, judging by the way one of them cracked his knuckles. One stepped forward, twirling a knife around his fingers.

"What do you want?" I ground out.

Scarlett peered out from behind me. I gave her a warning look before eyeing the men again.

"We want the girl."

"Why?"

The one with the knife was taller than the other two. He cocked his head to the side. It was shaved, and he had what looked like a tattoo of a bulldog on one side of it. I almost shook my head at his appearance but decided it wasn't worth it.

"None of your business, mate. Just hand her over and we'll be on our way."

I raised an eyebrow.

"If you want her, you'll have to go through me."

He scoffed and gave me the once over. I might not look like I could take them, but they had no fucking clue who they were dealing with.

"Three against one, mate. Are you sure you like those odds?"

I felt Scarlett press herself against my back, reassuring me she was right there.

I don't care what it takes. I will protect you, little wisp. These fuckers aren't having you. Over my dead body.

"You clearly don't know who I am."

"Doesn't matter who you are. We only came for her."

I gave them a smile.

"Oh, I see. He didn't tell you who you'd be trying to take her from now, did he?"

The man with the knife looked a little uneasy at my statement while the other two bristled at his sides.

I knew very well who sent these fuckers. It had to be Stuart. If he came himself, he wouldn't leave alive. Our message had been very clear when we sent them Mason's head. You fuck with us. We will fuck with you right back. Not to mention he must know by now we'd blackmailed Garrett into backing off.

"You think you know who sent us?"

"I don't think, I know. Stuart is getting sloppy."

The way the leader's eyes widened made it clear I'd hit the mark. Then he shook himself off and glared.

"Whatever. Just give her here."

"How much is he paying you to take her, huh? Because I'm telling you now, if you don't turn around and walk away, you'll be the ones paying."

One of his men tutted and nudged his friend.

"This bloke thinks he's tough. Stuck up rich pricks have no fucking idea."

"Next time, I suggest you do your research before you take jobs from men like Stuart Carver. You would have known my reputation precedes me if you did."

"What fucking reputation?" the leader spat.

I turned to Scarlett behind me.

"Get behind that tree," I murmured.

"Drake, are you sure we shouldn't just run?"

"Do what I said, little wisp. Let me deal with this."

I felt her let go of my coat, but she didn't move away. Turning back to the men, I offered them another smile as I straightened, widening my stance. They looked at me like I was crazy. Well, maybe I was. The thing about love was you did everything in your power to protect the one you felt it for. Scarlett was my love. Anyone who threatened her threatened me. I wasn't lying when I told her I'd be her executioner. These men were going to die for trying to take her from me. No one would ever steal my woman away again. Never a-fucking-gain.

We'd made a promise to Scarlett. I intended on sticking to my word no matter what.

"I've been very remiss in introductions."

I stepped closer to them.

"Drake Ackley."

I pressed a hand to my chest before dropping it back to my side.

"You may have heard of my friends and me. People like to call us the Four Horsemen of the Apocalypse. And I'll bet you want to know which one of them I am. Well… you're about to find out."

EIGHTEEN

SCARLETT

The moment the words about him being one of the horsemen left Drake's lips, he walked towards the three men who were after me. The man with the knife struck first, trying to throw a punch at Drake, who sidestepped it with ease. I put my hand over my mouth, backing away slightly. He'd told me to get behind the tree near us, but I wasn't going to hide and cower away from what was happening. Not to mention the fact Drake was crazy for taking on three guys at once.

What the hell is he thinking?

He had to be out of his damn mind, but something told me Drake wouldn't let them take me, no matter what. I couldn't deny it was hot even if I should be scared out of my mind by the danger right now.

The second guy, the one with a black tracksuit, threw himself fists first at Drake. He caught the guy's hand mid-strike and threw his fist off. The third one, a short man with blonde hair, tried to jump on Drake's back. Before he had a chance, Drake elbowed him in the stomach, then spun around and put his fist in the guy's face. The blonde man's head snapped back and he let out a grunt.

Drake didn't have time to stop, as the bald guy with a tattoo on the side of his head swiped at him with the knife. Drake stepped back, the man narrowly missing his coat with the blade. The way Drake moved with such grace had me riveted to the scene playing out. It was as if he was anticipating all their moves and dancing out of the way before they could get a grip on him.

"Get him, Jim," knife man barked at the tracksuit guy.

The blonde man was holding his nose with one hand as blood spurted from it. I saw Drake's nostrils flare before tracksuit came at him, swinging his fist and clipping my man around the ear.

"Oh, you should not have done that," he ground out.

Drake grabbed him by the shoulders and head-butted him in the face before throwing him into knife man. The two of them toppled over together and fell in a heap on the floor. Drake cracked his neck, seemingly unfazed by the hit landed on him. While the two men on the floor tried to extract themselves from each other, Drake's attention went to the blonde. He smiled, his expression turning rather sinister.

The man took a step back as if realising a predator had him in his sights. I swallowed as Drake pounced, taking the man by the neck and backing him into a tree. It was at that point I realised he wasn't going to allow these men to walk away with their lives. His hand tightened around the guy's neck. The blonde man tried to push Drake off him, but my statue of a man stood strong. His other hand came up and joined its twin. The blonde wheezed, trying to pull Drake's hands off his neck.

My attention went to the others who had both got up now. The one with the knife was walking towards Drake while tracksuit man was still looking a little dazed.

"Drake!"

His head whipped around and he let go of the blonde man, turning just as the tattooed guy raised his knife. I don't know how the fuck he did it, but somehow, Drake was on him, gripping the guy's wrist and snapping it backwards. The man with the knife yelped, dropping his blade on the ground.

"You think this is a game, hmm?" Drake said with deadly calm. He hadn't even broken out into a sweat or anything. "Let me make something very clear. I don't show mercy."

He punched the guy in the face before throwing him to the ground. Tracksuit had shaken himself off by then and tried to come at Drake again. Drake merely grabbed hold of his arm, spun him around and wrapped his arm around the guy's throat. He struggled against him, but Drake was looking around on the floor for something. A moment later, he threw tracksuit into the blonde man who was nursing his broken nose. He dived for the knife the tattooed guy dropped. He rose to his full height and turned to the man on the ground with a grin.

I couldn't look away as he tried to scramble backwards, but Drake caught up to him, grabbing him by the front of his clothes.

"Death comes to all," he said, his voice so calm, it was terrifying.

Then Drake slit the man's throat. Blood seeped from the wound, covering his hand in red liquid. He dropped the guy's shirt, straightening and turning towards the other two. Drake slid the back of his hand across his face, smearing blood over it. It almost felt like a purposeful act. As if he wanted the others to see.

Holy fuck!

Before they had a chance to run, Drake practically pounced on the one in the tracksuit. The knife slid into his body with so much ease, it looked effortless on Drake's part. He shoved the guy away before grabbing hold of the blonde-haired man and slitting his damn throat too. But Drake didn't stop there. He came for tracksuit again as the man held his stomach, blood seeping into the white of his top. The blade slashed across his throat before Drake threw him to the ground.

Drake stood there, breathing a little heavier than normal, as he stared down at the three men bleeding out. He had blood on his face and both his hands. And to me, he'd never looked more like a god. Like the man who controlled who lived and who died.

"You're Death."

Drake's head turned ever so slightly towards me. His lips curved up at the sides, his indigo eyes flashing with what could only be described as murder-filled delight.

"You missed out a word there, little wisp."

"What word?"

"My."

I swallowed as he stalked towards me, blade still clasped in his palm. He stopped inches from me, staring down at my small form like I was the most precious thing in the world to him.

"My Death."

He leant closer.

"That's right, Scarlett. I'm your reaper."

Then I was caught up against his chest and he was kissing me so hard, I forgot to breathe. If there was one thing in this world Drake was an expert in, it definitely had to be kissing. The man could probably kill a girl just by kissing her. And the irony of it was not lost on me.

He's literally Death.

But he wasn't the fourth and final horseman for just anyone. He was it for me. My horseman. My Death.

I clutched his coat, aware he was getting blood on me but not caring in the slightest. I wanted him so badly, my legs were shaking.

"Take me home, please. I need you."

He kissed his way down my jaw, making me tremble all the more.

"I will, but we have a little issue to deal with first."

"What?"

He pulled away, straightening to his full height. I almost protested at the lack of contact until I saw the grim look on his face.

"We need to get rid of the bodies."

The bodies. Right. He just killed three people. Why am I forgetting that? Oh yeah, he just kissed the living shit out of me and now my brain is all fucked.

"We?"

"Mmm, you stay here. I'll get the car."

"You've got blood all over your face and your hands. What if someone sees you?"

He pointed at my bag.

167

"Wet wipes."

I was having a very hard time processing all of this. I'd watched him kill three men, and he'd been barely out of breath doing it. This man was absolutely lethal. Especially for my heart. It was pounding so hard, I thought it might explode on me.

"Scarlett."

I shook myself before pulling open my bag and extracting my makeup wipes. Drake took them and cleaned himself up while I stood watching him. He'd told me we would need to deal with the bodies. We. Together. Me and him.

"Wait, hold on... you just killed three people. How on earth are we meant to get rid of them on our own?"

"Just do as I say and we'll manage."

He took my face in his hand and cleaned off the blood he'd got on there.

"Now, hold these whilst I get the car. Do not go anywhere unless someone other than me comes along, okay? Then you run."

"But, Drake—"

"We do not have time to discuss this. Wait here."

He handed me the knife and the wipes. I took them and watched him stride away towards the road. I needed to get my shit together. Drake needed my help. I wasn't going to let him down. Taking a deep breath, I looked over at the men, wondering how Drake intended to get rid of them.

You can do this. You can help him. Drake doesn't need you freaking out or losing your mind, okay? He'll look after you when we've sorted this out.

I took that and ran with it. Setting down the wipes and the blade together, I walked over to the men and checked them to make sure they were dead. Then I used their clothes to mop up the excess blood before dragging them closer to the road. They were fucking heavy, but I managed. Now I could see how much blood had got on the ground.

"Fuck."

Drake deciding to cut their throats wasn't the smartest idea, but it was neither here nor there. We were going to have to deal with it, regardless. Not like we could leave a ton of evidence or it might arouse suspicion.

"I see you've been busy."

I jumped at the sound of his voice, spinning around and finding Drake standing over the bodies.

"You told me we had to deal with it. I was trying to be practical."

He had a bunch of cleaning materials with him, which made me raise my eyebrows.

"Take this and mop up as much of the blood as you can."

He handed me a bunch of absorbent cleaning cloths. I'd killed two men, so I wasn't particularly squeamish about blood, not to mention I'd cut myself for Drake. I did as he asked while he picked up the smallest man, the blonde one, and carried him away.

I worked as quickly as possible while the blood was still wet. It wasn't perfect, but Drake had something to wash it down with. Then I helped him with the other two men, getting them situated in the back of the car. He'd put the blonde man in the boot. We stuffed one in the footwell and laid the other across the backseat. Drake had put down plastic sheeting and covered them in a blanket. I wondered why he had all this shit in the car with him, but then again, West told me they'd killed quite a few people in the past ten years. I got the impression they all knew the best ways to deal with dead bodies.

Drake made me wait by the car while he dealt with everything else. I kept looking around to make sure no one else was coming along. My nerves were firing on all cylinders. I rubbed my clothes with my fingers, trying not to freak out. This whole thing was fucking crazy.

By the time Drake got back, I could see two people walking along the road towards us. I jumped into the car, did my seatbelt up and tapped on the dashboard, hoping he wouldn't take too fucking long and those people caught up to us. He got in a minute later, eyeing me with a frown before he turned on the car and set off.

"Are you okay?" he asked after a minute.

"You just killed three people and made me help you clean up what is essentially a crime scene and you're asking me if I'm okay? No, Drake, I'm not okay."

He reached over and stroked my hair back from my face, tucking it behind my ear as he pulled up at the entrance to the cemetery.

"Which part are you not okay with?"

"The part where we could have and still could get caught."

"I won't let that happen, little wisp. You're safe with me."

I looked at him. The softness of his expression made my stomach twist in itself in knots. Then he leant over and kissed my forehead. I didn't say a word when he pulled away and set off again. He'd reassured me the back windows were tinted when we were putting the bodies in the car, but I was still a bundle of nerves.

"Where are we taking them?" I asked after a few minutes.

"Landfill."

"We can't just dump three bodies there, they'll get found."

"You don't need to worry. I called Penn when I was getting the car and he knows a guy."

Why I was even surprised by this knowledge was beyond me at this point. Penn was some kind of madman genius who seemed to know everyone. Maybe I should tell West I wanted a tattoo. Then I could sit and question Penn about himself the whole time. For some reason, he fascinated me. Not because I was attracted to him, but he was on a similar level of fucked up to West. Guess I was drawn to the misfits and those who didn't play by society's rules.

I sat back and watched the houses go by while Drake drove and wondered when my life had got so crazy that killing people and disposing of bodies was becoming something of a normal, everyday occurrence. I guess when you have four psycho boyfriends who have adopted the moniker of the Four Horsemen of the Apocalypse, it was par for the fucking course.

I glanced over at Drake again. He hadn't been lying about being my executioner. He'd protected me and kept me from being taken. And if I was being completely honest, rather than making me scared of him, it had only made me fall deeper in love with the man I'd come to know as Death.

171

NINETEEN

DRAKE

When I'd agreed to take Scarlett to her mother's grave, I did not imagine it would turn into a bloody mess. We'd finally made it home after dealing with the three men I'd ended up killing. We'd stopped at a drive-thru on the way back. We'd both been starving after cutting up the bodies, bagging them and having Penn's man take them deep within the landfill site. Money had quickly exchanged hands, and we'd been on our way. Scarlett hadn't exactly been happy to be involved in the process, but she didn't complain too much.

Scarlett had a tight hold of my hand as the lift doors opened. I tugged her towards the stairs when I realised none of the boys were downstairs. I'd texted them earlier to let them know what had happened. I'd had one back from West who was pouting about not being involved, but I'd ignored him. Not like I planned on getting into a fight with three men today or anything.

"Where are we going?" Scarlett asked when we were walking up the stairs.

"To get cleaned up."

"In…?"

"My room."

I found myself pulled to a halt as Scarlett stopped dead in the middle of the hallway.

"You're letting me in your bedroom?"

"Why wouldn't I?"

She stared up at me with wide eyes.

"Let me see, you've kept me out of there for months and now, without any warning, you're taking me in there."

I tugged her along, shaking my head at her statement. She wasn't exactly wrong, but I didn't think letting her into my room was a big deal. Apparently, to her, it was.

"Well, you should consider it a privilege in that case."

"Drake!"

I opened the door to my room and pulled her inside, shutting it behind us.

"I want you in here, little wisp. Now, come along."

She didn't immediately start walking when I did, her eyes darting about the place. I let out a sigh.

"You can look around later. First, you're getting in the shower."

She followed me, her eyes still wandering around the room. It was of a similar layout to the others, with a big window along one side. My bed was on one end. A big set of wardrobes with black doors sat on the wall opposite the windows. I'd had the walls painted a deep navy blue. Everything was ordered, neat and in its place.

"Promise?"

"Yes, Scarlett. I promise you can snoop around to your heart's content if that's really what you want."

I pulled her into my bathroom. It had a slate floor and black tiles on the walls. I had a separate bath to the shower and a large counter for the sink with a big mirror above it.

"Strip and put your clothes in a pile there."

I pointed at a space underneath my heated towel rack. I would dispose of all our clothes later. Scarlett took a long minute to look around the bathroom, leaving me impatient for her to get on with it.

"Scarlett, clothes off and in the shower. Now."

She put her hands up.

"Okay, okay, Jesus. Calm down, bossy boots."

I watched her take her clothes off, unable to help myself from admiring her curves. She glanced at me as she stepped into my shower and flipped it on.

"Are you coming?"

I tugged my clothes off and dumped them in the pile with hers. She watched me walk towards her, her eyes wide when I grabbed her around the waist and hauled her against me under the spray. My fingers ran down her wet skin, savouring the softness of her body.

"I'm going to smell of you now," she murmured, staring up at me with a smirk on her lips.

"What do I smell like?"

"Sin."

I chuckled and leant down, capturing her mouth and cupping her face with my hand. When I pulled away, I grabbed the shower gel and squirted some on my hands. While I was just about ready to fuck the living daylights out of Scarlett, I had other ideas for how and where I wanted to do it.

"I think you must like the smell of sin," I told her as I washed her body. "You seem to like me."

"I more than just like you," she mumbled as I turned her around and washed her back.

I didn't want to read into that, even though my heart fired off at her words. Picking up the shampoo to distract myself, I started washing her hair. I'd managed to get blood in it earlier and wanted to make sure she was clean of all traces of those men.

"I'm going to have to get a set of toiletries for your room too now, like I have done with the others."

"Who says you'll spending a lot of time in here?"

She let out a little huff and crossed her arms over her chest.

"If you don't want an equal share of my time, that's your loss. I'm sure Pres, West and Frankie will be happy to take your nights off your hands."

I tugged her back against my chest and ran my hands down her front, stroking them across her breasts. She shivered but continued pouting.

"Such a brat," I whispered in her ear as I cupped her pussy and slid my fingers along her lips. "I'll get Francis to tie you to my bed so you can't leave if you start with that line of thinking."

"Then don't be out here trying to withhold bedroom privileges from me. I already have to put up with not having my own one."

I had ideas of how to create a space for her in our penthouse, but it was something I was going to discuss with the others, so now wasn't the time.

As much as I wanted to continue playing with her, we needed to finish washing. I let go of her to condition her hair after rinsing the shampoo out. She let me without complaint and gave me a shy smile when I allowed her to wash me in return.

I pulled her out of the shower, flipping it off before wrapping a large towel around her small body and drying her thoroughly. I set Scarlett on the counter while I dried myself. She used a smaller towel to dry her hair enough so it was no longer dripping.

Picking her up off the counter, I took her into my room and strode across to my bed. I set Scarlett down in the middle of it and crawled over her. My fingers traced a line down her chest, watching her skin prickle from the contact. She stayed perfectly still, allowing me to explore her stunning body, scars and all. I stroked her 'war' brand. It had healed up, leaving pink lines across her skin that would eventually turn white. West now had a matching one she'd given him on his chest. It was a little like the binding of two souls, which I had to admit felt apt for her and West. They were both as unhinged as each other at times.

"You're beautiful," I murmured, settling my fingers across the biggest scar on her abdomen. "I've always thought so, but now… now you're more so. All of your imperfections are perfect to me."

"Drake…"

"Shh." I put my finger to her lips. "Don't say anything."

I sat up and reached over to my bedside table. Scarlett was suitably distracted from looking around my room right now, but she could later after I'd had my way with her. I dug out a small knife. She watched me use it to make a small nick on my wrist. Blood pooled around the cut. I coated my finger in it before leaning over her. Her eyes followed the path of my finger across her chest, painting a word on it in blood.

Scarlett swallowed when I was done. Her eyes went to mine after she read it, even though it was upside down for her.

"You branding me too?"

"In my own way."

Smeared across her chest in my blood was the word 'mine'. She was mine. All fucking mine. Scarlett belonged to me.

"I'm already yours, Drake." She reached up and stroked her fingers across my face. "I've been yours for a while, in case you hadn't noticed."

"Is that so?"

She nodded.

"I helped you get rid of three bodies. I think that proves my loyalty."

I grinned and leant closer.

"It does."

"There's something else that belongs to you as well."

I raised a brow.

"And what would that be?"

She licked her bottom lip, then her eyes clouded over. Her hand dropped from my face and she looked away.

"Scarlett?"

"How do you really feel about me? I mean, you said you've always wanted me, but what does that mean?"

Catching her by the chin, I turned her face back towards me to make her meet my eyes. I didn't like seeing fear in those beautiful hazel-greens.

"It means…" I leant closer, brushing my mouth over hers. "It means, little wisp, that you are the owner of what you'd probably describe as my cold, black heart."

Her bottom lip trembled against mine.

"You love me?" she whispered, her voice shaking on the words.

"I love you."

"Fuck."

I kissed her, stealing away any other words she was thinking about saying. She wrapped her arms around me, pulling me flush against her. I tried not to groan as my cock slid against her wet little pussy.

"Such a dirty little mouth you have," I murmured against her lips.

"All the better to wind you up with."

"Brat."

"I'm your brat, sir."

I pulled away from her and grabbed her by the waist, flipping her up onto her hands and knees. Running my fingers down her back, I pressed kisses to her spine.

"You have a lot of punishments pending, little wisp. I intend to collect."

She shivered but didn't tell me no or to stop. I got up off the bed and walked over to my display on the wall across from my bed. It was black metal crisscrossing bars with hangers at different intervals. On those hangers were my various whips and crops.

I selected a small crop, testing it against my hand before moving back towards the bed. Scarlett looked back at me, then down at the implement in my hand.

"Drake…"

"What's your safe word with the others?"

"Red."

"Then you say that and I will stop, okay?"

She nodded but didn't look entirely convinced. I knelt on the bed and stroked her hip.

"What's wrong?"

She turned over and crawled into my lap. I set the crop on the bed and cupped both her cheeks as she held onto my shoulders. She searched my face for a moment.

"Nothing. I want you to punish me, but first…"

"First?"

"Kiss me and say it again."

I almost denied her. The truth was, I couldn't help myself when it came to my little wisp. Not any longer. I wanted her smiles and her laughter more than anything else. Leaning closer, I ran my nose along hers.

"I love you."

"Again."

I pressed a kiss to her mouth.

"I love you, Scarlett."

"I love you too."

I swallowed at her statement. My heart hurt in a good way. In the best fucking way. My mouth was on hers, demanding entry until she relented and kissed me back with as much passion as I gave her. She gripped my hair in her fists, rubbing herself against me. I found myself so desperate for more contact. More of her. I let go of her cheek and dug a hand between us. Scarlett shifted, then she was sinking down on me and moaning in my mouth. My hand curled around her hip and directed her movements, forcing her to slow down as she took me.

My other hand slid from her cheek to hold her jaw and tip her face up, stretching her neck out. She looked at me with wide, lust-filled eyes. I framed my mouth over hers, not quite touching her lips.

"I'm going to cover you in marks, little wisp. I want you to be a good girl and take them."

"Yes, sir."

I ran my thumb along her bottom lip before slipping it between them.

"Your wet little pussy has made a mess of my dick. You're going to clean it up before presenting me your pert little behind. Do you understand?"

I slid my thumb from her mouth.

"Yes, sir."

Scarlett might be my little brat, but right now, she would be my good girl. I knew what she wanted most in the world was to hear me give her praise. And if she took her punishments like I'd told her to, she would.

TWENTY

DRAKE

W hen I let go of her, she slid off me, leaving a trail of kisses down my chest as she bent over me. Her tongue curled around my cock, licking up her arousal. I couldn't stop staring at her. The way her mouth parted and her tongue darted out. And when she covered my dick with it, that was fucking everything.

She sat up and turned around, getting up on her hands and knees in front of me after she'd cleaned me. I slid off the bed, picking up the crop before I ran it over her behind, watching her shiver from its touch.

"Safe word, Scarlett."

"Red."

"Good girl."

The little sigh she let out had me smiling, not that she could see.

"Keep your eyes on the headboard."

She centred her gaze on it, adjusting her hands and knees so she was more comfortable. I gave her a light tap with the crop, signalling I was going to start. I watched her suck in a breath. Then I laid into her, sending the crop sailing through the air. The smack as it struck her skin was so fucking satisfying. She exhaled on the first strike, her fingers curling into the covers. They were the only outward signs of the pain it had caused her. But I knew my little wisp liked it. She thrived on it.

The crop smacked against her skin, again and again, painting her behind with red marks. I was gentle at first, but the strikes got harder, leaving darker marks each time until they turned into little welts. Her breathing was heavy, and she kept making these little whimpering noises, but not once did she tell me she didn't want it. She didn't tell me it was too much or to stop. She knew she could, but my girl was so fucking brave and strong.

When her behind was suitably red and raw, I moved to her thighs. Then she cried out, lurching forward after I pulled the crop back. I ignored her new sounds of pain while I continued to punish her skin.

"Fuck," she yelled a minute later, her elbows buckling.

"Too much for you, little wisp?" I asked, pausing for a moment while she caught her breath.

She shook her head before resting it on her hands.

"No. No, it's not."

I ran the crop over her raw skin, making her hiss.

"Are you sure?"

"I'm not going to lie. It fucking hurts, Drake, but I want it. I want you to make me scream from the pain."

I removed the crop and leant down, pressing a kiss to her abused skin.

"I'll make it better afterwards. Good girls get to come."

She trembled as I pressed more kisses to her red, welted behind. And to reward her for being such a good girl for me, I slid my tongue along her rather wet little pussy, curling my tongue around her clit a few times.

"Oh god," she whined.

"God isn't here," I murmured. "Just Death and he isn't remotely merciful."

That only made her moan more as I continued to lick her clit. She pressed back into my mouth like it was instinctual to seek me out. I curled my free hand around her hip, holding her in place.

"You're… you're going to make me come if you don't stop now."

I pulled back, watching her raise her head from her hands and take a long breath.

"Is pain your drug of choice, little wisp?"

"Yes, sir."

I straightened, gripping the crop in my fist and getting ready to start again. My fingers released her hip. I stood back, giving myself room. The first strike across her thigh made her cry out as if she wasn't ready, but she gripped the covers and kept her eyes on the headboard.

Such an obedient little brat.

The crescendo of her cries grew louder as I continued to assault her red skin with the crop. She'd told me to make her scream. I hit her harder, making welts appear on her thighs. I didn't want to break her skin, but I was getting close to doing so.

"Fuck," she screeched, lurching forward again as I hit a particularly sore spot for her. "No more, please... please, no more."

I ran the crop over the seam of her pussy, coating it in her arousal. It glistened when I pulled it away. I moved closer and shoved it in her face.

"This says otherwise, little wisp. You want me to hurt you."

"I hate that you're right."

I dropped the crop and knelt on the bed instead, leaning over her and kissing her shoulder.

"I think my good girl has been tortured enough, don't you?"

"If you say so, sir."

I clasped her chin between my fingers and turned her face, finding it tear-streaked along with her teeth digging into her bottom lip.

"I'll make it hurt in other ways," I whispered in her ear before I dragged my teeth over the lobe. "Just think of how much it will burn every time my skin meets yours whilst I fuck you."

Her whole body shook. I couldn't hide my smile as I released her and straightened again. Reaching over to my drawer, I pulled it open and extracted lube. I'd told Scarlett one of her punishments would include me making her little behind raw before I fucked her tight little arse. It was time to deliver on it.

I gripped her arse, making her cry out with the pain as I exposed her little hole to my view. Flipping the cap with my thumb, I dribbled it down over her. I set the lube down and rubbed it in, making her jerk under my touch. While this might be a punishment for her, I wasn't going to skimp out on preparing her to take me. Scarlett had got used to being fucked six ways from Sunday, so she didn't need as long, but I never liked to risk things. I worked her up until she could take three fingers with ease. She was whimpering and bucking in my grasp, her red flesh so fucking enticing. I'd take care of it when we were done, making sure I looked after her.

I let go of her to coat my cock before gripping her hip and notching it to her tight little entrance. She let out a breath as I pressed forward, and bore down, making it easier for me to slide into her. I grunted at the sensation of her gripping me. Her head dropped down onto her hands and I could have fucking sworn I heard her mutter, "Shit, Death," under her breath.

I leant over her, pushing deeper with my movement.

"Are you trying to tell me something, Scarlett?"

"What?"

I nuzzled her hair.

"Is there something else you'd rather call me other than sir?"

"No."

"As long as you're sure."

She looked back at me, her face flushed red.

"I want you to be sir and maybe sometimes Death. Okay… so more than sometimes. Is that okay?"

My cock throbbed inside her, making me jerk forward and impale her completely. She let out a long breath before she groaned.

"I'll take that as a yes," she said a moment later, giving me a wicked grin.

I pulled back and thrust inside her again.

"It's a please do," I murmured, wrapping an arm around her and pulling her flush against me as I sat up, forcing her to straddle my lap.

From this angle, all of me was touching where I'd spanked her. She hissed at the contact.

"Jesus, you feel so fucking big like this."

"I'll take that as a compliment."

She snorted and wrapped her hands around my back, holding onto me as I gave her shallow thrusts, rubbing her raw skin against mine.

"Don't let it go to your head."

"Too late."

I bit down on her earlobe, listening to her harsh pants and feeling her body relax into mine. Looping my arm around her, I held her stomach to give me more leverage to fuck her with. The way she moaned with each thrust was fucking music to my ears.

"Do you love me, little wisp?"

"Yes," she whimpered, her nails digging into my skin.

"Say it."

I needed to hear it again to be sure she meant it.

"I love you, Drake."

I groaned in her ear, my other hand diving between her legs to stroke her clit. She rocked back against me.

"And I will stab anyone who tries to flirt with you."

I choked out a breath.

"What?"

"You're mine. I won't tolerate anyone encroaching on my territory."

Of all the times for her to start acting possessive of me, this wasn't the one I expected. And I had to admit, it only made me fall harder for her.

"I think you've been spending too much time with West if choosing violence is your first port of call."

"The reaper needs a dark queen to ride by his side. I suggest you don't complain about it and accept you're mine. I will hurt anyone who says otherwise."

I gripped her tighter and rubbed her clit harder.

"He also needs a queen to fuck and punish to his heart's content. She needs to be his brat and his good girl. Do you know where he can find such a goddess?"

She practically purred against me.

"Right here. You already have her. She's yours. And she loves you to the stars and back."

"I love her too, very much." I pressed a kiss to the shell of her ear. "Come for me, little wisp."

Shifting her in my lap, I adjusted the angle to hit deeper and circled her clit the way I knew she liked. She cried out when I gave it to her harder. The pain of my skin against hers sent her over the edge. I felt it hit her as she clenched hard around my cock. Her body tensed and released, her nails digging harder into my skin.

"Fuck, Drake, come for me too... please, fuck, please."

I pressed her forward on the bed, covering her body with my own before giving it to her harder than before. She cried through it, her body writhing beneath me until I grunted with my own eruption. I collapsed on top of her when I was spent, pinning her to the bed with my much larger body.

It took a few minutes for me to regain my equilibrium and move off her. She lay there quietly as if she needed more time to come down from her high. I slipped off the bed and went into the bathroom, cleaning myself up before gathering up supplies to take care of her.

I sat next to her when I came out and stroked her back.

"Do you want to lie in my lap whilst I take care of you?"

She nodded but didn't make a move. So I took it upon myself to shift her into my lap. I checked over her welts to make sure I hadn't broken the skin anywhere. Then I rubbed soothing ointment into her red skin. She sighed as I did it. When I was finished, I cleaned the blood off her chest and the cum from between her legs. Then I laid her back down on the bed while I got a t-shirt for her out of my cupboards. I pulled it over her head and tucked her under the covers, pressing a kiss to her forehead.

After that, I tugged on some clothes and went downstairs, pouring two glasses of water and putting a bag of dried fruit snacks she liked between my teeth. As I got back to my room, I found her clutching my pillow, her face buried in like she was breathing in the scent of me. I couldn't help but grin at how fucking cute that was as I set down the glasses and the snacks.

"Little wisp."

She popped her head up, flushing red with embarrassment. I got under the covers and made her sit up so she could eat and drink. She let me feed her and make sure she was full before I allowed her to curl up by my side with my arm wrapped around her back. Pressing a kiss to her forehead, I watched her fall asleep. It wasn't very late. I was intending to get up after she was settled, but I found I couldn't leave her. Instead, I lay there stroking her face and wondering how I'd got so fucking lucky. I had the woman of my dreams in my bed and she loved me. It was a mind fuck, but a good one.

Her soft breathing soothed to my anxiety-ridden mind. I pressed my face into her hair and closed my eyes, savouring her warmth against me. Savouring every part of Scarlett. And somehow, without meaning to, I fell asleep hours before midnight for the first time in years. All because I had the love of my life next to me.

TWENTY ONE

WEST

My body jerked awake to the rush of cold air before a warm body curled itself around my back. A small hand appeared and wrapped around my stomach when I cracked an eye open. A hand I knew intimately. I closed my eye and settled into her embrace. There was no threat. It was just the owner of my heart crawling into bed with me as the morning sun dappled across my sheets. Lips pressed to my spine before a tongue traced the line of it. Then she settled, nuzzling her face against my skin. She knew I was awake but didn't make an attempt at conversation or say good morning. It was almost like she merely wanted to be in my space. And I was content to let her.

If it had been before she came back into my life, I would have jumped up the moment I awoke, ready to spill blood. None of the others came into my room without permission for that very reason. With Scarlett, my body instinctively knew it was her. She was my lifeline. My whole soul. At least, what counted for my soul since I was lacking in humanity at times. She made me feel. And what a fucking revelation not to wake up wishing for violence.

I turned in her embrace until her messy hair came into view. She blinked as she looked up at me. I didn't give her a chance to speak, diving down to catch her lips in mine. Who cared why she was here. My heart just cared that she was. Here in my arms, her mouth where it belonged and nothing to stop me from feeling her small frame against mine.

I ran my hand down her back to the curve of her arse, finding her without underwear beneath the t-shirt she wore. However, the moment my hand settled over her bare skin, she let out a small cry of pain in my mouth. I immediately let go of her, sat up, ripped down the covers and pressed her onto her front. My eyes were searching and what I found had me almost smiling.

"I see someone was a bad girl last night," I murmured as I took in the welts across the backs of her thighs and behind. Drake clearly hadn't held back.

"I had punishments pending from days ago," she responded, her voice muffled by the pillow her face was pressed into. "And it was worth the pain."

I ran my finger over one of the welts on her thigh. She tensed at the contact.

"My dirty girl likes a little pain with her pleasure."

"I was a very naughty little slut last night," she whispered, turning her head to the side.

I leant down, pressing a kiss to the angriest looking welt on her behind.

"Mmm, did my naughty girl come from all the pain he caused?"

"Yes."

"Good little slut."

The way her body trembled at my words made my dick hard. The sight of her was making me a little crazy. A little like I wanted to sit her in my lap and make her ride me while I pressed down on the welts Drake had left on her skin.

"And does he know you left his bed?"

"He's asleep."

I looked over at my clock on the bedside table. It read past ten in the morning.

"Drake's asleep at this hour?"

She shifted, turning on her side to meet my eyes.

"I was surprised too. He looked so peaceful. I didn't want to wake him, but I was starving. I went downstairs, had breakfast and he was still dead to the world when I came back."

"So you sought me out?"

She nodded, giving me a shy smile. I sat back, gripped her by the arm, and tugged her into my lap. She wrapped her arms around my neck.

"You're his remedy."

"Remedy?"

"For his inability to sleep. You should get back to him before he wakes up."

The pout she gave me had me wrapping my hands around her behind and squeezing her abused flesh. She yelped, jerking against my body and making my dick throb. I didn't want her going back to Drake's room. I wanted her to sit on my cock and ride me until she came so hard, she cried. Perhaps I'd send her back to him with my cum leaking from her pussy. I'd quite like to know what he would say about it.

"Are you sure you want that?" she asked as I wrapped my hand around her throat and stroked her soft skin.

"No, I want you to slide that sweet little pussy down on my cock whilst I choke you until you come."

Her eyes widened slightly at my rather blunt statement of my desires. Not sure why she was surprised.

"I suggest you do as I say, little Scar. I'm not a patient man."

And didn't she know it. The way she scrambled to pull off my shorts and rip the t-shirt from her body had me chuckling. Before she had a chance to mount me, I grabbed a hold of her body and buried my face in her tits, kissing and licking her skin until I bit down on her nipple so hard she cried out in shock.

"West, fuck!"

I gripped her throat again, squeezing the sides to restrict her airway. Then I smacked her arse, making her cry out again.

"Give me what I asked for."

She fumbled between us, her fingers gripping my cock. When she slid it between her lips, I could feel her wetness coating the crown.

Always so ready for me, little Scar.

She moaned when she sunk down on me, not stopping to let herself adjust until she'd taken the whole thing. Then she leant towards me, brushing her mouth over mine.

"Do you remember what we talked about when you let me scar you?"

"Mmm, I do."

"I know what promise you don't want me to break."

"Oh yeah?"

Her hand curled around my jaw as she pressed a kiss to the corner of my mouth.

"Forever. I promised to give you forever."

My hand around her throat tightened. The way her eyes twinkled as she leant back slightly to look at me had my fucking heart in knots.

"Are you going to keep that promise?"

She rocked her hips into me, clenching around my cock in the most delicious way. Her hand curled around the back of my neck before she leant her forehead against mine.

"All of my forevers are yours."

I couldn't answer, so I kissed her instead. My tongue tangled with hers, creating a fucking mess between us, but it was what we needed. We'd found our way back to each other.

My forever is your forever. There is no me without you, little Scar.

She filled all my empty spaces with her light. She saved me from the dark by making a home for herself in it next to me. This woman was my goddess of the night. And I loved her with every inch of my being.

When she pulled away, her hazel-green eyes twinkled, and she pressed kisses down my jaw and neck.

"Who do you belong to?" I asked, tugging her back by her neck to look into her eyes.

By fuck, the way she smiled at me set my body on fire.

"War."

"My little warrior goddess."

I squeezed her throat again, making her buck into me.

"Touch your little needy clit for me. Show me you're mine by giving me your climax."

Her hand snaked between us, finding her clit and stroking it. She rocked her hips against me in time with her stroking. Her eyes were fixed on mine as I kept a hold of her throat, the other hand wrapping around her behind to rub over her welts.

There was no more need for words. We surpassed those. The only communication between us was through our emotions reflected in each other's eyes. My Scarlett was back. She felt the same connection we'd always had with each other. It had changed, morphed into something stronger, deeper. My soulmate had found her way home to me. And I was ready to give up everything for her. Give up my fucking life if that's what it took to keep her safe. To keep her by my side. I'd give my woman the world even if I had to burn it down to ashes and dust.

"Forever," she mouthed to me right before she came.

"Forever," I echoed, watching her fall over the edge.

There was nothing but me and her in the moments she clenched around me, her body going slack against my grip. I released my tight hold on her throat to give her air but kept stroking her skin with my thumb. Everything could be burning around us and I wouldn't give a shit. The only person I had any care or appreciation for was her.

She pitched forward, leaning her forehead on my shoulder when she was spent, her breathing harsh and laboured. Carefully, I pressed her down onto the bed, rolling on top of her as I gripped her thigh for leverage. She closed her eyes as I thrust inside her, letting out a little sigh of happiness. Her hands gripped my back, keeping me there with her. My pace increased with my own need to find a release. And right before I did, her eyes flew open, catching me unawares.

I fell so hard, I thought I might fucking die with the pleasure. It raced up my spine with an intensity I had rarely experienced. Scarlett brought out these feelings inside me. It was all her. No one else ever had the ability to make me vulnerable. Make the dam burst around me and the floodgates rip open so wide, I didn't think they would ever sit right inside me again.

I'd known this would happen if I fucked her when I could see her face. I'd barely managed to keep my head straight when we'd fucked Scarlett together the last time, but now we were alone, I was drowning in her. In those beautiful eyes holding the keys to my entire soul. She broke me and put me back together every time, just as I did her.

I buried my face in her neck to hide my emotional state from her scrutiny. In response, she pressed a kiss to my hair and stroked my back with her fingertips, as if reassuring me it was okay. She had me. She wouldn't let me go or fall apart.

"My beautiful little Scar," I whispered in her ear, "you make me happy. I hope you know that."

She let out a breath, her hands flattening and tightening around me.

"Don't make me cry. And you make me happy too."

"I like making you cry."

She snorted. I lifted off her but not before pressing a kiss to her forehead.

"I want you to go see his highness before he wakes up and surprise him with your cum-filled pussy."

The blush spreading across her cheeks had me grinning as I sat up on my knees between her legs.

"You are incorrigible."

"You wouldn't have me any other way."

"Fine, I'll tell him it's your gift to him."

I laughed, rubbing my hand over her bare thigh.

"I'm sure he'll appreciate it."

She shook her head and sat up, pressing a kiss to my mouth.

"We all need to talk."

Nothing good ever came with that statement. I stroked her cheek, not wanting her to think I was too concerned.

"About what?"

"Something Drake told me yesterday."

Before I could question her further, she picked up her discarded t-shirt, tugged it over her head, and slipped off my bed.

"Scar…"

She looked back over her shoulder.

"I'm not mad. I just don't like the secrets."

Then she flounced out of my room, leaving me wondering what secrets she was referring to. And asking myself what the fuck Drake had told her. It's not like I thought we should have any further secrets between us, but it could be anything.

I got off the bed and went into my bathroom to shower, then I'd go seek out Francis and Prescott to warn them of the impending conversation. They were likely going to freak out over it too, but it was neither here nor there. We were a family. And we'd deal with things like a family. Because that's what you did for the people you loved. You heard them out and fixed shit between you. We would keep doing that with each other, no matter what.

TWENTY TWO

SCARLETT

D rake was not entirely impressed with his gift from West. In fact, he told me the next time I helped West prank him, he would put me over his knee and spank me in front of the others. I'd told him that wouldn't be much of a punishment. He responded by pinning me to his bed, telling me how much he loved me and kissing me until I was breathless. To say I wasn't completely won over by his playfulness would be an understatement. The Drake of my past had returned and I couldn't be happier.

After he'd taken care of my welts, cleaned me up and let me go to grab some clothes from Francis' room, I'd found him and the others downstairs with breakfast laid out. I sat down, took a sip of my tea and noticed West, Prescott and Francis were looking at me with expectant expressions on their faces.

"What?"

"You wanted to talk," West said.

I put my mug down and dug my spoon into my cereal, stuffing it into my mouth and chewing. Setting my spoon down, I levelled my gaze on my four men.

"Drake told me you knew about my medical history. Now, I'm not mad about it, but I do think we need to stop keeping secrets from each other. Not to mention we need an actual conversation about our relationship and what it means for the future."

Prescott reached out across the table and took my hand, stroking his thumb along mine. I didn't strictly need his reassuring touch, but it grounded me all the same. The five of us needed to be realistic and clear about what we wanted from each other. I wasn't scared of what they would say. Being on the same page was important to me after everything we'd been through.

"No more secrets," he said with a nod.

I took a deep breath and let go of Prescott's hand.

"I want to see my medical records."

No one said anything as Drake got out of his chair and went over to the coffee table to pick up his tablet. He brought it back over, flipping through it for several minutes before he set it in front of me and took a seat again. I had expected him to say no or question why I needed this. He hadn't. Instead, he gave me what I asked for without hesitation. And hell did it make me want to go sit in his lap to kiss him until he was breathless to show my appreciation. Instead, I met his eyes and gave him a nod.

My attention went to the tablet. I picked up my mug, sipping at my tea as my fingers hovered over the screen. I steadied myself internally and began looking through everything. They'd never let me see any of my x-rays from the accident nor show me the extent of the damage. This made it all clear. The fact I'd even survived was a miracle.

It confirmed what they'd told me. After the surgeries, the scarring had left me with severely damaged fallopian tubes and my ovaries barely functioned. The only reason they'd left them in place was not wanting to put me into early menopause. It was hit or miss whether I'd even get a period. I didn't want any more surgery if I could help it. They couldn't fix what had been broken. And it was just my reality.

Seeing it laid out brought it home. The accident had taken a lot from me. And yet, strangely, I was no longer sad or mourning the loss of it. Before, I had no hope. I had nothing but a big fat void inside myself. Four voids. Four missing pieces. Now, the void was no longer there. It had been filled and with it brought a sense of peace and acceptance. I wasn't lesser or damaged. I was me. Scarlett. A woman who had survived many ordeals. It made me strong, not weak. It made me powerful.

I stared at the tablet for a long moment before turning off the screen and going back to my breakfast.

"I'm okay with the fact I can't have kids," I said, making them all look at me with startled expressions. They hadn't been expecting me to announce it. And I hadn't either, but the thing was, I was okay. Now all was said and done, it didn't feel like I was drowning in misery any longer. I was whole.

"I mean, I don't think I was before, but I felt like I was missing something… when in reality, what I was missing was all of you. I feel like myself again because I have my family back. That's what I need. My family. Biological urges are all very well, but it's what I want that matters. And I want you four. That's it. Nothing more, nothing less... just you."

I looked down at my hands resting on the table.

"What I need to know is if you all feel the same. I mean, I know you do, but we've never said it to each other when we're all together. I need to know you're okay with it only being us for the rest of our lives."

The first person to take my hand was West, who was sitting next to me. He rubbed his thumb down the back of my hand and gave me a look that spoke volumes.

"I've never wanted anything else other than the five of us."

And if that didn't say something about West's feelings towards us, I didn't know what would. We'd been dancing around the fact we loved each other and strangely, I was okay with it. He wasn't ready to tell me. Sometimes words weren't necessary when you could look into a person's eyes and see the truth. West didn't hide his feelings from me. He just struggled to openly admit them.

I squeezed his hand to reassure him. He gave me a nod, then turned towards Drake, who was sitting at the head of the table as usual. He laid his palm out flat on the wooden surface. I could see the cogs turning in Drake's head, but he didn't hesitate to put his hand on West's, as if this was his connection to me too.

"I didn't go through ten years of fighting to get you back to make our family whole for nothing," he said with a low voice, emotion radiating off all the words. "I just want us."

Apparently, my prodding and insisting Drake open up to me had shifted something inside him. Or maybe it was because we'd shared our feelings finally. Either way, my heart was full seeing him be so willing to declare how he felt and what he wanted.

Drake turned to Francis, putting his hand out to him. As expected, there was no hesitation on Francis' part to hold Drake's hand. He looked over at me, his silvery-grey eyes glinting. I ran my tongue over my bottom lip. Something about the way Francis looked at me had my body heating like he was stripping me bare in his mind and imagining all the dirty things he wanted to do to me. While it might not be entirely appropriate given the conversation we were having, I didn't care. It was layered with love too. The love he felt for me. The unfathomable depths of it weren't overwhelming. I felt the same way. I did about all of them.

"You complete us, Scar. I don't have need or want for anything else other than this."

Francis gave me a wink before putting his hand out to Prescott, who took it, then leant across the table to take mine again. Prescott stared at me with those beautiful blues of his. The smile he gave me had my heart racing.

"You four and Mum are the only people who have never willingly walked out of my life without a backwards glance. My loyalty is here and there's nothing else I could ask for or need other than this."

He squeezed my hand tight in his. It made me want him so badly, I was up and out of my chair, letting go of his hand and West's. I was around the table and gripping his face the next moment.

"I love you," I whispered before I kissed him.

It wasn't chaste or restrained. I poured out my love and appreciation into it, showing him my feelings. How I would never abandon him, even when things were tough. Never give up on the two of us, no matter what happened in the future. He deserved my devotion. He loved me in a way I couldn't describe. Gave me things I never knew I needed or desired. He was my king.

"I love you too," he told me when I released him.

I walked around him to Francis and sat in his lap, wrapping my arms around his neck and nuzzling my nose against his.

"You made me blush with the way you were looking at me," I whispered.

He ran his hand down my chest, making me wriggle in his grasp before curling his fingers around my waist.

"Can't blame me, can you?"

I chuckled before kissing him. Admittedly, I adored the way he made me feel beautiful and wanted without words. My safety and my home were with him.

"No," I replied when I pulled away. "But that wicked mind of yours is clearly running riot. No doubt you won't tell me what you're planning."

He grinned and bit his lip.

"Never."

I pressed a kiss to his cheek.

"I love you for it."

"I love you more."

I stroked his face before extracting myself from his lap and going to Drake. He curled a hand around my waist, pulling me against his side as I leant down towards him. Drake tipped his face up to catch my mouth in a searing kiss that had my toes curling.

"My little wisp," he murmured against my lips.

"My reaper," I whispered back.

He smiled, stroked my side, and then released me. We'd already made love declarations earlier, so I wasn't put out by the fact he didn't say anything further. I skipped around the table to West instead, who looked up at me with his beautiful amber eyes shining with happiness.

I reached down, tucking my fingers under the collar of his shirt and brushing them over the scars I'd given him. He took my other hand and pressed it to his mouth, giving my palm a series of kisses. I craved the reassurance of his embrace.

West didn't object when I sat in his lap. No, he wrapped his arms around me and let me rest myself against his chest.

"Can I stay here whilst I finish eating?" I asked.

"As my little Scar wishes."

It didn't matter if I'd had soul-destroying sex with him earlier. The way I wanted to be close to West couldn't be quantified. Being near him made me feel... alive. There was a certain rush to having a man like him be utterly obsessed with you. I feared and desired him at the same time. A heady rush of mixed emotions that set me on fire.

For now, I was content to be held by him. And to remember the way he looked at me as he came apart earlier. How he couldn't hide the depths of his devotion to me. His love. It was like being suffocated but in a good way. In the very best way. I liked it when West choked me during sex and this feeling was no different. I wanted to be drowned in his abyss of violence and destruction, pulled so deep inside I could never find my way out.

As I leant over to drag my bowl and mug towards me, I heard Drake clearing his throat. I turned to him when I'd got settled, raising my eyebrow.

"I spoke to the others about this before you came down… after what happened yesterday, I think we all agree we don't want you leaving Fortuity without one of us with you. In fact, I'd prefer it if you stayed here out of harm's way entirely."

It took me a second to gather my thoughts and feelings on that little matter.

"You want to lock me up here?"

Drake frowned.

"No, I would never lock you up, Scarlett. I want you to have your freedom. I'm worried about what Stuart will do next. You know you're not safe alone, right?"

I hated it, but he was right. While I could get away if it was one man, I didn't think Stuart would send just one. It would be multiple. Especially when he realised sending three men after me hadn't worked. Drake had killed them all himself without breaking a sweat.

"I don't like it, but fine, I'll stay here. Will that make you happy?"

"It doesn't make me happy at all, but I need you safe where he can't get to you."

I went back to my food, disliking the prospect of not being able to leave Fortuity, but knowing it was in my best interests. It's not even like I felt safe going anywhere without one of them, anyway. They were my protectors. My guardians. My Horsemen. While I could handle myself just fine, I didn't trust Stuart at all.

"You know, we might as well have Penn on retainer at this point," West said. "We use the fucker's services enough."

"Will he give us mates rates since you two are so friendly?" Prescott asked.

West snorted.

"We're already getting them."

"Maybe we should invite him around for dinner to show our appreciation," I said.

"I'm not having him at our dinner table. He will simply flirt with you all evening," Drake said, giving me a stern look.

I batted my eyelashes at him.

"Don't worry, I would never stray even if he's rather handsome and the tattoos do it for me."

Prescott, Francis and West started laughing while Drake glared at me. I was already sat on the only tattooed man I wanted between my legs.

"Brat."

"If you're that worried, I promise I'll tell Penn he's not allowed to flirt with me at the table."

Drake turned back to his food, but not before giving me a suspicious look, as if he was wondering what exactly my game was.

"I'll consider it," he said after a few minutes.

I couldn't really ask for more from him. Drake might be prickly and stubborn, but he bent to my will more often than not. I didn't like to tell him he'd become soft when it came to me, no matter how many times he punished me. The care he gave me afterwards spoke volumes. The man loved me and he would do everything in his power to keep me safe. And it's why I'd decided not to object to his request to stay in the building for my own safety. It would only be until we'd dealt with Stuart. I could deal with that... couldn't I?

TWENTY THREE

FRANCIS

My head was buried in my computer, running numbers for a meeting I had tomorrow with Viktor Bykov's accountant. We'd almost secured his daughter's account, but there were a few unresolved issues between us and the owners of the Syndicate. I hoped to have them sorted soon.

I was so busy, I didn't notice my office door open, nor the two people who walked inside until they were right up at my desk. My head whipped up, my eyes falling on my parents.

"Hello, Francis," Mum said with a smile. Her grey eyes that matched mine were full of joy.

It had been months since I'd seen them. I hadn't been expecting them to just walk in here.

"Oh shit, I completely forgot about lunch," I blurted out, smacking my hand against my head.

My dad chuckled and shook his head.

"Always busy, I see."

"I'm sorry."

I got up from my desk and came around to embrace both of them. I'd mostly taken after my father. We were matched in height and stature, with dark brown hair. Mum was willowy with blonde hair and I'd got her eyes. Eliza and Jasper Beaufort were the most normal parents a person could have. Mum had been a stay at home mother until I flew the nest, and Dad worked for a gas company. She worked a part-time job in an office now. They were proud of me for what we'd built with Fortuity. I'd paid off their mortgage when we made our fortune, but they'd refused to take anything further from me. Instead, I spoiled them on their birthdays and for Christmases. It was my way of giving back. And probably why I liked to give Scarlett everything I could. I wanted her to know how much I loved and needed her.

"Don't be," Mum said. "We wanted to surprise you, so we asked them not to call up. And we know you boys are always working."

I shrugged as I let her go.

"How are they, anyway?"

"They're fine," I said as I walked back around my desk to save what I was working on.

"May tells me Drake has a girlfriend."

I paused what I was doing to look up at her.

"Um, yeah, he does…"

Drake had told me about his conversation with his mother. No surprise she'd blabbed to mine, considering the two of them were best friends. I was going to get the third degree over it, no doubt. Not something I particularly wanted to deal with considering they were both wondering when I would settle down too.

"Frankie, do you need me to arrange that meeting with Mr Knox? He said he'd be bringing Mr Nelson this time… oh, I didn't realise you had… oh…"

My eyes went to Scarlett, who was standing in the doorway with a tablet in her hands, staring at the three of us with wide eyes. I left my desk when I saw the fear in them. This was completely my fault for forgetting my parents were coming to lunch. Now I was going to have to explain why Scarlett was here.

Fuck.

Yet, the person I was most worried about was my girl herself. I ignored my parent's shocked expressions and went straight over to her. My first instinct was to cup her cheek and stroke it to soothe her.

"I didn't know your parents were here," she whispered.

"It's okay. We'll deal with it together, okay?"

She nodded, leaning into my touch as if it was grounding her. Scarlett might be strong as fuck but seeing people from her past couldn't be easy. Especially when they happened to be my parents.

I dropped my hand from her face and turned to my parents, taking a breath before I dived in.

"Mum, Dad… you remember Scarlett, right?"

"Well, of course we do, Francis," Mum said, looking between us and trying to guess at our relationship and what was going on.

"But the last we knew, she was missing," Dad put in.

Scarlett tucked the tablet up against her chest and sought out my fingers, gripping them tightly between hers.

"I can explain... sort of."

I felt Scarlett take a breath next to me before giving both my parents a smile.

"It's so nice to see you. I'm afraid I only just remembered the past, so you have to excuse my shock at seeing you again."

"The feeling is mutual," Dad said, but he smiled back at her.

Scarlett let go of my hand and went over to them, shaking my dad's hand, and Mum gave her a hug.

"We never expected... well, that's neither here nor there. It's good to see you again, Scarlett," Mum told her as they drew apart.

I fidgeted, then Scarlett looked back at me with eyes full of fucking love and I knew what I had to do.

"Should we eat upstairs? Scarlett can join us then."

I wasn't going to take them out to a restaurant and air my private life where anyone could hear.

"Yes, that might be for the best," Mum replied, giving me a nod.

Scarlett popped her tablet down on my desk and followed me and my parents out into the lobby towards the lifts. None of us spoke as we rode up to the penthouse. My parents rarely came here. I usually went to them, but maybe we should change that now Scarlett was back. Maybe I should be more involved in their lives and them with mine. I was their only son, after all.

Scarlett followed me into the kitchen after we got my parents settled on the sofas. The two of us started preparing something simple together. She leant over to me as I was stirring a pot.

"What are we going to tell them?"

It wasn't something we'd spoken about, how we were going to address this with our parents. How we would explain what happened to Scarlett and the fact we were all in a relationship with her. Guess I was going to have to come up with something to appease them.

"A stripped back version of the truth, leaving out anything to do with Stuart. They can't know what we've done… they wouldn't understand."

She wrapped an arm around me, pressing her face into my shoulder.

"No. I'll just go with your lead, probably safer that way."

I pressed a kiss to her forehead, forgetting entirely it was in full view of my parents. Restraining myself when it came to Scarlett wasn't exactly my forte. Being with her felt so natural. Touching her was something I couldn't go without when she was in my space. When her attention was on me and me alone. There was nothing in this world like being loved the way Scarlett Nyx loved me.

"Go set the table… and maybe text the others as a heads up. They probably won't come up here, but they'll need to know."

She nodded, stroking my back before she moved away to get the plates and cutlery. I watched her for a moment before going back to preparing lunch.

Twenty minutes later, we were all seated and tucking in. Mum and Dad kept giving Scarlett glances like they couldn't believe she was there. They asked me about how business was going and we talked about mundane things until I couldn't hold it in any longer. So I told them Scarlett had come to work for us. How she hadn't remembered who we were at first and slowly, things changed when she did. And how she lived with us here now.

They didn't ask Scarlett where she'd been or about the kidnapping. I think they were afraid of upsetting her by bringing it up. They just remarked on how pleased they were that we'd all found each other again.

I left Scarlett talking to Dad while I cleaned up the dishes. Mum came into the kitchen and leant up against the counter, eyeing me with concern. I sighed as I straightened after closing the dishwasher.

"Are you and Scarlett in a relationship?"

I nodded, unsure of what else to say about it. We hadn't hidden it. Scarlett had constantly touched me throughout lunch and I, her. It was like we couldn't stop. For her, I knew it was a reassurance thing. I was her safe place. There was no fucking way I would stop her from taking what she needed from me.

Mum looked over at Scarlett and Dad, who were laughing at something she'd said. The way my girl's eyes lit up had my heart racing. Seeing her happy was all I needed. All I ever fucking wanted.

"You love her."

My eyes went back to Mum, who was looking at me now.

"Yeah, I do, Mum."

"Will you explain why May told me Drake's girlfriend is also called Scarlett?"

I rubbed the back of my neck before looking away. It was better to just come out with it.

"Scar is his girlfriend too… and West's… and Prescott's." I looked at her again. "We're all with her."

For a minute, Mum didn't say a word, clearly processing what I'd told her. She didn't look shocked or put out. It wasn't an easy thing to admit to your parent, that you were in what was essentially a polyamorous relationship with Scarlett at the centre of it.

"I always wondered if the four of you loved her as more than just a friend. I guess I didn't expect… well, I never expected her to come back after all these years, let alone for the five of you to find each other. But you were always very attached, so I suppose I can't be too surprised this has happened."

I moved closer to her and took her hand.

"It's not like we meant to, but it's Scar… she's…"

"She's your one. I can see that, Francis. Did you think I wouldn't understand?"

"I don't really know, Mum. With her being back and it being so complicated, I wasn't sure what to tell you, so we decided we shouldn't until we were sure of everything."

She squeezed my hand.

"Are you sure now?"

"The only thing I'm sure of is the five of us being a family and her. I'm sure of her. Scar gets me. We take care of each other like it should be, you know… a partnership. And so what if she shares those things with Drake, Pres and West too? Doesn't make her love me any less. She doesn't make me feel second best… ever."

Mum dropped my hand, only to stroke my hair back from my face. She smiled when she noticed it wasn't gelled. I didn't wear it any longer. Not when it made Scarlett happy to run her fingers through my hair. I couldn't deny it made me feel good too.

"You were never second best, Francis."

"I know but having her makes me see that clearly."

"If being with her this way makes the four of you happy, then it's all that matters. I won't pretend to understand it, but all I want is your happiness in whatever form it comes."

I almost shook my head. That was the thing about my parents. My mum was so easygoing and accepting. Probably why she and Drake's mum were friends. Eliza was the calm in the storm that was May Ackley.

"There's something I do have to ask you to do though."

Her eyes narrowed.

"What?"

"You can't tell May she's back."

Mum's eyes widened.

"You are not seriously asking me to lie to her?"

"It's not lying, it's withholding the truth. I think Drake deserves a chance to tell her himself. It's his life, Mum."

"He never tells her anything."

I snorted.

"Are you surprised? I know she's your best friend, but May is kind of scary when she gets going."

Mum rolled her eyes but smiled.

"I suppose you're right. And Drake does need to tell her himself. I hope he does soon."

"When he finds out you know, I don't think he'll have much of a choice. Neither Pres with Rosie. She's going to be…"

"Angry you kept Scarlett from her."

"Yeah."

Mum nodded and dragged her fingers across the kitchen counter.

"I hate to ask this, Francis, but where has she been?"

I shifted on my feet. The question I didn't want to answer. Mostly because I couldn't. There wasn't an easy or simple explanation for her disappearance. Not without revealing things better in the past. They didn't need to know their son was a killer, nor the type of shit I enjoyed.

"I can't tell you, Mum. It's not my place to talk about it."

"Do the police know she's no longer missing?"

I shook my head.

"Francis…"

"We will tell them when Scar is ready to. She's still working through things, you know. She's spent ten years without her memories. It's difficult for her."

Mum looked over at Scarlett and Dad.

"I can imagine it is. Well, you have my word this will stay between me and your father."

"Thank you."

She pulled me in for a hug. I looked over her shoulder at Scarlett, who was smiling at me. Seeing her happy made my heart lurch. She was so fucking beautiful. Nothing in the world mattered more to me than her.

Mum pulled away from me and saw me staring at Scarlett.

"Go."

I couldn't help but be pulled by the thread binding me to Scarlett. When I arrived next to her, she stood up and put her arms around me. I stroked her cheek and smiled. Then I pressed her face into my chest and breathed her in. Her cinnamon scent surrounded me, soothing every part of me from the inside out.

"She's happy you're home with us," I whispered.

"Doesn't think I'm crazy for wanting all of you?"

I laughed.

"No, I think you'll have more trouble convincing May and Rosie than Mum."

Scarlett shuddered before clutching me tighter.

"I'm not looking forward to that part."

They would have to accept it eventually because no matter what, we were sticking together. We'd promised each other as much. No one in this world could tear us apart except for Stuart Carver. And we had a plan to make sure he never did.

TWENTY FOUR

PRESCOTT

"Seriously, I'm going to die of boredom at this rate," Scarlett huffed, pouting at me with those deliciously sensuous lips of hers.

"You've been inside for just over a week, hardly a death sentence."

I knew she hated being locked up. It wasn't fair on her. Not after everything she'd been through. I just didn't think she'd be on my case over it so soon. Her ordeal with Mason had affected her more than she liked to let on. The free spirit inside her who liked to be chased was chained up, begging to get out. I could see it in her eyes.

She crawled towards me across the bed and sat in my lap, plucking my phone from my fingers and tossing it on the bed. Someone wanted my full attention on her.

"Please, Pres. I'm trying to be good and do what Drake asked, but I need to get out of this building. Even if it's just for a couple of hours."

I cupped the back of her neck, running my thumb along her skin. My poor lamb was suffering. I despised seeing it. It tore at my heartstrings every single time.

"Well, it's very lucky for you I've got a surprise outing planned then, isn't it?"

The way her hazel-green eyes lit up had me grinning.

"You do?"

"Yes, so you better go put a dress on."

Fuck, her joy was utterly infectious. She was practically bouncing in my lap, vibrating with excitement. She leant forward and plastered my face with kisses.

"You are literally the best boyfriend ever, but don't tell the others."

I laughed, knowing she'd been asking West and Francis too, but neither of them had budged. She knew better than to ask Drake, even if she had him wrapped around her finger. The way he conceded to her desires was a fucking miracle to watch. Then again, Drake always had a soft spot for her, even when we were kids.

"Wait." She deflated all of a sudden. "Does Drake know?"

I removed her from my lap and got off the bed. There was no fucking way I was taking her out of the building without informing Drake of my plans. He would string me up by my balls if I did that.

"Yes. Now, get dressed, West has dinner on and we don't want to be late."

Like a little kid in a sweet shop, she scrambled off the bed and went over to my wardrobes, pulling them open. I watched her select a dark, forest green dress and change into it. Then she was looking over her shoes. She selected a pair of smart, dark trainers. She didn't like to wear heels outside of the office and even then, she'd started wearing ballet flats most of the time. Past Scarlett had emerged in small but significant ways, changing things she did and liked. I was all for it. Seeing her come into her own was a joy in itself.

She braided her hair while I changed into something smart but casual. A dark shirt, chinos and dark trainers to match hers. She grinned when I took her hand and pulled her downstairs with me. She was animated throughout dinner, making Drake suspicious, but I told him not to worry. I'd take care of our girl. Besides, the place we were going to was safe. Probably one of the safest places I could take her with all the security protocols in place.

Scarlett was quiet on the drive. She watched the city go by, dragging her fingers over the window every so often. I pulled up in a car park nearby, paid and took her hand, leading her along an upmarket street. She had a curious expression on her face when we arrived outside a nondescript building. I pulled her inside, only to be greeted by a huge graffiti-style sign proclaiming the name of the club. Desecration. You had to know someone to gain access to this place. And lucky for me, I knew a certain Fixer who lived in the owner's pocket.

"What is this place?" Scarlett hissed as we walked by a bouncer over to the reception desk.

"A sex club," I murmured before greeting the girl behind the desk.

She was a pretty redhead with a bright smile, but that was all I noticed. When Scarlett was in the room, she was the one who radiated beauty and sin. My eyes were for her and her alone.

Scarlett fidgeted next to me as I checked in. I was concerned she didn't want to be here. Her eyes were curious as the girl waved us into the club after checking our coats and told me someone would be along soon to take us to our private room.

I tugged Scarlett into the main club. There was a bar, so I drew her over to it. It was a decadent space full of red velvet and black. In the centre of the room stood several stripper poles with huge velvet-covered padded seats along the walls. For a weekday night, the place was pretty full. There were people seated, clearly waiting for something to happen.

"Do you want a drink?" I asked Scarlett, who was gazing around the room in awe.

"Water is fine."

I didn't get a chance to speak to the bartender. A girl with green eyes, bronze skin, and dark hair approached us.

"Mr Ellis?" she asked with a shy smile.

"Yes."

"If you and your date would like to come this way, your room is ready."

I pulled on Scarlett's hand as the girl started towards what looked like a set of double doors on the other side of the club.

"I'm Remi. If you need anything, you just have to ask."

I nodded, my attention going to Scarlett, who was staring at a man lounging near the corner of the room surrounded by women. He had dark hair and dark eyes with tattoos down his neck and on his right hand, which lay on his thigh. I got the distinct impression he was someone by the way people were glancing at him.

"Who is that?" Scarlett asked, nodding her head towards him.

I noticed Remi looking at the man before she pushed the doors open.

"Mr Villetti. He owns the club."

Zayn Villetti. The mafia prince. No fucking wonder. He looked the part. A king presiding over his kingdom.

"Didn't expect him to be here," I said as Remi led us down a corridor with numbered doors.

"It's a special club night. He always attends those." She paused at a door. The number plate said ten. "Here we are."

She opened the door and ushered us inside. It was a small room but contained everything you would need to watch. A sofa. A bench right in front of the two-way mirror. A mini-fridge stocked with water bottles and alcohol. And a set of drawers Remi mentioned contained a variety of toys, lube, and condoms.

I thanked her after she indicated the button on the side of the window to start the show and the second button if we needed something brought to the room. She left, telling us to enjoy ourselves. Scarlett turned to me when the door closed.

"What is this?"

"We're going to watch."

It took her a second to understand my meaning.

"How did you know I wanted… oh, Pres."

She jumped into my arms and kissed me.

"You are the perfect man. My king."

I chuckled as I set her down on the sofa. Grabbing a couple of water bottles from the fridge, I put them down on the side table and pressed the button to start the show. Scarlett squirmed next to me as I took a seat.

A moment later, the lights in the other room came on, giving us the full view of a bed set right in front of the mirror. Remi told us no one could see into our room. I'd made very specific requests. They'd been more than willing to accommodate.

Scarlett's fingers slid into mine as three people entered the room. Two men and one woman. The way her pupils dilated told me she was excited by the prospect. I wanted to show her what I saw when she was sandwiched between the others. Wanted my girl to experience the things I did. The high I got from watching. Who knew if she would enjoy it, but I could only hope.

The two men bracketed the woman between them, one kissing her while the other pressed them to her neck. She writhed between them, enjoying the attention.

"Fuck," Scarlett hissed.

She let go of my hand and put it on my thigh instead, giving it a squeeze. I leant closer, still watching the people in the other room.

"Does my little lamb approve?"

"Yes, a hundred times yes." She glanced at me. "Am I allowed to touch you?"

"Of course, but you have to pay attention to the show. I want you to see what I see."

She nodded, turning her eyes back to the other room. They were on the bed now, undressing the light brown-haired woman slowly, removing each piece of clothing with care. I may have asked for someone who looked similar to my girl.

"Imagine it's you being undressed like that by Francis and West."

Scarlett's mouth parted on a breath, but she didn't make a sound. She'd been sandwiched between those two a few times during our group sex. I knew she liked them fucking her together. She loved all of us doing it.

One of the men took his clothes off, and the girl mounted him, rubbing her pussy over his cock.

"Oh... fuck," Scarlett whimpered when the woman took him inch by inch, giving us a perfect view.

Her hand on my thigh drew higher until she was brushing her fingers over my cock.

"Come here," I practically growled, hauling her into my lap with her back plastered to my front. I held her chin in place when she tried to look at me. "Watch. Don't take your eyes off them. See how they fuck her the way West and Francis fuck you."

The other man was at the girl's back, his fingers delving into her tight little hole. An open bottle of lube sat beside him.

"Pres," she moaned as I stroked my fingers up her bare thighs, watching the threesome in front of us over her shoulder.

We could hear the low grunting and moaning sounds of the room echoing around ours through the speakers at the corners of the mirror.

"Is this making my lamb wet?"

"Yes," she hissed when my fingers met the soaked fabric of her underwear.

"Mmm, so I see."

Her arousal was mine and mine alone. I would never want anyone but me and the boys to see her this way. Worked up and needy for us.

"Does my little lamb need her wolf?"

She ground back against me, forcing a grunt from my chest with her movements.

"Please."

The second man had his cock out now, his hand rubbing lube over it. When he notched it to the girl and pressed forward, my fingers curled beneath Scarlett's knickers and plunged into her wet pussy. She whimpered and gripped the sofa arm with one hand, her nails digging in while I pumped my fingers into her.

We watched the second man push deeper, impaling the girl on his dick. The way she moaned from the stretch made my dick throb. It reminded me of the sounds Scarlett made when we fucked her together.

"Do you see that, lamb? That's how you look when you're taking two of them. When you're stuffed full of cock."

"Oh god, Pres. Please, please fuck me."

Scarlett was rocking on my fingers now, her eyes fixed on the scene in front of us.

"Mmm, does my dirty lamb need filling like she is?"

"Please."

As if I would deny myself the opportunity to fuck her little pussy. I'd never taken a girl to watch with me before. Never wanted to until Scarlett. Besides, I got my kicks from watching the others fuck, so never needed to go anywhere else. They were happy to let me watch, so what was the point?

Now we had Scarlett. My kinky little lamb was just as deviant as the four of us. Our perfect goddess of the night. She wanted to try everything. This was for me and her. Something we could share together. There was no fucking way I could involve the others in this. Scarlett was possessive. She wouldn't want to see them fuck another girl. But this? We could watch people we didn't know fuck in private for a price. One I was more than willing to pay for the safety and security of a club catering to your basest desires. I would do anything to make Scarlett happy.

Drake said yes because he knew Zayn's club was one of the most secure places in the city. The mafia prince was known for running a tight ship. Privacy and security were his top priorities.

I removed my fingers from Scarlett's pussy, pressing her forward enough to undo my trousers and get my cock out. I pulled her knickers down her thighs to give me access but didn't bother tugging them off her body. My chin settled on her shoulder a minute later.

"If you want my dick, lamb, take it. Show me how much you need me."

She shifted back as I held it for her. And slid down on it just as the door in the other room opened, revealing a third man. I smiled at the shocked gasp emitting from Scarlett's mouth. He was completely bare, with dark hair and dark eyes. The way he smirked as he approached the threesome on the bed made Scarlett squirm on my dick as she sunk further down.

"Room for one more?" the man asked as he climbed on the bed.

"Holy fuck," Scarlett moaned as he took the girl by the hair, pulling her closer and shoving his dick in her mouth.

I couldn't help but be pleased with Scarlett's reaction.

My girl loves this as much as I do. What more could a man ask for?

TWENTY FIVE

SCARLETT

W hen I begged Prescott to take me out of the penthouse, I did not imagine I would end up in a sex club sat on his dick while we watched four people fuck. I got it now. Completely understood his fascination. It was the most erotic thing I'd ever seen in my life. Watching three men go at this woman like she was their plaything. They gave it to her with wild abandon, heedless of the fact they were being watched.

"That's what Francis, West and Drake look like when they fuck you, little lamb," Prescott whispered in my ear. "When they make you take them all at the same time."

He gripped my hips and made me rock against him, fucking me while we watched them. And what a sight it was. The dark-haired man had the girl's hair in his fist, pumping his cock down her throat and making her gag on it. I could hear the sounds of it through the speakers. The chestnut-haired one, who was fucking her pussy, was running his hands up her body, pinching her nipples while she rocked on his cock. The man with the auburn hair gave it to her from behind while he held onto her shoulders as leverage. I was riveted. There was a rawness to the way they fucked each other, to the passion between them.

I knew this was a show, and they'd been paid to act this out for us, but it didn't stop it from feeling real. It was so fucking hot, I thought I might combust. My body was on fire with the scene in front of us. Prescott had understood what I needed. He'd surprised me with this. He wanted to show me what he saw. What he desired. Watching people fuck in the rawest and most animalistic way. No wonder this turned him on so much.

"Pres, please, I need more. Touch me."

I don't think I could have got through watching this scene without him there, his cock buried deep inside me. He pushed me forward slightly so he could unzip the back of my dress. I let it fall off my body, pooling at my waist. His fingers pulled down my bralette and cupped my breasts. I moaned when he pinched my nipples and pressed kisses to the side of my neck.

"Do you like it, my lamb? My gift to you."

I moved my hips faster, needing more friction between us.

"Yes, fuck, it's the hottest thing I've ever seen in my life."

The dark-haired man pulled his cock from her mouth and rubbed her saliva around her lips. His dick was covered in it. Then he leant down, taking her chin between his fingers and spat directly in her mouth. I shuddered, feeling Prescott dig his teeth into my bare shoulder.

"Dirty girl," the dark-haired man said. "Such a dirty little whore."

"Yes," the girl moaned. "I'm your dirty whore."

She wrapped her hand around his cock, stroking her saliva into it. The auburn-haired man bit down on her shoulder the way Prescott was doing to mine. She yelped, pushing herself back into his embrace. I didn't know what to do with myself other than to watch them and let Prescott touch me. Let him drive me higher.

"Look at our slut, she's so desperate," the chestnut-haired man taunted. "You need dick, don't you, slut?"

Prescott had to have told them to say those things. And he must have asked them to get someone with the same hair colour as me. I could picture myself there getting fucked by Drake, West and Francis while he watched us.

"This is what you like... watching them give it to me," I said, arching my back as he pinched my nipple again.

"You take them so well, little lamb. Spread wide open by their cocks. It's the best sight in the whole fucking world. I could watch you every day and it would never be enough. You are the most beautiful creature I've ever beheld. The way you come apart for us is stunning. I don't think you realise how much we desire you. How much we need your body wrapped around ours. You are our queen. The one we need to debase over and over again until you're a panting mess."

I moaned, wanting more. Needing him to fuck me harder. This position was great for watching, but not to be fucked in the way I needed.

The fact three of my men had such dirty mouths turned me on so damn much. Drake had been a little more vocal the last time we'd had sex. Admittedly, I enjoyed the times he said nothing. It made me want to wind him up, so he'd crack.

"I need you to fuck me harder," I panted out, not caring how desperate I sounded.

I heard Prescott chuckle before I found myself pulled off him. He pushed me up to my feet. It was disorientating, but Prescott was behind me, pressing me forward until my knees hit the bench in front of the window. Then he made me kneel on it.

"Put your hands against the glass."

I obeyed, knowing they couldn't see me. They knew we were watching, but it made it hotter to know they weren't able to see Prescott fucking me as they fucked each other. My dress was still pooled at my waist and my knickers halfway down my thighs. He didn't bother removing them. He merely stood behind me and bent me forward slightly to give him a good angle. The moment he thrust inside me, I moaned and my breath misted the glass.

"Look at them, little lamb. Can you see their dicks pumping in and out of her?"

He was close to my face, running his teeth along the shell of my ear.

The dark-haired man's cock was now back in her mouth. She was being ravaged by the three men. They weren't giving her body any mercy as they fucked her in unison.

"Yes," I hissed when he gripped my hip and pounded into me the way I needed.

"They're going to make her come all over them. Make her come the way they make you."

"Pres," I whined as his fingers rubbed over my clit.

"Mmm, that's right, lamb. You're going to come with her."

Prescott shifted his angle, making me cry out from the way he was thrusting into me. My breath kept fogging the glass, but I could still see what was happening in front of me. Prescott pressed his free hand on one of mine, holding me there.

The three men were fucking the girl ever harder. She was gagging all over the dark-haired man's cock, her saliva dribbling down her chin.

"Fuck," he grunted as he erupted down her throat, spilling his cum.

The chestnut-haired one was rubbing her clit and making her squirm on him and the auburn-haired man's dicks. The dark-haired one pulled his cock from her mouth, rubbing his cum all over her lips and chin. She didn't swallow, just kept her mouth open and turned to us, showing me and Prescott what he'd given her.

"Jesus," Prescott hissed in my ear.

The girl swallowed and smiled before turning her attention back to the two men still fucking her. The dark-haired man sat down and watched them. I couldn't help but wonder if he enjoyed watching as much as me and Prescott did.

"Does our dirty whore want their cum filling her holes?" the dark-haired man said with a smirk.

"Yes," she moaned, "please."

"Then be a good little girl and come for them."

Prescott circled my clit harder, rubbing me in the way he knew would make me explode all over him.

"Hold on for me, lamb," he whispered. "Hold on until she comes."

I squirmed on his cock, trying to stop from coming. All the orgasm denial Francis had done with me made it easier to keep myself from falling too quickly. I panted against the glass, wanting to see it. Needing to watch the moment she fell apart.

"Oh, fuck, I'm… I'm going to come," she cried out.

"Not yet, lamb, just wait," Prescott told me.

I moaned at the same time she did. Her body bucked with her climax. The men were grunting and cursing as she rode the wave.

"Let go. Come for me, little lamb. Come all over my dick."

I bit my lip as the two men started erupting inside the woman. Then I was lost to my own orgasm wreaking havoc through my body. I let out a low whining sound, my breath covering the glass as I panted out my release. Prescott grunted behind me, continuing to rub my clit until it was so over sensitised, I cried with it.

"I can't," I gasped. "Please."

He seemed to understand as he stopped, pressing his hand against my other one instead. Then he was fucking me into the window, squishing me against it. I was in no state to complain, not that I would have. Feeling his body pounding into mine with his desperation was intoxicating.

"Fuck, little lamb," he groaned when he came, spilling inside me with hot pulses of cum.

I pressed my cheek to the glass, not even caring about the people on the other side. All I cared about was Prescott and me locked together after our mutual releases.

"I love you," he whispered, pressing a kiss to my neck.

"Love you too."

He pulled me away from the glass and walked us back to the sofa, settling me down in his lap. He hugged me close, pressing kisses to my face.

"Do you understand now?" he asked after a minute when we'd caught our breath.

"Yeah, I do… that was quite something."

"I can't say it's as good as when I watch you, but it was pretty fucking amazing."

I grinned.

"Nothing beats me?"

"No one in this world is more beautiful and as responsive as you, sweetness. You're everything."

I turned to him and pressed a kiss to his cheek.

"My sweet king."

"I'm not sweet."

"You are to me."

He rolled his eyes and shook his head, but I knew he was secretly pleased by my praise. My king liked to be admired, even if he refused to admit it.

When we'd both recovered, we cleaned up and got our clothes in order. We drank the bottles of water Prescott had got out of the fridge, then made our way out of the room. The four people had left after they'd finished, presumably to clean themselves up, and the other room was dark.

Prescott led me back into the club. Neither of us felt inclined to linger to watch the show going on. There were a couple of women on the poles, but I was more interested in staring up at my man who'd just entirely rocked my world by bringing me here and giving me an experience to remember.

We collected our coats from the reception area and pulled them on before stepping outside into what could only be described as a downpour. Prescott tried to hurry me along to the car, but I looked up at the sky as the rain pounded down on my face.

"Sweetness, come on, it's pissing it down."

I turned my head and smiled at him but didn't say a word.

"We're going to get soaked if you don't come along."

I allowed myself to be pulled towards the car park, but not before the idea of what I wanted Prescott to do to me in the rain consumed me. We ran through the rain, me laughing as Prescott cursed. When we got under the cover of the car park, he shook his head, his hair all wet. I tugged at his hand to get his attention.

"I want you to chase me."

His mouth twitched, his blue eyes darkening at the prospect before he frowned.

"Right now?"

I pressed myself closer.

"Yes, right now."

Perhaps it was the freedom I'd felt in the moments we'd shared together in the club, watching other people fuck. Or perhaps I was just high off the whole experience. Either way, I needed this. I was desperate to have him chase me down, press me into the mud, and fuck me. I wanted him to be my wolf. The one who would catch his lamb in the middle of the night in the pouring rain.

"Drake is going to kill me."

I went up on my tiptoes and pressed a kiss to his lips.

"So what? You won't let anything happen to me."

Prescott wrapped his arms around me.

"No, I won't. You're safe with me."

"Then please take me somewhere you can chase me."

He sighed and pressed a kiss to my forehead.

"I can't deny you when you ask me for something."

"You know you want to."

He let me go and took my hand, pulling me over to the car.

"I will never turn down chasing you, sweetness. Never."

Those blue eyes of his glinted as he opened the car door for me.

"Now get in. I have just the place in mind."

I jumped in the car, vibrating with excitement and adrenaline. Tonight, pretty much all my fantasies with Prescott were coming true. I was one lucky girl to have this man who owned my heart and my soul. The one who was so willing to do anything to make me happy.

My Pestilence, you're king in my heart.

TWENTY SIX

PRESCOTT

S carlett was going to get me into so much shit with
Drake, but I no longer cared. No fucking way I was
going to let that fuck, Stuart Carver, ruin our lives. We
deserved to live the way we wanted, regardless of what he was
up to. Besides, we were going to destroy him. Murder the man
in cold blood, so we would be safe. I wanted him dead for
everything he'd done to Scarlett. The way he'd fucking abused
her sickened me to my core. I couldn't wait until he got what
was coming to him. Until we gutted him and anyone else
who'd aided him when it came to abusing my woman.

I found on-street parking as the park was closed to cars at
night and pulled up. We both slid our coats off as there was no
point wearing them when we were about to get very dirty
together. Scarlett got out with me, looking like the cat who got
the cream. I took her hand, and we walked towards the park
together in the downpour.

By the time we reached the woods I was aiming for in Richmond Park, both of us were soaking wet. I'd kept an eye out the whole way in case anyone was following us, but there was nothing suspicious I could see. Didn't hurt to be careful, especially when Stuart had sent three men after her when Drake had taken her to visit Lylah's grave.

We'd meticulously planned the visit to Desecration. I'd taken one of our lesser-used cars that weren't in any of our names. This impromptu chase was unplanned, but I was incapable of denying Scarlett the things she wanted, not when I wanted them too.

I turned to her as we stood together just under the cover of the trees and cupped her face with one hand.

"Stay in the woods, okay? We don't want to get caught here."

"I will. I promise."

I stroked her face and pressed a kiss to her forehead.

"Run."

My hand dropped. She gave me a smile, then she turned and ran into the trees. They were closer together than the woods we'd run through before. I gave her a minute before I gave chase. Given the danger of us being out here, I wasn't going to draw it out. I was going to catch my lamb, shove her down in the mud, and give it to her without restraint. It had been raining hard for quite some time, so the ground was soggy, even in the densely packed trees.

I could see her up ahead, scrambling through the trees and trying not to trip over the undergrowth. It made me smile. Scarlett didn't like to make things easy on herself.

There was no calling out to each other this time. We didn't require taunts. She needed to run. I needed to chase. The rain was heavy. The trees creaked with the wind and I could hear thunder rolling in the distance. It made it a little eerie. The atmosphere was dense and unyielding, making me really feel like a wolf hunting down his prey. And what delightful prey she was. Her wet dress clung to her body. It was lucky it wasn't long or it would be harder for her to run.

I wasn't going at full pelt, wanting her to feel the mix of fear and adrenaline that came with the hunt. The closer I got, the more I could hear her heavy breathing and her feet pounding against the wet undergrowth. She could hear me too. Scarlett kept looking back to see if I was there. And when she spied me, she tried to run faster but was hampered by the weather and the trees surrounding us. The moan of fear she let out had my heart pounding harder against my chest. I wanted to grab her. I needed to feel her against me again.

The show at Desecration had been pretty fucking incredible. The experience I shared with her was unlike anything else. But this? Chasing her? It was my favourite. The primal, animalistic need inside me wasn't often sated. Scarlett was the perfect prey. She was all of my fantasies rolled into one. The way she accepted and embraced the things I desired was unparalleled. She was everything.

I reached out, my fingers brushing her braid and narrowly missing her dress. She ran harder as if she realised she was about to get pounced on, making a sharp turn left to throw me off. I let out a growl as the thunder rumbled.

My hand went out again, catching hold of her braid this time and yanking her backwards into me. She slammed into my chest, sending me a few steps back to keep balanced. I spun her around, catching sight of her scared expression before I was shoving her down in the undergrowth and covering her body with my own. She panted against me. I could feel her heart hammering against her ribcage. I pinned one of her hands in the mud before catching her mouth in a bruising kiss. The moment our lips met, it was a wild frenzy of pulling at each other, wanting to be closer, needing more, desperate for everything.

I shoved up her wet dress as her free hand fumbled with my clothes. She whined in frustration when she couldn't unbutton my chinos. The wet fabric was making everything so much harder. I let go of her hand to help her, tearing at my clothes to free my aching dick. Once tonight wasn't enough. It would never be enough with Scarlett. Never.

"Pres," she gasped as I pulled aside her knickers and shoved my fingers inside her.

I covered her mouth with mine, kissing her as I pumped my fingers into her wet pussy and got my cock out. She wriggled in the muddy ground, getting herself all messy. My knees were already squelching in the mud as I moved closer to her. I didn't care one fucking bit about the mud and the rain. All I wanted was her. My beautiful little lamb who was already clawing at me, needing me to fuck and claim her all over again.

I ripped my fingers from her pussy and replaced them with my cock, thrusting deep. She cried into my mouth at my roughness. Her legs wrapped around me, encouraging me to give it to her harder. I bit her bottom lip, making her pant and shove her hands under my shirt to scratch her nails down my back. I groaned, pressing kisses down her jaw and neck. My lips brushed over the scars West had given her. The neckline of her dress was low enough so everyone could see it. Scarlett was proud of wearing his mark now. She wanted to show everyone she belonged to War just as she belonged to Pestilence, Famine and Death.

"Bite me," she panted. "Make me yours."

I nuzzled the top of her breast before digging my teeth into her skin. Her nails dragged down my back, marking me in return. I growled against her skin, biting harder to bruise her. To show her she belonged to me.

My knees started sliding in the mud, so I slammed a hand down to steady myself, fucking her harder. I couldn't help myself, acting on sheer fucking instinct and need. There was nothing but me, her, the trees, the mud and the rain hammering down on my back through the canopy. Scarlett was right. We needed this experience together. We needed it to set us free. She might run from me, but she always allowed herself to get caught. She wanted it. My girl would never abandon me.

"Mine," I growled, letting go of her skin so I could crash my mouth to hers again. "All fucking *mine.*"

She couldn't respond with my tongue in her mouth, tasting and devouring her whole. Scarlett did something to me. She made me wilder. She set me free from my burdens and shame. I might hold her heart, protect her and be the one she came to for comfort, but she did the same for me. This woman had the power to heal me from the inside out just by being her.

I let go of her mouth to press my face into her neck, so close to the edge of everything.

"I love you, sweetness," I choked out.

Scarlett wasn't just my little lamb, she was the sweetest thing I'd ever tasted. The sweetest woman who opened her heart to four broken men, who needed her more than they needed air to breathe. She was dark like us, but she was brilliant and bright too. She was our light. There in the spaces where I ended. And I was there in the spaces she began. We were destined for each other.

Her nails drew down my back as I adjusted the angle between us. I shoved a hand down, finding her clit and rubbing it while I fucked her pussy. I fucked my woman into the mud, getting her dirty. It stuck to both of us while the rain battled to wash it away.

It was almost poetic, this moment. A symbol of our relationship. How we were so in tune with each other and yet the passion between us burnt so hot, it was an inferno blazing, devouring the two of us in a pit of twisted desire.

"Pres, fuck," she gasped right before she exploded, her body bucking and trembling beneath mine.

The moment she went limp, I pulled my hand away, gripped her hip and drove into her, seeking out my own end. I kissed her lips despite the fact she was holding onto me weakly as if I'd sucked the life out of her. I would look after her and make it all better when we were done.

My climax hit like a fucking freight train. It raced up my body, ripping me apart and knitting me back together in the same breath. I collapsed on top of her, pressing her deeper into the muddy mess we'd made of the ground. She held me to her as if she didn't want me going anywhere.

"I love you," she whispered against my rain-drenched neck, "I love you so much."

Now we were spent, both of us trembled with the cold. I needed to get her back to the car and warmed up. I cupped her face with my palm, still needing to catch my breath. Still needing to regain my equilibrium.

"You're shivering," I murmured.

"So are you."

I chuckled.

"We're wet, muddy and cold, I think it figures."

Her arms around me tightened as if she was trying to give me her limited body heat. Was there anything my beautiful girl wouldn't do for me?

I was about to pull away from her when I froze at the sound of voices.

"You saw them come in here?"

"Yeah, I swear it, mate."

"It's too fucking dark, man, I can't see them anywhere."

Scarlett's fingers dug into my skin.

"Let's split up. Can cover more ground that way. The things we fucking do."

"Too right."

The noise of them moving off in different directions met my ears. I was up and off Scarlett the next moment, pulling her with me and pushing her behind the nearest tree. I covered her body with mine, pressing her into the bark.

"Help me with my clothes," I hissed in her ear.

She fumbled between us, tugging her wet dress down her legs before she got me put away too, zipping up my chinos in the process.

"Stay quiet, okay? Don't move."

She nodded. Her body shook against mine, but she was holding herself there, trying not to make a sound. I could hear one of the men moving through the undergrowth despite the rain. He wasn't being very stealthy. Peering out, I could see him walking a few feet away with a light in his hand. My hand slid into my pocket, gripping a knife I kept in there. I pulled it out and then I left Scarlett, stalking after the guy with quiet steps. Knowing she would stay unless someone found her, I didn't look back to check on my girl. She wasn't stupid. Scarlett knew the risks.

I watched him as I moved after him. The man was so unaware of his surroundings. The rain didn't help, but even his fucking flashlight wasn't doing him any favours. Stuart was seriously getting sloppy if he sent these idiots to do his dirty work. Then again, Drake had said the men who came after him and Scarlett weren't the brightest sparks, either. Hired muscle didn't need to be smart, but Stuart knew we weren't stupid men. Clearly, he was desperate to get us. Desperate enough not to be clever about it. It would be his biggest mistake, underestimating the Four Horsemen and their goddess Nyx.

I got close enough to the guy to catch him unawares. I was on him the next moment, dragging him up against a tree with my knife pressed to his throat and my other arm locked around his chest. Before he could say a word, I growled low in his ear.

"You better stay silent or I'll slit your fucking throat and leave you to bleed out."

TWENTY SEVEN

PRESCOTT

T he man shook in my grasp but didn't say a word.
There was nothing I wouldn't do to keep Scarlett
safe, including killing this man. I'd known coming
out to the woods was possibly a bad idea, but I couldn't help
it when it came to my girl. We'd needed this. And now we were
going to fight for our survival. Fight to stay safe, regardless of
Stuart's fucking plans.

"You listen here," I murmured in the man's ear, "you're
going to find your little friend and you're going to leave these
woods. You won't come after us. If you do, I won't hesitate to
gut you. Is that understood?"

Before the man had a chance to respond, I heard a high-
pitched scream echoing through the woods.

Scarlett.

"Fuck!"

Then I was moving, dragging the guy along with me as I
ran through the trees to get to her. The other guy must have

found her. I'd known leaving her was risky, but I needed to get rid of this guy so we could escape. If she was taken away, I would never fucking forgive myself.

A minute later, I could hear the other man cursing and grunting. There was clearly a struggle going on, as the light he was holding was moving around wildly. I slammed the man I was dragging up against a tree.

"You fucking stay there, you hear me."

He nodded, fear lacing his features. Then I was running towards the light. The scene I was met with had me in a full-on fucking rage. The guy was struggling with Scarlett in his grasp. She was fighting for her life, kicking out and trying to bite his hand over her mouth.

"Listen here, you little bitch, you better fucking quit it."

No one, and I mean no fucking one, got to call her that except me and the others during sex.

I leapt, crashing into both of them. My knife slid into the guy's back, piercing through flesh. He howled in pain. Then I ripped him away from Scarlett, pulling him backwards with me while tugging the knife out and stabbing it into him again, right where his kidney was.

"You think you can take her from me? You think I'm going to fucking let you have her?"

He struggled against me, but I kept stabbing him again and again, making very sure he would bleed out and die. There was nothing else but the need to destroy him for having the audacity to try to deprive me of the love of my life. No one got to touch her. She was fucking mine.

"You came after the wrong fucking people. I'm your worst fucking nightmare."

I threw him on the ground and knelt down on his back before shoving the knife between his ribs and piercing his lung. I did the same to the other side. He was wriggling, clawing at the dirt, but I didn't give a shit. He wheezed as I pressed him harder into the mud. Digging the knife into his other kidney for good measure, I kept him there, knowing he was going to bleed out. His lungs would collapse too.

"Pres," came Scarlett's voice.

I looked up, finding her watching us without any sort of judgement.

"He has to die."

She nodded and pointed to the other man. He was staring at me in absolute horror like he had no idea how vicious and unrelenting I could be. The fool didn't know the lengths I would go to keep Scarlett from harm. She was mine to protect. Fucking mine.

"I told him to stay the fuck where he was. If he moves, I will chase him down and kill him too."

There was no way this guy beneath me was surviving what I'd done to him. The man against the tree looked like he was about to piss himself at my words. Well, he better take me the fuck seriously. I wouldn't hesitate if he tried anything.

"Get off me," the man below wheezed.

"Shut the fuck up and die quietly, you piece of shit."

I pushed his face into the mud with a hand to the back of his head. He struggled harder, the mud clearly getting into his mouth and airway as he tried to get me off him. We were silent as the rain continued to batter down on us and the man's movements grew sluggish. I let him go the moment he stopped, checking his neck. There was no pulse.

I stood and faced the man against the tree. Walking towards him slowly, my bloody knife still clutched in my hand, I saw how pale he looked. Scarlett had her arms wrapped around herself, and she was shivering. Every part of me wanted to go to her, warm my girl up and look after her, but right now, I had to deal with this fuck.

I reached for him and put my knife to his throat, pressing against it, but not hard enough to break the skin.

"Listen here, fuckhead, if you want to walk away with your life, you're going to do exactly as I say."

He didn't respond, but he'd seen me kill his friend. He knew I wasn't playing around.

"You're going to take a message to Stuart. I fucking know it was him who hired you, so don't even try to deny it. You tell him we're coming. We're fucking coming for him and he's not going to walk away with his life. He stole what was ours and hurt her. We don't take kindly to anyone causing pain to what's ours. Is that understood?"

He nodded and whimpered.

"Good." I turned my attention to Scarlett. "Search his pockets for me, little lamb."

She came over to us and started going through the man's jeans without hesitation. From his back pocket, she pulled out a wallet. Then she was looking through it. She tugged out his driving licence and showed it to me.

"Now, Terrance, is it? I have another task. You're going to take care of him for me." I nodded over to the dead man in the mud. "You'll get rid of his body and make sure you leave no fucking traces of what happened here."

The guy swallowed at my words, but I wasn't fucking done.

"If I find out you didn't follow through, I will hunt you down and gut you like a fucking pig. I will feed you your fucking guts and choke you to death with them, you hear me? I will do it in front of your family if you have one, then I'll kill them too."

The stench of urine hit me a moment later. I smiled at him. I'd clearly scared him half to fucking death. Served him right. He tried to come at me and my woman. I wouldn't let that stand.

"Do we understand each other?"

"Y-y-yes."

"Good. Now, you're going to let me and her leave whilst you deal with him."

He nodded and I released him. Scarlett gave the wallet to me and I tucked it into my pocket.

"I'm taking this just in case you decide to make the wrong decision, Terrance. There is no fucking place you can hide from me and my friends, so don't disappoint me."

I took Scarlett's hand, giving him one last significant look before I pulled her away from the scene. She didn't hesitate to run through the forest with me until we made it out onto open ground. The two of us didn't stop running through the park, both aware of the urgency. We needed to get the fuck away from here as soon as possible. Neither of us spoke. I had blood and mud all over me. This was an absolute fucking nightmare. I swear to fuck if that shit didn't do as I said, I would lose it on him. There would be no holding me back.

When we reached the car, I got Scarlett inside and turned the engine on, whacking the heating right up to warm her. I didn't see to her straight away. Something had me wondering how the fuck they'd found out where we'd gone. My first instinct was to check the outside of the car despite the rain. I looked around it and underneath everything. Pausing, I saw something sticking to the underside of the bumper that shouldn't be there. I reached out and ripped it off the car. They'd fucking stuck a tracker on it. I cursed, threw it on the ground and stamped on it several times until it smashed. Then I got in the car, put my seatbelt on, connected my phone up to the Bluetooth and set off.

"Are you okay?" I asked her, knowing we had to leave immediately.

"I'm just cold."

Scarlett was curled in on herself on the seat.

"I need to call Drake. They had a fucking tracker on the car, so I'm guessing they might have put them on all the ones we own."

She nodded. I hit dial on Drake's number. He answered after the second ring.

"Where the fuck are the two of you? You were meant to be back well over an hour ago."

"You have to promise me you won't get mad at Scar for what I'm about to tell you."

"Prescott."

"Promise me, Drake."

"Fine, I promise. Now, what the fuck is going on?"

I sighed, rubbing my face as I navigated the streets of London. Then I explained what happened after we left the club, not leaving out a single thing about what happened with the two men. Drake kept silent the whole time, letting me get it out without interrupting. And when I was done, I could practically feel his anger bleeding through the phone.

"Fuck. For fuck's sake. Jesus Christ, this is a fucking mess."

"You're telling me."

"Are you on your way back?"

I'd thought about taking Scarlett home, but I wasn't sure it was safe given they were clearly watching the building and tracking our fucking vehicles.

"No, I'm taking her to Mum's. You and the others have to make sure the building is safe, check all the cars and up our security. We're not letting anyone take her from Fortuity again, you hear me? I won't let it happen."

"Are you sure that's a good idea? Rosie is going to question why you've turned up at her place in the middle of the fucking night with Scarlett in tow."

Mum was going to give me such a fucking hard time over it, but to keep Scarlett safe, I would do anything.

"Eliza and Jasper know about us. It's only a matter of time before Mum finds out. I might as well get it over and done with now."

"Fine. You keep her safe, Pres. We'll deal with shit here. You sure that guy will get rid of the body?"

"I'm pretty fucking sure. Doubt he wants me coming after him and his family. Not after what I threatened."

Scarlett snorted from beside me. She'd heard every word of what I'd said to the guy.

"Is our girl okay?"

"I'm fine, Drake," she replied for me, "I promise. I'm just cold and tired."

"I love you, little wisp."

"Love you too."

"Take care of her, Pres. I'll call you tomorrow."

He hung up. Scarlett looked at me.

"You sure about taking us to Rosie's?"

I reached over and stroked her thigh.

"Yes. It'll be fine. You'll see."

We lapsed into silence as I drove. What happened tonight was fucked up.

Scarlett fell asleep during the journey. When I pulled up at Mum's house, I had to wake her. It had stopped raining by then. We'd be safer here than anywhere else, considering Mum didn't have any close neighbours. I held Scarlett's hand as we walked up to the front door and rang the doorbell. We were met with the sound of dogs barking. Boxer, Bean and Bone were Mum's Labrador Retrievers.

The door was pulled open a minute later, revealing Mum in a dressing gown with her blonde hair up. She'd clearly locked the dogs in the kitchen, as they weren't on her heels. Her blue eyes widened when she took me in. I'd put my coat on and wiped the blood from my hands and face, but there was still mud all over my trousers and trainers.

"Prescott? What on earth are you doing here? What happened?"

Then her eyes fell on the girl beside me and her mouth dropped open. Our clothes were still damp. Scarlett had muddy streaks all over her legs and arms.

"Who is... oh my god."

"Hi, Mum, listen, I know this is a shock, but could you perhaps let us in? Scarlett's freezing and I need to put her to bed."

Mum stood back to allow the two of us into the house. I didn't lean down to kiss her cheek as I usually would. She shut the door behind us and locked it.

"I'm going to put her in the shower and myself too. I'll talk to you after I've put her to bed, okay?"

She gave me a nod, but I could see her wanting to ask me a million and one questions. Right now, my priority was my girl. I tugged her away to the bathroom on the ground floor, glad my mum had tiled floors. Easier to clean the mud off them we were traipsing in. Scarlett came willingly and let me undress her after we got into the bathroom. We walked into the shower together when we were both bare. Scarlett's eyes were drooping. My girl was absolutely exhausted.

We washed thoroughly before I turned off the shower and bundled her up in a towel. Then I carried her from the bathroom after slinging one around my hips and took her upstairs into the bedroom Mum kept for me here when I visited. Setting her down on the bed, I dug out one of the t-shirts I'd left here and pulled it over her head.

"Pres…"

"Shh, it's okay. Get into bed and try to get some sleep. I'll be up soon, okay, sweetness?"

I tucked her up underneath the sheets and pressed a kiss to her forehead. I'd done my best to dry her braided hair, but it was still damp. She didn't seem to mind as she closed her eyes and drifted off.

I pulled on some jogging bottoms and a t-shirt before making my way downstairs. I gathered up all of our wet, muddy and blood-soaked clothes, taking them into the utility room next to the kitchen and stuffing them in the washing machine before turning it on. Then I grabbed our trainers and put them in the sink, washing away the mud and grime with the water. I set those on the side when I was done.

Taking a breath, I made my way into the kitchen. The dogs barked at me and I petted them so they'd settle down. Mum was sitting at the kitchen table with a mug between her fingers. I took a seat and dragged my fingers through my hair.

"What's going on, Prescott?"

"It's better that you don't know details."

"My son turns up at the door covered in mud with a girl who disappeared ten years ago in tow and you expect me to not ask questions?"

I sighed and looked away. The three dogs curled up around Mum's feet when they realised I wasn't going to give them more attention.

"I expect you to trust me when I tell you if I involve you in this, you won't like what I have to say."

Mum had no clue what me and the others had engaged in for the past ten years. We'd all made sure our parents were none the wiser about our activities. It was better for them that way. And yet today, I'd brought Scarlett here for her safety.

"Are you in trouble?"

"Yes, and no. The only thing you need to know is Scarlett is back." I paused, hating keeping things from her but knowing I had to, for all our sakes. "We need to stay a couple of days... if that's okay."

Mum reached out across the table and took my hands.

"You can always stay, you know that. And Scarlett is welcome too."

"Thank you. Is it okay if we talk tomorrow? I don't want to be away from her."

Mum scrutinised me for a long moment.

"Are you and Scarlett…?"

"Together? Yes."

"I always thought it was her and West."

I shook my head and smiled.

"It's a long story. One I'll tell you tomorrow."

"Okay. You get off to bed. My questions can wait."

I got up and gave her a kiss on the cheek before making my way upstairs. Scarlett was dead to the world as I slid into bed next to her. I wrapped my arms around my girl and held her against my chest before I fell into oblivion myself. Things had got far more fucked up than we needed them to be. There were no two fucking ways about it. We needed to go after Stuart and bring him the fuck down. He wasn't going to stop until we were dead. We had to get to him first before he destroyed us all for good.

TWENTY EIGHT

SCARLETT

I awoke to the sound of birdsong. Prying my tired eyes open, I didn't recognise the room I was in. I twisted in the bed, finding it empty. My hand stretched out to find lingering warmth there. I hadn't been alone for long.

When I looked around the room after savouring that warmth for a long moment, I found a little black cat sleeping on the end of the bed next to a larger ginger one. It made me smile. Prescott told me Rosie had six cats.

I sat up abruptly, making both cats give me evils. Last night came flooding back to me in waves. We were at Rosie's house because Stuart was tracking us and had sent men to find me. Prescott had viciously stabbed one of them to death right after we'd gone to watch a sex show, then he'd chased me down and fucked me. It has been the rawest and most wild sex I'd ever had with him, cementing our bond with each other so deep, I could never tear him out of me. I didn't want to. Not even after I'd watched him kill and threaten another man to protect me.

I rubbed my face and gave the cats an apologetic look. Not like I intended to disturb them, but last night's events were fucking crazy in good and bad ways.

Next to the cats sat a pile of clothes. Presumably, Prescott had left them for me. I hauled myself out of bed and pulled them on. They were his, so miles too big for me, but being wrapped up in his scent comforted me. I tightened the drawstrings on the shorts and snuggled into his hoodie. Clearly, Prescott kept clothes here for when he visited his mum.

I ventured out into the hallway, finding an upstairs bathroom and going about my business. Then I padded downstairs, following the sound of voices into the kitchen. It was a big space with a huge kitchen table off to one side. Prescott sat with Rosie, both with mugs of tea in their hands. They looked so alike, it was uncanny.

At Rosie's feet sat three brown Labradors, who all looked at me as I entered. Prescott noticed me next. He immediately got up and came over to me, tucking a hand under my chin and stroking my skin.

"Sweetness, did you sleep okay?"

"Like the dead."

I crashed out the moment my head hit the pillow last night. My hair wasn't too worse for wear this morning, still tamed by my braid.

"I noticed."

I wanted to wrap my arms around him, hold him tight, and tell him how much I loved him. Thank him for keeping me safe last night. However, I was conscious of the fact his mother was staring at the two of us. It made me wonder what he'd told her.

He drew me over to the table, giving his mother a tentative smile.

"Hi," I said, trying to remain calm.

While Francis' parents had been very welcoming and accepting, I wasn't sure what Rosie would think of me being back. Not to mention her feelings on the matter of her son being in a relationship with the same woman as his three best friends. Rosie was a free-thinking spirit, but even I understood this wasn't the most normal of circumstances.

Rosie got up out of her chair and wrapped me up in her arms. Her patchouli scent surrounded me, reminding me of my childhood spent in and out of her flat as we lived in the same building.

"It's so good to see you, Scarlett."

"You too," I murmured, unsure of what else to say.

She pulled away and gave me a bright smile.

"I'll make you some tea. Would you like breakfast too?"

I nodded.

"Thank you."

"Oh, it's quite all right. Please make yourself at home."

She bustled over to the kettle, leaving me with Prescott who took me in his arms and buried his face in my braided hair.

"My lamb," he whispered, rubbing my back in slow circles.

"I'm fine, Pres."

It wasn't a lie. I was fine. Last night didn't bother me. I'd seen enough death now. And I certainly wasn't scared of

Prescott for what he'd done. If anything, I only fell deeper in love with him, if that was even possible. He protected me. It made me aware I had a seriously skewed sense of justice, right and wrong, but I no longer cared about any of those things. Not when I was with them. The loves of my life.

He let me go and pulled me over to sit down next to him at the table. His blue eyes were intent on mine as he placed a possessive hand on my thigh.

"What did you tell her?" I whispered, looking over at Rosie, who was busy preparing breakfast.

We had turned up on her doorstep, rain-drenched and muddy. It was a good thing she hadn't seen the blood on Prescott's polo shirt. That would have raised alarm bells and we couldn't afford for Rosie to find out what he'd done last night.

"That you came to work for us and things happened… then you were pissed after you remembered us, but we're all okay now. She doesn't know about Stuart or any of the other shit we've done. It's going to stay that way."

"Did you tell her we're all together?"

"Not yet."

I gave him a look.

"You can't keep it from her."

"She knows we're together."

I snorted.

"Well, I think that's pretty obvious."

He leant closer and pressed his forehead to mine. I slid my hand along his shoulder and cupped the back of his neck.

"Is it? Should I make it even more obvious?"

"Pres—"

I couldn't finish my sentence. He kissed me, making me sway into him. Then I pulled away, putting space between us. Rosie was watching us. I couldn't read her expression. Was she okay with me being with her son? We'd been inseparable as kids, but we were grown up now. I didn't know if it might be weird. It wasn't for Eliza and Jasper, but they were different. They only wanted Francis to be happy when he'd spent so many years tortured over the fact he felt like second best. They saw the way I raised him up when we were kids and how I did the same for him now.

I could only hope Rosie would see how much I loved Prescott. How I would do anything for him. He was my entire world.

"What's wrong?"

I looked at Prescott who was frowning at me.

"I'm just worried she will hate it," I whispered when Rosie went back to making breakfast.

"What? You being with us?"

I nodded. He stroked my cheek, those blue eyes of his softening.

"Listen, I don't need her approval. I love you, little lamb. I couldn't leave you even if I tried."

He let go of my thigh and wrapped an arm around me, drawing me against his chest. His warmth and reassurance bolstered me. We'd been in this bubble between the five of us and now reality was intruding, reminding me our relationship wasn't something society would look upon favourably. It wasn't normal. But I didn't care about normal. I cared about us.

We drew apart when Rosie brought breakfast over. She'd made a full English for us, something I appreciated after all the energy I expended last night. She didn't ask where I'd been, only querying how I was now and if I was glad to be back with my best friends. Prescott and I skirted around the issue of the real nature of our relationship until I nudged him with my foot after she asked if we were happy together.

"Mum, I feel like I need to explain something," he said, rubbing the back of his neck with one hand.

"About what?"

"Me and Scar... and the others."

Rosie raised her blonde eyebrows, eyeing the two of us with concern.

"Drake, Francis and West?"

"Yeah."

"So tell me."

She looked between the two of us when he didn't immediately respond. I leant forward on my elbows.

"You asked if we're happy and we are," I started, trying to think of the right words to say. "Pres, West, Frankie, Drake, and I are happy together... as a family."

When Rosie frowned, Prescott took one of my hands, entwining our fingers together.

"What Scar means to say is we're all in a relationship with her and it's okay if you're not on board with that, Mum, but we're not going to hide it from anyone. We love her and she loves us. I won't abandon her. Not now. Not ever."

She didn't speak for a long moment, her eyes remaining fixed on her son. Then she got up and came around the table before wrapping Prescott up in her arms.

"Do you have any idea how proud I am of you?"

Prescott froze as if he wasn't expecting her reaction.

"Mum?"

She pulled back and clasped his face between her hands.

"You've always worried you'll turn out like your father, but you're nothing like him. You're loyal, kind, and caring. Ezra doesn't deserve to be called your father. He doesn't deserve you. I might wish I'd never laid eyes on the man, but he gave me you. I love you so much and I want you to take care of Scarlett. I want you to love her the way I know you can. Make sure those three take care of her too. Francis is a good egg, but I know what West and Drake are like. You keep them in line."

"Scar does that well enough herself."

"I imagine she does. Never let you boys get away with anything, that one."

Rosie pressed a kiss to Prescott's forehead, giving him a bright smile. Tears welled in my eyes at the sight of it. Then she came around to me and I found myself caught up in her arms.

"If there's anyone who can keep those boys and my son from doing anything stupid, it's you, Scarlett." She drew away and looked at me. "You were always saying you were destined for each other. I suppose this isn't really surprising under the circumstances."

I didn't like to tell Rosie they'd done a lot of stupid and fucked up things, regardless of my presence or intervention. Instead, I smiled and nodded. She patted my shoulder before going back to her own chair. The three of us finished up breakfast, the tension in the air somewhat dissipated from earlier.

Prescott and I stayed in the kitchen to deal with the dishes while Rosie took her dogs out for a walk. Prescott washed and I dried. He leant up against the counter when he was done, watching me as I put the plates away.

"What?" I asked when I folded up the tea towel and placed it on the counter.

"That was easier than I expected."

"Telling her about all of us."

He nodded. I reached out and took his hand.

"She watched us grow up together, Pres. It's not like I'm some random girl you all decided to share between you. What we have is different. It's special."

He looked conflicted, making me wonder what was going through his head. When he let go of my hand, I almost protested, but he took his phone out and fiddled with it.

"I'm ready," he said after a moment, staring down at the screen.

"For what?"

"To delete Ezra from my life."

I moved closer and peered at his screen. His thumb hovered over the delete contact button.

"Yeah?"

"Mum's right. He never deserved me. He's a shit excuse for a man, and I don't respect him. I might not be perfect, but I know I'm a damn sight better than him. I would never abandon my family."

He pressed down, erasing Ezra's contact details from his phone. Then he let out a breath and looked at me.

"I have you to thank, you know."

"Me? I didn't do anything."

He shook his head, popping the phone on the counter and capturing me up in his arms.

"You came back to me, little lamb. For ten years, I hoped I'd get to see your face again. To see you laugh, smile and tell me when I'm being an idiot. You never abandoned me. You fought your way back even if you didn't know that's what you were doing at the time. Every day, you show me how strong and brave you are in the face of all the shit you've been through. And you love me, flaws and all. You've done everything, sweetness, absolutely everything just by being you."

I reached up and cupped his face, letting a tear fall down my cheek from his words. He had no idea how proud I was of him for being able to let go of his father for good. Ezra had done nothing for him other than be his sperm donor.

"I just love you, Pres. All I've ever done is love you."

He pressed his forehead against mine.

"That's all I need you to do, sweetness. Keep loving me no matter what happens."

I kissed him, melting into his embrace. Loving him was effortless. And I'd keep doing it until the very end.

TWENTY NINE

FRANCIS

D rake and West weren't downstairs when the lift
doors opened to reveal Prescott and Scarlett. The
first thing she did was run across the room and
barrel into me, almost knocking me off my feet from the
impact.

"Hey, steady on there," I said, walking a few steps back into
the counter to regain my balance.

The next thing I knew, she'd climbed on me, wrapping her
legs around my waist and burying her face in my neck as she
clung to me.

"I missed you so much."

She'd only been away for two days and yet our place felt
empty without her. I stroked her back and breathed her in.

"I'm here. I'm right here."

She pulled away to look into my eyes.

"Take me upstairs please."

I raised an eyebrow, but she continued to look at me with an unreadable expression. Not wanting to deny her, I carried her towards the stairs. I caught Prescott's eye on the way, but he merely shrugged as if to say she hadn't told him what she wanted from me. She'd sounded perfectly okay on the phone last night when I'd spoken to her about when they were coming home.

"Don't you want to say hello to Drake and West?"

"I will later. I need you right now."

Her words made me move faster. There was nothing in this world that would stop me from giving Scarlett exactly what she needed when she asked for it.

When we got into my room, I set her down and shut the door. She stared up at me with an almost pleading look on her face.

"What is it, Scar?"

She reached out and took my hand, pressing it to her cheek.

"Will you bind me, please?"

I stroked her skin with the pads of my fingertips.

"Of course… in what way do you need it?"

"To feel safe."

I nodded, knowing exactly what I needed to do. Taking her hand, I pulled her towards the bed. Scarlett came willingly and allowed me to take her clothes off, setting them aside before I encouraged her onto the bed. Going over to my wardrobe, I opened the door and selected a few lengths of rope.

"Arms behind your back," I told her as I approached the bed again.

She did as I said. I knelt behind her and started binding her arms and chest. Then I created a harness at her back stable enough to hoist her up with. It was very similar to the way I'd bound her the first time I'd fucked her in the ropes. This time it would be to give her a sense of safety. I'd ask her why she needed it when she was settled.

She didn't protest when I encouraged her to stand up so I could tie her ropes to the pole suspended above my bed. Nor when I bound her legs and ankles and pulled them up so she was left hanging in place, not exactly face down, but almost. I stroked her skin, making sure all the knots were perfect, and she wasn't going anywhere.

Scarlett let out a breath when I lay beneath her on the bed so we could look each other in the eye. I reached up and touched her face, reassuring her I was right there before dropping my hand to my chest. For a few minutes, she didn't speak as she settled into her bindings. She barely shifted in them. She couldn't move much, anyway, but to know this helped her was everything to me. I always wanted her to feel safe.

"What's wrong?"

She closed her eyes and sighed.

"Being away from you, Drake and West reminded me of when Mason took me. I know I had Pres, but it's still so raw for me. I don't feel right in myself when I don't have you all near me."

If she hadn't been suspended from my ceiling by ropes, I would have wrapped myself around her. As it was, I shifted up onto my elbows and rubbed my face against hers. She opened her eyes and looked into mine.

"Am I weak for needing you all so much?"

"No, we need you too, Scar." I kissed her cheek. "And you've been through so much. You don't have to be strong all the time. We're here to catch you when you fall."

A tear dripped onto my face. Fuck, she was clearly more emotional about all of this than I realised. I moved, wanting to get her down, but she let out a little sound of protest when my hands went to the ropes.

"No, please, I need it. Just stay with me."

"Are you sure?"

"Please, Frankie. I'm just overwhelmed."

I settled back down, but it didn't stop me from reaching out and touching her shoulder, stroking her skin with my fingertips. A part of me needed the physical connection as much as she did.

Scarlett didn't stop crying, allowing silent tears to drip down onto me. I didn't wipe them away. They were evidence of her feelings. Her pain. And I would wear them to show her I wanted to rip the hurt from her chest. I would make it my own, so she didn't have to carry the burden alone. No matter how much pain it caused me to see her this way, I'd let her get her feelings out.

After a few minutes ticked by, she let out a little choking sound.

"Frankie."

I cupped her face, brushing under her eye with my thumb.

"What do you need?"

"I…"

"Should I get Drake and West in here? And Pres?"

She nodded, pressing her face into my palm. I held it there until she relaxed and then pulled it back to grab my phone

274

from my pocket. I sent them a group text, warning them of the circumstances they'd find us in. Not like they hadn't seen me bind her before, but her being suspended from my ceiling was different. This wasn't for sexual gratification. Shibari was an art form and provided mental relaxation as well as stimulation. It was the part that initially attracted me. When I was tying the knots, it calmed me. I went into a different space. It was similar for the model, the feeling of being constricted provided safety and security. Not to mention the ropes looked beautiful on a body.

I pressed a kiss to Scarlett's face after I'd dumped my phone on the bed. She strained for more, so I gave her my lips, allowing ours to mould together as I cupped her face.

"I love you," I whispered against her mouth.

"Love you too," she murmured back before seeking my tongue with hers.

I vaguely heard the bedroom door open, too focused on giving Scarlett what she needed. The pad of footsteps had me pulling back and stroking her cheek. When I finally turned to look at the three men standing at the end of the bed, Scarlett let out a soft sigh.

Prescott was the first to kneel on my bed and reach for Scarlett, stroking her hair, which she'd French braided. I moved back slightly to allow the other two access to her. West came around to look into her eyes while Drake knelt on her other side, stroking his hand along her bare thigh. None of them questioned what was happening or why she needed this.

She smiled when she saw West. He didn't say a word, just touched her face to let her know he was right there. The silence spoke volumes. None of us wanted her to feel unsafe with us when she was at her most vulnerable, tied up and suspended from the bar above my bed. Her emotions on full display after her heart bled.

Another tear spilt from her eye. West leant down and licked it away, making her let out a shuddering breath. He cleaned her tears with his tongue. She shifted in her bindings. Drake held her steady as I put my hand on her calf.

The four of us waited when West pulled back. We didn't want to rush her. Her breathing evened out after a few minutes. Then she looked at me.

"Let me down, please."

I sprang into action, getting the others to hold her while I undid the bindings connecting her to the pole. Then we settled her on the bed, all kneeling around her as she lay there on her front, her hands still tied behind her.

"Do you want me to release you?"

She nodded, resting her cheek on the covers. I did as she asked, unbinding all the ropes from her body. The indents all over her skin calmed me. They were a symbol of our connection to each other. The safety she felt with me. Scarlett had let herself be at her most vulnerable with me and the others today.

She sat up and looked between us.

"I forgot to say hi."

Raising up on her knees, she grabbed a hold of the back of Drake's head and kissed him. He stroked her side but didn't move to touch her further.

"Welcome home, little wisp," he told her when they drew apart.

She practically pounced on West next, almost knocking him over. He didn't seem to mind when she kissed him, wrapping her arms tight around his body. His hand went to hair, stroking the braid. She pulled back to look into his eyes.

"My beautiful little Scar."

Her fingertips went to his mouth, stroking along his lips as if memorising them. Like she needed to trace the words he said. The two of them silently communicated for a long minute, then she moved closer to me. The way she looked at me spoke volumes.

I moved back against the headboard, settling myself against the pillows. She curled up in my lap, letting me hold her and stroke her skin. Drake and West took places next to me while Prescott put his head on her thigh as he sat between my spread legs.

It was reaffirming our bond with each other. Being without her had been as hard for me, West and Drake, as it had been for Scarlett. We were still settling into our relationship. We'd only just established we wanted a future with each other. None of us wanted out. It was more than fate and destiny. It had everything to do with who we were as people. Who we were as a family.

"Fletch wants to see me tomorrow for lunch," Drake said, breaking the silence as he settled a hand on Scarlett's shoulder.

"Do you want to go?" she asked, turning her head to look at him.

"No."

"What if I went with you?"

He contemplated it for a moment before letting out a sigh and leaning his chin on her shoulder.

"You offering to hold my hand?"

"No, well… yes, but I meant going as your partner to support you."

We'd spent the past couple of days removing all the fucking trackers on our cars, making sure our security was increased further and acknowledging no matter what we did, Stuart was coming for us. We'd finalised the plan between us. It was a question of enacting it. Drake wanted Scarlett home before we did anything. She was just as much in this as we were. It was all together or nothing.

"And before you say no because of the danger of me leaving Fortuity poses, may I remind you of the three men you killed to protect me? You won't let anything happen to me."

I almost laughed. Drake would never allow anyone to take Scarlett again. Not after Mason kidnapped her from under our noses. He took it personally as he was the last person to see her that night, even if he didn't like to show it. I swear losing her a second time had cracked the ice casing around his emotions and brought them all out to the forefront. At least around us and Scarlett.

"I won't."

"Well then." She twisted in my lap and took a hold of his hand, pressing a kiss to his palm. "You don't have to deal with your family alone. You have me now."

"She's right, you know," I said, earning me a hard stare from Drake.

"She's always right when it comes to you, Drake," Prescott put in.

Drake sat up and looked at West as if he was going to add something. West's amber eyes glinted with amusement as if seeing us give Drake a hard time was the highlight of his day.

"What they said."

"I hate all of you," Drake ground out, which only made Scarlett laugh.

"You do not. Don't be such a big baby. I've already met your step-uncle once. What's the worst that could happen this time, huh?"

I swear his eyes practically popped out of his sockets at her words. Then he crossed his arms over his chest.

"Fine. I'll let him know to expect both of us."

Scarlett leant over and pressed her lips to his cheek.

"See, that wasn't so difficult."

"You're walking on very thin ice, Scarlett."

She sat back against me and grinned. I put an arm around her waist, holding her closer.

"I think I earned myself a punishment," she whispered to me.

"Do you think he's going to do it in front of us?"

"Maybe... if we provoke him enough."

"That's it," Drake announced before he grabbed a hold of Scarlett, tugged her out of my arms and put her face down across his lap. "You asked for this, brat."

She turned her head up to look at him.

"Oh, I know. Punish me so I can get my reward, sir."

Drake ran his palm across her bare behind.

"And what reward might that be?"

"You, me, them and the playroom."

I bit my lip as Drake smiled.

"I see someone has been missing her horsemen a little too much. We can't have that, can we?"

He looked at the rest of us. I was certainly not going to complain, and neither was Prescott nor West. When he got our approval, he turned back to Scarlett.

"Well, let's begin."

Fuck did the night take a rather unexpected but pleasant turn for all five of us. Scarlett might have needed the ropes to calm her down, but us together, locked in ecstasy, was the very best way to celebrate her coming home.

Soon, things were going to get dicey. And it would be life or death for all of us in the end.

THIRTY

DRAKE

S carlett had been right last night. I would protect her if anyone tried to take her. And forcing her to hide out was taking a toll on her. The whole incident with Prescott and her had only proven it was fucking futile. No matter what we did, Stuart would come after her. So we were going to bring the fucking pain to him. No more waiting. No more biding our time.

Well, we would go after him once I'd dealt with what Fletcher wanted. If Stuart's men saw us out and about without a care in the world after what happened a few days ago, it would piss the man off. Flaunting it in his face was better than keeping my girl locked up in an ivory tower. Rattle his cage to force him into making more mistakes. His biggest one was yet to come. Thinking we wouldn't have the balls to kill the motherfucker. Idiot. We killed his children when we were sixteen. What made him think he wouldn't be next after everything he'd done to us? To Scarlett? The cunt was far too secure in his position. Not any longer.

If we had to go down, he would be coming with us. Only he would be in his fucking grave.

I had to admit, it felt nice to have someone by my side as we walked into the restaurant to meet with Fletcher. Scarlett looked fucking amazing in a rather demure black dress and little peep-toe heels. It was the way she carried herself that had me enraptured. She was my queen, holding her head up high with her light brown hair falling in perfect waves around her shoulders.

The reaper and his goddess of the night. Heads turned as we weaved through the tables after the waiter, who was showing us to our table. I never cared what people thought of me, so I ignored it.

After last night in the playroom, we were all feeling a little... brighter. It certainly showed with the way she kept throwing me these little secret smiles. Her hand tightened around mine as if to reassure me this would be fine.

It was just lunch with Fletcher. I'd had them countless times before. However, something was off. He'd been incredibly insistent and wouldn't tell me why he wanted to see me. After he'd blabbed to my parents about Scarlett, I wasn't feeling particularly charitable, but curiosity had got the better of me. And I should have fucking known not to trust the cunt.

The moment we arrived at the table, my eyes narrowed on the second occupant. Now I knew exactly why he'd wanted me to come here. I had a hard time holding in my anger.

Sat there looking like my fucking older double was my father. Oscar Ackley. The man I hated almost as much as Stuart Carver himself.

Scarlett put her other hand on my arm when she saw him as if she couldn't believe her eyes. Of course, she remembered him, but it would be pretty fucking impossible not to notice we were related. Oscar might have greying hair at his temples, but his indigo eyes and dark hair mirrored mine. If he stood up, we'd be matched evenly in height. I hated it, but you didn't get to choose who you got your genes from.

"You came," Fletcher said, getting up and walking around to me. "It's nice to see you again, Scarlett. I'm glad he brought you."

The way he leered at her had me gritting my teeth. I'd already warned him about the way he'd been staring at my woman before. Now, I was plain fucking pissed off. At him. At my father. At the whole fucking situation.

"What is he doing here?" I asked, keeping my voice low.

Making a scene in a restaurant was not my style. And yet, the rage building in my gut needed an outlet. By fuck did I want to smack that smug smile off Fletcher's face.

"I told him you didn't want to see him, but he insisted."

I stepped closer to him, staring down at the man with no small amount of hatred.

"You know what, I don't have a good reason not to walk out of this place."

"Drake."

Scarlett's voice cut through the tension between me and Fletcher. My head whipped to her. She was giving my father a rather venomous look as if she couldn't believe he had the audacity to turn up here. I had told her what kind of man he really was.

"We don't have to stay if you don't want to." She looked up at me then. "You don't have to hear either of them out. You don't owe them anything."

I could have kissed her in the middle of the busy restaurant right then. Everything inside me screamed at me to do so. The gnawing urge grew stronger until I was unable to resist pulling her closer. She understood. She knew. And she wasn't going to force me into speaking to my father.

My hand curled around her face, tipping up towards me.

"My little wisp," I whispered, leaning closer. "Love of my life."

Then I kissed her in full view of everyone, not caring in the slightest about the level of PDA as my tongue slid into her waiting mouth. She gripped the lapels of my jacket, letting out a small mewl of pleasure as if she couldn't help herself.

When I let her go, her cheeks were flushed and her pupils dilated. I smiled, knowing I'd done that to her. Made her fucking weak at the knees. Well, she affected me in the same way, but I wasn't about to show it. She knew the power she had over me. How she could make me do what she wanted with her words and her body. I'd followed this woman down the rabbit hole willingly and I was never coming back out.

I swiped my thumb over her mouth before releasing her. Then I walked over to my father, who hadn't risen to his feet. He stared at me like he'd never seen me before. I was a changed man now I had the woman I loved and my three best friends who'd all promised me forever.

"I remember telling you I never wanted to see you again, Oscar," I said, keeping my voice fairly calm and even.

"Drake—"

I held a hand up.

"I don't care if you're sorry. In fact, I couldn't fucking care less what you have to say to me. I don't think I made myself clear enough before, so allow me to remedy that."

I leant closer and lowered my voice.

"You are not welcome in my life. I have a family and it doesn't include you. If you wish to keep your life, then I suggest you stay away. Next time, I won't be so nice."

I put my hand on the table, getting even closer.

"You don't know a single thing about me, and that's probably a good thing. If you did, trust me, it would make your blood run cold to know what type of man I've become. What type of man you brought into the world. They don't call me and the others the Four Horsemen for no reason. Just think about which one your son is next time you think it's a good idea to darken my door, hmm? Maybe it will make you think twice."

I didn't let him speak. In fact, I didn't look at him as I pulled back, turned around and walked away. My hand slid into Scarlett's as she followed me. The reaper and his little wisp made their way out of the restaurant without a backwards glance. And I felt a lot lighter for it. I was done with my father for good.

I sucked in a breath of air when we got outside and realised for the first time my burdens were no longer hanging over me. I wasn't alone.

Scarlett tugged on my arm. I looked down at her and smiled when I saw her eyes were full of pride.

"Let's go see my mother."

I pulled her away to the tube station nearby without letting her say a word. Fuck knows what had come over me. All I wanted was to re-introduce my mother to the woman I would spend forever with.

It took us thirty minutes to get across the city. Scarlett hadn't asked any questions or even brought up my father on the journey. Instead, we talked about our childhood. The little things that made us happy. I told her about all the music I'd written for her, including the song I'd played her on the rooftop when she'd first found me up there. She wanted to hear more, to know everything. I promised her when all of this was over, I'd give it all to her. I'd play each and every song, explain to her why I wrote them and what they made me feel.

I rang the doorbell and fidgeted, suddenly wary of turning up at my mother's house without telling her. She would be home as it was her day off. She was a nurse at the hospital nearby. The one we'd all been born at.

The door was pulled open, revealing the woman who'd given me life. May Ackley was short, with dark brown hair, brown eyes, and a stern expression on her face. When she saw it was me, she broke into a smile. I was still pissed she'd decided not to change her name after the divorce but right now, I was riding on a high. Nothing would get me down. I had my girl. The rest didn't matter.

"Now, to what do I owe this pleasure?"

Then her eyes fell on Scarlett and widened almost comically.

"Hello, Mum. You asked to meet my girlfriend, so I brought her around for you."

Mum was momentarily disarmed by my words and seeing the girl who had disappeared ten years ago on my arm.

"Hello, May," Scarlett said. "It's lovely to see you again."

Mum cleared her throat, gave me a look, then smiled at Scarlett.

"Well, this is quite the surprise. Come in, come in, it's chilly outside and you're letting the draught in."

I kept a straight face as Mum stood back to allow the two of us in. This was the house I'd grown up in. Oscar had moved out, leaving it to her.

Mum led us through into the kitchen, waving at the table for us to sit down.

"Now, have you two eaten? I was just about to make some tea, but I can whip something up for you."

"We haven't. That would be nice. Thanks, Mum."

I took Scarlett's coat and mine, hanging them up in the hallway while she sat down at the table. Pulling out a chair, I sat next to her and enfolded my hand in hers on the wooden surface. Mum busied herself in the kitchen but kept throwing glances at me as if she was trying to work out what happened to her son. The answer sat next to me. The girl who'd freed me from my locked cage and awoken the past version of myself.

"I'm not going to beat around the bush here. You turn up with Scarlett, tell me she's your girlfriend and expect me not to ask where on earth she's been." She looked at Scarlett. "Sorry, dear, I should direct that at you. Where have you been?"

I squeezed Scarlett's hand, reassuring her I was right here.

"I'm afraid I can't tell you that," Scarlett said. "It's better for everyone involved if I keep it to myself. All you need to know is I came to work for your son with my memories of the first sixteen years of my life missing. He and the others helped me remember what I'd lost. Now we have each other back. That's the important thing, not what happened to me."

While I knew the story we were telling our parents, I didn't expect Scarlett to inform my mother in such a calm and collected manner. Like she wasn't remotely scared of Mum or what she might say in response.

Mum pursed her lips and went back to making us lunch. I could see the cogs working in her mind as she poured three mugs of tea for us all.

"Okay, I can respect that. So tell me, how long has this been going on for?"

"A few months," I said, saving Scarlett from having to. "And I need you to know something before you ask us any further questions. Yes, Scarlett is my girlfriend, but she's also Francis, Prescott and West's girlfriend too."

The teaspoon Mum was holding clattered on the work surface. There was no point in me hiding it. It was better to tell her these things straight away, or she'd accuse me of keeping shit from her. And I knew I was in for one hell of a talking to the moment she turned around and met my eyes.

THIRTY ONE

SCARLETT

W hilst I didn't know what to expect when Drake said he wanted to go see his mother, I certainly didn't think he would just come out with the whole me being in a relationship with all of them straight away. Judging by May's reaction, she wasn't entirely happy to be informed of our unconventional arrangement. The way she stared at Drake with disapproval written all over her face spoke volumes. May Ackley wasn't known for keeping her opinions to herself. Likely why Francis had told his mother to keep silent about it until Drake told May himself.

"If this is some kind of joke, Drake, it isn't a very funny one."

"It's not a joke." He squeezed my hand tighter. "Why on earth would I make light out of something as serious as informing you the woman I'm going to spend the rest of my life with is also in a relationship with my best friends?"

SARAH BAILEY

May shook her head. I knew she was going to be against this. I hadn't blamed Drake for not wanting to tell her. It seemed May hadn't changed much in the past ten years if this was anything to go by.

"You mean to tell me you are okay with… excuse me, Scarlett, I don't want to insult you, but how on earth are you okay with being with the same woman? That's…"

"It's what, Mum? Unorthodox? Unconventional? Have I ever not been either of those things?"

May looked at him with a raised eyebrow and put her hand on her hip.

"You've never had a girlfriend before, Drake, and now you're telling me you're in some kind of, what, polyamorous relationship with four people?"

Drake snorted, stroking his thumb down the back of my hand to let me know he had this. He wasn't going to be browbeaten by his mother over his relationship with me and the others. He loved me and he'd proven to me just how much by protecting me against all the odds.

"I'm still straight, Mum, and I'm not having sex with the boys if that's what you're worried about."

"I did not… that's not what I was…" She let out a breath. "I wouldn't have an issue with you being… intimate with them if that was the case. This is just not what I expected from any of you."

Drake sat back in his chair and shrugged.

"It's not the first time we've shared."

I couldn't believe he was admitting this to his mother. I had to put my free hand over my mouth in an attempt to hide my smile.

290

"It's not the... lord have mercy, I'm not sure I want to ask what that means."

The way her face coloured up made me want to hide under the table and clutch my stomach. It was so difficult not to laugh at this situation and her reaction.

"This is why I don't tell you things, Mum. You clearly don't approve, but it doesn't stop this from being a reality." He waved at me. "You, of all people, should understand why we can't stay away from each other with the way you go on about how Francis and I were born on the exact same day. It's the same for all of us. We belong together. It's always been Scarlett for me. Always. It will never be anyone else. I can't stop loving her and I don't want to try. Not when she makes me happy. She completes all of us. We weren't okay without her. None of us were. And now we are. We're a family. I won't let anything come between us. Nothing will tear us apart. Never again."

He looked at me then. The love in his eyes almost knocked me off the chair. The intensity of those indigo eyes had me dropping my hand from my mouth and reaching out to touch his face. The fact he was standing up to his mother over me had my heart in absolute knots.

He pressed a kiss to my palm, making me practically swoon. There was nothing like being wrapped up in Drake's gaze when his full attention was on you. It was overwhelming, exhilarating and oh so fucking everything.

"Death needs his little wisp," he whispered. "I'm keeping you this time. Eternity isn't long enough, but it will have to do. I cannot imagine a world where you don't exist next to me."

I leant closer and rested my head on his shoulder.

"Listen, I love you and you're my eternity too, but your mum is staring at us and I'm kind of worried if I kiss you, she'll blow a blood vessel," I whispered back.

He chuckled and pressed a kiss to my forehead.

"Don't worry, I'll handle her."

He made me sit up and let go of my hand before rising from his seat. Drake dug his hands in his pockets and walked over to his mother, towering over the woman like he did most people. She stared up at him without compunction. May never backed down from a fight.

"You're allowed to feel whatever it is you want about the five of us, but you don't get a say in my life and who I choose to spend it with. If you have a problem with me and the others all being with Scarlett, then I'll take her and walk out of that door. I've already been ambushed by Oscar today. You know I have no issues cutting my family out of my life."

"Your father ambushed you?"

He sighed and removed his hand from his pocket to place it on her shoulder.

"Fletcher decided to trick me into lunch with them. We walked out of the restaurant."

May looked incensed.

"That man knows absolutely no bounds."

"Why do you speak to him?"

"He's still your father, Drake. It's easier this way."

"Easier for who? Him?"

She shook her head.

"No, for me. I will never forgive him for everything he put us through, but I have no wish for animosity between us."

She let out a sigh. There were so many things written across her face, but she took a long minute to voice them.

"I want you to be happy, Drake. The fact you're here and in a relationship... well, I may need some time to deal with my personal feelings on the matter, but it doesn't mean I want you and Scarlett to leave. Please, sit and let me make you lunch."

Drake nodded at his mother before returning to me, taking a seat by my side. May went back to preparing us lunch. I leant into him, wanting his warmth surrounding me. He wrapped his arm around me, pulling me against his chest.

"Are you okay?" he murmured

"I'm with you, of course I'm okay."

"Scarlett..."

"It's fine. I knew she would have a hard time with it. Besides, I've dealt with Eliza, Jasper and Rosie's feelings on the matter. What makes you think I can't cope with your mother?"

He cocked his head to the side as I stared up at him.

"It's less about me thinking you can't deal with it and more you shouldn't have to. I don't want anyone making you feel bad for choosing us."

I stroked his chest, adoring the fact he felt that way.

"Hate to break it to you, but a lot of people aren't going to be very receptive to this."

"Does that bother you?"

I shook my head.

"Is it weird that I didn't really question it when I ended up with all four of you? It was barely a fleeting thought about what it might mean. It has always felt right. Like we're meant to be together. Fighting it seemed futile, you know… like what would be the point in denying ourselves what we need."

It was the truth. I hadn't thought much about it. Being with the four of them had been instinctual. A part of me recognised them as my four best friends. When I remembered them, it was far too fucking late. I'd gone and fallen in love. I couldn't turn back. Couldn't tear them out of my soul. They were too important to me.

"Denying fate is always futile."

"Says the man who thought we were a curse."

He gave me a dark look until I smiled at him.

"If you think I won't punish you because we're at my mother's, you're mistaken," he whispered, leaning closer and nuzzling my hair. "I'll tell her I'm taking you upstairs to see my old bedroom, push you down on my bed and lick your little pussy until you're about to come, then bring you back down here all wet and unfulfilled. You can explain to my mother why you're all flushed and embarrassed."

I was under no illusions about Drake and his punishments. He would carry it out without a second thought if I pushed his buttons hard enough. The thought of sitting through lunch with May when all I'd want was for him to make me come was enough to bring me up short.

"What do I get if I'm good?"

He put his free hand on my thigh, stroking the bare skin.

"Then I'll reward you when we get home, although, I'm quite partial to the idea of fucking you where I used to fantasise about doing so as a teenager."

I buried my face in his shoulder to prevent May from seeing how hot my face was at his words. The thought of Drake touching himself over me was making me want to rub my thighs together.

"Please stop talking, you're making me want things I shouldn't."

"Like what?"

"Watching you touch yourself over me."

"Oh yeah? You want to watch me wrap my hand around my aching dick and stroke one out for you? Will you lick the cum from my stomach afterwards?"

I nodded against his shoulder, absolutely dying with need and embarrassment clashing inside of me. His mother was right there. We weren't speaking loud enough for her to hear what was being said, but even so.

"I think I'm going to need to take you upstairs."

"Drake!"

He laughed. I lifted my head away from his shoulder in time to catch his mother staring at us. That made it all worse. I glared up at him and those blasted indigo eyes twinkling with amusement. Damn this man. Damn him for making me want him so much. And in front of his mother, of all people.

"You are on thin ice, mister," I hissed, sitting up properly to regain my composure. "I do not need you making me wet in front of your mother."

"Does that mean if I touch your pussy, I'll find you wanting?"

He moved his hand higher up my thigh, pushing my dress up with his exploring. I grabbed hold of his fingers and subtly pulled them away, placing his hand back in his own lap. It was then I realised he was in a similar state of arousal to me. The smile playing on my lips at it couldn't be helped. Especially when I looked into his eyes to find desire rippling and threatening to undo everything.

"Later."

"Promise?"

"I'll sit in your lap at your desk and you can do whatever you want to me then."

"Deal."

May came over with lunch a few minutes later, making Drake and I pull apart. She didn't give me a look of disapproval, something I could only be thankful for. The three of us enjoyed a quiet, reminiscent lunch without any further drama. I imagined she didn't want to alienate her son when he was being open with her.

When Drake and I left, May gave me a hug and told me to take care of her boy. I barely got a chance to tell her I would before my sir was whisking me out of the house. Someone was rather impatient to get me back to the office. And I couldn't deny I was looking forward to being alone with him.

THIRTY TWO

FRANCIS

My hands dropped as I finished securing Scarlett's hands above her. Two metal cuffs were around her wrists, attached to chains suspending her from a ring on the ceiling of the playroom. Her knees rested on the bed, spread apart for my viewing pleasure. She couldn't close them as I'd cuffed both of her ankles to a spreader bar.

"Okay?" I asked.

She gave me a nod, as she couldn't talk. I'd given her a ball-gag. Her muffled protests about what was going to happen next would be so sweet.

"And how do you safe word out?"

She clicked her fingers twice.

"Good girl."

Scarlett told me she wanted to play this evening after her encounter with Drake's mother yesterday. She wanted to feel safe under my command, hence why she'd chosen me, but she'd not specified anything else. I had free rein. It's why I'd chained her up the way I had. She wouldn't be able to do anything but watch and take what was given to her.

I got up on the bed in front of her and sat back against the headboard. She eyed me with an intense gaze as if she was trying to work out what I would do next. Picking up a little remote control from the side table, I turned on some sensual music, keeping the volume low.

"You like watching me, don't you, little whore?"

She nodded. This wasn't just for her. A part of me still needed to embrace the way she saw me. I'd fought so hard to stop feeling like I was second best. Scarlett had helped me. This would be another step forward. One that put me slightly out of my comfort zone, but what the fuck was the point in living in a world where you didn't grow. Where you didn't face the things holding you back.

"Keep your eyes on me. I'm going to reward you for being such a good girl."

I shifted up onto my knees and moved closer, within touching distance, but the way she was restrained made it impossible for her to reach out to me. My fingers went to my shirt buttons, undoing the top one as I bit down on my lip. Never in my life did I think I would be giving someone a striptease, but Scarlett was the girl I would do anything for.

Her eyes widened when she realised what I was doing. I undid the next button, taking it slow as I moved to the music slightly. The muffled moan she made kept me going. Each button exposed more of my skin. Her pupils had fully dilated. She shifted, making the chains above her rattle.

"Do you want to touch me, little whore?"

She nodded vigorously, letting out more muffled noises from behind her gag. I smiled and shook my head.

"Not yet."

The whine she made had me undoing the last button. With extra care, I tugged my shirt off, letting it fall onto the bed below me. Then I ran my fingers down my abs, showing her what she was missing. Now the chains were really rattling as she strained towards me. My fingers went to my belt, teasing the buckle.

"Is the sight of me making that pussy wet, hmm?"

Oh, but the sounds she made, trying to talk when she knew she couldn't. Spit dribbled down her chin. I reached out and swiped at it with my thumb before sticking it in my mouth. Her eyes almost bugged out. Her knees shifted. She wanted friction between her legs. Too bad. It was impossible for her to close them.

I tugged the buckle open, undoing my belt to gain access to my zipper. Scarlett's eyes zoned in on my movements. My fingers ran over my straining cock.

"Do you want to see how hard I am for you?"

She tried to move towards me again, her need coming across in her muffled moans of agreement. I reached out and stroked my fingers across her stomach to tease her. The way her chest rose and fell had me running my fingers up to her chest and stroking around her breasts. Her whines were so needy like she was begging me for more. I pulled my hands away and unzipped my trousers.

"Look." I stroked my cock through my boxers. "See how much I want you."

More spit dribbled down her chin. She thrashed in her chains, twisting herself to try to get to me. I smiled at her before shifting off the bed to shuck my trousers. Her eyes followed me, watching as I continued to stroke my cock, but I didn't reveal it to her.

"I'm going to reward you soon, little whore. Give you everything you need." I looked over at the chair in the corner. "We both will."

Scarlett tried to whip her head around to see who I was referring to. She had no idea we weren't alone. She couldn't stretch that far. Her protest behind the ball-gag had me reaching out to stroke her side in order to settle her.

"Be a good girl and keep your attention on me."

Her eyes immediately went to me as I pulled down my boxers, allowing my cock to spring free. I knelt on the bed again, right in front of her as I fisted it between my fingers.

"That's it, watch me. Look at what you do to me."

My hand moved up and down my shaft. She couldn't keep her eyes off it. I couldn't deny I wanted all of her attention. My need unshackled those final chains wrapped around my wrists, holding me back. Her desperation for me made it very clear. I was at the top of her podium. I was first place.

With my free hand, I reached out and cupped her jaw, stroking my thumb across her bottom lip. Then I indicated with my head to the person in the chair they should join us. Drake rose to his full height and stalked towards the bed. His indigo eyes glittered as he came to a standstill behind her. The crop in his hand rose and struck out across her behind, making her cry out as I held her steady.

"Good girl," I soothed, my fingers leaving her chin and wrapping around her neck instead. "I've got you."

He struck again. She took it this time, only a muffled whimper sounding from her throat. She shifted against me, her eyes intent on mine. Then they dropped to where I was still stroking myself. The desperation in her expression had me stroking her throat.

"More?"

She nodded. Drake slapped her with the crop again and again. Her moans were a mixture of pleasure and pain behind the gag. He kept going for a few minutes, then he dropped the crop on the bed and knelt behind her, careful not to disturb the spreader bar. His hands ghosted over her shoulders, making her skin prickle. Then he reached up and unbuckled the gag, discarding it on the bed next to us.

"Frankie," she gasped, "please."

"Do you want me... or do you want him?"

"Both. I want both."

"Well, as much as I'd love to give that to you, it's not what we have planned, my little whore."

Drake shifted out from behind her, moving up the bed and not saying a word as he settled himself against the headboard facing the two of us. I ran my finger down the centre of her chest.

"What... what are you doing?"

"Wait and see."

I moved behind her, pressing myself against her back and cupping her throat with my hand. My other hand slid along her stomach. Drake wasn't wearing anything. His hand was circled around his cock. He'd told me about their conversation yesterday. About how she wanted to watch him. This went one step further. She couldn't touch him. The only relief she'd get was from me.

"Look at him," I murmured in her ear. "Watch him like you wanted to."

While me and Drake weren't into Prescott's kinks, we recognised Scarlett liked to watch and be watched. We were willing to give her anything she wanted, including this.

Before she could say a word, I stuck my fingers in her mouth, making her suck on them in time to his stroking. She shifted against me, my cock slipping between her red cheeks. She moaned around my fingers, rubbing against me the best she could. Her attention was on Drake, but I was the one who could touch her and give her pleasure.

"Do you want me to fuck you?"

Her moan of agreement made me slide my hand lower, delving between her legs and finding out for myself just how wet she was for us. Avoiding her clit, I pressed two fingers inside her. The aim wasn't to let her come but to let her imagine we were both fucking her. One of us in her mouth and the other in her pussy.

Drake's eyes were fixed on her, watching the way she moved against me, trying to gain more friction. My thrusts were shallow and slow as he stroked himself for her. She moaned around my fingers, clearly enjoying what I was doing and the little show she was getting.

"Pres told us how much you liked his surprise. We wanted to give you our own version."

Her whimper around my fingers told me she wanted it too. She needed it.

"Here's what's going to happen. He's going to make himself come for you. Then you're going to clean his cum from his stomach whilst I fuck you. And if you're really good for us, Drake's going to suck your clit until you come all over my cock."

I pulled my fingers from her mouth. She gasped for air for a moment before turning her head slightly.

"I want to be good for you."

My hand wrapped around her throat.

"Watch him."

I pressed kisses to her shoulder as her attention went back to Drake. He didn't speak as he stroked his cock for her viewing pleasure. I kept up my pace, pressing my fingers deeper inside her wet pussy.

"Frankie, please," she whimpered after a few minutes, shifting against me. "It isn't enough."

"You need my cock in you?"

"Please."

I shifted behind her, removing my fingers from her pussy to grab hold of my cock. Pressing it between her lips, I rubbed it back and forth, making her moan as it knocked her clit.

"Shall I fuck you whilst he comes all over his stomach, little whore?"

"Yes, fuck, please."

"You've been such a good girl."

I lined myself up and pushed inside her, groaning at the way she fluttered around me. No doubt, I loved to tease the fuck out of Scarlett and deny her orgasms until she was fit to bursting, but it was pure fucking torture on my end too. All I wanted was to be wrapped up in her this way.

She moaned as I began to fuck her. I kept one hand around her throat as leverage and my other hand angled her body to give me better access.

"Tell him how much you want to see him come," I whispered in her ear. "Give him an incentive to spray his cum all over himself for you to clean up."

Scarlett ran her tongue over her bottom lip as if she was imagining how he'd taste on her lips.

"Sir... I want you to come for me. Show me how much you desire me," she said a moment later, causing Drake's eyes to darken further. "Paint yourself with it so I can clean it from your body. I want to run my tongue over your skin and taste every inch of you."

Drake's hand moved faster and his lips parted on a breath like he wanted to say something, but he had no idea what. As if the driving need to come for her had short-circuited his brain. To be honest, this entire situation was making mine a little fucking loopy too.

"That's it, come, sir, please. I want to see you. Show me."

And on her last word, Drake erupted all over himself, letting out a groan of satisfaction while ropes of cum splattered all over his stomach for Scarlett's personal pleasure.

THIRTY THREE

FRANCIS

Scarlett shifted against me, clearly wanting to go to Drake as he slowed his strokes and stared at her with lust-drunk eyes. As if he'd totally got off on her watching him. Guess we all had an exhibitionist streak. After all, our best friend was into voyeurism. You kind of had to be okay with being watched when Prescott was around.

"Sir, please… I want to taste you," Scarlett panted out.

Drake was slow to rise, taking his time to stand up and walk across the bed to us. He stood in front of Scarlett. His head canted as he took her in as if assessing whether he was going to help her lick the cum from him or not. Then he put his hand out to her, offering the sticky liquid he'd got on it to her first. Scarlett didn't hesitate to suck on his fingers, cleaning every last drop from his hand like it was her finest meal.

"Did you like that, little wisp?" he murmured, shifting closer. "Do you want some more?"

"Please."

He wrapped his hand around the back of her head and directed her towards his stomach. With the way I'd chained her up, he was going to have to help her reach his body. He held onto the chains above her with his other hand and angled himself to allow her to lick the cum from him. Scarlett watched him as she did it. The way they stared at each other was almost mesmerising. The love and desire written all over their faces had me swallowing hard from the intensity of their feelings.

You'd think it would make me jealous to know how much she loved Drake and the others, but it didn't. We were meant for each other. All four of us were hers, completely and irrevocably. We were each other's too, forged in friendship and blood. Bound for life in a way few would understand.

When she'd cleaned up every part of him, he let her go to kneel in front of her. He cupped her face above my hand around her throat and brushed his thumb over her bottom lip.

"My good girl deserves her reward."

She watched him lower himself further, his fingers sliding down her body until he circled her hips with his large hands. She shivered as he bent his head. There was no hesitation as his tongue sought out her clit. I continued to fuck her, groaning in her ear with each stroke.

"Oh god," she cried out.

"That's it, little whore, let him make you come."

"Please, sir."

Drake didn't let up, licking her like a man fucking starving for a taste of his woman. And it pushed Scarlett over the edge. She shook with her climax, clenching down hard on my cock. I tightened my fingers around her throat, holding back from spilling my cum inside her. It was a heady experience having her come apart on me like this. The very best kind of ending.

Her head lolled when she was spent. Drake sat back on his hands, staring at her with a smug smile. I merely hammered into her harder until I was coming apart too, unable to help myself.

"Little whore," I grunted, pressing my face into her hair.

I pulled away after placing a kiss on her shoulder, dropping down on the bed to catch my breath. She hung there, watching Drake, who was rubbing his thumb over his bottom lip. Reaching over to her ankles, I undid the cuffs and tossed away the bar, letting her close her legs even as my cum leaked from her pussy. I shifted up the bed to sit back against the headboard, leaving her there to wonder why I wasn't letting her go.

"Frankie?"

The frown on her face made me want to wipe it away.

"Did you think it was just me and Drake?"

"What?"

There was a reason I'd only turned the lights above the bed on. Scarlett had no idea all four of us had been in the room the entire time. West and Prescott emerged from the shadows and knelt on the bed behind her.

"Hello, little lamb… you gave us quite the show."

She turned her head, spying him coming around to her side and pressing a kiss to her shoulder. Prescott wasted no time leaning lower and covering her nipple with his mouth. She let out a moan as West came up behind her and pressed her back against him. I leant over, picked up the lube and chucked it over to him. He caught it before popping the cap open and giving me a wink. Drake shifted up to sit next to me, allowing Prescott to come around to her front and continue playing with her tits.

Prescott left her nipples a moment later to adjust the chains to give her more slack. Then he lowered her into his lap, forcing her to slide down on his cock. She didn't have time to say anything as he kissed her, cupping the back of her head to angle her face. Scarlett let out a sharp gasp in Prescott's mouth as West prepared her for what would happen next.

"You've been such a good little slut for Drake and Frankie," West told her. "You're going to be one for us too."

Prescott released her mouth, his hands on her hips to move them at the pace he wanted to set.

"Yes, I want to be good for you… be your good little slut too," she panted.

West wrapped his hand around her neck, turning her face to him with his thumb. Her mouth was claimed a moment later in a bruising kiss that was West all over. He never did anything by halves. It was all or nothing.

When he let go, he grinned at her.

"Are you ready to take my cock too? I can feel how much you want it. My dirty bitch is in heat, isn't she?"

"Yes, yes, please. Fuck, please, West."

"Good girl."

He shifted back to coat his cock, leaving Prescott to kiss her again, his hands running over her body while she took over and rode him the best she could with her hands chained above her head. West gripped her hip and pressed inside her. She whined but didn't tell him to stop as he slowly worked his way up into her tight little hole. I couldn't take my eyes off them.

The raw passion between those three was enough to make my dick twitch. Getting hard again wasn't the goal here, but fuck, anything to do with Scarlett had me rising to the occasion. Especially hearing the neediness in her voice. The way she moaned as they fucked her. I couldn't get enough.

"I never thought I would understand Pres' fascination with watching… until her," Drake murmured low enough so only I could hear.

"Could it be because you're in… luurrve?"

Drake gave me a dark look.

"Fuck off."

I poked his side.

"Go on, you can admit it. I won't give you a hard time."

"You literally just did."

"You do love her though."

"And?"

I grinned. He was just being stubborn for the sake of it.

"We're all glad you got with the fucking program."

He rolled his eyes, but I could see him trying not to smile.

"She's hard to say no to."

"Or perhaps you just don't want to."

He shrugged.

"That too."

I turned my attention back to the others. I couldn't help it. They were a sight I didn't want to miss a second of. Scarlett was in the midst of being bitten on the shoulder by Prescott while West held her neck and pounded into her from behind.

"That's it, slut, take it… let him claim you."

"Please, harder."

Prescott responded by shifting lower and biting her right underneath her war scar. She cried out with a mix of pleasure and pain. Just as I liked to see her skin covered in indents from ropes, Prescott liked to leave bite marks and bruises all over her. For him, it was a primal instinct. For me, the patterns of the ropes were my form of art, a painting on her body of my claim over her.

"You ready for tomorrow night?" I asked, hesitant to bring it up, but knowing all of us were a little on edge because of it.

"Yes, and no." Drake sighed and rubbed his face. "We're relying on things going to plan. Nothing ever does."

I slapped his arm before shifting onto my knees, wanting to get closer to the threesome in front of us. Drawn to the sexual energy radiating off them.

"Pres always tells us to take risks."

Drake raised an eyebrow.

"Since when did you gain a devil may care attitude?"

I moved closer to Prescott, West and Scarlett.

"Since I realised we're stronger together than apart and we have a bigger incentive than Stuart does." Reaching for Scarlett, I stroked her face as she turned it to me. "Her."

I looked back at Drake. The contemplation on his face had me grinning. I pressed a kiss to Scarlett's mouth, wanting to get lost in her and leave Drake to his own thoughts. Much to my surprise, he arrived on her other side and stole her mouth from me. I put my hands on her instead, pressing one between her and Prescott to seek out her clit. She bucked against him and West, jerking in their hold and moaning in Drake's mouth.

"You're going to come all over them, aren't you, little whore?"

She moaned again. I moved my fingers faster, circling her clit the way I knew she liked. It was the catalyst. She released Drake's mouth and threw her head back on West's shoulder, crying out with her release. It had Prescott gripping her hips and slamming her down on them until he was grunting. That was shortly followed by West, who couldn't contain himself either.

I sat back, watching the three of them come down from their highs. When West and Prescott let her go, I sat up again. My fingers went to her cuffs, getting them undone so she could lower her arms. Drake was there, catching her and cradling her against his chest. Prescott took one of her wrists and rubbed down her arm before doing the other. Then Drake took her up to the top of the bed and stroked her skin until she'd fully recovered.

"That was... unexpected," she said, looking around at us.

"In a good way?" I asked.

"In the best possible way."

She gave me a smile and reached out her hand. I placed mine in it, letting her squeeze my fingers. Then I let go to get wipes for Drake to clean her up with. The five of us sorted ourselves out. Prescott and West each kissed Scarlett goodnight before retreating to their rooms, leaving me with Drake and Scarlett.

I put my hand out to her as I stood next to the bed. She crawled out of Drake's lap and took it, letting me help her up. Her eyes went back to Drake as if she didn't want to leave him. I leant closer, brushing her hair over her shoulder and kissing one of the bite marks Prescott had left on there.

"Do you want us both tonight?"

Her attention came back to me.

"I already had you both."

"I meant to sleep in between."

She chewed on her lip. I straightened, then my eyes went to Drake.

"Your room or mine?"

He rubbed his cheek.

"Mine."

I took hold of Scarlett's hand as he rose, snagged my boxers from the floor and tugged her towards the door. She glanced back at Drake as if she was surprised by him allowing me to spend the night with them. Drake passed us as we walked to his bedroom and opened the door. I pulled Scarlett in with me, shutting the door behind me and pressing her towards the bed. Drake was getting a clean pair of shorts from his wardrobe as I slid my boxers back on. Scarlett sat on the end of his bed with her eyes intent on both of us as we approached her.

"Get in, little wisp."

I tried not to smile at his commanding tone. She scrambled back and got under the covers. He got in on the right side and me, the left. I immediately cuddled up to Scarlett, not giving a shit what Drake had to say. As far as I was concerned, the moment he agreed to this, all bets were off. Scarlett put her arms around me, nuzzling my bare chest with her nose.

It took Drake a minute to curl himself around her back, resting his hand on her waist above where I was holding her. She let out a soft, contented sigh, pressing a kiss to my skin.

"I love you."

"Which one of us?" I asked, knowing full well what she actually meant.

"Both. I love you both with all my heart."

"Love you too, Scar."

I closed my eyes, feeling relaxed and wanting to fall into oblivion to forget what we were going to do tomorrow. Scarlett shifted, burrowing herself further into both of us. I could feel her pressing back against Drake, clearly wanting more of him against her. I could hear him let out a huff and couldn't help my smile.

"Comfortable?" he asked a moment later.

"No, you're being a statue again. You didn't have to agree to sleep with both of us. Relax, or you can go sleep over there and I'll stay here with Frankie."

That made him let out another huff. I cracked an eye open to watch him shift against her, clearly trying to get more comfortable himself. He pressed a kiss to her shoulder and curled his hand around her stomach, stroking it with his fingers. It meant he was touching me, but I didn't give a fuck. Drake had been in my life for as long as I could remember. He was my best friend.

"I'm sorry," Drake whispered against her skin. "Can I kiss you goodnight?"

Scarlett turned her head to look at him, her eyes soft.

"Of course you can."

He did just that, giving her a soft kiss. With each stroke of his mouth against hers, I could see the tension leaving him until he sagged against her. Then he let her mouth go and Scarlett rested her cheek back on the pillow, a small smile playing on her lips. All of us lapsed into silence. I closed my eyes again, starting to drift off with her soft breaths lulling me to sleep.

Before I dropped off, I heard Drake whispering, "I love you, little wisp," to Scarlett. And I knew he was as invested in this relationship with her as the rest of us.

THIRTY FOUR

SCARLETT

W est looked over at me as we turned into the private road that led up to the estate where I'd spent ten years locked up and unable to leave. I tried not to fidget in my seat, knowing I had an important role to play. Being here again made my stomach twist into knots. It brought back horrifying memories I wanted to push down into the recesses of my mind. And I hated everything about it.

"Little Scar."

"I'm fine."

"No, you're not."

I sighed and worried the seatbelt at my chest with my gloved fingers. I wore all black, just like the others. Tonight would be messy and the blood would be less conspicuous on black.

"I keep thinking about it… about what he did to me here."

West stroked my shoulder with his free hand while keeping his eye on the dark road. We were about to come up to the security gate. Two people were stationed there twenty-four-seven. The fence around the estate loomed, making me tremble. It was built high to keep people out, like this was some kind of fucking military base. Stuart was far too paranoid for his own good. When you make enemies of the Four Horsemen, you should be concerned about your safety. And keeping them away from the girl you kidnapped. Stuart was stupid enough to let me out of my cage. He made a grave error of judgement, thinking he'd done enough to keep me on his side. Fear didn't breed absolute loyalty. Love did.

"Take a deep breath and remember I've got you."

I did as he said, dropping my hand to grip the syringe sitting in my lap and hiding it beneath my sleeve. The planning we'd done for the past couple of weeks was all coming to fruition. We'd had to create a diversion when we left Fortuity to make sure Stuart's spies wouldn't discover we were coming for him tonight. That required enlisting Penn's help.

His men had driven all four of the boy's cars out the car park under Fortuity and had them all go off in different directions to send them on a merry chase. We'd left the building on foot and made our way to the cars Penn had provided for us a few streets over with all our supplies already inside. Then we'd left London behind us to travel to Stuart's estate in Kent.

West pulled the car up outside the security gate. One of the men inside came out and looked the car over before tapping on the window. The floodlights on the gates were shining in our damn faces, but I turned and wound down the window. Then I smiled at him when he recognised me, his blue eyes bugging out.

"Hello, Sam."

Before he had a chance to say a word, I reached out through the window, grabbed a hold of his shirt and pulled him down. I stabbed him with the hidden needle, pressing down on the plunger.

I shoved him back, causing him to stumble. The other man was coming out of the building, but he was met by Francis, who had been hiding in the back and had slipped out while Sam was occupied. He had a needle in his gloved hands. Francis grabbed hold of the other guard from behind and stabbed him in the neck. The man cried out and struggled against him, but Francis ripped the needle out and kicked him on the ground, holding him down with a foot to his back.

West got out of the car, putting his phone to his ear to let Drake and Prescott, who were in the car behind us, know we were ready for them. Then he looked up at the camera sitting above the gate and smiled. We weren't taking any prisoners tonight.

I slid out and walked over to Sam. He'd dropped to his knees. I stared down at him with disgust. Then I shoved him over onto his back and gave him a smile.

"You can go to hell, you sadistic fuck."

I'd injected him with cyanide, as had Frankie with the other guy. He would be dead within minutes. I didn't give a shit. He'd said some pretty nasty things to me while shoving me in the cell for Stuart. Not to mention the times he'd kicked me in the stomach for good measure. He deserved to die painfully. To be honest, everyone on the estate deserved it. They were all complicit in holding me captive.

West walked into the security building to work out how to open the gate. Francis looked over at me, a slight look of concern on his face.

"You okay, Scar?"

I shook my head. I wouldn't be okay until this was over with. Until everyone was dead. Until I'd destroyed this place where I'd been brainwashed and held against my will for ten years. It would be my fucking reckoning. I'd never believed in revenge or an eye for an eye, but what Stuart had done to me... it was unforgivable. This wasn't revenge. It was justice.

I put my hand up when he made to walk over to me. If any of them comforted me during this, I might break. They could catch me when I fell, but only after we'd destroyed Stuart Carver for good. Right now, falling apart was not an option.

"Let me do this. I need to."

Francis gave me a nod, but the concern didn't leave his face.

This was personal for me. I was the one who'd been kidnapped. I'd been stolen from my life. I was the one who'd make them all fucking pay.

Drake and Prescott pulled the second car up behind us, both getting out. Prescott immediately came over to me. My eyes were on Sam, whose breathing was shallow now. He'd passed out a minute ago.

"Take him to the car," I said, my voice hollow.

Prescott put a hand on my arm and gave it a squeeze. I turned away and got back in the car to wait for them to deal with the men and the gate. My hands splayed out over the dashboard as I took a deep breath, bowing my head to try to regain some semblance of control over my warring emotions.

I vaguely heard the gate opening before West and Francis got back into the car. West started it and then we were moving. I looked up, watching the dark road ahead of us and the trees surrounding the estate.

The moment the main house came into view, I sat back and put my hand over my mouth, bile rising up in my throat. My prison held ugly memories. Being back at the scene of the crime was horrific. My low moan of fear had Francis reaching forward and squeezing my shoulder. He said nothing, just gave me the reassurance they were all here for me.

West pulled the car up near the fancy turning circle in front of the house with a fountain in the middle of it. Drake and Prescott stopped next to us, getting out of the car a moment later. The two men we'd poisoned were in the back of their car.

I stared at the building in front of us through the windscreen. It was strange to see it all lit up, given it was nearing eleven o'clock at night. Dark deeds were best done at night when the country was sleeping. When no one would be any the wiser until the morning light arrived.

"Ready, little Scar?"

My eyes flicked to West. Seeing his amber eyes so full of love had me taking another deep breath and unbuckling my seatbelt. I could do this. I had my boys with me.

"As I'll ever be."

The three of us got out of the car, joining Drake and Prescott, who stared at the estate with thinned mouths and angry expressions on their faces. They knew what had gone down in the walls of this place.

You'd think we would have had a party to meet us with all the security Stuart had for this place. I smiled. He didn't account for how much I knew about his fucking estate. Instead of guards, there was a single man waiting for us at the front door.

I walked over to him as the boys got the two men out of the car. Gio had a tight smile on his face when I stood before him.

"Hey."

"Miss," he replied with a nod.

"Is it done?"

"Yes. It wasn't easy, but you shouldn't have any trouble."

I hadn't told him what we were going to do to everyone, but I'm sure he was more than aware. After all, the boys had threatened his life if he didn't help us. This had been the hardest part of our plan, getting Gio alone so we could have a conversation with him. Of all the people in Stuart's employ, his chef had been the only one who was nice to me. Everyone here was complicit in what had been done to me, but I had no interest in harming this man. He'd given me comforts no one else had, like the birthday cake he'd made for me last year when I'd been locked in the cell. The memory of Mason giving it to me was sour, but that wasn't Gio's fault.

"You should get out of here."

He reached out and squeezed my shoulder.

"Live well, Scarlett."

Then he walked away towards the car nearby. If he said a word or revealed his involvement in this to anyone, the boys would hunt him down and end his life. He knew that. They hadn't wanted to let him go. Gio wasn't innocent, but his help had meant we could destroy this place and get away with it. At least, that was the plan.

I watched him start the car and drive away towards the road leading off the estate. The one we'd just driven along.

The boys joined me, Prescott and Drake, carrying the two men who were now dead. I stared up at the house, dreading having to walk inside. It wasn't a place I had any interest in returning to, but soon it would be gone. Eviscerated from the world. I kept that in mind as I stepped into the lobby through the open front doors.

The building had two large wings on either side of the centre part. One of them was for the staff, the other for Stuart and Phoebe. The middle part held all the entertaining rooms, places for the public when Stuart held dinners and parties here. I was never allowed to attend those, but I'd snuck out and watched on several occasions just to see something outside of my limited worldview. I got caught a lot, landing me in the cell, but it didn't stop me. My need for something more outweighed the risk.

The lobby was a grand affair with a staircase curled around each side ending in a landing overlooking the marble floor below. My footsteps echoed around the vast space as I made my way into the centre of it and looked up at the painted ceiling. Stuart had commissioned the artwork when I was still in my teens after he'd visited the Sistine Chapel in the Vatican. He liked over the top shit to demonstrate his wealth and influence. Everyone always admired it when they walked in. I personally thought it was excessive, but there was no accounting for taste. Everything about Stuart Carver was lavish and fucking gaudy if you asked me.

West came to a stand next to me, his eyes darting around the place as he rested a sledgehammer on his shoulder. His face was a picture of disgust.

"What the fuck is this shit?" He waved at the ceiling with his free hand. "Who does he think he is? The lord of the fucking manor? What a cunt."

"You could say that. He likes to show off his wealth."

"This is a fucking neon sign blaring in your damn face saying look at me, I'm so far up my own arse, I can see the fucking sun. Jesus, if I didn't hate the guy already, this would make me want to bash his head in on sight." He spat on the floor. "Fucker knows no bounds."

I couldn't help breaking out into a smile at his words. His words shoved their way through my paralysing fear of being back here. Reaching out, I laced my fingers with his, making him look down at me as Francis dumped a bag down next to me.

"You can bash his head in later. First, let's make sure Gio did what we asked. I'm ready to end this."

West grinned at me. This was it. There was no going back. We had committed to ending Stuart for good. And nothing would stop us now.

THIRTY FIVE

SCARLETT

The first place we needed to check was the security room. This was key to our plan going off without a hitch. Not that I imagined any plan we had would end up the way we envisioned, but we couldn't afford to go off script unless circumstances changed.

Prescott and Drake dumped the two dead security guys in the lobby and shut the front door. I squatted down, opened the bag Francis had brought and pulled out a crowbar, swinging it between my fingers when I stood up.

"Careful with that," Drake said.

I turned to him.

"Why? Do you think I'm going to hit you with it?"

The way he smiled had my heart thumping.

"No, but if you're planning on bludgeoning anyone to death, warn us first."

I winked, then took a deep breath, reminding myself I had nothing to fear here. We had the upper hand. We'd done everything in our power to make sure this was as painless as possible… for us. It wasn't going to be painless for them. We planned to make it hurt.

"If you want to kill someone that way, I brought the sledgehammer. Much more effective," West said as I started towards the staff wing.

I shook my head, trying not to imagine what kind of damage West would do a human being with it. The house was eerily quiet, even at this time of night. I could only hope for the best and expect the worst. Gio wouldn't have been able to get to everyone. We knew that, but the important people would be none the wiser as to who had just entered the main house.

The security room wasn't far off the lobby and, as expected, was locked. There was one thing about this old house no one had thought to replace. The fucking wooden doors. I stepped back, waving at it. West gave me a grin before stepping up to it. Then he looked up at the camera blinking above it.

"Did you think this flimsy piece of shit would keep us out?" he said before his foot slammed into the door, making it groan under the impact.

He took a step back, taking the hammer off his shoulder, and proceeded to smash the door repeatedly. It lay in pieces by the time he'd finished. I was the first one to step through, holding the crowbar tight in my fist.

The man in the room scrambled back away from the safe he was trying to get into and looked like he was about to shit himself.

"Well, hello, Alex. I bet you didn't think you would see me again."

I looked back to find West had followed me in.

"Tell Drake it's bludgeoning time."

Then I turned to Alex, head of fucking security and the biggest cunt out of all of them. I swung the crowbar back and forth as I approached him. He backed up into his chair, his knees buckling under him.

"Scarlett…"

"You fucked with the wrong girl."

West came around and forced him into the chair. He stood behind Alex, holding the man down for me. I pressed the crowbar into his chest, making him wince.

"Who knows we're here?"

"N-n-no one."

I canted my head, pressing the points of the bar harder against him.

"Are you sure about that?"

"Yes! Everyone else is…"

"Is what, Alex?"

He looked towards the screens.

"Passed out. I was going to phone the police, then you all barged in here."

"A likely fucking story."

Pulling the bar away from his chest, I brought it down on his hand instead. He screamed at the impact, the sound of bones snapping filling the air.

"How long until you noticed, huh? Or were you too busy wanking over porn as usual?"

The only reason I knew about Alex's proclivities was due to overhearing two guards complaining about walking in on him masturbating in here. There were a lot of things I'd heard in the past ten years I probably shouldn't have. I stored it all away. When you lose your memory, keeping your new ones becomes imperative. I never wanted to forget anything again. Guess it worked in my favour. I could tell the boys information about the estate they couldn't have found out any other way.

"I... I... only a few minutes before you got here. I was..."

"Wanking."

"Yes."

West snorted but didn't say anything. Why was I not surprised? For all Stuart's paranoia and security protocols, he hadn't employed the most vigilant of men to do the job.

"Well, it's too fucking bad for you. If you'd been paying attention, maybe you would have seen us kill your fucking security at the gate. Now... you're going to die too because of your own stupidity."

I brought the crowbar down on his other hand, making him scream again. Tears slid down his cheeks, but I didn't care. This man wasn't worth my pity or regret. He was worthless scum. He'd taunted me more times than I could remember. Sometimes when they threw me in the cell, he came in and beat me further for good measure. He made my life hell. I wasn't going to let him get away with it. No one here deserved my mercy.

"That's it, Alex, cry like a little fucking baby. Maybe in your next life, you won't try to manhandle women like they mean nothing, you worthless piece of shit."

The way he blubbered had me watching him for a moment. I gripped the crowbar at the end with both hands and swung it, smacking him across the side of the head. The crack of his skull sent a shiver down my spine, but I didn't stop there. Blow after blow came until he was bleeding profusely from the shattered side of his face. His eyes were open, but dull and lifeless.

I looked at the bloodied crowbar. A sick sort of satisfaction washed over me. Francis' words from the day I first killed clicked into place. The thrill of taking another life. One who had hurt you. Who had given you too much pain.

Justice. This is justice. Every part of it.

Reaching out, I used Alex's shirt to wipe away his blood from my weapon. West had let go of him after the first blow came, knowing it would have knocked him out. He leant back against the desk, watching me with pride.

"My little warrior has sharp claws."

I shoved the chair with Alex in out of the way before stepping up to West. Placing the crowbar on the desk, I looked up at the man I'd loved my whole life.

"Your little warrior is a goddess."

He brushed my cheek with his knuckles.

"My goddess of the night."

"If you two are quite done mooning over each other," Drake's voice came from behind us. "We've got to find out where the fuck that cunt has got to."

West wrapped an arm around me, pulling me away from the desk to give Drake room. He strode right up to it, but not before giving me a smile as if he was proud of me too.

Prescott whistled as he walked in and saw Alex. He nudged Francis when he followed and indicated me and West with a nod of his head.

"Peas in a pod, those two."

Francis rolled his eyes and went over to help Drake. They'd obviously heard Alex screaming and knew what to expect when they came in.

Prescott came over to us. West kept his arm around me, holding me to his chest as if letting go would tear him in half. Prescott, on the other hand, leant down and pressed a kiss to my forehead.

"My brave little lamb."

"More like your murderous little lamb."

He laughed.

"That too."

"For fuck's sake," Drake ground out, making me turn to the screens.

"What is it?"

He pointed at them.

"They're all over the place, not in their rooms. We're going to have to stage everyone and that's going to add time."

My eyes scanned over the screens, finding he was right. The staff had all passed out where they stood. Gio had drugged the food and spiked drinks. We'd got him the drugs to knock everyone out, but we knew there would be outliers like Alex he wouldn't be able to get to. I was sure there would be other security guards in the building too. We just had to find them.

"There's a plan for the building, along with everyone's room assignments," I said, pointing at the board to their right. "We can't afford to leave them where they are. Now, where's Stuart?"

Drake flicked between more cameras until we came across a room with two people passed out inside. Stuart and Phoebe were both slumped on a sofa. It would have taken time for the drugs to work through their system.

"Here."

"That's their private sitting room."

Drake stared at the screens for a long moment. Then he straightened and turned to all of us.

"We only have limited time before the drugs wear off. Francis, I want you to restrain Stuart and Phoebe. Take Pres with you. If you find anyone along the way, you know what to do with them."

We needed to take their lives. Everyone here would die. It was the only way we could guarantee no witnesses. No one would ever know the truth of what we'd done.

"West and I will start dealing with the rest of the staff and make sure all the security is dead. Scarlett, you can direct where everyone goes. Remember, we need to make it look like they were all in their beds, okay?" He pointed at Alex. "This fuck can stay here. He was meant to be watching the screens all night."

"We need to search Stuart's office too," I put in.

"We can do that later... after everyone is dead."

I nodded and gave him a smile. We weren't going to leave without going through his shit. This man had haunted our lives for ten years. He'd made mine a living hell. We needed to find out everything we could before we razed this place to the fucking ground.

Francis dug the things we needed out of the bag and handed them to Prescott and Drake. Then we were looking over routes and moving out. I held West back for a moment, eyeing the safe with suspicion.

"Do you think we can get this open?"

He looked at it, then at his sledgehammer.

"We're better off finding the combination. Would take too much time."

I nodded and followed him out. While I wanted to know what Alex was trying to access, in the grand scheme of things, it wasn't important.

"What are you two doing?" Drake asked, crossing his arms over his chest as we emerged from the security room.

"Nothing, let's go," West said, adjusting the hammer on his shoulder and walking off in the direction of the staff living room where we'd identified a few people who had lost their battle with consciousness.

Drake and I walked after him, me gripping the crowbar tight in my fist. I wasn't planning on killing anyone else with it, but it made me feel safer.

"Are you okay?" Drake asked after a moment.

"I guess so. Being back here is… difficult."

I was keeping my memories at bay, trying not to think too hard about what was done to me here. Killing Alex had been cathartic, but I wouldn't feel okay until everyone who had hurt me here was eradicated from the world.

He reached out and tucked me up against his side as we continued walking. I nuzzled his jumper, feeling his warmth and presence surrounding me. Drake could be cold, but with me, he'd changed. There was tenderness and affection in his gestures. He had more than proven he was willing to do anything for me. The fact he'd stood up to his mother in the face of her disapproval over our relationship spoke volumes. Not to mention him allowing Francis to sleep in his bed with us last night. After he'd relaxed, he'd drifted off quickly, leaving me between two slumbering men I loved fiercely. They were my shelter. My safety. And I'd fallen asleep knowing they'd protect me until their dying breaths.

The five of us would be each other's guardians. We'd fight until the very end.

"I know this isn't easy for you, little wisp. I want you to know I'm proud of you for coming here."

I held back the emotions swirling in my gut from his words.

"You're going to make me cry," I whispered.

He leant down and kissed my forehead before straightening.

"When we're done, you can fall apart and we'll put your pieces back in place together as a family. Okay?"

I nodded, knowing I had the strength of my four men behind me.

We reached the staff living room and stepped in after West, who was surveying three of the people in here.

"Who are they?" he asked, swinging the hammer down and placing it on the floor with the handle sticking up.

I walked over and checked each person.

"Norman, Granger and Mirabelle." I pointed at each of them in turn. "Why?"

"Do you want to kill any of them?"

I bit my lip and shook my head. They were the groundskeepers and had never given me any trouble. West cracked his knuckles and dug out his knife.

"Then allow us to do the honours."

Drake flicked out his own knife, then the two of them approached the three groundskeepers. They were dispatched with ease. One quick strike between the ribs to the heart. Drake taking the first two and West the last one.

"Right, where do we put them?" Drake asked, looking over at me with a smile.

I tossed my crowbar from hand to hand, having memorised the room assignments. It was time to stage the bodies.

"Follow me."

THIRTY SIX

SCARLETT

After we'd deposited the bodies in their bedrooms, we walked out and heard a noise. The three of us froze. Drake put a finger to his lips and signalled to West he was going to check it out. I moved closer to West as Drake broke off from us, creeping in the direction of the noise. West took my hand and pulled me in the other direction towards the stairs. We still had a job to do. Drake could handle whatever that was alone.

When we were far enough away after making our way downstairs, West pulled me into the kitchen, somewhere I'd been many times in the past. We made our way over to the pantry, finding Cecilia, Gio's assistant, passed out there. West set his hammer down, pulled her out of the pantry and placed her on the large kitchen island. His eyes went to me.

"This one?"

I shook my head. She wasn't that bad compared to the other staff. The housekeeper, Moira, was the one I hated the most. Stuart had a fucking butler too. Gendry. He was a cunt who gave me shit for anything I did wrong. When I found him, I wanted to cave his head in with West's sledgehammer, not that I thought I could wield it. Maybe I would find another way of ending his sorry existence.

West took out his knife and ran it along her throat, staring down at Cecilia with a dark gleam in his eyes.

"How would you like me to kill her, little Scar?"

I looked her over. She'd merely turned a blind eye to the abuse dished out by the others. It didn't make her any better than them.

"We can't have her bleeding out everywhere in here."

He set his knife down and pulled out a syringe from his pocket, flipping the cap off.

"Cyanide it is then."

I watched him inject Cecilia in the neck. She was unconscious so wouldn't feel any pain. I suppose that was a small mercy, not that I believed she should have any. In this situation, beggars couldn't be choosers. We were here to dispatch them all with efficiency.

He put the cap back on the syringe, pocketed it with his knife, then indicated the hammer with his head. I took a hold of the handle while he put Cecilia over his shoulder. Then we left the room, me dragging the sledgehammer long behind us.

We walked down the hallway towards the stairs leading up to the staff bedrooms where we'd just come from. I left the hammer at the bottom of the stairs for West to collect later.

We deposited Cecilia in the room she shared with one of the maids, Jemma, who had been asleep in her bed. West had taken a knife to her, uncaring about the bloodshed. I'd said

334

nothing, merely watched him kill her with a fatal wound to her heart.

"Is there anyone specific you want to kill yourself?" he asked me when we were walking back down the stairs.

"The butler and the housekeeper."

"Did you see where they were on the cameras?"

I nodded. They were in the family wing. We could circle back if there was anyone else left when we were done.

"Let's go find the fuckers then."

We made our way back to the lobby, where West deposited his sledgehammer, knowing we had no further use for it right now, and across to the other wing. I swung the crowbar as I walked. West kept checking me to see if I was okay. Keeping my mind off the memories of this place was difficult, but I kept my shit together. Being in the family wing was worse. This is where I'd lived for ten years. Where everything had happened to me.

"What did they do to you?"

"Gave me shit all the time. They said things... called me names and made me feel worthless."

I swallowed as we entered the family sitting room. In the far corner, the two of them had passed out with their clothes in disarray. My lip curled up in disgust as we approached them.

"Well, well, looks like these two were having quite the party in here," West said, looking them over with a sneer. "Would they be in their rooms at this hour or should we fuck them up and leave them here?"

Seeing Gendry's limp dick hanging out of his clothes made me sick. Made me see fucking red.

"We need to move them into his bedroom."

I didn't tell West what I was planning to do when we got them into the butler's room. We heard a noise behind us and found Prescott walking in. He had blood on his face.

"Just in time," West said. "Help me with these two."

"Where's Frankie?" I asked as Prescott came over to us. "And what did you do?" I pointed at his face.

"He's keeping an eye on Stuart. We ran into some trouble on the way, a couple of guards who were still awake." He grinned, blood-lust written all over his face. "Don't worry, they aren't breathing any longer."

Prescott and West lifted up Gendry and Moira. West waved at me to lead the way. We retraced our steps to the staff wing. I noticed the two guards were no longer in the lobby.

"Did you move those two?" I asked Prescott.

"Yeah, we took them to the big dormitory bedroom you said the guards stayed in."

I nodded as we walked up the stairs and got to Gendry's bedroom. Before the boys could put them down, I dragged a chair into the middle of the room.

"Put him here. Do you have any rope or something to secure him with?"

"Why?" West asked, depositing the man down in the chair.

"I'm going to wake him up. I would rather he be witness to his own demise."

"What about this one?" Prescott asked.

"Put her on the bed. He can watch me kill her."

Prescott did as I asked, looking over at West with a raised eyebrow as if he wasn't expecting me to be quite this ruthless. Well, those two were in for quite the experience. He pulled out a couple of cable ties from his pockets and squatted behind Gendry, securing his arms for me. It would have to do.

I went into his bathroom and poured a glass of water before coming back out. Then I threw it in Gendry's face.

"Wakey, wakey," I shouted at him, slapping him across the cheek.

He jerked into consciousness, spluttering and blinking. It took him a minute to recover from being drugged. Then he stared at me with wide eyes when he realised we'd secured him to the chair.

"Scarlett?"

"Yeah, it's me. And before you ask, no, I'm not answering any of your fucking questions."

I slapped his face again for good measure before walking away towards Moira.

"You see, Gendry, we're here to kill you. But first, I'm going to gut this bitch."

"W-w-what?"

West came over and handed me his knife, giving me a smile before he stepped back with Prescott. I'd told them all before we came here I wanted to be in on the murder. I didn't want them to stop me from taking lives.

Before Gendry could say another word, I stabbed Moira in the guts and twisted the knife, tearing it through her flesh. She would bleed out all over the fucking bed, but I no longer cared. My gloved hand was covered in blood as I turned around. Gendry looked white as a fucking sheet when I approached him again.

"She called me a dirty little whore and made me feel like shit. You, on the other hand, tried to force yourself on me.

337

Don't think I've forgotten. You're fucking lucky Stuart didn't want me sullied or no doubt that cunt Alex wouldn't have pulled you off me."

His bottom lip trembled as I looked down at where his dick was still hanging out.

"Do you know he's dead now? I bashed his fucking head in. But what you deserve… well, that's so much worse."

I didn't want to touch him like this, but my disgust with this man made me do it. Reaching down, I grabbed a hold of his dick and then I was sawing through the flesh with West's knife. The horrific screams emitting from Gendry's mouth were ignored. When I severed his dick from his body, I smiled at him before shoving the limp organ in his wide open mouth.

"That's it, take it like a good fucking boy."

He choked and tried to spit it out, but I refused to let him. While I held his dick in his mouth, I stabbed him between his ribs right where West had explained to me the heart was. I did it again for good measure before stepping back and watching him choke on his own dick while he bled out.

"Well, remind me never to get on your bad side," Prescott said from next to me.

I looked up at him with a smile.

"He deserved it."

He leant down and kissed my forehead.

"He more than deserved it."

I turned to West, noting the way his amber eyes gleamed with violence.

"I think that's everyone… we should meet up with Frankie."

West gave me a nod before he strode over to Gendry, hauled him off the chair and threw him on the bed on top of Moira, not giving a shit about how he was placed. I put the chair back where it should be by his desk and washed my bloodied gloves off in the bathroom.

"Let's go."

The three of us made our way across to the family wing and upstairs to the private sitting room. Francis was sitting in one of the armchairs scrolling through his phone. He looked up when the three of us entered. Stuart and Phoebe were both tied up. I noted Francis had shaped harnesses around them using ropes and chains. His attention to detail made me smile.

"Have they woken up?" Prescott asked, leaning against the wall.

"Not yet," Francis replied as he got up, stuffing his phone back in his pocket.

I looked around the place.

"Have you seen Drake?"

"No, I thought he was with you and West."

I shook my head.

"He was until he heard a noise and went to investigate."

Retracing my steps, I walked back outside the room and looked down the hallway. A door opening caught my attention. I froze in place as the person exited the room. My breath whooshed out of me, spying familiar the black hair of the man I loved dragging someone out with him. My feet were immediately carrying me over to him.

"Drake!"

He looked at me and smiled.

"Where have you been?" I asked when I reached him.

He abruptly closed the door behind him. It was the master bathroom. I frowned, wondering why on earth he would be in there.

"Dealing with a stray guard and a couple of other staff members."

I looked at the man he had a hold of. His throat was slit, but there was no blood dripping from it any longer.

"What were you doing in the bathroom?"

Drake looked behind him, then back at me.

"Nothing really."

I waved at the man.

"That does not look like nothing."

He shrugged.

"Where are the others?"

"In with Stuart and Phoebe. We think we got everyone."

He started towards the open doorway I'd come out of, dragging the man behind him.

"We'll deal with this guy, do one last sweep of the place, make sure everyone is where they should be and then we can wake Stuart up."

I wanted to ask Drake further questions about the bathroom but decided it wasn't worth it. We had more important things to do.

He left the dead guy outside the sitting room and walked in.

"Right. We can leave those two here. They're not going anywhere. Let's all walk the building, then we'll deal with them, okay?"

The others nodded and followed him out the door. Drake picked up the dead guy and strode off in the direction of the staff wing.

It was time to make sure everything was handled here before the final act.

The one we'd all been waiting for.

The deaths of Stuart and Phoebe Carver.

THIRTY SEVEN

SCARLETT

After we walked the house, the boys carried Phoebe and Stuart from the main house to one of the outbuildings nearby. It was an old barn with beams running across it. From there, Francis and West secured a meat hook to a chain and hoisted Stuart up onto it, hanging him on the hook. He was left dangling in the middle of the space. They did the exact same thing to Phoebe.

Drake had been looking around the barn for something. He appeared next to me with two large plastic containers. I raised my eyebrows as he placed them underneath Stuart and Phoebe's hanging bodies.

"What are those for?" West asked as he stood back to make sure their handiwork was secure.

"I want their blood," Drake said with a shrug.

"Why am I not surprised?"

West rolled his eyes and came over to me and Prescott, who was laying out a few implements on an abandoned table we'd found in the barn. Drake's statement, combined with the whole keeping me out of the master bathroom before we left the main house, made me suspicious about what he had planned.

West put his hands on my shoulders and gave them a squeeze.

"You ready for this, little Scar?"

I leant back into his chest and turned my face up towards him.

"As I'll ever be."

He bent his head, seeking out my mouth with his and kissing me. Then he stroked my neck when he let go, giving me a wicked grin. I'd put my hair up in a braided bun to keep it out of the way.

"Do you want to go first or last?"

"Last."

"As my little Scar wishes."

He released me. I curled myself into Prescott's side. He wrapped an arm around me, giving me a half-smile as he stroked his fingers down the handle of the butcher's knife.

"You planning on using that?"

Prescott snorted and picked it up, swinging it a few times.

"Perhaps."

He set it back down and leant closer, capturing my mouth in his. I turned and gripped his jumper between my fingers to keep him there while he took his fill of my lips. I smiled when he let me go, smoothing down his clothes.

"Time to get this show on the road, little lamb?"

"Yeah... just give me a minute."

He stroked my face and let me go, giving me a nod.

Drake and Francis were conversing in low tones as I approached them. I brushed my hand against Drake's arm to get his attention. His indigo eyes were dark as he turned to me.

"Ready, little wisp?"

I went up on my tiptoes, wrapping my hand around the back of his neck.

"Kiss me first."

He did as I asked, pressing his mouth against mine and devouring me with one of his heated and toe-curling kisses I would never get enough of. I was breathless when he pulled away. The smirk on his face told me he knew how he affected me.

I shifted closer to Francis, who had a pensive expression on his face as he stared up at Stuart and Phoebe.

"Frankie."

His eyes darted to mine as I curled my arms around his waist. His hands moved to my behind, pulling me tighter against him.

"Are you okay?"

"Just thinking about how this is almost over."

"Is that a bad thing?"

"No." He squeezed my flesh. "I'm ready to leave this chapter of our lives behind and start a new one. But first, I want to make him pay for the things he's done to my family."

"You will."

He bent his head to mine, brushing his mouth along my lips.

"And then you'll be free of him forever."

I nodded, pressing my mouth firmly against his. Francis kissed me like I was his sun, moon, and stars. He had me locked up in his arms, demonstrating to me I was his everything in the moments before we would show the man who'd hurt us his rule was over.

When he released me, he smiled and reached up to stroke my cheek.

"It's time."

I nodded and turned to find the others had joined us. Drake moved over to Phoebe, flipping out a knife and grabbing a hold of her wrist. He made a single cut down the centre of her forearm. Blood flowed when he dropped her arm, dripping down to her hand and then into the container below. He did the same to the other side.

"Wake him up."

West had a bucket of water and threw it at Stuart's head. It had been ice cold and the shock of it jerked him awake.

"W-w-what's going on?"

His eyes were wide as he tried to focus on us and his surroundings. It took him a minute, then his face paled when he realised he was hanging from a hook and the five of us were standing below him.

"Hello, Stuart," Drake said with a sneer. "Nice of you to join us."

"What the fuck is this?"

Prescott stepped forward, the butcher's knife swinging between his fingers.

"This? Oh well, it's our little surprise for you."

"Surprise? A fucking surprise?"

He wriggled in his restraints, which only made him swing back and forth. I tried to suppress a smile. He looked utterly ridiculous trying to get out of the harness Francis had fashioned.

"You bastards. You mother fucking bastards."

"Well, that's not very nice," West said. "What did we ever do to you?"

"What did you do? What did you fucking do? You killed my sons!"

West shrugged and smiled at him.

"You still harping on about that? Wow, you're like a broken fucking record, aren't you? Boo-fucking-hoo." He took a step towards Stuart. "What about the lives you stole from us, huh? From her." He pointed at me. "You took everything you could from her, but you couldn't take us. No, you tried to destroy what we had, but you didn't succeed. And now? Well, now you're going to pay."

The way Stuart seethed at West's words had him swinging vigorously in his harness. The veins in his temples were popping and his face had gone puce. He was about to open his mouth when his head turned sharply, and he caught sight of Phoebe next to him.

"What did you do to her? What the fuck did you do to my wife?"

"She's not dead… yet," Francis said, stepping closer to Phoebe. "But you see here?" He pointed at the cuts Drake had made, the blood steadily flowing from her hands into the large container below her. "For every one of your crimes against us, we'll make another cut. She's going to bleed to death because of you." He shrugged as he looked at Stuart. "But I don't know why you care. Not like she was faithful to you."

Stuart was so enraged by Francis' words, the spittle from his mouth sprayed out with his shout.

"You worthless fucking piece of shit. Let her go!"

Drake tutted and took hold of Phoebe's wrist. He dragged the knife down, making another slice next to the first one.

"We can't do that." He took her other wrist and slid the knife down it too. "You see these? Well, the first one is for when you kidnapped Scarlett. The second, for when you had her mother killed." He indicated her arm. "This is for the beatings you gave her. And this? Well, this is for locking her in a cold, dark cell to nurse her wounds." He cut Phoebe again. "You're lucky she's unconscious for this, not that she would stay awake for long. Too much blood loss."

It was dripping down faster now. A red river flowed down her hands.

"This is for when you decided you were going to give her to that cunt Mason." Drake looked up at Stuart. "She killed him, you know. Stabbed him to death. It was beautiful watching her butcher him after all the pain he'd caused."

He sliced Phoebe's other wrist.

"And this one? It's for you trying to take her again." He made another cut. "And again."

Then he stepped back and stared up at the woman I'd been made to call mother for ten years.

"It's such a pity you underestimated us, Stuart, but your worst mistake was underestimating the girl you stole from us."

Stuart had been raging at Drake's actions, but I'd been too busy watching my man explaining each cut he made. It was almost poetic when I thought about it. Phoebe wore his crimes on her wrists.

"Begin," Drake said, waving at Stuart.

Prescott grinned as stepped up to Stuart and took a hold of his leg. The man tried to kick Prescott away, but West was there, holding onto his free leg, preventing him from doing so. Prescott cut down Stuart's trouser leg, exposing the flesh. Then he used the butcher's knife to flay the skin from his leg. Stuart's scream made me flinch, but I kept watching as Prescott left the flesh attached but hanging off Stuart's leg. Blood ran down it, dripping into the container below.

"That's for taking her from us," Prescott ground out before he spat on Stuart's bloodied leg and stepped back.

West took the butcher's knife from him and proceeded to flay another piece of skin from Stuart's leg. He then gave it to Francis, who did the same, followed by Drake. Stuart was screaming and crying by the time they were done. I could see his bone. It was kind of gruesome, but I didn't care. The fucker deserved it.

The boys repeated the same steps on his other leg. The blood was flowing heavier now from both Phoebe and Stuart. It was mesmerising.

West took his knife and dragged it down Stuart's stomach, slicing through flesh to expose his guts. They fell out of the wound. I could see Stuart's horrified expression. I smiled at it.

"I would feed you these, but I don't really want to deal with the fucking smell," West spat at Stuart before stepping back.

I watched Drake, Francis, and Prescott slice through the tendons in the exposed parts of Stuart's forearms, not bound by Francis's ropes. He was beginning to lose consciousness now with all the blood loss.

The three of them stepped back. West set a chair in front of Stuart and gestured to me. I walked over and took a hold of his knife. He helped me up onto the chair. Stuart hung there, half-conscious and blubbering incomprehensibly. I patted his cheek.

"There, there. It's almost over now," I crooned, my voice mocking. "We thought we'd leave you with one last little parting gift before we send you to hell."

I gripped his chin between my fingers and pushed his face up, exposing his fat neck. Even so, I met his eyes and smiled.

"They did kill your sons. They killed them for me. And you know why? They tried to rape me. They were going to force themselves on me like they did to all those other girls. The rapes you covered up along with Mason's dad."

His eyes flared with pain.

"And they're buried beneath the foundations of the building you never checked. They drowned them in concrete. I just thought you should know. Goodbye, Stuart. This is for everything you did to me and my men."

"Death comes to all," Drake murmured from behind me.

The words settled over me. He was my reaper, but this was my kill. I was the executioner today. Destroying the man who'd abused me for ten years was only right and fair. It was justice.

I sliced the blade across Stuart's throat, cutting through flesh to end his sorry existence. It took several slices because his neck was so fucking big. After I'd watched Drake slice those guys throats, I knew exactly what to do. It was satisfying seeing the blood pouring down his body.

I stepped down from the chair, set the knife down on it and stood back with the boys, watching Stuart gurgle as blood flowed from the wounds we'd made. We watched the life drain from his eyes together, knowing we'd finally brought an end to this man. The one who'd caused us nothing but pain. It was done. We'd killed him. He was gone.

The boys crowded around me a moment later, holding me against them to reassure me it was over. I breathed out a sigh of relief, sinking into them as silence descended over us.

The silence in the wake of death brought upon the world by the Four Horsemen and their goddess, Nyx. The silence to end it all.

THIRTY EIGHT

DRAKE

O nce we got Stuart and Phoebe down from the hooks when the blood had stopped dripping, the four of us carried them back into the house. We laid them down in their bed together, Francis removing the harnesses so we could dispose of the ropes and covered the bodies with their sheets.

"Go get the containers and bring them to the master bathroom," I told Francis and Prescott who gave me a look but left the room as I'd requested.

I had to admit, this was a diversion we could do without considering this whole thing had taken longer than I expected, but I couldn't pass up the opportunity. In a sick sort of way, I needed this.

"I knew you had something planned in that room," Scarlett said, crossing her arms over her chest and giving me a look.

"And you will find out very soon what it is."

"We don't have time to waste."

I raised an eyebrow and stalked over to her.

"It won't be wasting time, little wisp."

She didn't look as though she believed me. To be honest, I hardly believed myself. This was going so far off book, I wasn't sure I recognised myself. It was reckless. Maybe Prescott had rubbed off on me. He had almost got Scarlett caught by Stuart's fucking men after agreeing to chase her in the rain. Thankfully, nothing had come our way because of the man he'd killed. We'd checked up on the guy who was meant to dispose of him when Scarlett and Prescott had been at Rosie's. He'd taken Prescott's warning to heart. We would have killed him if he hadn't got rid of his friend.

"Since you decided you wanted their blood, I have an idea of what the fuck you're up to," West said as he left the bedroom.

Scarlett stared up at me for a moment before retreating from the room too. I shook my head as I exited the bedroom. West and Scarlett stood outside the bathroom door. He rubbed her back and nuzzled her hair with his face. I sighed and leant against the wall outside. Scarlett didn't like me keeping anything from her. I wasn't sure she'd agree if I told her in advance.

Prescott and Francis appeared at the top of the stairs, each carrying a container with care. I shoved off the wall and opened the bathroom door, stepping inside the bright, white-tiled room. In the centre of it stood a huge Victorian-style claw-footed bath. And in that bath, I'd drained three people of their blood before I'd taken them to their rooms.

Scarlett came to a standstill next to me, taking in the rest of the space. There was a huge rainfall shower on one side of the room and the other had double sinks on the counter. The huge window looked out over the dark garden beyond.

Her eyes went to the bath. Then she took a step towards it, cocking her head to the side.

"A blood bath," she said without any inflection in her voice. "You made me a blood bath."

"Yes."

West whistled as he walked around to the bath and then rolled his eyes.

"You really are a kinky little shit, Drake."

I shrugged and continued to watch Scarlett. She dragged her fingers along the lip of the bath as she circled it.

"You want to bathe me in the blood of our enemies."

"Yes."

She nodded, then walked over to the sink counter and ripped off her gloves, setting them down. Next, she began to remove her clothes as if she wasn't going to question this any further.

"Put it in the bath," I said to Prescott and Francis, who had joined us.

"This might be the most fucked up thing we've done," Prescott said as he walked over to the bath and carefully poured out the blood into it.

"We just flayed a man's skin from his body, and you think Scarlett taking a bath in blood is fucked up?" Francis asked as he walked around the other side and poured in his container, making sure not to spill it.

Prescott shrugged and looked at Scarlett, who was still undressing and placing her clothes in a pile on the counter.

"I suppose you have a point."

"My argument would be us not having time to do this shit." Francis looked at me with amusement. "But if the boss says it's okay."

"I'm making time," I said, closing that line of conversation down as I looked at my watch. "It's just past midnight."

"You haven't forgotten what else we need to do, right?"

I shrugged.

"No, but you know how to run, don't you?"

Francis gave me a look but set the container aside and walked over to the window where West was standing. None of them were against this happening. Francis just wanted to give me shit because he could.

Scarlett stepped up to the bath when she was bare and looked at me. I made my way over to her. Prescott stood back, leaning against the counter and crossing his arms over his chest. I took Scarlett's hand and helped her step into the blood. She shivered but lowered herself into the red liquid. Watching her submerge herself in blood had my dick rising to the occasion. The way it slid over her skin was more than I could take. As she settled in it, I rolled up my sleeves and dipped my arms into the blood before running them along her arms. It had got cold in the intervening period since we'd killed the owners of it, but I didn't care. It was fucking everything.

"Little wisp," I ground out through my teeth, aching for her in a way I never had before, "so fucking stunning."

She looked back at me, her hazel-green eyes wide. Then she reached up and stroked my face, getting blood on it. I let out a breath and wanted to steal hers. I wanted to get in there with her. To impale her on my length and fuck her until she came all over me. My hand rose out of the blood. I gripped her chin before I caught her mouth with mine. She let me part her lips and slide my tongue inside, tasting every inch of her sweet little mouth.

"Fuck, I want you," I whispered, "I can't wait until later."

"Then have me."

I let her go and then I was practically tearing off my clothes. I could feel Prescott, West and Francis staring at us, but I didn't give a shit. I bundled them up, kicked my shoes away, and dumped my clothes on the counter. Then I stepped into the bath behind Scarlett, who moved to give me room. Sinking down into the liquid, I shuddered at the sensation of it on my skin. Scarlett turned around and straddled my lap, her hands wrapping around my neck before she kissed me. Her body rubbed against mine, making the blood slosh around the tub.

"Take me, Drake," she whispered against my mouth. "Take me the way you need. I want you to."

Maybe it was the events of this whole night making us both lust-drunk for each other, but I shifted us out of the liquid for a moment, allowing her to sink down on me inch by inch. She moaned, continuing to kiss me until she was fully impaled on my cock. I lowered us back into the blood. Scarlett started to ride me, making the blood slosh even more. Some of it ran down the sides of the white tub.

She pulled away and arched her back, holding onto my shoulders to keep herself steady. The way her eyes glinted had me gripping her hips, my fingers digging into her skin.

"Well, fuck," Prescott hissed from near us.

I noticed West and Francis had come closer and were standing next to him. They could do whatever the fuck they wanted as long as I could have this. Have her this way. There would never be an opportunity like this again. Not if I had anything to do with it. We were going to have a normal life together when this was done.

Well, normal for us. We would never conform to society's whims. We made our own. And we revelled in it.

My hand ran up from her hip along her body, dragging more blood across it. I pinched one of her nipples between my fingers, making her mewl in response. Her gaze was still fixed on mine as she rode me faster.

"That's it, you're such a good girl."

"Drake," she moaned, her voice all breathy and filled with desire, "more. I want more."

I smiled, leaning towards her and kissing my way down her throat. My mouth met hers again, and I bit down on her lip, making her whine in response. My teeth dug harder until she bled for me. Then I sucked at the wound, groaning in her mouth.

It never occurred to me I'd want to fuck her when I bathed her in blood. Sure, I'd thought about doing it afterwards, but this was far beyond any fantasy I'd ever had of my little wisp. We'd killed together. Now this, clinging to each other, desperation lacing our veins in our lovemaking. There was nothing like this adrenaline rush.

Letting go of her mouth, I pulled her against me, our chest brushing together as I thrust up into her. I buried my face in her neck as she panted out her pleasure, her nails digging into my shoulders.

"I love you, little wisp. You have my heart. You have it all. I will never belong to anyone but you."

She shifted, then she was biting down on my earlobe, making me grunt. She sucked it into her mouth to soothe away the sting. I shuddered, holding back the need to come inside her. The woman had just discovered what would make me detonate on her within minutes. I dug my fingers harder into her skin, locking her in place as I continued to thrust up into her.

"Fuck," I hissed.

"I love you too," she murmured, pressing kisses down the side of my neck.

It was then I understood what it meant to be destined for each other. What it truly felt like to know you had found the person you'd spend eternity with. Who embraced everything you were and gave you what you needed without hesitation. Scarlett was my destiny. She was our fate. Our birth wasn't a coincidence, it was a sign we belonged with each other. People had tried to tear us apart. They hadn't succeeded. They had only strengthened our bond because we'd fought for it. We'd jumped through so many hoops to come to this moment. And it was everything.

She was everything.

"Drake, harder, please… I need it."

I encouraged her to get off me, turned her around and made her grab hold of the sides of the tub. Getting up on my knees, I pressed inside her tight little pussy once more, holding onto her hips as leverage before I pounded into her. Scarlett cried out, her fingers whitening around the tub. Then one of her hands left it and snaked between her legs. She stroked herself, letting me fuck her until she exploded around me. Her garbled cries were music to my ears.

"That's it, good girl, come over my dick."

"Drake."

"That's not my name here, is it?"

She tipped her head back.

"No… you're my Death."

My hands tightened around her hips.

"Good girl."

She arched her back and shuddered against me. Then she was slumping down, only holding herself up by one hand. Letting go of her hip, I stroked a hand down her back, wanting to soothe her as she came down.

"I think one of you needs to join them," came Prescott's voice.

My head turned, finally looking at the three of them leaning against the sink counter. Their eyes were fixed on us. The blood had got on the floor, soaking the white tiles. It was quite the fucking sight, seeing this perfectly pristine bathroom marred by red. I couldn't help smiling. It was exactly as I had envisioned it when I'd come in here. I wanted to paint it red.

"You want us to fuck her in the blood too?" Francis asked, raising an eyebrow.

Prescott looked down at where Francis was clearly sporting an erection.

"I think that says you wouldn't be averse to it."

Francis shifted, his cheeks going red. Then he waved at West.

"He's more into blood than I am with all his knife shit."

West was too busy watching Scarlett with a dark gleam in his amber eyes to respond to Francis' dig.

"Both of you can join in."

The next thing I knew, West was pulling off his clothes, clearly unphased about giving it to Scarlett in blood. Francis stared at him for a long moment.

"Well, shit."

Then he was tugging his clothes off too. Scarlett's head raised, her eyes widening at the sight of them stripping off. Her gaze went to Prescott who hadn't moved to do a thing.

"If they're going to join us, then you need to get naked too," she said a moment later, giving him a significant look.

Prescott straightened, dropping his arms from his chest.

"Is that so?"

She smiled as she straightened and rested her back against my chest.

"Yeah, Pres… it's all or nothing with us, remember?"

He nodded slowly. Then he was pulling his clothes off too.

I guessed Scarlett was right. It was all of us or nothing. We weren't known for doing anything by halves. And fucking in blood? Well, that was going all the fucking way and then some.

THIRTY NINE

FRANCIS

West moved to the bath, placing himself on the edge of it before reaching down into the red liquid and coating his forearm in it. He stroked his palm up Scarlett's body, cupping her breast to flick her nipple with his thumb.

"Look at you, little Scar, covered in the spoils of war," he murmured.

She let out a pant as he leant closer and brushed his lips along her cheek.

"Beautiful."

His hand slid higher and curled around her neck, angling her jaw to his advantage. He stroked his lips across hers.

"Make him come. Work his dick with that little pussy until he coats you with cum. Mix it with the fucking blood, you hear me? Make Death feel good. He made this happen. Without him, we'd never have found you. Show him how much you appreciate his hard work."

He kissed her, pushing his tongue into her mouth to taste our girl. She put her hands on the sides of the bath and started to move up, rocking herself back on Drake. His hands were guiding her, helping set the pace. West released Scarlett's mouth and smiled before looking at me.

"I think you should reward Famine too, little Scar. He needs your pretty little mouth wrapped around him."

West shifted away and pointed at the bath. Given Drake had embraced all of our kinks when we shared, I wasn't going to complain about the blood. I had to admit I was turned on watching the two of them fuck in it.

I climbed into the tub, feeling the cold liquid against my skin, and stepped up to Scarlett. She looked up at me with lust-filled hazel-green eyes. Then she reached for me, pulling me closer as her hands curled round my hips.

"Make me take it, Famine. Deprive me of oxygen when you fuck my mouth."

This position reminded me of when we'd first all fucked Scarlett. She took Drake while I fucked her mouth. This time I could see desire written all over her face. And I wasn't about to deny her anything.

My hand wrapped around the back of her head. She'd put it up in a braided bun. I was careful not to disturb it as we didn't want her getting blood in her hair. Scarlett opened her mouth for me to slide my aching cock in. I groaned as she curled her tongue around me.

"Fuck, little whore."

She moaned around my cock. I pressed deeper, wanting to make her take it all. This woman was a goddess, giving us everything we needed and so much more. She continued to ride Drake, making him grunt and let out a series of harsh pants. Then he nuzzled her neck, pressing kisses to her blood-soaked skin.

"Good girl. That's my good little wisp. Suck him harder."

We were all running off an adrenaline-fuelled high after what we'd done tonight. Death hung in the air. We'd finally orchestrated our revenge against Stuart Carver. And after this kinky little interlude, we'd destroy the place Scarlett had called her prison for good. We'd make sure there was nothing but a shell left.

Prescott remained by the sinks, watching the four of us with evident need in his eyes. West stroked his fingers down Scarlett's chest, dipping his hand into the blood again. Scarlett moaned around my cock. Her fingers dug into my skin. I forced my dick further into her mouth. She swallowed and allowed me into her throat.

"Go on, make them come, little Scar. Let them paint you with it. I want to see it running down your fucking face."

I almost came right then with West's words ringing in my ears. Scarlett hummed around me. I fed her more until my dick was jammed so far down her throat, she choked around it. My hand held her in place, revelling in the way she swallowed repeatedly around it, trying to breathe. My woman had told me to deprive her of oxygen. I pulled back and pumped in again, listening to her gagging sounds and the way the blood sloshed around the tub.

"Fuck," Drake ground out through his teeth.

Scarlett rode him harder. His head fell back against the lip of the bath, and he let out a low grunt. I pulled out of her mouth, allowing her room to breathe as Drake came inside her.

Her gasps echoed around the room. She gripped my hips in an iron hold, clearly trying to stay upright while West continued to stroke her. His eyes were intent on her face, watching each and every one of her little tells. We'd all become so in tune with our girl, knowing exactly what made her tick in the bedroom.

"Oh, god, fuck," she panted. "Jesus, West!"

Scarlett fell back against Drake, her whole body twitching with her second climax. West pulled his hand from the blood and cupped her throat.

"Good girl," he told her. "My good little slut."

She shuddered, closing her eyes as Drake stroked her shoulders and down her arms with his palms to soothe her. When she recovered, Drake lifted her off his cock, making her move closer to me.

"Up on your knees, little whore," I ordered her as I took a few steps back.

West let go of her throat to let her crawl towards me. She curled her hands around my hips and ran her tongue up my shaft.

"Pres, find something we can use as lube," West said over his shoulder before he put his hand to Scarlett's throat again. "And you, little Scar, you're going to take his dick down your throat. I want to feel it against my palm."

I held onto her braided bun and placed the head of my dick at her lips. She opened her mouth to me, allowing me to slide back in. The angle she was at made it easier for me to shove it down her throat. She gagged but didn't complain. West watched my cock disappearing with complete rapture. Seeing her take it and feeling it.

Prescott rummaged around in the drawers and then approached us with a bottle of coconut oil. He handed it to Drake and sat on the edge of the bath next to West. Then he ran his hand down Scarlett's back. She arched into his touch as I began to fuck her throat.

Drake leant forward, popping the cap on the oil and drizzling it on his fingers. I watched him rub her tight little hole before pressing a finger inside. I had a perfect view of what he was doing from where I was standing. If anything, it only made it harder not to come. Feeling Scarlett's tight throat encasing my cock was more than I could take.

"Fuck, I don't know if I can't hold on. You feel so fucking good, little whore."

"Paint her face," West said, "make it drip down her chin."

I gripped her braid harder, ramming my cock into her mouth with short, hard thrusts. She was holding on for dear life at this point, her eyes watering with the force I used. That sight pushed me right over the edge.

I pulled out of her mouth, fisting my cock, and then I erupted. My cum sprayed over her still open mouth and chin. I pulled her head back and directed it all over the bottom of her face. It ran down her skin and dripped into the blood. I released Scarlett, my chest heaving with my climax. She turned her head to look at West and Prescott, showing them both her cum-drenched face.

"What a messy little lamb," Prescott said.

Her tongue darted out as she licked it from her chin. Prescott's blue eyes heated. She let go of my hip and dragged her fingertips through the cum. She grinned as she crooked a finger at him.

"Come infect me, Pestilence."

I stepped out of the bath, making room for him and West if they wanted to play with her. Seeing the blood running down my legs didn't bother me. Drake shifted out of the blood and sat on the edge of the bath to give them more room too.

"Turn around, little lamb."

She did as he asked. He took her cum covered fingers and put them in her mouth, making her suck on them. Then he made her clean up the rest of her face, directing her fingers with his own.

"Good girl, you wouldn't want to waste what Famine gave you."

She shuddered at his words. He released her and stood up, walking away to the space between the bath and the window.

"Come here."

Scarlett rose from the blood. West stood and helped her out of the bath. The blood clung to her skin as she walked over to Prescott. He drew her down on the tiles, making her straddle his lap. Drake gave the coconut oil to West, who grinned at him. I sat on the lip of the bath, watching Scarlett impale herself on Prescott's dick as she held onto his shoulders.

"Do you remember when we fucked you together the first time?" he asked, stroking her bloody skin.

"Yes."

"We're going to fuck you like that again."

West walked over to them and knelt on the tiles behind Scarlett. He coated his fingers in oil before sliding them into her. Drake moved back into the blood and then leant his arms on the end of the bath, watching the three of them from his position.

Prescott lay back, pulling Scarlett down with him to give West better access. She moaned as Prescott gripped her hips and made her ride him. Her hands were flat on the tiles by Prescott's head, the two of them staring at each other with lust and love radiating from their expressions.

"Good girl, little wisp. Let them make you feel good," Drake said, a smirk appearing across his lips.

He knew what he'd done by initiating this whole thing. A fivesome in the blood of our enemies was at the top of the most depraved acts we'd engaged in. This would probably make most people squeamish but fuck it, I'd long since stopped caring about right and wrong. I'd embraced who I was. There were no more chains holding me back. No fucking way I'd pass up an experience like this. It's why I'd even got in the bath with Scarlett and Drake. I wanted to have this moment together.

It was a fucked up form of celebration, but that was us all over. We weren't named the Four Horsemen for nothing.

"Please, War, I want your cock," Scarlett whined as she continued to fuck Prescott while West had his fingers in her arse, preparing her for his dick.

"Do you? Mmm, I don't know if you deserve it yet, slut. I think I need to hear you beg a little more."

"Please, I want you so fucking badly. I need you inside me. Stretch me out... make it hurt, War. I need you to make it hurt."

When she begged, it made it very hard for any of us to think straight. The sound of her voice was like a fucking beacon, guiding us to her, pulling the four of us under her spell. Our goddess would not be satisfied or tamed. She was as wild and free as her horsemen. She didn't take no for an answer.

West gripped her hip and shoved a third finger inside her.

"You want the pain, slut? Are you thinking about that night when I made it hurt so bad you screamed against your gag, hmm? Did you like tasting yourself whilst I fucked you?"

"I loved it… every moment. Please give it to me. I want you to hurt me again, War. Break me."

Drake looked at me with a raised eyebrow. We'd heard West say some pretty fucked up things to Scarlett since the night after she'd run to him. To hear her want it just as much. Well, our girl was full of fucking surprises.

"You've been such a good girl tonight. You did so well." He stroked her back. "You deserve to get fucked the way you need."

Releasing her, he poured the oil over his cock, coating it thoroughly, then pressed it against her. Scarlett cried out when he breached her. He didn't give her any time to adjust, but she'd told him she wanted the pain. He shoved deeper, making Scarlett grip Prescott's shoulder, her nails digging into his skin. He grunted and stroked her arms, trying to calm her as West impaled her completely on his dick.

He leant over her, ghosting his lips over her ear.

"That's a good girl, you've taken us so well… now, little Scar, War and Pestilence are going to fuck you until you scream. Until you come all over our cocks from the pleasure and pain. Is that understood?"

She nodded, her eyes still fixed on Prescott's.

"Good girl." He straightened and gripped both her hips. "Let's begin."

FORTY

PRESCOTT

The feel of Scarlett impaled on both West and I was the highlight of my fucking night. Yes, I'd enjoyed all the death and violence we'd engaged in and ridding the world of Stuart Carver. But this moment with Scarlett? This was what I longed for. The times when we were all together like this. Where I could watch them fuck her and then take my fill of the woman we loved. The woman we'd devoted our entire lives to.

My little lamb.

West gripped the back of Scarlett's neck, pulling her upright to press her against his chest. I wrapped my hands around her hips, directing her movements. West circled her neck and nibbled her ear.

"Make your tits bounce for Pres," he told her. "Show him how much you want him to touch you."

Scarlett let out a harsh pant, placing her hands on my chest as leverage. Then she was riding us harder. I watched the way her breasts moved with each rise and fall of her hips against mine. I couldn't deny how fucking alluring it was, watching her use us for her own pleasure. Showing us exactly how much she needed our cocks inside her.

"Good girl, such a good little slut you are for us."

She bit her lip, staring down at me with such intensity, it threatened to undo me. The way this girl loved us. The fierceness of it. The absolute pure devotion she had for us. It was fucking awe-inspiring. Everything we did was for her. Even this evening had been for Scarlett.

Yes, we'd killed Stuart, his wife and all his fucking staff because he would never stop coming after us. But we'd exacted justice for her. He'd abused our girl. Made her life a living hell. When she explained the extent of the damage inflicted on her, I'd been utterly incensed. The need to destroy everything Stuart stood for burnt in my veins. Soon, this place would be fucking ashes.

One of my hands left her hip and ran up her abdomen, stroking her bloody skin. Drake and his blood kink. Admittedly, watching him fuck her in it was a sight to behold. She was our queen, wearing the blood of our enemies on her skin. I may have been slightly hesitant before she told me to get naked, but now I was all in. There was nothing I wouldn't do for Scarlett and the boys. Nothing in this world would stop me from giving them everything they needed.

My fingertips grazed her scars. The ones painting a picture of the trauma she'd been through. Scarlett was so fucking strong. She was still healing, but you could see when you looked into her eyes, she would fight through anything thrown at her. We'd be right by her side as she did it. Our woman could take on the fucking world if she wanted to.

"Look at you, little lamb. Our goddess bathed in blood," I said, cupping her breast and pinching her nipple between my fingers. She moaned and her nails dug into my skin.

"You want to tell Drake and Frankie what you did to the butler, little Scar?" West asked a moment later, gripping her throat tighter.

Scarlett looked at the other two. Drake was leaning on his arms watching us while Francis sat on the edge of the tub.

"I cut his dick off and fed it to him for the time he tried to force himself on me. I don't know if I'd call Alex pulling him off me as lucky since Stuart didn't want me sullied, but I made that fuck pay for even trying."

Drake raised an eyebrow.

"Such savagery," Francis said with a smirk. "Tell me more. How exactly did you do it?"

"You want to know exactly how she severed a man's cock from his body?" Drake asked, looking at Francis with a frown.

"Yeah, I do. You got a problem with that?"

Drake put his hands up.

"No. I can't really since you just let me fuck our girl in blood. Whatever floats your boat."

Francis gave him a wink before turning back to Scarlett, who was grinning at him.

"Pres cable-tied Gendry's hands behind his back on the chair," she said, stroking my chest and not faltering in fucking me and West. "Then I woke him up by throwing water in his face and screaming at him. He was all disorientated, but I got his attention by killing the housemaid, Moira. She was a bitch to me and those two had been fucking each other for as long as I can remember."

Francis leant forward as if he was completely enthralled by what she was saying. This wasn't something he'd expressed finding a turn on before, talking about the killings we'd carried out, but apparently, it was a thing for him and Scarlett. Who the fuck knew.

"I stabbed her in the guts using West's knife, twisting it to mess up her insides. Then I went over to him, told him why I was doing it before grabbing hold of his dick and sawing through the base of it. He screamed the whole time, but I didn't care. I stuffed his limp dick in his mouth and held it in there before stabbing him in the heart and leaving him to bleed out."

West stroked her neck.

"You missed the best part, little Scar," he murmured.

She turned her head slightly.

"What's that?"

"When you told him to 'take it like a good fucking boy'."

Francis shifted off the bath and knelt down next to us before taking Scarlett's face between his hands.

"My savage little whore. I'm so proud of you."

Then he kissed her, his tongue tangling with hers. Her hand left my chest and curled around Francis' neck. He pulled back slightly to lean his forehead against hers.

"I love you," he told her, staring into her eyes as he did it.

She stroked his face, pressing her lips to his once more.

"Forever," she whispered, "you're my forever."

Then he let her go and sat back, allowing her to concentrate on me and West again. Scarlett looked at West, who was continuing to give it to her without missing a single beat. There was nothing like being inside her this way. Having Scarlett take us both. I would never get enough.

"I want to make you come. I want to feel you both inside me, coating my insides. Bring me War."

The way West smiled would be chilling if I didn't know him so well. It was sinister in nature. The desire for violence ran through his veins. But this wasn't the type of violence where we would pay dearly or with our lives. It was the kind where raw passion and lust mixed with brutal fucking.

"As my little Scar wishes." His free hand went to her pussy, stroking her clit as the hand around her neck tightened. "Give it to her, Pres, make her fucking feel it."

I held onto her hips and thrust upwards, making her take more of me with each movement. It was clear he was depriving her of oxygen, but she didn't struggle against him. She took it, her eyes wide as she clutched West on one side and kept her other hand on my chest.

"Is this what you need, hmm? Want us to use you like our own little fucktoy and give you our cum?"

"Please."

"Such a dirty little slut, all covered in blood, begging for dick like you can't get enough. So wanton and needy. Don't worry, I'll give you what you need. Make it hurt so bad, you cry. Your pleasure is my fucking purpose."

It was getting harder to hold back with the way we were both fucking her. Everything in my body was taut. I strained against the urge to explode, keeping up my pace. A tear leaked out of Scarlett's eye. West licked it from her cheek. She moaned and struggled then, clearly feeling the effects of our brutality.

"Please," she whimpered, "please."

"Go on, infect her, Pestilence, give her what she needs."

His words brought it on, tipping me over the edge. I groaned with it, feeling my body shake as I came inside her, giving my woman exactly what she asked for.

"Feel that, little Scar?" he hissed in her ear. "Feel him coming for you?"

"Yes, fuck, yes."

"Now I want you to come for me, then I'll give you War."

As I came down from my high, I could feel her getting closer to hers. The way she clenched and strained as West held her throat tight and stroked her clit was a clear sign. Her nails dug into my skin, making me grunt from the pain, but I didn't care. She could claw me all she needed if it meant she came. Because Scarlett always came so fucking sweetly.

The moment West pushed her over the edge, she fell, bucking and writhing in his hold.

"Good girl," he murmured, pressing a kiss to her cheek. "Such a good girl."

Then he was fucking her almost violently, pursuing his own end like there was nothing else in the world he needed more. He growled when he came, making Scarlett take it all. Take everything he had to offer her.

He released her and Scarlett collapsed on me, resting her face on my chest. The three of us were spent, all needing to catch our breath for a few long minutes.

Francis was the one who helped Scarlett up off the two of us as West shifted backwards. Drake had got out of the bath and unplugged it, draining the blood. The place was a mess, with blood all over the tiles. We were covered in it too. Drake stepped up to the shower and turned it on, rinsing the blood off him. We all took turns to do so, drying off and dressing again. We didn't have time to linger now we'd done this. Not when we had shit to get on with.

Drake held Scarlett for a moment, whispering something in her ear and kissing her forehead before he looked up at us.

"We need to clean this room with bleach. I'm not taking any chances no matter what we're planning on doing to the house."

West and Francis disappeared to get us new gloves and cleaning supplies. Scarlett remained curled around Drake as if she needed his comfort and security. I went over to them and rubbed her back as she nuzzled her face on his chest.

"You're okay, little wisp," he murmured, "I've got you."

I gave him a curious look.

"She just needs a minute," he told me. "This is a lot, you know."

I nodded. It had been. Her being back here in the place where she'd experienced so much pain. While this might have been cathartic for her, it was also hurting her too.

I moved closer and pressed my face to her hair.

"You're okay, sweetness, it's almost over. We're almost at the end now, okay? We can go home soon."

She nodded and continued to hold on to Drake until West and Francis got back. Then the five of us cleaned the room, removing all traces of the blood and piled up all the towels and cleaning supplies into bags. We didn't want to risk traces of us being found here.

We made our way downstairs and out to the cars, stuffing everything in the boot of one of them. Drake opened the other one and stared down at the large jerry cans we had in there. We lifted them out, setting them down in front of the house.

West had snagged his sledgehammer along the way and had it hoisted over his shoulder. He looked at Scarlett with a pensive expression on his face.

"You know the plan," Drake said, picking up one of the jerry cans and unscrewing the cap. "We cover every room and the outbuildings. Make sure that barn is done too, okay?"

Inside those jerry cans was petrol Penn had sourced for us. It was all untraceable, so even if they suspected arson, and they would, there was no fucking way they would find out how we got hold of it.

"Scar will come with me," West said, his tone brokering no objection. "We'll do the outbuildings and join you in the house when we're done."

Scarlett looked up at him with a frown.

"Just don't take too long," Drake replied before striding off into the main house.

Francis and I picked up our own cans, watching Scarlett take one and follow West towards the outbuildings.

"What do you think he wants to do with her out there?" I asked as I walked into the house with Francis.

He shrugged.

"Fuck knows. This is West we're talking about. Let's just get this done, then we can leave. I'm sick of the sight and stench of this place already."

I grinned. I was about done with this place too. And he was right. We should get this over with. Whatever West needed from Scarlett, I was sure it wouldn't take up more time we didn't have to waste after our little bit of fun with the blood bath. At least, I hoped. You never knew with West. I trusted Scarlett to make sure he didn't do anything stupid. She was the only one who could keep him in line.

"You're right. Let's get ready to burn this place down. I'm sick of it too."

And with that, the two of us parted ways, each walking into opposite wings to cover the place in petrol. The blaze it would create would leave little trace of what we'd done here tonight.

Good fucking riddance.

FORTY ONE

WEST

When we were out of earshot of the others, Scarlett turned her face towards me and gave me a look. I knew she was suspicious of why I'd asked her to come to coat the outbuildings in petrol with me.

"What?"

"You could do this bit by yourself, so why do you want me here?"

I adjusted the hammer on my shoulder.

"We went through the whole house, including your bedroom, and there was no room like the one you described. The concrete cell. I'm guessing it's out here somewhere. I want you to show me. I need to see it."

Maybe it was fucked up and twisted of me to force her to take me to her concrete prison. I had to see the place. Needed to know what she'd gone through. Seeing her bedroom wasn't enough. Scarlett hadn't wanted to go inside, so we hadn't made her. She told us there was nothing for her other than memories of screaming at night and the metal bars across the windows. Her bedroom was on the ground floor of the family wing at the back of the house. It made me sick to see the bars keeping her inside. The whole place made me violent, but I was keeping a lid on it. I couldn't afford to lose control when we had shit to do.

Scarlett faltered in her steps, shifting the can in her hands.

"You want to see the cell?"

"Yes."

"I don't want to go in there, West."

"You don't have to. Just take me to it and you can wait outside."

She almost shook her head, her eyes full of sadness and pain.

"Okay, but we need to go deal with the barn first. It's furthest away from the house."

I touched her arm with my free hand, but I don't think it reassured her. It made me feel like a dick for forcing this on her. She'd already dealt with so much this evening, being back in the place holding most of her worst memories. We'd made new ones for her. Killing all the people who'd wronged her. Not to mention the fuckery in the bathroom. That was unexpected, especially for Drake, who was so fucking anal about everything. Our girl had changed him. Brought out the old Drake. I'd known she could. Only Scarlett had the power to set us all free from the trauma and pain of losing her. She was the key to everything.

She was quiet as we reached the barn. I set the hammer down and took the can from her, going into the place and coating the area with petrol. I came out and drew a line from the barn to the first outbuilding. Scarlett brought my sledgehammer over and we swapped, so she didn't have to carry it.

We dealt with the first outbuilding together. It was a storage unit filled with all sorts of crap, like old furnishings. The second contained gardening supplies. And the last building made her hesitate in her steps.

"This is it, isn't it?" I asked, giving her shoulder a squeeze and pulling her to a stop.

"It is."

"You don't have to go any further."

She looked up at me.

"Why do you want to see it so badly?"

I set the hammer down and took the can from her, placing it on the floor too. Then I put both my hands on her shoulders and came down to her level, meeting her eyes.

"You went through some of the worst experiences in your life in that place. I need to see and feel it for myself. Your pain is my pain. I need to live it and breathe it with you. Only then can I help take away the hurt and suffering lingering inside you."

Tears welled in her eyes.

"West…"

"You're mine and I'm yours. We're half alive when we're apart. We don't exist without each other. Let me carry your pain."

Her hand came up and settled on my jaw.

"You want to share my burdens?"

"Yes. That's what soulmates do, little Scar. You don't need me to stand on your own two feet, but it doesn't stop us from belonging by each other's sides, breathing the same air and our hearts beating in tandem. It doesn't stop us from needing each other to feel alive."

Those threatening tears burst through, spilling down her cheeks. I gathered her up against my chest, stroking her back and pressing my face to the top of her head. Little sobs erupted from her mouth, showing me how much she struggled with her memories and the past. Scarlett had come so far with us, but there were still miles to go, so many things she had to heal from. I would help her in whatever way I could.

When she settled down, her sobbing abating, she pulled away and wiped her eyes with her sleeve.

"Let's go see the cell," she told me in a small voice as if she was unsure of herself and the decision to take me to it.

"You can stay outside, I promise."

She nodded and picked up the can. I placed the hammer back on my shoulder and guided her into the building. Scarlett turned the light on when we entered. There were shelves and shelves of canned goods and other food supplies. We walked by them until we reached the end. There stood a metal door. She didn't need to tell me this was the place.

"Will it be unlocked?"

She nodded, placing the can down next to us as she stared at the door. I moved closer to it. Reaching out, I grasped the handle and pulled it open. It swung back without any resistance. Then I stepped inside. The ghost of her pain hit me like a ton of bricks. My eyes darted around the bare concrete walls, floor, and ceiling. There were no windows. Not even a fucking lightbulb hung on the ceiling.

"You were in the dark here."

"Yes," she replied from behind me.

I walked around the concrete cell. The only light was coming from the open doorway. On the floor, there were several old bloodstains. Seeing them made me want to destroy this place. Made me want to smash it into tiny pieces. That was her blood. My girl had been made to stay in here while she was bleeding from wounds inflicted on her by that cunt we'd killed and his fucking security guards.

I took the sledgehammer off my shoulder and gripped it between both of my palms. While I wouldn't be able to obliterate it, I could do some fucking damage. There was a primal need inside me, begging to get out, begging me to fucking well erase her hurt from these walls.

I let out a roar before swinging the hammer into the wall, causing the concrete to smash. That first hit brought more. I kept swinging and swinging, smashing the room each time the end of the sledgehammer hit the concrete.

"Fuck!"

The more I destroyed the room, the more I wanted to end this shit for good. I needed to see this fucking place burn, razed to the damn ground. To know their fucking bodies would be completely unrecognisable. Everything needed to be gone. I wanted only ashes and dust to remain.

My fight left me when I saw the mess I'd made of the walls and floor. I stood there in the middle of the cell, panting, with concrete dust settling all over me. There was a certain sort of catharsis that came from such destruction. At least now, the place was unrecognisable.

My head turned to find Scarlett standing in the doorway. Her eyes darted around the ruined room before they came to a standstill when they met mine. Her hands fisted in her clothes at her sides. Her lips parted, but no sound came out. We stared at each other across the small expanse for a long minute. I thought she might turn away at that point, but she didn't.

Scarlett licked her bottom lip, released her clothes and put her hand on her heart.

"I love you."

Her statement slammed into me, almost knocking me off my fucking feet. And without thinking about it, my mouth formed the words I'd struggled with for so long.

"I love you too."

I let go of the handle of the hammer and stalked across the room. The next thing Scarlett knew, she was whisked off her feet, and I was kissing her like my life depended on it. I held my woman against my chest, devouring her mouth with each stroke of my tongue against hers, proving to her once and for all she was mine and I was hers. That our love had never disappeared. It had been waiting for us to grab hold of it all along.

She wrapped her legs around my waist as I moved out of the cell. I pressed her up against the wall outside, continuing to kiss the life out of her. Her hands were in my hair, disturbing the dust and debris. One of mine circled her throat, laying across her skin where it belonged. The only necklace she should ever wear was mine.

"I love you, West," she choked out as I kissed her jaw. "I've loved you my whole life. I never stopped. My heart has always and will always belong to you. I don't know why it took me so long to tell you, but I love you."

I captured her mouth again, tasting her words from her tongue and the desperation in her voice. The feeling was entirely mutual. Telling her I loved her felt like a fucking impossibility until she said it. Until she set me free with her declaration.

Words had never felt quite adequate to describe the way I loved Scarlett, but I had to try to explain it to her. Pulling back, I stared into her hazel-green eyes. The ones that had captured me from the day I set my own eyes to hers.

"From the moment I saw you, I knew you were the one, little Scar. I knew you were the only person in this world I belonged next to. You are the other half of me. You're my strength, my ambition, my joy and my light. You are my heart."

Her hand slid from my hair to my neck.

"I will never love another. I can't when you're buried so deep inside me, tearing you out would kill me. I refuse to let you go, no matter what happens. No matter how much life continues to throw at us because you are mine. My love. My only love. Fuck, little Scar, I'm so in love with you, it hurts my fucking heart. It hurts so bad and yet I will endure the pain to be by your side. I will endure anything for you because I love you with every inch of me."

She swallowed then pressed her forehead to mine, staring at me with such love and affection, it fucking killed me. As if on instinct, the two of us touched the places where we'd scarred each other. A reminder we belonged together. You couldn't have me without her.

"We're each other's forever."

I nodded and smiled at her. My beautiful, perfect girl who ruled my world. There was nothing and no one better or more important to me than her.

Neither of us moved. Both savouring this moment. Allowing our declarations to settle into our bones. It was a fucking miracle we'd found our way back to each other. That we'd put the hurt, pain, and strife behind us. Sharing it with each other so we no longer felt so alone. Now we were one again. We were together with nothing holding us back.

"We should get back to the others," she whispered. "We still have to finish this."

I reluctantly set Scarlett back on her feet. She gave me another lingering kiss before she picked up the jerry can and unscrewed the cap. I went back to get my hammer and took it out of the cell, allowing her to throw petrol into it. Then we coated the rest of the building. Scarlett stopped me outside, brushing off the concrete and debris from my clothes and hair. I did the same to her, as I'd got it on her when I'd kissed the living shit out of my girl. Then we walked back towards the main house together, trailing a line of petrol behind us.

We found the other three outside the house waiting for us. Scarlett poured the petrol right up to the front door, then down towards where the boys were standing.

"You took your time," Prescott said, crossing his arms over his chest.

"We had something we needed to do," Scarlett said with a shy smile in my direction.

She handed me the can when I approached her. I put the hammer and final jerry can in the back of the car, closing it and walking over to them. The five of us stood staring at the house for a long minute.

"Are we ready?" Drake asked, taking a box of matches out of his pocket. "You get to do the honours, little wisp. This is your fight, not ours."

He handed them to Scarlett, who took them, staring down at the box. She stroked her fingers along it.

"I'm ready."

FORTY TWO

SCARLETT

The box shook as I opened it and slid a match out. My hands were trembling, but I ignored them. This was how it had to happen. I stared at the house. The one to cause me so much hurt and pain. Then I remembered only a few minutes ago West and I had told each other about our feelings. He'd destroyed the cell for me. My heart swelled, and I took a deep breath.

I struck the match against the box, lighting it. The flame was so small, but it would create havoc the moment it hit the petrol. It would engulf the whole building in flames.

I threw the match into the line of it I'd trailed here. The match hit the ground, the flames rising up a moment later. The five of us watched it streak up towards the house. It branched off towards the outbuildings too. It took a few minutes before flames appeared in the windows of the place.

"I opened the safe in the security room," Drake said, startling me.

"You did?"

He nodded.

"I found the combination for it in Stuart's office. I copied the data from his computer whilst we were dealing with the rest of the house. We have everything we need now."

The flames were mesmerising. I couldn't stop staring at them as they grew higher. The sound of glass cracking under the intense heat from the blaze made me smile.

"What was in it?"

"Two guns with their licences and bullets. I left them there. Good thing we got into the security room when we did."

So that's what Alex had been going for. Drake was right. We were lucky. I didn't know those were on the property, but it was hardly surprising. Stuart kept a lot of shit from me.

"Thank you for looking. I would have wondered otherwise."

He set his hand on my shoulder.

"You're welcome."

We fell silent then, all five of us contemplating the blazing building. Then I turned to Drake, staring up at my man, who stood tall, the dancing flames reflecting in his indigo eyes.

"I've seen enough. We should go."

"It's over now."

I smiled.

"Yeah… almost."

He gave me a nod, dropping his hand from my shoulder and walking towards the cars. I followed him and got in the one I'd come in. The others joined us, West getting into the driver's seat as Francis got in the back. My eyes fixed on the burning house as West started the car and set off. Francis reached forward and stroked my neck, resting his forehead on the headrest behind me. I sighed and put my fingers on his.

"You're okay, Scar. You're going to be okay."

I knew I would be, eventually. It would take time to put this all behind us.

My eyes darted to the building one last time as West drove back down the long driveway. Then I closed them, leaning my head against the window and drifted off, exhaustion settling over me.

I jerked awake when the car stopped. West stroked my leg and smiled at me.

"Time to switch cars."

I stretched and got out, finding the others opening the doors of Prescott's Jeep. Inside was a change of clothes for all of us. We were at the back of a dark car park, so no one could see us undressing and switching out our clothes. Drake put them all in one of the cars we'd brought, then encouraged me to get into the Jeep. I slid into the back, getting settled in the middle as West joined me. Prescott got in the other side and pressed a kiss to my temple.

"My little lamb."

I curled up against him as he wrapped his arm around me. I must have fallen asleep again because the next thing I knew, he was shaking me awake as we were home. I climbed out of the Jeep and followed the four of them to the lift. The cars we'd gone to the estate in would be taken care of by Penn and his men. There was one thing we had left to do after this, but for the most part, everything was wrapped up this evening.

We were finally free of Stuart Carver once and for all.

"What time is it?" I asked as we rode up to the penthouse in the lift.

Drake looked at his watch.

"Almost three."

No wonder I was tired. We'd been at this for hours.

"You can go to bed if you want. We were talking about having a drink on the roof, but it can wait."

I shook my head.

"No, I'll come up… just want a proper shower first. I stink of petrol."

West snorted.

"We all fucking do."

"You have dust in your hair," Francis said, nodding at West's head. "Dare I ask why?"

He shrugged.

"Smashed up the cell they kept Scar in."

Drake shook his head and rubbed his face.

"That wasn't the plan, West."

"Nothing about tonight went exactly to plan. It is what it fucking is."

Drake dropped his hand and looked up at the metal ceiling.

"You're right. What's done is done."

The doors opened a moment later and the five of us piled out. I joined West in his room. He made no complaints about me taking a shower with him. In fact, he was gentle when he undid my braid so I could wash my hair. The two of us stepped into the hot water after stripping off. It was soothing against my skin. He wrapped his arms around me from behind under the spray and pressed his cheek to mine.

"How are you feeling?"

"Tired, but okay. Guess it hasn't fully hit me yet, you know, that he's no longer a threat to us. That he's gone for good."

"You ended him. We're safe now."

I nodded. We were. I would be forever grateful to my men for giving me this. For letting me help them take the lives of the people who'd stolen mine. It was surreal to think it was all over.

West turned me around and pressed me against the tiles. His hand curled around my throat, thumb stroking down my wet skin. Those amber eyes of his glowed in the low light.

"You never have to live in fear again, little Scar. Not whilst you're by my side."

His other hand stroked down my chest until his fingers met my pussy. I shuddered, unable to help myself from arching into his touch.

"I love you."

Leaning down, he kissed his way down my neck until his lips met the scars he'd given me.

"You're mine."

His tongue ran over them.

"You belong to War."

I gripped his arms, my knees almost buckling. The way West loved me was overwhelming. It consumed me, filling all my empty spaces and making me whole again.

"I love you too," I panted as his fingers slid inside me, the heel of his palm grinding into my clit.

"Good girl."

I was lost in him as the water beat down on his back. West kissed me, his fingers working inside me until I was crying out my pleasure against his lips. Then he hooked my legs around his waist and fucked me. The two of us needed this after we'd declared our love for each other. Needed to reconnect. Have a moment of passion and possession. And when we came together, it was a meeting of two souls destined for each other.

West washed me afterwards, shampooing and conditioning my hair with gentle fingers. The way he could be so tender after all his brutality made my heart sing. I was the only woman who saw this side of him. The only one he granted it to.

We dried and dressed after we got out. West left me to blow dry my hair, telling me he'd see me up on the roof. I didn't want to go to bed later with wet hair, so I took my time with it.

I padded out of West's room and made my way up to the roof. The door was open, and I could hear their voices. I slid on some sandals before I came up here, so I wasn't wandering around with bare feet. The boys were sat out on the benches in the garden area with bottles of beer in their hands.

When I reached them, Francis handed me a cider, as he knew I didn't drink beer. He was sitting on the bench. I sat in his lap and put my feet on Prescott's legs. Drake was on one of the loungers, with his guitar resting on his lap. West leant against the wall, staring out over the city with his beer bottle dangling between his fingers.

Francis curled his arms around me and kissed the top of my head as I rested it on his shoulder, breathing in his hypnotic scent. The one that soothed me. Cinnamon and apples. My fingers curled into his hair as I held the bottle against my chest with my other hand. He let out a noise of contentment.

Prescott slid my sandals off, setting them on the floor before he began to massage my feet. His smile as he caught my eyes was electrifying. I was a very spoiled woman having these four. They took care of me in a way no one else ever had. And I did the same for them.

"Will you play me something, Drake?" I asked, turning my attention to him.

"What do you want to hear?"

"The one you wrote about me."

He chuckled.

"They're all about you, little wisp. You'll have to be more specific."

I looked over at him. His indigo eyes twinkled in the moonlight.

"The one you haven't let me hear yet."

He didn't hesitate, putting his fingers to strings as he continued to watch me. He'd mentioned he was writing something new the morning after he told me he loved me for the first time. The melody wasn't haunting like the others. It spoke of acceptance and understanding. It told me of his love for me. I could see it in his eyes. And it made my heart hurt.

I didn't know it was possible to love four people so intensely. We'd built bonds with each other that would last an eternity. We were made for each other. That's how I saw us. Fated to be with each other for life. As Drake had once said... we were born together and we would die together.

When the song was over, Drake set the guitar on the lounger and rose to his feet, digging his hands into his pockets. He looked over at West, who hadn't turned around yet. Then he met Francis' eyes before turning to Prescott, who'd finished massaging my feet and was merely stroking my bare legs with his fingertips.

"We going to ask her?" he said with a raised eyebrow.

"Ask me what?"

Francis encouraged me to sit up and drop down on the bench next to him. West turned around and came over to us, swinging his bottle with his movement. Prescott got up along with Francis and the four of them stood before me, their eyes all fixed on mine.

"What?" I asked again, wondering what they wanted from me.

We'd already had sex together tonight. I didn't think I could take another round. Not after West had fucked me in the shower.

"We have a proposition for you," Drake said. "One we hope you'll agree to."

My fingers curled around the edges of the bench.

"Planning things behind my back again?"

"No, we just wanted to surprise you."

I let go of the bench and waved a hand at them.

"Okay, well, tell me what it is and I'll give you my answer."

Drake stepped closer.

"We wanted to know if you would consider what would be, for all intents and purposes, a marriage between us and you. We know it wouldn't be legal. It would just be for us. To show our devotion to each other. And if you say yes… we'd like to do it now."

FORTY THREE

SCARLETT

M y ears started ringing the moment Drake said the word marriage. My hand went to my mouth as I tried to process it. The idea of it. The implications. And I had no idea what to say. It's not like I expected them to ask me for this, considering it wouldn't be legally recognised. It never even crossed my mind. The only thing I'd ever been sure of was spending my life with them.

What did Drake even mean by right now?

Did they want to do some kind of ceremony?

What exactly were they expecting from me?

I dropped my hand from my mouth and frowned.

"We can't get married."

"It wouldn't really be a marriage, little lamb, more of a lifelong commitment to each other with vows and stuff," Prescott said, cocking his head to the side. "We want to show you how much we love you and we're in this for life."

"We want to hold a commitment ceremony... of sorts," Francis added.

I looked at West, as he hadn't said anything. He smiled at me, his amber eyes glinting. Then he put his beer down on the bench and knelt at my feet. He took both my hands in his.

"We've made so many promises to each other over the years. Let us reaffirm them. Your forever is our forever. You're ours and we're yours." He pressed a kiss to my fingers. "Are you in this with us, little Scar?"

He knew I was but that wasn't what he was asking. It was about tonight and the things we'd shared together. Would one more step towards the future be too far? I'd already devoted my life to them. It was quite frankly adorable, sweet and completely romantic that they wanted a commitment ceremony with me. These four men were so dark and depraved, but with me, they could be kind, understanding, and loving. They treated me like their queen now we'd moved beyond our past. Now everything was out in the open and we were no longer burdened by lies and secrets. They were everything I could ever ask for and more.

"I'm in."

West smiled, placing another kiss to my fingers before he let go of my hands and stood. He turned his attention to Francis.

"Did you get everything?"

He grinned and moved away to Drake's glass structure. They'd planned this. I didn't mind them hiding it to give me a surprise. It was a good one, not some nefarious shit they'd been involved in.

Francis came back with a box of things and set it down on the bench next to me. He took out a small box, which he opened and placed in my lap. Nestled inside it were five platinum rings. One of them was smaller than the others, clearly meant for me. I picked it up and looked on the inside, finding a little horsehead had been carved into it. It made me smile. Next, Francis took out a long length of rope that was braided with different colours. Green, red, purple, blue and black woven with silver thread. The final items he extracted were a knife and bandages.

I had an idea of what all of this meant and who had chosen these things, but I smiled up at him as he put his hand out to me. He helped me to my feet and pressed me closer to Prescott.

"How is this going to go?" I asked as Prescott took my hand and kissed my knuckles.

"Follow Frankie's lead," West said with a shrug as he dug his hands in his pockets.

No surprise Francis was the one who had planned out the ceremony part.

"Okay, we all need to get in a circle for this to work," Francis said, giving me a wink.

The boys herded me into the circle. I was standing next to West and Prescott with Drake and Francis in front of me.

Francis picked up the rope and slid the knife into his pocket. He made us place all our forearms together in a circle, so our hands were pressed to each other, then proceeded to bind our hands and wrists together with Drake's help.

"This cord represents the binding of our souls. The knots are a symbol of our love and devotion to each other. May the five of us bring each other peace through the years. May we grow stronger with each passing day bound by our vows and commitments to each other. May the cord running between us never break. May we always be together as one."

We all stared at the cord as Francis tied it off.

"Okay, Scar, you're going first. So repeat after me… I vow to be your guiding light in the darkness, to cherish every moment we spend together in this lifetime and the next, to give you my heart and soul to keep safe, and to love you no matter what life brings our way."

I repeated the words, smiling at all of them in turn.

"Thank you, Scar." He turned his attention to Prescott. "Now you, repeat after me… I vow to be your protector in the darkness, to cherish every moment we spend in this lifetime and the next, to give you my heart and soul to keep safe, and to love you no matter what life brings our way."

They all repeated after him and he said the words himself when it was his turn. Then he untied us and made us all put our hands out with our palms facing upwards. He took the knife from his pocket and set the point of the blade in Prescott's palm.

He sliced across Prescott's hand, then moved to West's, cutting his hand too before his own. He took Drake's, slicing through it and, finally, mine. I winced from the cut but didn't complain about it.

"May our blood bind us for eternity."

He made each of them rub their bloody palm against mine, mixing all our blood together. No doubt this was Drake's contribution to this ceremony. The handfasting was definitely Francis. The knife, so very West. And the rings with the horse

404

carvings in them? That was Prescott all over, with his little obsession with the horsemen.

Lastly, Francis picked up the box of said rings and had me place them on their ring fingers. West was the one who slid the ring onto mine, giving me a devious smile as he did it. It felt fitting for it to be him. We had fallen in love with each other when we were kids. He was the one I'd envisioned spending my entire life with. I just had four men now instead of one. And it was everything to me. They were my life, my loves and my home.

"May these rings symbolise our commitment to each other and guarantee no one else will hit on our woman because we will gut them if they do."

I snorted and shook my head.

"That's not very romantic, Frankie."

"It's what we do," West said with a shrug. "You're ours."

Prescott took my hand and rubbed the ring.

"No one gets to touch or take what's ours, little lamb. Never again."

I gave him a look.

"So you'll just kill anyone who does? I thought we were done with that after tonight."

"Drake will. He's our executioner."

I rolled my eyes and glanced at Drake, who merely shrugged and rubbed his face.

"If I have to kill again to keep you safe, I will."

Why on earth was I not surprised our commitment ceremony had included talking about murder?

"Can we please get back to this rather than talking about killing?" I waved between us. "I know it isn't a wedding, but I think kissing the bride should totally be a thing."

The words had barely left my lips when I was gathered up in Prescott's arms and his mouth was on mine, tasting me like a man starved. I melted against him, letting him have his fill of me until he pulled away and smiled.

"My sweet little lamb can have whatever she wants whenever she wants."

He set me down and pushed me towards West, who kissed me next. It was hot and heavy. His bloody hand wrapped around my throat to remind me who I belonged to.

"Mine," he murmured against my lips. "Forever, little Scar."

When he released me, my knees were a little weak. Francis was there to catch me as I stumbled. I found myself bent over his arm as he kissed me, his fingertips in my hair, stroking my scalp. His scent surrounded me, making me feel at home in his arms. He smiled when he pulled away to look at me.

"My little whore, so beautiful," he whispered.

He set me upright and pushed me towards Drake, who stared down at me for a long moment without moving. He lifted his hand and curled a lock of my hair around his finger. Then he was tugging me towards him and bending down to capture my mouth in one of his searing kisses. I was a puddle of goo by the time he let me go.

Francis made me sit down so we could all bandage up our hands where he'd cut them and clean away all the blood. I smiled at him before I picked up my bottle of cider.

"Can I make a toast?"

They all grabbed their beer bottles and held them, giving me an expectant look.

"I just want to say thank you for giving me tonight. We've been through so much shit in our lives, and today we can put it all behind us." I looked at them each in turn. "Also, it just occurred to me it's technically our birthday, so happy birthday." I raised my bottle. "To us."

"To us," the boys said in unison, raising their bottles before we all took a drink.

"Did you deliberately choose last night to be the day we did everything so we could do the whole commitment thing on our birthday?"

Francis smiled.

"Maybe."

I pointed at him.

"You, mister, are a sneaky, deviant little shit."

He came closer and stroked my cheek.

"You love that about me."

I rolled my eyes.

"I suppose I do."

The next thing I knew, I was yawning, as if everything had finally hit me all at once. Exhaustion washed over me, making me feel like I'd aged a hundred years. We were only twenty-seven today, so I suppose that might be a slight exaggeration.

"I think someone needs to be put to bed."

I set my bottle down and took Francis' hand.

"Mmm, and so do all of you."

An idea formed in my mind. One I was pretty sure certain people wouldn't like, but I didn't care. They could deal.

"We're all going to go down to the playroom and sleep together. That's the only bed big enough for the five of us."

"Excuse me?" Drake said, his eyes widening.

I tugged Francis towards the door to the roof, expecting them to follow suit.

"You heard me, and I will have no objections raised by any of you. We've fucked together. We can sleep in the same bed together."

I heard Drake grumbling behind us, but he didn't say anything else.

"You need to teach me how you do that," Francis murmured in my ear.

"Do what?"

"Get him to agree to anything you want."

I smiled.

"You'd have to make him fall in love with you."

Francis made a face. I laughed, the sound of it echoing around the stairwell as we entered it.

"Look, he's my best friend and all, but I'm not sure I want him being that devoted to me. He's kind of a lot to deal with."

"Lucky for you, I know how to handle him."

"Mmm, you have mellowed him out a lot. We're all very grateful for it."

I leant my head against his shoulder as he pushed open the door to the penthouse. We made our way to the playroom, stopping to get extra blankets on the way. I busied myself making up the space for the five of us, while the others went to get ready for bed. When I was done, I wandered into Drake's bedroom, as it was closest to the playroom, to brush my teeth. He was leaving the bathroom when I entered. My eyes roamed over his bare chest. There was no question about it. This man was a god. And I loved him for it.

"Do you really not want to spend the night with us?" I asked when he paused to stroke his fingers down my arm.

"It's not that. You know I have trouble sleeping."

I stepped closer before wrapping myself around him, my fingers tracing a line down his spine.

"That's why you have me," I whispered into his chest. "I make it better."

He chuckled.

"I won't deny that, little wisp."

When I pulled away, he pressed a kiss to my lips and left me to finish getting ready for bed. I brushed my teeth and pulled my dress off, leaving me bare. I walked back into the playroom to find all four of them already on the bed. Their eyes went to me, darkening when they realised I wasn't wearing anything.

"Sleeping only. I'm exhausted and you've already had your fun with me tonight," I said as I crawled on the bed and nestled myself between West and Francis. Prescott was next to West and Drake next to Francis.

Prescott leant over and gave me a kiss goodnight. Then they tucked me under the covers and one of them turned out the light. I snuggled up to West, pressing my face into his chest while Francis curled himself around my back, pressing a kiss to my cheek. I let out a contented sigh and rubbed my thumb across my ring. A part of me felt more secure knowing we were all together like this. We devoted ourselves to each other tonight after committing what could only be described as a massacre.

It's over now. You don't have to be afraid any longer. You can heal in peace with them.

The thought had me relaxing deeper into the embrace of my men and drifting off into oblivion. I was finally safe and free to choose my life. And I'd chosen to live it with them.

FORTY FOUR

SCARLETT

M y feet practically dragged along the damn lobby as I made my way across it towards the lifts. The whole day had been exhausting. I wanted to curl up in a ball and fall asleep. Who would have thought you'd get grilled so much for being a missing person. The victim of a kidnapping. Although, I supposed, given the circumstances of my captor's death, I kind of had to give it to the police for being thorough.

I rode up in the lift, leaning against the mirrored wall, and closed my eyes. Three days ago, we'd set fire to Stuart's estate, having killed everyone inside. Today, I'd turned up at a police station near the estate looking worse for wear with a story about how I'd escaped during the fire.

In order to get my life back on track, I had to deal with the whole being a missing person business. I'd spun them a story about me being held against my will for ten years, missing out the fact I knew exactly how and why Stuart had taken me. They didn't need to know I'd forgotten everything all that time. There was no one around who could tell them otherwise. Anyone who could was either dead or had left the country. We'd made it possible for the chef, Gio, to disappear and start a new life in exchange for keeping his mouth shut.

The police had little choice but to take what I'd told them at face value. There was nothing to prove my story otherwise. We'd made sure of that when we'd burnt down the estate.

When I got up to the penthouse, I went straight upstairs and took a shower, washing away the hours I'd spent in an interview room. Drying and dressing, I made my way up to the roof where I knew the boys were. They'd finished work for the day an hour ago, and they weren't anywhere else in the penthouse.

I found them in Drake's glass structure, talking and drinking. They all fell silent as I entered. Drake put his hand out to me. I went and curled up in his lap. He was in his favourite armchair. He petted my hair and let me bury my face in his neck.

"How was it?" he asked a minute later.

"Shit."

He rubbed my back and kissed the top of my head.

"I'm sorry."

"It's not your fault. They just asked me so many questions. It was exhausting going over everything, but it's okay. At least I'm no longer considered missing. Means I can go on with my life, you know. I don't have to worry about being on their records or anything else."

I sighed, rubbing my face against his skin.

"It got tense when they started asking me where I would go, what with Mum being dead, but then this lady officer came in and told them she would take it from here. She drove me home without any questions being asked. Like she'd been told to get me out of there when they'd finished questioning me."

I turned my face up to his so I could meet his eyes.

"It's a relief it's over even if it was a lot to deal with."

"You did so well, my good girl."

My heart fluttered at his praise. He knew when I needed it and gave it freely. I would always be Drake's brat, but right now, I wasn't in the mood to push his buttons. All I wanted was to breathe him in. To let him comfort me and help me feel more at ease.

"You don't have to worry anymore, Scarlett. We'll take care of the rest."

I smiled and rested my head on his shoulder again. There wasn't anything to worry about. The thing about having dirt on the police commissioner was you could get him to do what you wanted. That included making sure I never had to deal with any repercussions regarding my disappearance after this. Not to mention he would make sure the investigation into the fire would be wrapped up quickly.

Stuart's estate straddled the border between Kent and Greater London, meaning jurisdiction could technically fall under the Met's purview. Drake had a conversation with the commissioner the day after fire, essentially telling him to make sure the investigation was handled by his force, otherwise, we'd release the evidence we had against him. Safe to say, it had made the news because of who Stuart was. Good thing none of us had been linked to it. And they certainly weren't going to find out about me, either. Drake had been very clear about my name being kept out of the public eye. He didn't want me being all over the news and getting harassed. I guess I had the commissioner to thank for getting me out of that interview room and home safe.

"We have something for you," he said after a few minutes had gone by.

"Another surprise?"

"You could say that."

They'd already sprung the commitment ceremony on me. What was one more thing?

I sat up and gave him a look.

"I'm beginning to not like surprises."

He stroked my cheek.

"You'll like this one, little wisp."

He encouraged me off his lap so I could say hello to the others. Then they were dragging me back downstairs into the penthouse. I fiddled with my ring on the way down. Prescott had informed me it contained a tiny tracker embedded in the metal. They didn't want to be in a position where they couldn't find me again after everything with Mason. I could hardly blame them for that. It made me feel safe and secure, so I hadn't given them any shit for it.

When we got into the living area, Francis took my hand and pulled me closer to where the war room was. It was then I noticed there was no longer a bookshelf in front of it. A white door stood there now. Drake opened it and gestured for me to enter. I gave him a curious look before dropping Francis' hand and stepping inside.

My hand went to my mouth. On one wall there was an open wardrobe space with all of my clothes hanging in neat lines. A whole section was dedicated to all my shoes and trainers. Then there was a beautiful chest of drawers. I walked over to them, finding a framed photo of the five of us when we were teenagers. It brought tears to my eyes seeing us like that. We'd been through so much since it was taken, but it was a reminder of a time when we were innocent of things to come.

I set it down and continued looking around. There was a dressing table on the opposite side of my clothes with a mirror on the wall and all my makeup set out. A large rug covered half the room. It was black with little silver stars running across it, representing the night's sky. There was a huge dark blue sofa by the window facing the cityscape. I went over to it, running my fingers along the soft fabric. My eyes darted up to the picture hanging above the sofa on the wall. It was a painting of Nyx, the goddess of the night, and four horses below her, each representing the horsemen.

I'd complained to Drake about not having a space in the penthouse. And they'd made me one. They'd changed their war room with its creepy photo display into a room for me. A space of my own. It not being a bedroom didn't bother me. It would mean my clothes were all in one place. My very own personal dressing room and somewhere I could come when I needed space.

I turned and practically sprinted across the room. Then I was jumping on Drake, who had to take several steps backwards to stay upright. My legs wrapped around his waist as I buried my face in his neck.

"Thank you, thank you, thank you."

He put his arms around me. I shifted my head back and started planting kisses all over his face. Not sure how he felt about it, but he was smiling by the time I was done.

"You're welcome."

It was definitely him who had made this happen. When Drake got an idea in his head, he usually followed it through.

"I won't tell anyone else how sweet you are to me. I mean, they know already." I waved at Prescott and Francis. "But it'll stay between us."

He laughed and set me down, pressing a kiss to my forehead.

"Well, you can thank those two. They designed the room for you. I merely suggested we should."

"When on earth did you have it all done?"

"We had people up here whilst you were at work to install all the wardrobe space. Today, we had all the furniture delivered and the finishing touches added."

For Drake to be so thoughtful was a miracle in itself, but he'd changed so much since I'd broken down his walls. He'd become more like the boy of our youth while still maintaining the man he'd grown into. I got to see all sides of him and it made me appreciate him all the more.

"I love you so much."

He bit his lip and stroked my cheek.

"My heart and all its love are yours, little wisp."

I rushed to Prescott next, who gathered me up in his arms, his blue eyes glinting as he smiled down at me.

"My perfect king made me a perfect room."

"I'm glad you like it, little lamb. We wanted it to be special for you."

"I love everything about it."

He kissed me, making my heart melt. The way I loved this man and all his beautiful imperfections made my chest swell. He might like to think he was bad, but in my eyes, he was kind, caring, and compassionate. He loved me fiercely, knew exactly what I needed before I did, and never failed to give me whatever I asked him for.

"I love you," I whispered against his lips.

He nuzzled my nose before he pulled away.

"I love you too, sweetness."

His arms fell back to his sides. I stepped up to Francis. The way his silver-grey eyes glittered as he took me in had my heart soaring.

"Let me guess, you chose the colours and the furniture."

"How did you know?"

"Because it's you, Frankie."

He took my hand and tugged me against his chest.

"Me, eh?"

"Yeah, my sneaky deviant who knows me so damn well, it's scary sometimes."

He rested his forehead against mine and cupped the back of my neck.

"I'll take that as a compliment."

"It's a compliment of the highest order because I'm so in love with you, I don't know what to do with myself."

His smile could have lit up the whole damn room. Francis deserved all my love, praise, and compliments. He was my safety in all the madness of our lives.

"My beautiful little whore, I love you to the stars and back."

I didn't want to leave his embrace. Never wanted to be apart from him. And I had him for life, along with the others. What more could a girl ask for? What more could she want? They had given me everything and so much more.

Francis pressed a kiss to my lips and let me go, stroking his hand down my arm. I looked around and frowned.

"Where's West?"

He appeared at the top of the stairs just as I spoke. I watched him descend them and come right up to me. In his hands, there were a bunch of papers. He grabbed my hand with his free one and tugged me back into my new room. I found myself deposited in his lap on the sofa a few seconds later. He set the papers down next to me and cupped my face in both of his hands.

"My little Scar."

"What part of this room is your input?"

He smiled and nodded up at the painting of Nyx and her horsemen. I couldn't help grinning.

"It's perfect."

"No, you're perfect. My little warrior."

"And you're the love of my life."

West kissed me, reminding me of why I'd fallen in love with him all those years ago. And the breach between us was healed after all these months of being in a strange sort of limbo. Repairing what had broken between the five of us was tough, but every second had been worth it. I wouldn't change our lives for the world.

Francis, Prescott, and Drake joined us on the sofa when West released me. It was big enough for the five of us to sit comfortably. They'd made sure we could all be in here together whenever I wanted.

"We have one final thing for you," West said, picking up the papers he'd set aside. "These are the deeds to your mother's flat. We were able to buy it after we made Fortuity a success. We've taken care of it for all these years, and now, we want to give it to you."

I took the pages from his hands and looked them over.

"When you're ready, we'll sort out transferring it into your name, but it's yours, little Scar, to do with what you wish."

I remembered when I'd gone there to search for my mother. The guy next door told me someone came to visit it regularly. It had been the boys all along. It made me happy to know they'd done this for me. They'd made sure I had a home if I wanted it. The home I'd grown up in. Was there anything they wouldn't do for me?

"Thank you… I don't know what I'll do with it but thank you. I appreciate it so much."

I set the pages down and curled up in West's lap, holding him close, and kissed his neck. He pressed his lips to my forehead.

The five of us watched the sun setting over the city together. There was a certain sort of peace in knowing all the things and people who had caused your suffering were gone. One that left you content and safe. And I couldn't have asked for more from the taxing day I'd had to come home to these four, surprising me with such a beautiful space.

FORTY FIVE

SCARLETT

M y hand tightened in West's as we trod down a path we'd been along before many times when we'd been younger. I tipped my head back to look up at the night's sky. It would be dawn soon, but for now, the moon shone above us. There were a few stars out, but most were obscured by the light pollution in the city.

Perhaps this was an absolutely crazy idea, but neither of us were known for taking the sane route in life. We'd always played by our own rules. Done things our own way. This was no different.

West and I had come here with one specific purpose. To fix what had broken almost eleven years ago after the most traumatic event of our lives. Because, really, both of us were deeply affected by the night of my accident in the worst possible way. We'd lost each other. The person we thought we would spend our life with. And, although we were together now, it was our own personal trauma related to what happened we wanted to address.

West led me into the shell of the building and up the three flights of stairs to reach the place where it had all come to a head. Someone had cleaned away the sick from when I'd thrown up here last time. I'd learnt from Drake this site was owned by the same man who ran the club Prescott had taken me. Zayn Villetti, the son of the mafia kingpin, Gennaro. A man I wasn't sure I wanted to be properly introduced to.

Before I'd come back into the boys' lives, I had no idea what lurked beneath the surface of polite society. The criminal underworld was not something I ever expected to be involved with. I guess from the moment I became a killer, it became a part of my life even if we were done with that side of things now.

It had been a couple of months since the fire at the estate. The police had wrapped up their investigation last week. It had been deemed an accident, and the case closed. I was pretty sure if it had been fully investigated, they would have opened a homicide and arson case, but it never got that far, thanks to the commissioner. He made sure any evidence of foul play wasn't brought to light. We were in the clear. Not that they would have had evidence of our involvement as we'd been thorough, but you could never be too careful.

West set down the bag he'd brought and kissed my forehead. He left me to look out over the city while he prepared things. Being here made me feel all sorts of things, but I kept a lid on it. Having West there helped me stay in control. His presence was my grounding force.

We'd talked about this for weeks before making the decision to return to the scene of my accident one last time. Some places had the power to keep you captive in your own mind. I didn't want to be afraid any longer. I wanted to take back my power and set myself free. It was lucky West felt the exact same way.

"Little Scar."

I turned to find he'd set out a blanket on the concrete along with several items we would need. Now we were here, there was no going back. I had no qualms about doing this with him.

"Come here and kneel at my feet. Now."

I hurried towards him, dropping down to my knees on the blanket and bowing my head. We'd already talked about how this would all go earlier. He'd given me the option of a safe word and we'd agreed if I really wanted out, I would say red or click my fingers twice like I did with the others. We both knew I wouldn't use it regardless because I wanted this. I needed it. And he did too.

"I would call you a good girl for obeying me, but we both know that's not true. You're not my good girl today, are you? You're my dirty little slut."

He pointed at something on the floor.

"Put that in your mouth."

I reached out and picked up the gag, securing it in my mouth with a buckle at the side. His hand went to my hair, gripping onto the braid, but he didn't tip my head up to look at him.

"Did you do this so I had something to hold on to?" He laughed in such a cruel way, I almost flinched. Then he tugged on the braid. "My bitch wants her hair pulled whilst I fuck her, doesn't she?"

I couldn't reply with the gag in my mouth. His hand tightened around my braid, pulling my hair until my scalp burnt.

"You think I don't require an answer because you can't talk, do you? Mistake number one."

I yelped as he tugged my hair again, this time harder.

"Let's try that again, and this time, you're going to answer me. My bitch wants her hair pulled, doesn't she?"

I nodded. The pain made me feel alive. Reminded me I was in control of all of this, even though I was at his mercy right now.

"Mmm, that's better. Don't fuck with me, slut, or I'll make this worse for you."

The darker part of me wanted him to make it worse. Wanted him to hurt me so I cried and purged everything holding me back. To exorcise my demons in the place where all our heartache and pain started. To heal me once and for all.

"Now, you're going to bend over and put your hands behind your back. I want your chin on the blanket so you can stare out at the view, you hear me?"

My moan behind the gag was his answer. He let go of my braid. I did as he asked, leaning on my chin with my hands behind my back, facing the city. It was super fucking uncomfortable, but this wasn't about my comfort. It was about pushing me right out of it.

He took a hold of my hands and cuffed them, making it ten times worse for me. I whimpered behind the gag, but it was ignored. My skirt was pushed up over my behind, exposing my skin to the air. A chuckle burst from his lips.

"Look at this bare little pussy, just waiting for cock." Then he ran his thumb between my cheeks, knocking the little plug he'd inserted earlier. "And this? Mmm, I think someone wants to be fucked here, doesn't she? What a cock hungry little bitch you are."

I shifted, growing ever more uncomfortable leaning on my chin and because of the ache between my legs. Being degraded by him had me desperate for his body against mine. To feel all of his brutality.

"Mmm, yes, you are, waving this pretty pussy at me. If you think that's going to make me fuck it quicker, you're mistaken."

The slap across my behind radiated up my spine a second later, the sharp sting of it making me cry out against the gag.

"You see, you've been a bad girl. Bad girls get punished before they're fucked. Especially dirty little sluts who want nothing more than to be railed to within an inch of their lives. That's what you are, isn't it? A slut. A bitch desperate for all her holes to be filled at once. You want to be used until you're crying from shame, pain, and despair. Only then will you ever be satisfied."

More slaps came. I cried out from each of them, trying to keep my chin in place. He stopped, giving me a second's reprieve before my braid was in his fist and he pulled me upright by it. His other hand circled my neck as he pressed his front to my back, pinning my arms between us.

"Look. Look at the place it happened. Do you feel it, slut? Do you feel how much pain is in this place? How much we've fucking suffered for our sins?" He stroked my neck with his thumb. "You do, don't you? You know how much it fucking hurts."

I whimpered, straining against him. His words dug into the parts of me still shattered by what happened that night. They shone a light on the wounds, making them visible to both of us.

"That's right, my little slut, you know how it feels. How much we've burnt for each other in ways no one should. Feel it. Fucking feel it. Let it rip through you."

My heart hurt, the memories surfacing and slamming into me. The way he'd shouted my name when I fell. The pain in his amber eyes. The horrifying sound my body made when it hit the floor. All of it burst through, leaving me defenceless and utterly at his mercy.

"That's it." He tightened his hand around my airway, squeezing the sides. "Let it out. Show me your pain. Let me have all of it."

Tears slid down my cheeks. They dripped onto his hand. He pressed his lips to my ear, his tongue tracing the line of it. I tried to talk behind the gag, but it was impossible. Spit dribbled out of my mouth as I struggled against his hold on me.

"That's right. You know you need this. Give me your fucking pain."

I wanted to scream and tell him I couldn't do this. Tell him I wasn't strong enough. West held me through it, allowing me to purge the memory of the worst experience of my life. Even as he used harsh words, they soothed me. They made me whole again.

"Scream it, my little slut. Tell the whole fucking world how much it hurts."

No matter how loud I tried to scream, no matter how much it burnt my throat to do so, the noise was hampered by the gag. It's why he'd given it to me. To allow me to purge my pain without anyone but him hearing the sound.

I sobbed, shifting against him and my bindings. I let it all rip, the pain seeping out of my pores onto the concrete floor. West took my pain. He took it all. The memory replayed over and over in my mind. The moment my hand slipped from his and I fell. How I'd told him I loved him. How he screamed for me. And how I'd landed, passing out from all the pain.

When I was finally spent from the crying and screaming, I slumped against him, closing my eyes. It was done. The memory dissipated, leaving just me and him alone in the building where our lives had split apart.

"Good girl," he murmured. "You're my good girl, little Scar."

Then he removed the gag from my mouth, tossing it to the side.

"I'm going to make it better for you. I'll heal you, my little warrior."

He laid me down on the blanket on my back with my arms still cuffed behind my back. My eyes opened, staring up at him looming over me with a dark glint in his eyes. His hands slid up my legs, making me bend my knees for him. My skirt was bunched at my waist, leaving me utterly exposed.

"West…"

His finger traced a line along my pussy, making me shiver.

"My little slut is still so wet for me. I think I should take care of this little pussy, don't you? Then I'll take care of this too." He knocked the plug. "You can't stop me from taking whatever I want, can you?"

I shook my head. No part of me wanted to. Not even after I'd sobbed my heart out. The memories of the past no longer clung to my skin. West had torn my suffering out of my mind, laid it bare for both of us to see. He set me free, just like he told me he would. He exposed the burden I carried. The burden I'd thrown away. This place couldn't hurt me. It couldn't do a single thing any longer.

"I'm going to take all of your little holes, my dirty whore, and I'm going to make them mine."

He reached over and stroked the scars he'd given me.

"Tell me who you belong to."

I swallowed hard.

"I belong to War."

His deviant smile was the only warning I got before West did what he did best.

Broke me to fix me all over again.

FORTY SIX

WEST

Had it hurt me to go through this experience with Scarlett? Of course, it fucking had. I purged my pain right alongside her as she cried and screamed behind her gag. It poured out of me with the memory of the night she fell crowding my brain. The way she shook and struggled against me, experiencing it all over again was horrifying but necessary. We both had to go through it together so we could finally lay our demons to rest.

I stared down at my woman, my fingers resting on her scars as her chest heaved with her harsh breaths. My little warrior had come into her own, proving once and for all just how strong she was. How she endured no matter what was thrown at her.

My goddess. The light of my life. How I fucking love you with every part of me.

There was no one else in this world who understood me like Scarlett. No one else loved me the way she could. My destiny was right here with her.

Her beautiful eyes were bloodshot from her tears, but she stared up at me with so much love, trust and affection, it threatened to undo me.

"Remember, we're forever, little Scar."

I straightened and undid my clothes, freeing my aching dick. One hand went to her knee, and the other wrapped around my cock. I pressed the head of it to her wet entrance, teasing her with it. She let out a little whimper but didn't move. She didn't try to force me to give her what she wanted. How I loved her all the more for her patience. I could see her need in her eyes. The desperation to feel the connection between us. She didn't have to worry. I would give her the world because she deserved it.

Pressing forward, I slid inside her, taking it achingly slow. Too fucking slow. I let out a breath, trying not to feel so fucking overwhelmed by the pleasure of this moment. The feeling of contentment and belonging washed over me from being with her like this. It was breaking me apart on the inside in the best fucking way possible. Every inch she took knitted those shattered pieces together. My little Scar made me whole again.

Her mouth parted on a little exhale when I was fully encased inside her sweet, wet little pussy. She pulsed around me. A small smile played on my lips at the deviancy in her eyes. I placed my hands down on either side of her head, leaning over her delicious little body.

"Desperate, are we? Do you want me to fuck you until you're crying all over again?"

"Please."

"Dirty girl."

"I'm your dirty girl."

"Mmm, yes, you are *mine*."

I lifted one hand and stroked her neck with my finger, making her shudder. Pushing myself upright, I gripped the backs of her thighs, pressing them against her chest. Then I pulled back and slammed inside her, making her yelp. There was no reprieve. My thrusts grew ever harder, the pace I set leaving her panting and crying from the intensity.

"Fuck, yes, West, please, fuck, don't stop."

The bond between us flared as we stared at each other. The heat and raw passion reformed our souls, entwining them together the way they were always meant to be.

This place had once broken us. Now, it would cement us forever. Scarlett and I as one.

"Mmm, my dirty little slut is taking it so fucking well. You're such a good little slut for me, aren't you? Your pussy loves my cock."

"Yes, yes, yes."

My eyes darted towards the city. The light was creeping along the edges of the horizon. Dawn was breaking on us and I couldn't think of a more perfect moment than this.

My attention went back to Scarlett. I gripped her throat in one hand. Her eyes flared with heat.

"My fist is your necklace."

Then I tugged her upright, sitting myself on the blanket with the movement. Scarlett settled her knees on either side of my legs so she could ride me. I kept her steady with my hand around her neck.

"That's it, show me how much you want it." I ran my tongue up the side of her face, licking away her tears. "Show me you want my cock, slut."

She rode me harder, whimpering with each movement. I could feel the vibrations of her little sounds against my palm.

Such perfection. You were made for me, little Scar. A goddess to ride through the world with me.

"Good girl. You're my good little slut. I think you deserve a reward."

My free hand dug between us, my fingers circling her clit. She moaned with the movement, pressing against me as she rode my dick.

"Mmm, come for me. I'm going to make you clean it when you're done. Then you know what'll happen next."

She whimpered with her agreement. She fucking knew. I'd promised to fuck all her little holes. I planned on seeing it through.

"West," she cried when she came, her body trembling and bucking against mine.

Her head fell back, her eyes closing as it washed over her. The beauty of this woman as she climaxed was indescribable. My goddess was everything, and so much more. The depth of my devotion to her couldn't be explained. I would endure the worst life had to throw at me as long as I had Scarlett.

I pulled her off me when she was spent, then forced her head down to my dick. She opened her eyes and looked up at me, her tongue darting out to circle the head. Her mouth opened and enclosed over it a moment later, making me groan.

My hand gripped her braid, not to force her, I just needed something to hold on to. Needed to touch my beautiful girl to remind me she was here. She was mine.

After she'd cleaned my dick of her cum, she sat up and waited for me to move. To put her in the position I wanted. I turned her around, unlocked her cuffs, then put her on her hands and knees.

"You're going to stay right there and take it like a good little slut," I told her as I pulled out the plug from her tight little hole.

Tossing it aside, I picked up the lube and pressed some inside her with my thumb. I coated my dick next before notching it to her. She let out a sigh as I entered her as if it was what she wanted all along. To feel me here, claiming the last part of her she had to offer me. I wrapped a hand around her hip, stroking her skin with my fingertips.

"Take me, little Scar. Impale yourself on my dick."

She backed herself onto me, taking inch by inch. When her cheeks were flush with my body, I held her there, revelling in the feel of her surrounding me.

"Good girl."

Scarlett looked back at me, her hazel-green eyes full of emotion. I grabbed a wipe to clean my hand off before reaching forward and gripping her braid.

"Now fuck yourself on my cock. Show me you deserve to come again. Be my slut."

She moved, sliding my cock from her and taking me back inside her again. The tight sensation of her made me groan. This woman had my fucking heart in a chokehold. She gave me so much pleasure. So much happiness. So much fucking joy.

My lips parted on the words wanting out of my head, but they wouldn't come. Instead, I watched her fuck herself on me. The way she sighed with her pleasure. How she took me without resistance or complaint. She worked herself against my dick, increasing the pace with each thrust. I could not be more awed than I was by her.

I tugged on her braid, pulling her up to me and wrapping my arm around her waist to hold her body against mine. Then I took over, thrusting up into her. She moaned and curled her arm behind us, wrapping her hand behind my head. Her fingers speared into my hair as her head fell back against my shoulder.

"Good little slut," I murmured. "My good girl taking me so well."

I thrust harder, wanting to dive off the edge of the fucking cliff with my woman.

"Stroke that needy clit, little Scar. Come with me."

Her free hand curled between her legs. She panted as she touched herself and met my eyes. There it was. Our bond filling the space between us. Our eyes reflecting our feelings of love for each other. It was the only thing I needed in this world. Us. Me and her.

"Give it to me. Give me everything."

Before she could say a word, I caught her mouth with mine, kissing her like my life depended on it. Because it did. It depended on her. She was my air. My sustenance. The very fucking essence of me. I couldn't do anything but give in and let her carry me under.

CATACLYSM

We came together in a fucking crescendo of passion and pleasure. Our bodies trembled together. They became one. I didn't fucking know where I ended and she began. There was nothing but us. Just fucking us. We mattered. We were here. And we were fucking alive.

When our lips parted, our eyes fixed on each other, our breath mingling together with our exertion. I wrapped my hand around her throat, unable to help myself from doing so.

"I love you, little Scar."

She brushed her mouth against mine.

"I love you too."

The words settled between us, reminding me this was our moment. Our time together.

It started with us. We had been the catalyst for the events of our lives. Our desire to be with one another had cemented the path we'd all trodden along. It had dragged us all down to the very depths of hell. We'd had to pull ourselves out.

This proved it was all worth it. It showed me no matter what shit I'd gone through, I'd never given up on her. I never would.

We pulled apart to clean up with the supplies I'd brought. Scarlett rearranged her clothes and smiled at me as she stood. I wrapped an arm around her, drawing her against my side as we both turned to the lightening sky. It was streaked with oranges and yellows, signalling the dawn. A whole new chapter of our lives began today.

"It's beautiful," she whispered as if she didn't want to break the peaceful silence of this moment.

"Not as beautiful as you."

She nuzzled her face into my chest as she wrapped both arms around my waist.

"You're still a little obsessed with me."

"I'll never stop being obsessed with you, little Scar. You're my entire world and so much more."

"You're mine too."

I wrapped my other arm around her, cuddling her closer as the sun peeked over the horizon. The two of us had created a new memory here. One to replace the old. We'd taken our pain, broken it apart and filled it with love. Our love. The unbreakable kind. The one that would never shatter.

Scarlett looked up at me, her eyes shining with the purest happiness. It made my heart expand to encompass every part of her.

"My perfect little warrior."

She reached up and placed her hand on my cheek. I could feel her ring digging into my skin. The one I'd placed on her finger, making her my partner for life.

"My War."

I leant down, resting my forehead against hers and breathed in her cinnamon scent. I was content. I was happy. I was home. Because wherever Scarlett was, that was home.

The story of our life had begun with me and Scarlett. It ended with us too. It ended right here, where everything had gone wrong.

We weren't just Scarlett and West any longer. We were Nyx and War. And we belonged with the rest of our family. Pestilence, Famine and Death.

The Four Horsemen and their goddess, Nyx. Etched on each other's hearts forever as one. Fate had woven the strings of our lives and brought us together. And it would never tear us apart again.

EPILOGUE

SCARLETT

The breeze was cool against my skin. The sound of it rustled through the leaves of the tree above me as the sun dappled across the blanket below me. My eyes were closed as I lay back against West, who was propped up against the tree behind us. In between my crossed legs was Prescott. His head rested in my lap as he was currently using me as a pillow. On my right, Francis was laid out on his side, checking his phone. My fingers were tangled in his hair, stroking the soft strands as I often did. To my left sat Drake, reading a book on his tablet.

I opened my eyes, staring down at my left hand resting on Drake's thigh. The sun reflected slightly off the platinum ring. It was strange to think a year had passed since the day on the roof when we'd vowed to stay together forever. A year of learning each other all over again, settling into our lives, finding peace, contentment and, most important of all, happiness.

Our existence had perhaps become more mundane, but only in that we didn't get our kicks from death and destruction. Instead, we threw ourselves into building a life we all wanted. Fortuity was as successful as ever, if not more so. We worked hard and played even harder.

Our playroom had become our sanctuary. A safe space away from the outside world where the five of us could explore our sexual and non-sexual forms of kink to our heart's content. It was our outlet for the darkness we all craved since we'd left the underworld behind.

It was a perfect day to celebrate our twenty-eighth birthday together. There were no pressing matters for us to attend. Nothing for us to do but lie here in the sun and watch the world go by.

We were in Rosie's garden. Her three dogs were chasing each other on the lawn next to the table the boys had dragged out earlier for our birthday lunch. One of the cats was curled up on the end of the blanket near Drake's feet, enjoying the sun on his black fur. Ares had taken a liking to Drake. I was highly amused by the whole thing, especially the way Drake grumbled about the cat sitting on him when we visited Rosie and yet he'd quite happily pet Ares the whole time. I swear he liked the cat more than he was letting on.

Francis shifted next to me, drawing my attention to him. He rubbed his face on his t-shirt and set his phone down, letting out a sigh. His eyes darted over to Prescott, who had fallen asleep with his hand curled around my thigh.

"I see someone couldn't stay awake."

I grinned and continued stroking Francis' hair.

"Rosie made him get up early to take the dogs out so she could start cooking. He was grumpy as fuck about it," I replied, keeping my voice low so I didn't wake him.

We'd arrived here two days ago to spend the weekend with Prescott's mum. Drake and Francis slept in the twin room while West had shared with me and Prescott. It wasn't unusual for us to be three to a bed. Drake's, Prescott's and Francis' parents had got used to our relationship and the way we worked. Thankfully, Drake's mother had come around to the whole thing. The thought of Drake walking out of her life had given May an incentive to accept the way things were. Besides, she'd seen how happy we all made each other. No one could deny we belonged together.

"I suppose that one took advantage of having you alone."

Francis nodded his head towards West. I tried not to smile.

"Can you blame me?" West said, stroking his tattooed fingers down my bare arm. "You have a naked woman in your bed looking all sleep-rumpled and cute, you take advantage of the fact."

I rolled my eyes. Yes, I had enjoyed a morning quickie with West and I wasn't ashamed of it. He'd shoved his hand over my mouth to stop me from making too much noise. When Prescott came back, he'd found us in a post-coital haze and told us we should have waited for him. No doubt he would have enjoyed watching.

"Don't worry, you get me later," I said before Francis could reply.

We were going home after lunch. The five of us wanted to celebrate in our own way. The playroom would be involved, along with his ropes and chains.

He gave me a smile. I stroked my fingers down the side of his head and cupped his face, rubbing my thumb over his mouth. He poked his tongue out and licked me with a deviant look in his beautiful silver-grey eyes.

"Francis!"

He turned to look at the house, finding his mother standing by the table.

"Yes?" he called back.

"Your father wants to discuss the wedding anniversary arrangements with you."

"Okay, I'm coming."

Francis rolled his eyes and slumped back on the blanket. His parent's thirtieth wedding anniversary was next week. They were having a big party for it. Francis had paid for everything because we weren't exactly short on funds. He hadn't wanted to get too involved otherwise but had been roped into it by Eliza.

"I thought our birthday was supposed to be about us, not their fucking party," he muttered.

"It is about us and besides, you haven't had to lift a finger today so far."

He smiled at me, then sat up. The next thing I knew, he'd leant over and planted a kiss on my lips.

"Always keeping us in line."

"Someone has to."

"And you do it so well, little whore. Happy birthday, my stunning girl."

"Happy birthday, my fallen god."

He kissed me again and then hauled himself up. I watched him trudge off in the direction of the house, my fingers going to Prescott's head and stroking his hair instead.

"Is it lunchtime?" Prescott asked a minute later, turning his head to look up at me.

"Almost, sleepyhead."

"Mum will want me to help bring stuff out."

I leant down and pressed a kiss to his forehead.

"Then you should go offer your services."

"And leave you? Never."

I laughed and nuzzled his face with my nose.

"You're just going in the house and I'm still right here, silly."

He grabbed hold of my head and kissed me. I sat back when he released me, and he got to his feet.

"You three better make your way over before Mum hassles you."

"I'll make sure they take their seats."

He stroked my cheek and gave me a smile.

"Where would we be without you, sweetness?"

"Worse off."

He laughed.

"Happy birthday, little lamb, my goddess of the night."

"Happy birthday, my king."

I grinned as he walked off towards the house to help Rosie with lunch. He gave me a wink over his shoulder. I blew him a kiss. He caught it and tucked it in his pocket before he disappeared inside. I settled against West again, closing my eyes and savouring the warmth of the sun on my face.

"Drake, Scarlett, West, lunch is ready!" came May's voice a moment later.

Drake let out a little huff, setting his tablet down and stretching. I looked over at him, watching the way the sunlight caught his dark hair. The furrow between his brow had me reaching out and smoothing it away. His indigo eyes caught mine, and he smiled.

"Drake!"

"We're coming, Mum," he called but kept his attention on me.

"She'll be herding us like cattle if we don't get a move on," I said.

"Don't I know it."

I leant closer and pressed a kiss to his mouth. His fingers were in my hair, stroking my scalp and making me sigh. Letting me go, he picked up his tablet and rose to his feet.

"Have I told you how beautiful you look today, little wisp?"

I shook my head. He stroked my cheek with the back of his hand.

"You grow more beautiful every single day in my eyes. Happy birthday, my love."

"Happy birthday, sir."

He gave me one last longing look, then he walked away towards the table where May was busy telling Prescott and Francis where the dishes should go. Absolutely no surprises there. May always liked to take control of a situation, no matter what was happening.

West curled both of his arms around me and leant his chin on my shoulder.

"Look at our family," he murmured, watching Drake join the others as Rosie and Jasper came out of the house, followed by her three dogs, all wagging their tails.

"They're quite something. The best family we could have chosen."

"They kind of chose us."

I laughed. Eliza, Jasper, Rosie and May were like parents to me and West since neither of us had our own any longer. Our found family was all we needed.

"I don't think May would let us get away with not paying her regular visits. Drake would get lectured for hours."

"He might be a pain in the arse, he doesn't deserve that."

"No one deserves a May Ackley lecture."

He nudged me with his chin, letting go of my waist so I could get to my feet. I put my hand out and pulled him up with me. West looked down at me with a grin and his amber eyes full of affection.

"Especially not you. All you deserve is the world."

I reached up and touched his cheek.

"I have the world right here with you and the others."

He leant down and kissed me, making me melt against him. I'd loved this man since I was five. There was no question he made me feel like I had the world when he was by my side.

"Happy birthday, my little warrior," he whispered when he pulled back. "Owner of my heart."

His fingers traced a line across the scars on my chest. I sighed and reached up, touching the scars I'd given him over his t-shirt.

"Happy birthday, soulmate and love of my life. Now, come on, let's go celebrate with the others, hey?"

I took his hand and pulled him towards the table. Right then is when I knew nothing in this world would ever tear me away from the people I loved. We'd stuck together through thick and thin, fought so many battles, and now, life was peaceful. Just how we'd wanted it to be all along.

I looked back at West, taking in each and every one of his beautiful features. He smiled and made my heart swell at the sight of it.

"As my little Scar wishes."

ACKNOWLEDGEMENTS

Thank you so much for taking the time to read this book. I really appreciate all of my readers and hope this book gave you as much joy reading it as I did writing it.

My biggest thanks for this book goes out to my amazing friend and alpha reader, Ashley. You really have changed my entire life. I feel like I've gone through every single feel with you throughout bringing the horsemen's story to life. And I couldn't have done it without your support. I love you so much bby! No one else gets my characters quite like you. I can't wait to see what we do next together.

Thank you to Chrishawn for being an amazing friend and helping me get through this mammoth monster of a book. I'm so grateful to have you in my life.

Big thank you to my author bestie, Elle. We've grown so much over the years together and I'm grateful to have you in my life to share our writing woes and successes.

Thank you to my husband for being there for me no matter what and always putting up with my craziness. Love you to the stars and back.

ABOUT THE AUTHOR

Sarah writes dark, contemporary, erotic and paranormal romances. She adores all forms of steamy romance and can always be found with a book or ten on her Kindle. She loves anti-heroes, alpha males and flawed characters with a little bit of darkness lurking within. Her writing buddies nicknamed her 'The Queen of Steam' for her pulse racing sex scenes which will leave you a little hot under the collar.

Born and raised in Sussex, UK near the Ashdown Forest where she grew up climbing trees and building Lego towns with her younger brother. Sarah fell in love with novels when she was a teenager reading her aunt's historical regency romances. She has always loved the supernatural and exploring the darker side of romance and fantasy novels.

Sarah currently resides in the Scottish Highlands with her husband. Music is one of her biggest inspirations and she always has something on in the background whilst writing. She is an avid gamer and is often found hogging her husband's Xbox.

Made in the USA
Coppell, TX
01 May 2023

16275643R00249